Lips That Touch Mine

WENDY LINDSTROM

Winner of the Romance Writers of America's
prestigious RITA Award

"A heartwarming and passionate tale"
— *Road to Romance*

"Riveting – *Lips that Touch Mine* is a wonderful story. Couldn't put it down."
— *L. Benner*

"Beautifully written. Much more than just a romance."
— *Old Book Barn Gazette*

"Absorbing!"
— *Harriet Klausner*

"Beautiful love story... Wanted to keep reading and hoping [it] wouldn't end."
— *Cindy*

"I loved this Book, Boyd is such a fun loving man with a Heart of Gold."
— *I. Stukey "Bookworm*

"These books get better and better... really showcased the integrity and family values that the brothers share."
— *L. Christensen*

"The characters practically leapt from the pages, they seemed so alive."
— *Dafna Yee*

Books by Wendy Lindstrom

Shades of Honor
The Longing
Lips That Touch Mine
Kissing in the Dark
Sleigh of Hope
The Grayson Brothers boxed set

rustic studio
PUBLISHING

Originally published by Leisure Books
Copyright © 2005 Wendy Lindstrom
Digital edition published by Wendy Lindstrom
Copyright © 2012 Wendy Lindstrom
Second edition published by Rustic Studio Publishing
Copyright © 2013 Wendy Lindstrom

ISBN: 1939263093
ISBN 13: 9781939263094

Cover design by Kim Killion of Hot DAMN! Designs

Publishers interested in foreign-language translation or other subsidiary rights should contact the author at www.wendylindstrom.com.

Chapter One

Fredonia, New York
December 13, 1873

Boyd Grayson glanced over his shoulder at his part-time bartender and local distiller. "Karlton! Pour me an ale and charge it to Mr. Lyons. He's going to owe me a drink in about ten seconds."

Pat Lyons gritted his teeth as he arm-wrestled Boyd. He tried to force Boyd's knuckles the last few inches to the bar, but Boyd didn't budge. "Damn you, Grayson. You've got an arm like a lumberjack."

Boyd laughed. The description was more accurate for his older brothers, Duke and Kyle. Both topped six feet and were thick in the arms and chest. Boyd was their height but lean like their eldest brother Radford. It wasn't bulky muscle that was keeping his knuckles off the bar—it was stubborn pride. At twenty-three, Boyd refused to be bested by anyone, especially in his own saloon.

The regular patrons gathered around the bar, cheering and placing bets, crowding in as the intensity of Boyd's nightly arm wrestling match escalated. The noise roused his dog, Sailor, out from under the billiard table. The long-legged, mixed-breed mutt paced between the men, searching for the cause of the excitement.

Duke leaned his elbows on the bar to watch the match. "You're losing your touch, little brother. The life of a saloon owner is making you soft."

Boyd grinned. "Don't worry, Duke. I'll still be able to beat you when I finish here."

Jovial laughter filled the tavern, and Boyd's arm slipped back a couple of inches. Pat took advantage of his lack of concentration and gained another inch.

"Pay attention," Karlton said, nudging Boyd's shoulder. "I wagered a week's earnings on you winning this match."

Boyd grimaced at Karlton's frightening penchant for gambling, but leaned into the fight. "You're sweating, Mr. Lyons."

"And you're talking too much," Pat countered.

Boyd grinned and tightened his biceps. Shouts filled the smoky room as he lifted his fist upward, away from the bar.

Pat's arm trembled as their clenched hands arched toward the ceiling.

Slowly, Boyd dragged his opponent's hand over and down to the bar. A roar of male voices cheered as he successfully ended the match.

"Took you long enough," Karlton said, his relief so obvious that Boyd suspected he was trying to work his way out of another bad gambling debt.

Duke lifted his mug in a toast, but Boyd felt a deep pang of regret. He wasn't worthy of the pride in his brother's eyes.

"Bring him a drink," Pat called to Karlton.

As the short, stocky bartender placed a full mug of ale between them, Boyd reached across the mahogany bar and squeezed Pat's shoulder. "I earned this one," he said, complimenting his best friend's strength.

Two years ago, Boyd had bought the Pemberton Inn from Pat, who had turned the inn into a busy saloon. Pat hadn't been at home anywhere else, so like many of Boyd's customers, he now spent nearly every evening at the bar, often as the bartender.

Boyd raised his mug and toasted his friend then saluted his patrons who were earning him, and ultimately his distiller Karlton Kane, a small fortune. Karlton was in the business of distributing liquor, but he worked as Boyd's second bartender three nights a week. Boyd earned a good living from the family sawmill, which he owned with his three brothers. He didn't need the income, but he did need the nightly entertainment that his saloon provided.

Each night except Sunday the regulars would fill Boyd's homey tavern and line up along the bar to arm wrestle. Later, they would sprawl in chairs around the cast-iron stove to thaw the winter chill from their bones while they bragged with their friends and taught Boyd's dog ridiculous tricks.

The Pemberton Inn was more than a place to drink ale. It was a meeting place to discuss town business and commiserate with friends, a second home for many hardworking men who didn't have anywhere more welcoming to spend their evenings.

And it was Boyd's sanctuary. In the midst of the men and noise he could pretend he was happy.

He circled the bar and sat beside Duke, careful to avoid the revolver holstered at his brother's hip. Boyd himself kept a gun behind the bar, but weapons were forbidden in his tavern. Duke was the local sheriff, though, and not about to drop his piece at the door.

"You found a new deputy yet?" Boyd asked, signaling the bartender to refill his brother's mug.

"No." Duke accepted the ale from Karlton, gave a nod of thanks then glanced at Boyd. "Want the job?"

"Hell, no."

Duke's laughter was buried in an uproar of voices and pounding, scuffling feet.

Boyd jerked his attention to the middle of the tavern where Gordie and Louie Carson were tearing into each other. He and Duke shot to their feet. Karlton came out from behind the bar and Pat Lyons leapt off his barstool, but before anyone could get a hand on the Carson brothers, they careened toward the front wall. Their four hundred pounds of flesh and muscle slammed into Boyd's front door. The casing shattered and the door blew open, sending the Carsons tumbling outside and sprawling onto Main Street.

With a curse, Boyd bolted outside after them. His patrons and his brother ran out of the bar behind him, with Sailor yelping at their heels. The neighbors were not going to be happy.

Gordie and Louie Carson pummeled each other, grunting and huffing and kicking snow everywhere, while the patrons hollered and wagered on the outcome. Boyd exchanged an exasperated glance with Duke as they reached the fracas and pulled the men away from each other. They yanked the brothers to their feet and turned them toward Chestnut Street.

"Time to go home, boys," Duke said.

Gordie opened his mouth to argue, but Boyd nudged him in the shoulder. "Go, before I ask Duke to give you boys a room for the night."

The sudden quieting of the patrons drew Boyd's attention. The men were all gawking across the street at the widow's house. A slender young woman stood on the porch pointing a revolver at them. She clutched the gun with both hands, anger and fear marring her beautiful face.

"Where is the owner of this saloon?" she demanded, her voice shrill and trembling, the gun wobbling in her hands.

Boyd stepped forward, cringing as she carelessly swung the gun in his direction. From the way she nervously clenched the revolver, he suspected she was scared to death and had never touched a gun before in her life. "May I presume you are Mrs. Ashier?"

"Yes, and you may also presume that I am furious and fed up with the noise coming from that rum hole." She jerked the nose of the gun toward his saloon. "I haven't slept a night through since moving here. My boardinghouse is empty because of you, and I have no other means to support myself, Mr. Grayson."

So she knew his name. Good. That would make this little exchange much easier. He nodded toward the gun. "Is that loaded?"

"It most certainly is. I want these men to go home. Now," she said, sweeping the barrel of the pistol across the crowd.

"It's too early to send the boys home, but we'll head back inside for the evening. Sorry to disturb you."

Her jaw clenched and she glared at him. "Do you think an apology excuses your total disregard for your neighbors? I don't want your apology. I want these men gone and that rum hole closed!"

"It's Saturday night, Mrs. Ashier. I can't close this early. Now, be reasonable and put the gun down before you hurt somebody."

"Not until you and your inebriated friends go home."

"This *is* my home." He jerked his chin toward the saloon.

"You live there?"

He nodded and took a step forward, intending to remove the revolver from her shaking hands.

"Don't come any closer," she warned.

He stopped and lifted his palms. "No need to get jumpy, Mrs. Ashier." He worked up his most charming smile. "I'd just like to finish this conversation in private," he suggested, starting toward her again.

"Stay away!" She tensed and pulled the gun to her chest like a child protecting a coveted toy. An earsplitting crack ripped through the night. A window above his bar shattered. The men below ducked flying shards of glass and swung incredulous looks in her direction.

Boyd stared in outrage. "Are you crazy?"

Claire gasped and held her gun at arm's length. She didn't know what else to do with it; she hadn't meant to pull the trigger. Her heart pounded so hard she could only draw in half-breaths. But for the sake of her own survival, she gripped the revolver and stood her ground. She had to end the noise coming from the saloon before it put her out of business.

The Pemberton Inn was an attractive two-story structure on the corner of Chestnut and Main Street at the top of West Hill. But to Claire it was nothing more than a rum hole owned by an inconsiderate man. She wasn't sorry at all that she'd taken out a window.

A man stepped from the crowd, but Boyd signaled him to stop. "Give me a minute, Duke." The man nodded, and Boyd turned to face her.

He was taller than most of the men in the street, and at least five inches taller than she was. His hair was dark, probably black, but when she saw his face bathed in the light from her window, her stomach dipped. Not even the play of shadow and light could ruin the perfection of Boyd Grayson's face. If anything, it made him more dangerous.

"I understand that you're upset, Mrs. Ashier, but that doesn't give you cause to shoot at my patrons."

"I hadn't intended—I wasn't shooting at anybody."

He nodded toward her house. "Why don't we go inside and discuss this on more friendly terms?"

Never would she invite a man like him into her home. "Unless you're going to tell me that you're closing your saloon, I have nothing to say to you. I'm a widow trying to support myself. The noise from that rum hole has chased away every one of my boarders."

He stared back at her without a trace of shame on his handsome face. His look of appreciation and speculation made her glad that several feet separated them. "I'll be happy to rent a room this evening if it will help."

She gasped at his audacity and jerked her gun toward him, itching to pull the trigger and wipe the smile off his face. How dare he try to seduce her? Her late husband had used his looks and charm to lead her straight to hell. She'd vowed at his graveside that she would never again be manipulated by a man's charm or good looks.

She refused to waste any more words on the insufferable reprobate standing in front of her. She was nineteen dollars away from being destitute. She wanted his saloon closed.

Now.

She waved her gun toward the crowd of inebriates then folded her arms. "This is my last warning. Go home. All of you." "

Go easy with that, Mrs. Ashier, or you'll end up shooting yourself." Boyd nodded toward the gun. "If that's your grandmother's revolver, it has a touchy trigger."

"So do I, Mr. Grayson."

The men chuckled, so she brandished the gun again. Send those men home and close your bar," she demanded, "or I'm going to visit the sheriff in the morning. Your neighbors deserve some peace and quiet."

"I'm sure my brother would enjoy your visit, Mrs. Ashier, but he can't close a legitimate business."

"Your brother?" Her breath whooshed out, and she sagged against her front door.

"That's right." He gestured to the man on his left. "This is Sheriff Grayson, my brother, and he's a regular customer at the Pemberton."

To her shock, a bear of a man stepped from the crowd and held up his hands, making the badge on his chest flash in the light from her window. "Mrs. Ashier, these boys mean no harm. I'll get them inside and they won't bother you again tonight."

Shivering from fury and the frigid cold, Claire gave the sheriff a scathing look. "I'd suggest you step back, Sheriff, because I'm serious about closing this saloon. You should be ashamed of yourself for frequenting it."

"My job requires me to visit the saloons and keep the peace."

"Well, you've been remiss in your duty this evening. As long as this saloon is open, there is no peace for this neighborhood. And frankly, it doesn't impress me at all that the owner of this rum hole is your brother."

"I'm not overly impressed that he's my brother either."

She gaped at him, wondering if she'd heard him correctly.

The sheriff slanted a glance at Boyd gave her a half grin. "Boyd believes he can manipulate any situation to his advantage. It's embarrassing to the family, but the blame rests with my mother." The sheriff lowered his hands and shrugged, clucking his tongue as he walked toward her. "Ma had this burning desire to have a girl, but all she got were boys. So even after Boyd had grown out of wearing gowns to bed, Ma insisted on coddling him like a daughter. It's made him a bit odd, I'm afraid."

Boyd laughed along with his patrons as if they were all sharing a private joke at her expense. "If you're going to divulge my secrets, Duke," he said, "it's only fair that you share a few of your own. Tell her what you wear to bed."

Dumbstruck by the absurdity of the brothers' conversation, Claire shifted her gaze between them, wondering if they were drunk, insane, or both.

The sheriff looked her straight in the eye. "Actually I don't wear anything."

She opened her mouth, but was too shocked to come up with the reprimand the comment deserved.

The sheriff winked and plucked the gun from her hands. "Beg pardon for the rudeness, Mrs. Ashier. Go on in to bed now. I'll keep the peace tonight and return your gun in the morning."

Blast and damnation! The sheriff and his wretched brother had purposely distracted her with their nonsensical conversation in order to disarm her.

That she had been outwitted so easily infuriated her, but she held her tongue. She had something more potent than a bullet to put Mr. Grayson out of business. She had Dr. Dio Lewis, a powerful temperance speaker from Boston, who held as much disdain for intemperance as she did.

She'd written to Dr. Lewis shortly after moving to Fredonia and learning that the town was filled with rum holes like the Pemberton Inn. Dr. Lewis would be arriving tomorrow, and every church in Fredonia was going to cancel their evening service so the townspeople could gather at the Baptist church for his address. Boyd Grayson didn't know it yet, but he was going to attend that meeting.

Struggling to hide the mayhem raging inside her, Claire faced her neighbor, knowing he couldn't refuse the request she was about to make without being unpardonably rude.

"Mr. Grayson, if you would be willing to escort me to church tomorrow evening, perhaps we can find a way to make this situation tolerable for both of us." There wasn't a chance in Hades she would accept anything less than his closing the saloon, but that was exactly why she needed to get Boyd Grayson to church. Dr. Lewis had a message for the reprobate.

"In all fairness, Mrs. Ashier, it may not be in your best interest to keep company with me, being a saloon owner and all"

"I'm a respectable widow. I believe your reputation could benefit from the association."

Muffled laughter rippled through the crowd as Boyd moved to stand at the foot of her porch steps. "Are you sure it won't sully your own?"

"Quite."

"All right then."

At his nod of acceptance she turned to open her door, vowing she would soon be rid of Boyd Grayson and his abominable saloon.

9

"Mrs. Ashier?"

Gritting her teeth, she turned back to her reprehensible neighbor.

"I'm looking forward to discovering the benefits of our association." A slow smile spread across his face. He tipped an imaginary hat and gave her a courtly bow. "Good night, fair lady."

An involuntary flutter filled her stomach. No man, especially a drinking man, should have a face like a prince or own a smile with the power to mesmerize a woman. She couldn't begin to guess how many broken hearts Boyd Grayson had caused in his lifetime, but she vowed hers wouldn't be one of them. She closed the door in his face, and sagged against the mahogany-paneled wall of her foyer.

What had she gotten herself into?

She knew firsthand that men who drank alcohol were too unpredictable and could turn violent and deadly if provoked. But she'd *had* to confront him. Her last boarder had left earlier that evening because of the noise from the saloon. During the six weeks that she'd been running her boardinghouse, she'd had many guests, all of whom loved her home but eventually left because of the noise.

If she were simply renting to overnight guests, they would put up with the noise for a night or two. But the people she rented to were seeking a place to stay for several weeks or months. Traveling salesmen came to town to do business. Families came to visit relatives who didn't always have room to put them up. Newly married couples not wanting to set up housekeeping would rent by the year.

Unlike the Harrison Hotel or the Taylor House, Claire's boardinghouse was a home to her guests. They could visit her kitchen at any hour to make themselves a cup of tea and eat her fresh-baked tea cakes, cookies, or breads. They could sit by a warm fire in the parlor, or play the piano in her music room, or retire at their leisure to their own private bedchamber.

Taking boarders was her only means of supporting herself. She had no other options. Not one.

Her father had disowned her at seventeen for eloping with Jack Ashier, which had been the worst mistake of her life. She'd naively thought the reckless charmer loved her.

He'd only wanted the dowry he thought her wealthy father would provide.

But her parents had been outraged with Claire, and they'd blamed her grandmother Marie, whom Claire had been visiting, for allowing the elopement to happen. Instead of giving Claire a dowry, her father disinherited her and broke all ties with Marie, his own mother. Claire had spent four years in hell with a man who had promised her heaven.

Now all she wanted was to feel safe again.

She rubbed the chill from her arms, dreading the empty hours that invited nightmarish memories. She had to do something, *anything* to keep her mind occupied.

Hurrying upstairs to her bedchamber, she unlocked a small drawer in the oak chiffonier then moved aside her beloved grandmother's diary she'd yet to read. The letter her sister had written to her a month ago lay open in the drawer. Homesick, Claire picked up the letter and sank into the wing chair to read it again.

Dearest Claire,
I hope you and Jack are happy in your new home in Fredonia.

Claire groaned, the weight of her own lies burdening her conscience. She'd lied while Jack was alive that she was happy with him, and lied after he died that he was still alive and moving to Fredonia with her. She'd done it to keep her sister from worrying.

It must feel strange yet oddly comforting to live in Grandmother's house. I know how much you loved her. We all deeply miss her.

Joanna, Jonathan, and Joseph are growing too fast to keep them in shoes, but they are healthy, happy children. Michael has become a partner in Daddy's steel mill. I am busy with the unending household chores, but blessed with love and good health. I pray that you are, too, dearest sister. I miss you and wish you could come home for a visit, but as you must suspect, nothing has changed here. I'm sorry, Claire, but Daddy still refuses to speak of you. I continue to pray that one day his heart will know forgiveness, and you can come home.

Your loving sister, Lida.

Claire's throat ached. She would give anything to be welcome in her father's home again, but he would never forgive her for the embarrassment she'd caused the family.

For four years, she had longed to pour out her heartaches and fears in her letters to Lida, but she'd been too ashamed to admit her true circumstances. Instead, she'd filled the pages with false claims of happiness and love for Jack, feeling it was kinder to write fairy tales than truth.

Now it would be an even bigger lie to tell her sister that she was grieving Jack. She was relieved to be rid of him.

She wouldn't have wished him dead, but she was glad to be free of him, to have a chance to build a safe and decent life for herself. That's why she had allowed her new neighbors to think she'd been widowed for over a year, as uncomfortable as she was with yet another lie. But it would have been unseemly for a widow to bury her husband and open a boardinghouse eight weeks later. She would tell Lida the truth, of course, that Jack had drowned two months ago. But she would never tell anyone what had happened that dreadful night.

What a tangled mess of lies and broken dreams she'd wrought.

She placed Lida's letter in the drawer beside a small velvet bag—the only security she had left. She shook the contents onto the white lawn dresser scarf. The diminishing thickness of the pile sent a wave of panic through her. She should have had fifty dollars left. She *would* have had fifty dollars if she'd been able to keep her boardinghouse filled each night.

That scoundrel saloon owner was ruining her life.

She clenched her fist around her last nineteen dollars. She would not be forced into depending on a man again. Somehow she was going to shut down that wretched saloon.

Chapter Two

W hat a surprise the widow Claire Ashier had turned out to be. When Boyd had seen her standing on the porch last night, he'd never expected to find himself staring into the face of an angel with angry, starlit eyes.

He was certain she hadn't intentionally pulled the trigger on her revolver, but her daring in standing up to him and his patrons, and her ability to trap him into a church date, had thoroughly impressed him. Claire Ashier had an edge to her that warned people to stand aside. That drew him like a dog to a bone. He loved a good challenge.

Whistling, he tucked a small wood carving in his pocket and left his saloon. He strode across Main Street to Claire's house then took the steps of her front porch in a single leap.

Time to see what the lady was made of.

It took well over a minute for her to open the door, but only seconds for her disdainful expression to be replaced with surprise. A spark of appreciation filled her eyes as she surveyed his black wool suit and the Kersey overcoat he'd left open.

Boyd stepped into her foyer, pleased with himself. He'd gotten her attention.

A brightly burning lantern lit the hall and spilled into the surrounding rooms. A glance told him Claire hadn't changed anything in the beautiful house. The east and west parlors were still decorated in busy gold and burgundy wallpaper. Heavy draperies dressed tall windows, and chandeliers hung from high, tin-plated ceilings. The music room was also the same elegant decor of patterned carpets and rich, glowing woodwork in which her grandmother had taken such pride. More sheet music rested on the piano. He couldn't see the kitchen or pantry at the back of the house, nor the formal dining room from where he stood, but he suspected they were unchanged as well.

He had carted wood for Claire's grandmother so often during the past two years, and eaten Marie's baked goods at her kitchen table, that the place felt like home to him. He was glad Claire hadn't changed anything.

She reached for the closet door, but Boyd slipped his hand over hers, trapping it between the doorknob and his palm. She jerked her gaze to his, the message in her eyes deadly.

"I have something I want to give you before we leave." He released her hand and put his closed fists behind his back. "Choose a hand."

Her brow furrowed. "What?"

"It's a game, Mrs. Ashier. Don't tell me you've never played before."

"I don't play games." She turned back to the closet, but he raised one fist and held it a few inches from her haughty nose.

"I'll give you a hint. It's not in my left hand."

The slight twitch of her lips flooded him with satisfaction. She ignored him and retrieved an indigo blue wool coat from the closet. "I don't like surprises, and I don't accept gifts from men."

"It's not a gift. It's an invoice for replacing my window."

Her eyebrows jerked up with such surprise, he bit his lip to stop his grin.

"Well, in that case," she said, thoroughly flustered as she opened her hand. "I won't apologize for doing it, but I will accept responsibility."

Instead of an invoice, Boyd placed the carving on her palm.

She frowned, her gaze moving between his face and the small sculpted piece of wood. "What is this?"

"I couldn't find any wildflowers in my back yard, so I brought you this bouquet." He shrugged. "It was the best I could do in the middle of winter."

She lifted the carving closer to her eyes and let out a small gasp. "Where did you get this?"

"I made it."

"You did not."

"I did."

Wordlessly, she studied the tiny, intricately carved bouquet of roses that he'd dabbled with for the last few months, hoping to find the talent and desire to finish the statue he'd started seven years earlier. All he'd ended with was something he planned to feed to the stove.

"This is incredible." She met his gaze, her own unguarded for the first time. "Did you really carve this?"

"Yes. And it's really for you."

She studied it a moment longer then held the carving out to him. "I don't accept gifts from men. They always come attached with an obligation to return something."

"Do you accept apologies?"

"Of course."

"Then this is my apology, in material form, for disturbing you last night."

"I'm not looking for an apology, Mr. Grayson." She held out the carving as if to return it. "I want peace and quiet."

"Keep it," he urged.

She glanced at the carving then back at him. "I can't accept it."

"It's nothing but a piece of wood, Mrs. Ashier."

"It's a gift," she insisted.

"Well, I'm not going to cart it to church tonight." He took the carving from her and gestured toward the parlor. "Mind if I toss it in the fireplace?"

Her eyes widened. "You're going to burn it?"

"What else would I do with a bouquet of wooden roses?"

"Give it to your mother."

"Believe me, she doesn't need another carved piece of wood from me."

"Well, your shoes are wet with snow. Leave the carving on the cabinet, and I'll toss it out when I return from church."

"It'll only take a moment to remove my shoes—"

"I'll dispose of it *later*."

The crack in her voice surprised both of them. They stared at each other for several seconds before he smiled and placed the carving on the cherrywood silver chest that he'd always admired. "I'd appreciate that, Claire."

"It's *Mrs. Ashier*, and we're going to be late for church if we don't leave promptly."

⸻

Claire sat in an overfull pew at the Baptist church where that impudent saloon owner had deposited her before heading toward the back of the church. He'd whispered that he didn't want to start gossip by sitting with her, but the way he'd touched his lips to her ear as he whispered the warning was far more damaging. Already people were peeping at her then shifting their gaze to the back of the church, presumably to see if Mr. Grayson would nod and acknowledge their suspicions.

Well, he was here, and that was all that mattered at the moment.

She turned her attention to the pulpit where Dr. Lewis was telling about his heartbreaking childhood filled with abuse from an alcoholic father. Though he told his story to motivate others to abstain from the life-destroying vice, there wasn't an ounce of self-pity in the man. He was a strong and spiritual speaker whose words immediately began working magic on Claire and the people around her.

"There is a frightening change taking place in the converted Christian," Dr. Lewis said, his voice booming from the pulpit. "It is the shameful lack of temperance. Not only in bodily habits, but in intellectual, social, moral, and religious practices as well. Tonight I want to address one specific vice, the *worst* case of intemperance we know, namely the use of alcohol."

Amen. Feeling immensely proud of herself for summoning Dr. Lewis to their rum-soaked town, Claire glanced across the sea of inspired faces. Expressions of hope filled her vision, and her heart lifted. She had supporters here.

"Ninety-nine-percent of all the crime and poverty in this country can be traced to the same cause. Alcohol," Dr. Lewis continued. "Now, who is to blame for this?" He stared at the congregation as if they should know the answer, but not one person said a word. "The responsibility, my friends, belongs to those individuals of respectable position who indulge in drink. These people who set examples for the rest of us should be kicked out of respectable society, especially owners of the establishments that serve it. Encouragement of such a vice is as bad as self-indulgence."

"Do you honestly believe that?"

Amid shocked gasps, everyone turned to see who had spoken.

Boyd Grayson stood in the back corner of the church with his hat clasped in front of him, his dark hair glistening with melted snowflakes. He met Claire's shocked stare with a challenge in his eyes, demanding her attention even while her brain cautioned her to turn away. Last night the darkness had shadowed his face, but earlier this evening the light in her foyer had revealed gorgeous honey-brown eyes surrounded by dark lashes and a manly face that many women dreamed of.

But not her. She had married a handsome man like Boyd, and her dream man had become a cruel alcoholic. She was through dreaming.

The crowd murmured and whispered. Dr. Lewis folded his hands and addressed Boyd. "I speak only what I believe is true, Mister...?"

"Grayson," Boyd answered, seemingly undaunted at being the center of attention. "No disrespect intended, Dr. Lewis, but you and I both know the expression: You can lead a horse to water, but you can't force him to drink."

Dr. Lewis nodded, waiting for Boyd to expound. Claire secretly cursed Boyd for undermining her effort to improve the lives of people who desperately needed temperance from the vices that were tearing apart their families. She wanted to race to the back of the church and clamp her hand over his mouth.

"I'm asking how you can hold anyone but the imbiber himself accountable for consuming alcohol?" Boyd asked.

"I can answer best by posing a question. If a parent left a loaded gun and a four-year-old child unattended in the same room, would you not hold that parent responsible for an accident resulting from his negligence?"

"Of course, but we're talking about adults who knowingly consume alcoholic beverages of their own free will, not about unsuspecting children and loaded guns."

"Is that so?" Dr. Lewis turned to the congregation. "I ask you, who is most affected by alcoholism?" Silence greeted him and he shook his head with a sigh. "Our children suffer the most hardship. Drunken parents berate and beat their children. The money that should be used to clothe and feed them is spent at the saloons. I know because I experienced this firsthand. I agree that the imbiber is responsible for his own actions, Mr. Grayson, but every person who encourages him is as much at fault."

Boyd listened to Dr. Lewis in respectful silence, but Claire could tell he wasn't the least bit ashamed of owning a saloon. In his mind, the responsibility lay with the individual who chose to drink. She didn't disagree, but she also knew that many men wouldn't be tempted to imbibe if the saloons were closed. Whether Mr. Grayson wanted to accept it or not, he was part of the problem plaguing their town and ruining her business.

"What can we do to correct the problem?" one woman asked.

Dr. Lewis told them how other women had formed prayer bands and conducted nonviolent marches on the rum holes, shutting them down and taking pledges from the patrons to abstain from drinking. "I've seen it done in Dixon, Illinois, and Battle Creek, Michigan," he said. "You can do the same thing right here in Fredonia. All you need to do is organize a campaign."

Dr. Lewis looked straight at Claire. "Mrs. Ashier was courageous enough to request my help in stomping out intemperance. I ask you, the Christian people of this town, to stand with her and do the same."

In the sudden silence, Claire waited for satisfaction to flood her. Boyd Grayson now knew she'd trapped him into coming here tonight, that she'd summoned Dr. Lewis to help her put him out of business. But all she felt was her heart thudding like a sledgehammer against her chest. What if Boyd Grayson was as vindictive and vengeful as her husband had been?

"I'll stand with her." A rumble of excitement passed through the crowd as a woman stood up. "I'm Mrs. Reverend Beaton, and I would be honored to chair a committee," she said. To Claire's relief, a Mrs. Williams stood and pledged her support as well. Then Mrs. Dr. Fuller, and Mrs. Desmona Edwards followed suit. Before Claire's heartbeat calmed, nearly every woman in the church stood and volunteered her service.

Knowing it was time for courage, Claire rose to her feet, her back rigid, her chin high, her gaze fixed on Dr. Lewis so she wouldn't be tempted to glance at Boyd to gauge his reaction. "Let us take action," she said, "while our spirit of purpose is high and our mission clear."

To her surprise, enthusiastic applause greeted her. When the church finally quieted, Mrs. Beaton gave Claire a nod of acceptance and suggested that they hold a meeting at the church the following morning at ten o'clock.

"I'll help you start your meeting," Dr. Lewis said, "but then I must leave for Jamestown to continue our efforts. We're going to take our cause clear across the country!"

The buzz of excited voices again filled the church, and Claire finally dared to glance at Boyd. She expected him to taunt her in some way, but seeming admiration lit his eyes—and something more personal and much too intimate for her comfort.

Suddenly, she regretted asking him to escort her to church, because now he was going to walk her home.

Chapter Three

"You may as well say it, Mr. Grayson."

Boyd angled his head to see Claire's face as they crossed Barker Common and began walking up the section of Main Street they referred to as West Hill. Despite her ramrod posture and taller than average height, Claire was still four or five inches shorter than himself and he enjoyed having the advantage, however slight. "Say what?" he asked.

"That we're doomed to fail. That's what you were thinking."

"Are you a mind reader?"

"Your expression was speaking for you."

"If that's the case, Claire, I'm afraid I've offended your sense of decency a number of times since meeting you last night."

"And you have just done so again by using my given name without invitation."

He laughed. "Spoken with the honesty of a child."

"Don't mistake me for one, Mr. Grayson."

She stopped and met his eyes with a boldness he'd rarely seen from a woman. Her cheekbones were flushed with cold, her eyes sparked like blue fire in the glow of the gas streetlamp. The hood she wore framed the most interesting face he'd ever seen, and he felt a deep urge to tilt her chin toward the light.

Suddenly, her eyes narrowed. "You can forget whatever you're trying to suggest with that lazy look in your eyes. I'm not interested."

He arched his brow. "What do you think I'm suggesting?"

"That you're used to getting what you want."

"And you perceive that as a threat?"

"No, only an irritation I won't put up with."

The defiant tilt of her chin afforded him the view he'd been craving, but he could only smile at her. He hadn't enjoyed conversing with a woman this much in all the years he'd been involved with them. And he'd had more brief involvements than he cared to remember. "Tell me, Mrs. Ashier, is it me you despise or is it men in general?"

"I despise being manipulated and considered a fool. Whether you're willing to admit it or not, you were trying to hold my gaze long enough to form an intimate connection. I was merely forthright enough to express my lack of interest."

"Some men might misinterpret your comment as an invitation."

"Then they would be thinking with their ego."

A delighted laugh burst from him. "Touché. So, how does a man redeem himself from such a misstep?"

Her lips twitched and he knew she wasn't without a sense of humor. "The man could close his saloon and stop testing the lady's patience."

"Is that all?"

"That's all."

He offered his elbow to her, but she declined his assistance. They continued to walk up the incline of West Hill. "Just close his profitable business and do... what?" he asked.

"Help the lady close the rest of the town's saloons."

Laughter rose in his chest, but he held it back. "What if the man doesn't want to do that?"

"Then he'd be well advised to stay out of the lady's way."

He glanced down, expecting to see humor in her eyes, but they were filled with determination and warning.

"Women aren't wrong to want their husbands home at a decent hour with some money still in their pockets," she said, her voice quiet but firm with conviction. "We aren't wrong to want to feel safe in our own homes."

"Have I suggested something to the contrary?" It offended him that she assumed he wasn't aware of, or didn't care about, the families tormented by an alcoholic family member. The mere rumor of a patron abusing his family was enough for Boyd to prohibit the man from patronizing his saloon.

"I didn't intend to offend your character, Mr. Grayson. I'm merely stating my reasons for uniting the women against you and the other saloon owners."

"You're claiming to do it for the greater good of society, but I sense there's a more personal reason involved."

"Fighting for something you believe in is always personal." She climbed her porch steps, stopped at the door and faced him. "Thank you for the escort."

"Does this mean you're not going to invite me in for tea?" He offered his most charming smile. "Your grandmother always did."

Her mouth pursed in irritation. "There will be several of us visiting your saloon soon. Consider yourself fairly notified."

That was supposed to worry him? He grinned as Claire entered her house and closed the door in his face. He couldn't help himself. The idea of a few women thinking they could change the habits of an entire town was ridiculous. It would be like a colony of ants attempting to move a mountain.

⊷⊶

At ten o'clock Monday morning three hundred men and women of all religious denominations gathered in the Baptist church where they prayed, sang, and gave enthusiastic speeches on how to conquer the evils of intemperance. It was the first bright sunny day in weeks, and with high spirits, the ladies withdrew to the rooms below to plan the details of their march, while the men continued in prayer and pledged their support in dollars. Temperance meetings were arranged for every Sunday night and prayer meetings every night until their work was accomplished.

At precisely half past twelve, the procession of over one hundred ladies came forth from the basement and quietly walked across the park, with Mrs. Judge Barker and Mrs. Rev. L. Williams at the head.

Claire walked alongside Desmona Edwards and other wives and daughters of the most respected men in town, feeling a deep sense of pride in her mission. If her actions could save one woman, child, or family from suffering the pain she'd endured with Jack then her efforts would be worthwhile.

And if she could close down that den of noise across the street from her home, life would be almost perfect.

Just the thought of a quiet evening made her sigh. Her breath formed a long, frosty funnel in the cold air as she closed her fingers around the miniature carving she'd been unable to throw away last night. After the conversation she'd had with Boyd Grayson during their walk home, she had been determined to rid herself of his company and the gift he'd forced on her. But the tiny carving of roses was too magnificent to destroy. Each rose, in varying stages of bloom, was so perfectly sculpted that she could almost smell their fragrance. It intrigued her that the reprobate could have whittled something so exquisite.

The man intrigued her, too.

Boyd Grayson seemed every bit the charmer she disdained, but what she couldn't see clearly was the shadow he carried with him. There was another man standing behind his dashing personality, and she suspected he was totally unaware of it.

"All right, ladies." Mrs. Barker clapped her hands. "It's time to begin our work." She led the procession of women down the steps of the Taylor House and into the saloon. They filled the bar, surprising the three Taylor brothers, who knew that no self-respecting woman would enter such an establishment. Mrs. Barker immediately informed the men of the object of their visit, appealing to them personally to cease the sale of intoxicating liquors.

Mr. Taylor cast a helpless glance at his brothers. "We feel obliged to keep liquor in our hotel for our guests."

"We didn't come to argue, gentlemen. We're simply here to urge you by the promise of God to heed our pledge."

After more praying and gentle persuading, Mr. Taylor finally said, "If the rest will stop selling alcohol, we'll stop, too."

Claire stood with her mouth open, as stunned as the rest of the ladies. None of them had expected such easy capitulation.

"That includes the drug stores," Mr. Taylor said, breaking their stunned silence. "When every establishment selling intoxicating beverages ceases distribution, I'll stop selling it as well."

His maneuvering wasn't what they had hoped for, but it was a beginning. Mrs. Barker asked him to reconsider the matter and said they would call on him again the next day.

They called at Smeizer & Hewes next, but Mr. Hewes stated he had a license and would continue to sell according to its provisions. Next door, Willard Lewis said he would close his saloon if the rest would shut up their businesses as well. The ladies also visited J. D. Maynard's Drug Store. He argued that he couldn't run his shop without selling liquor, but promised not to sell to any drunkards. The ladies then walked to Baldwin's Drug Store, the Harrison Hotel, Duane Beebe's Saloon, Don Clark's Drug Store, and Wriensler's Saloon where they received similar replies.

Finally, they marched up West Hill to the Pemberton Inn. Claire sensed this would be the biggest challenge, and her own personal battle, but she was determined to win. Straightening her shoulders, she entered the saloon—and came face-to-face with Boyd Grayson.

He stood behind the bar, hip cocked, a crisp white towel slung over his arrogant shoulder as he filled a mug with ale.

He turned and smiled, saluting Claire and her fellow marchers with the foaming mug.

She tightened her stomach to stop the flutter. Why did she have to be battling the most handsome rakehell in town?

⊷⊱ ⊰⊶

A literal herd of women crowded Boyd's saloon. He whistled in amazement. Every woman in Fredonia must be marching. But the only face he could seem to focus on was Claire's. She wore her hood up, but thick honey-gold hair brushed her cheeks and fell softly across the breast of her coat. Her eyes held a silent challenge that warmed his blood.

Her face was pink from the cold, but he imagined it flushed with passion, her hair loose and her eyes half closed as he kissed her neck, her breasts, her...

Her naked image came to him so clearly it flooded his body with heat. He clenched his fingers around the mug handle, struggling for any thought that would drag his mind away from undressing her.

She smiled at him. "You look shocked, Mr. Grayson."

He was shocked all right. By his own desire. He'd never felt such intensity in his life. "I was expecting ten or twenty women," he said, struggling to regain his balance.

Her lips tilted in a superior half-smile. "There are over one hundred of us."

"And there'll be more," said Mrs. Barker. She and Mrs. Williams then pleaded with him to close his saloon and spare the poor wives and children any more suffering.

In the early afternoons, Boyd's saloon was usually quiet, but Pat Lyons, who was sitting at the bar drinking an ale, and Karlton Kane, who had been hauling in Boyd's weekly order of liquor, both stopped what they were doing and stared as if the women had lost their minds.

"Ladies," Boyd said, "I admire your efforts, but closing down drinking establishments isn't the answer to improving your home life. A man who neglects his family or beats his wife will do so whether he's a drunkard or not. Closing saloons will not make those men stop abusing their families."

"Can you prove that?" Claire asked. To his surprise, she seemed sincere.

"No. I can't. But do you suppose that man's family might be safer with him drinking at home?"

Understanding dawned in her eyes and she exhaled slowly. "No."

"Then you have my answer. I will not close my saloon." Instead of debating, Mrs. Barker turned to the ladies.

"Let's sing a hymn and pray that Mr. Grayson will reconsider his position."

Before he could tell her not to bother, the women filled his saloon with a mournful rendition of "Praise God From Whom All Blessings Flow." Sailor howled and scratched on the door of the storeroom where Karlton had quickly caged him after seeing the women marching toward the front door.

The deep baritone of a man's voice drew Boyd's attention to Pat, who was standing beside the bar singing loud enough to be heard in Barker Common. Boyd glanced at Karlton, but the burly distiller shrugged as if he had no idea why Pat had suddenly changed sides.

The hymn ended and Pat bowed. "Well done, ladies."

The women glowered at Pat, but to Boyd's astonishment, Claire was fighting a smile.

"We've done our best for this day." Mrs. Barker shooed the ladies toward the door. "Let's move on."

Boyd winked at Claire, but the humor in her eyes vanished. She marched out the door like a sergeant mustering her troops.

On Wednesday morning Claire began her chores with a renewed sense of purpose. The temperance cause was already gaining ground. Monday evening, after their first march, J. D. Maynard had signed their pledge and agreed to stop selling alcoholic beverages in his drug store. Of course, on Tuesday D. A. Clark warned them not to visit his drugstore again, as their visits were annoying.

Levi Harrison was more of a gentleman. He'd told the ladies he would consider their proposal if they returned to his hotel at eleven o'clock.

Claire and her fellow marchers would be there. Business by business, they were going to rid the town of alcohol. Day by day, bottle by bottle, they would tear down this mountain of evil.

She stepped from her warm kitchen into her cold woodshed and felt her spirits plummet. She loathed carrying wood.

Piece by piece, she stacked it in her arms then groaned as she carried it inside. This was only the beginning. After she filled the huge bin in the kitchen, she would have to carry three loads into her parlor, and another armload upstairs for the fireplace in her bedchamber. If she was lucky enough to get a boarder, she would have to carry wood for that room, too. It was enough to make a woman wish for a man.

Almost.

She dumped her load of wood into the kitchen bin with a crash then headed back to the shed. She would haul her own fuel each day for the rest of her life to avoid enduring another marriage like the one she'd suffered.

No job could belittle her or cause her the pain Jack had. Nothing could terrify her more than losing control of her life again, or subjugating herself to a man's cruel demands.

Nothing.

The thought of Jack shattered her calm. He'd been dead for weeks, but she couldn't escape him. His domineering presence lived within her, ruling her thoughts, keeping her scared. He was dead. She'd seen his gray, bloated body. She'd watched them lower his coffin deep into the earth and bury it. But Jack Ashier felt as alive as if he were standing behind her.

Spiders crawled up her back, and she shivered.

She would never forget that deadly look in his eyes, or the ice-cold fear that sliced through her when he pulled her beneath the brown river water.

Her knees weakened, and she lurched outside into the frigid morning air. She sucked deep gulps of cold air into her lungs as she slid down the shed wall. Her backside hit the top step and halted her downward plunge.

"Dear God," she whispered, clasping her stomach and rocking on the step. She squeezed her eyes closed, trying to block her last image of Jack's enraged face and the deadly intent in his eyes.

He'd wanted to kill her. He *would* have killed her.

A loud breath near her ear knifed terror straight through her heart. She screeched and recoiled, slamming her head against the shed wall. She opened her eyes and found herself nose-to-nose with a long-legged, panting white dog with brown spots and pointy ears that didn't quite stand up. He stared at her with huge chocolate-drop eyes, his tongue lolling from the side of his mouth.

Realizing it wasn't her late husband, and that the dog wasn't angling for her throat, she released a hard, trembling breath and clasped a hand over her heart.

"What are you doing here?"

The dog emitted a wheezy, whistling sound.

Her senses returned slowly, and she took two deep breaths before easing away from the wall. She rubbed the back of her head and stared at the dog with dismay, realizing it belonged to Boyd Grayson. "You scared the life out of me. Did your owner send you over here to do that?" After two days of marching on Boyd's saloon, she wouldn't have doubted his desire to make her pay for disrupting his day.

The dog wheezed again, but with his mouth parted and his tongue hanging out the side, he looked like he was grinning at her.

"Don't try to charm me, mister." She scooted to the edge of the step. "I've had enough of that from your owner."

Still wearing his brainless canine grin, the dog dropped into a sitting position and lifted his paw.

She gaped at him.

As if the dog understood she wasn't going to shake his wet, padded paw, he planted it on the snowy ground in front of him and sat watching her.

"Go on," she said, shooing him away with her hand. "Go *home.*"

He trotted in the direction she'd moved her hand, sniffed the ground then came back and sat in front of her again.

"I didn't throw anything. I was telling you to go home."

He stared at her with his big eyes, tilting his head and panting, not moving a toenail. She sighed and glanced toward the street to see if her neighbors were about. The street was empty. Just like her life.

"Can you carry wood?" she asked.

The dog's wheezy answer made her smile.

"Oh, bother. Come here." She held out her hand and the dog leapt forward, his tail swinging wildly behind him as she stroked his head. "I could use some company, even if you aren't much for conversation."

⟫⟪

"Sai-*lor*!"

Boyd shrugged on his coat as he stepped outside. He scanned Main Street in both directions, wondering which neighbor his dog was begging scraps from this time. The shameless mutt had become a mooch, and though Boyd admired Sailor's cunning, he didn't like him imposing on the neighbors, or having to chase after the dog each day. Still, he couldn't go to the lumber mill without the mutt. Who knew where the rascal would end up if left to his own devices.

Boyd gave a shrill whistle and followed a smattering of dog tracks down Chestnut Street, hoping they belonged to his dog. They trailed from the middle of the street to the edge then back again, as if Sailor had been trying to decide where his best chances lay. Suddenly, the prints veered left and climbed a small bank of snow to the rear of Claire Ashier's house. Boyd glanced across her yard and saw that they led right to her back door.

And stopped there.

He grinned in anticipation as he followed the tracks. If Sailor had wheedled his way inside, he had just earned himself a prime bone from the butcher.

When Boyd reached the back door to the shed it was open, but neither Claire nor Sailor were around. Having made this trip hundreds of times to carry wood for Claire's grandmother, he strode through the shed and knocked on the door that connected the woodshed with the kitchen.

Sailor's yelp and the sound of chair legs screeching across the hardwood floor told Boyd he'd guessed correctly. He loved that mutt. Sailor was the master of weaseling.

Claire opened the door, her eyes guarded and cool. Sailor barked and wagged his tail, wheezing like an overheated boiler. Boyd rubbed his dog's head, but spoke to Claire.

"Has Sailor picked out his own room yet?"

"What?" Her brow furrowed. "Oh." Her confusion melted instantly, and though she released a breath that resembled a gasp of embarrassment, she didn't smile. "He followed me inside while I was carting wood."

"Did he carry his share?"

Her lips pursed. "He tracked up my floor."

Boyd pointed to several chunks of wood beside the wood bin. "Where are your manners, Sailor? Bring in some wood for Mrs. Ashier. Go on."

Sailor lunged out the door. He swiped Boyd's knees then skidded to a stop before the wood scraps. After two seconds of rooting in the pile, Sailor bit into a hefty hunk of wood that he struggled to keep clenched in his mouth. He made it as far as the kitchen then dropped it on Claire's foot.

Her eyes shot open as she gasped, or maybe Boyd did—he couldn't discern who was more shocked. Her grip tightened on the door handle and she shifted as she extracted her slipper-covered foot from beneath the heavy chunk of wood. Her accusing eyes met Boyd's, but she didn't say a word.

"Claire—Mrs. Ashier—that wasn't supposed to happen."

She didn't look convinced. "Good-bye, Mr. Grayson."

She tried to close the door, but Boyd braced his hand against the hard flat surface, feeling terrible that she'd been hurt. "I'm sorry. Truly, Mrs. Ashier. Sailor lugs wood around all the time at the saloon. I'm always tripping over pieces of kindling that he drags out of the bucket." He reached down and grabbed the hunk of wood before Sailor could get his teeth around it again. He tossed it into the bin behind him then faced Claire, who was pale. "I'd better look at your toes."

She reared back. "You will not!"

"That was a heavy piece of wood, Mrs. Ashier. I really think—"

"My toes are *fine*," she said, but her voice was thin, as if she were in pain.

"Then it must be your slipper that's bleeding."

She jerked her gaze to her feet then gripped the doorknob with both hands.

He caught her elbow and turned her toward a small oak table in her kitchen. "At least allow me to help you into a chair." He nudged the door closed with his foot. "I hope your toes aren't too damaged. I'm not very good at stitching."

"I fail to see the humor in this." She tried to tug her arm free, but he maintained his grip as she limped toward a high back cane-bottom chair at the table.

The light sheen of perspiration on her forehead told him she was in far more pain than she was admitting. The split piece of firewood had been heavy, with a jagged edge that had hit her square on the top of her foot.

The instant she was seated, he knelt at her feet. "Would you mind lifting your gown?"

She clapped her hands over her knees and glared at him. "Take your dog and go home. I'm capable of tending to my own toes."

"I'm afraid I can't leave without making sure your foot isn't badly damaged."

"I told you, it's fine."

He ignored her and tugged the slipper off her foot.

"*Mister* Grayson!"

"Your toes are still attached. That's a good sign."

"How dare you be so... so impudent."

He fought to hide a grin as he sat back on one heel.

"Now, is there really cause here to malign my male prowess, Mrs. Ashier?"

"Your what?" As if she suddenly realized what he'd said, her face colored. "I suggested no such thing. I called you *impudent*, Mr. Grayson. That means arrogant, audacious, disrespectful—in case you didn't know."

He did know. He'd been accused of being impudent on many occasions, but he enjoyed getting her stirred up. "Well, it sounded like something far less desirable." He propped her foot on his thigh, but she gasped and yanked it away.

"What are you doing?" she asked in outrage.

"Trying to make sure your foot isn't broken."

"It's cut and bruised. Nothing more. Now please leave me to tend to my personal business."

"What if your foot is broken?" he asked, looking up at her. "If you can't walk, how will you hail the doctor? How will you care for yourself or your boarders?"

"I don't have any boarders, thanks to you."

"I'm sorry about that," he said, retrieving the clean handkerchief he'd tucked in his pocket before leaving the saloon. "Let me satisfy my curiosity, and I'll leave you in peace." He pulled her foot to his thigh, but she jerked away.

"I'm afraid your curiosity will have to go unquenched."

"Honestly, Claire, you would think I was trying to ravish you." He slipped his hand over her slender foot and smiled up at her. "Your pretty feet are most tempting, but I can control myself for a minute or two." He pulled her foot back to his thigh, and held firm when she tried to tug away. "If you keep kicking and tussling you *will* make me impudent, or whatever that word is."

She snorted, and he looked up in surprise, wondering if he'd really heard the hint of a laugh. Her lips were pursed, but her eyes... her gorgeous blue eyes sparkled.

"You look like your grandmother when you laugh." Because he knew she would deny her laughter, or reprimand him for using her given name, he lowered his head. "Please, Claire. Give me a minute to look at this. I need to be certain you aren't badly hurt." To his relief she gave in and let him feel her foot through her stocking. It was warm against his thigh, slender, and delicately sculpted at her ankle. He wanted to tug her stocking off and feel the smoothness of her skin, trace the line of her shinbone beneath his fingers.

"Is it broken?"

"I don't believe so. But I think the chunk of wood split the skin on your hallux."

"My what?"

"Your big toe." He smiled at her. "I assumed if you knew what impudent meant you would surely know the word hallux."

Instead of frowning, she tilted her head to study him.

"What truly baffles me is how *you* know the word."

He liked that she was turning the tables on him. "I took a bad fall in the gorge when I was nine. I'd broken a rib, but when the doctor told me I'd also broken my hallux, I thought he meant my back. After he told me I'd only broken my big toe, I was so relieved, I never forgot the word."

She studied him, and he returned her scrutiny. In the sudden stillness he could not only hear Sailor panting, but his own heart-pounding like a drum. He wanted to kiss her. Really kiss her. The kind of kiss that burns deep in the gut, that stops time, that makes two people cling and beg and go insane with lust.

"You're hurting my toe."

Her whispered complaint jolted him and he realized he'd been gripping her toes. "Sorry." He drew a shuddering breath and released her foot. "Do you have any iodine?"

"I'll put some on after—"

"Where is it?"

She sighed and pointed toward a door on the far wall of her kitchen. "In the water closet cabinet."

"Take off your stockings."

"I will not." She started to stand, but he caught her hips and pushed her back down. She gasped, her expression outraged. "You go too far."

"I'm doing what I have to." He winked. "Stay put. I'll get the iodine."

"You are insufferable."

"So I've been told." He stood up, and Sailor leapt to his feet. "Stay, Sailor."

Sailor's ears drooped and he blinked at Claire.

She held out her hand. "Don't let him bully you, too."

The dog's tongue flopped out of the side of his mouth and he ducked beneath her hand. She scratched his head and he horned in closer.

The mutt was right where Boyd wanted to be.

The unfairness of it rankled as he crossed the kitchen to retrieve the iodine. He could barely share a civil word with Claire, but his weasel of a dog was flopped against her sweet curves, basking in her affection like she owned him.

Well, maybe Sailor wasn't as smart as Boyd thought. If Boyd were a dog, he'd climb right into Claire's lap and start licking her from the neck down.

Whoa. The thought stopped him mid-stride.

Claire pulled off her stocking then glanced at him. "What's the matter?"

He stood in the middle of the kitchen, warning himself to calm down, to rein in and slow the horse before he frightened her away.

"Are you all right?"

He was ready to ride for the finish line, but he hadn't even gotten Claire out of the gate yet. But he would, he decided. If it was the only thing he accomplished in his life, he was going to make love to Claire Ashier.

He clenched the iodine in his fist and knelt at her feet.

"I'd like you to address me as Boyd," he said. He repositioned her bare foot on his thigh. She didn't fight him this time or comment on his request.

While he cleaned the blood off her toe, she continued petting Sailor. There was a tenderness in her touch, a warmth in the way she stroked the dog's head that was so natural and unguarded, Boyd couldn't take his eyes off her.

The shadow of loneliness dulled her eyes. He'd seen that same forlorn look in his mirror for years, but to see the pain and emptiness in Claire's eyes bothered him. In that brief glimpse, he knew that she'd experienced loneliness, that she'd suffered loss, that she knew fear.

What tragedy was it that left the residue of those emotions in her eyes?

"I know it's going to sting," she said. "Just get it over with."

He ducked his head and saturated a corner of his handkerchief with iodine. "You like Sailor," he said, trying to distract her from the sting as he dabbed at her toe.

"Does that surprise you?"

"Maybe."

"Why? I had two dogs when I was a girl, and I trained both of them myself. I could make them lie down just by snapping my fingers. I named them Shakespeare and—ouch."

"Sorry. Just a touch more," he said.

"Why?"

"Because I want to make sure it doesn't get infected. I think you're going to have a bruise on your instep."

"I was asking why you're surprised that I like Sailor?"

He finished wiping her toe, replaced the cap on the bottle and rose to his feet. "Because he's a weaseling, ill-mannered maniac. And because you seem to prefer your own company."

Her lashes lowered like window shades, and Boyd knew he'd struck a vein.

He set the bottle of iodine on the table. "Is it too forward of me to ask how long you've been a widow?"

"Yes." Her chin lifted and she met his eyes, but he sensed that behind her brave front she was hiding something. "It's not that I prefer my own company, Mr. Grayson. It's that I prefer not to subject myself to the games, petty judgments, and humiliating exchanges that most relationships contain."

"Relationships also contain companionship and joy."

"That's why I like Sailor. Despite being clumsy and a bit rambunctious, I don't have to wonder if his actions are sincere." She stroked the dog's bony back. "He just needs some training to polish his manners."

"Would you train him? If I brought him over each day, would you teach him some manners?"

The look on Claire's face told him she saw right through his ploy, but she didn't order him to leave. She gave him one of those looks women get just before they take you into the jeweler's shop and empty your pockets.

"Are you willing to fill my wood bins each day in return?"

There it was. Her payment for services rendered. He was used to this subtle maneuvering. And good at it.

"Of course." He could barely contain his grin. He'd had women eager to bed him, women eager to be wooed, but this was the first time he'd ever had to use Sailor as a go-between. Claire Ashier was only eager to get her wood bins filled.

Well, he would change that.

"You'll have to bring him first thing in the morning. We can start this Friday. Before breakfast."

"Before breakfast? I'm lucky if I wake up before lunch unless I've promised to work at the mill that day."

"Morning is the only time I'll be able to do it."

She was playing him, and he knew it, but he was playing her, too, and she knew it, so the only way for him to win—and he intended to win—was to agree to her terms. But before breakfast? That would be dawn for a woman like Claire. Not even Sailor got up that early.

"If that doesn't suit you—"

"It's fine," he said then gave her his most disarming smile. "But I was hoping we could arrange evening visits."

"I'm afraid that won't be possible. I'll be hosting prayer meetings in the evenings."

"Here?" he asked, unable to keep the disgust from his voice. The thought of a hundred righteous do-gooders, praying and caterwauling hymns only yards from his door, raised the hair on his arms. "Claire, it's bad enough having those women visit my saloon each day. It'll be torture having that noise seep into my life around the clock."

Her lips curved into a pleased smile. "I know."

Chapter Four

Wednesday evening Claire prowled her bedchamber, searching for something to distract her from the yawning emptiness of the house. She wished she had a dog like Sailor to keep her company, but she couldn't risk offending her boarders. Maybe a cat. No. No, she could never have a cat. It would be a constant reminder of... no. No cat.

The vast silence mocked her.

She rested her forearm on top of the chifforobe and looked out her window at the Pemberton Inn. With the noise coming from that rum hole, she would be lucky to rent out a single room this week.

Not only would that leave her without an income, it would leave her alone in the house. Without boarders, she had too much time to think, too much time to remember. She couldn't be alone, especially next week during the Christmas holiday. It would be unbearable.

A panicky feeling washed through her, and she closed her hand around the tiny carving. Was there anything she could do to convince Boyd Grayson to close his saloon? Was there *anything* that would touch his heart, or challenge his honor, or appeal to his sense of decency?

Failing that, how long would it take for her to find his Achilles' heel?

Her stomach tightened with dread. She would have to spend two dollars tomorrow to replenish the items in her pantry. That would leave her seventeen dollars.

She needed boarders.

She needed that saloon closed.

"What am I going to do, Grandma?" Sighing, she opened the dresser drawer and trailed her fingers over her grandmother's diary then raised the book to her nose. It smelled of leather and her grandmother's rose sachet.

Swallowing her anxiety, she took the journal downstairs to the parlor. She sat in a deep-seated rocking chair near the fireplace and hugged the journal to her chest. The rocking motion soothed her, and she envisioned herself as a little girl being rocked in her grandmother's arms. A sense of peace filled her and she felt more relaxed. She'd loved this creaky old chair and her grandmother's girlish laugh and the flowery smell of the house.

This was home.

Her home.

She needed to stay here. She *would* stay here.

"I could sure use your help, Grandma." The sound of her own voice made her sigh. She was talking to a book. Maybe she *should* get a dog.

The name Marie Claire Dawsen was written on the first page of the diary. Claire recognized her grandmother's handwriting—it was the same slanted script that filled the rest of the journal. She stroked her fingertips over the page and began to read.

I am overflowing with confusion and heartache, but I cannot share this inner torment with anyone.

This morning Abe—I dare not write his real name—pressed his cheek to my hair. His breath felt warm against my ear as he said my name... just my name, but oh, how he spoke it, soft as a prayer, his voice filled with pain and a passion we are forbidden. He is husband to another, father to four, prisoner to his obligations. I am a pastor's wife. But here, in the circle of Abe's arms, amidst the smell of coffee and wood shavings, I am a woman for the first time in my life.

A trembling breath of astonishment slipped from Claire's tight throat. In stunned disbelief she reread the first page.

Her Grandma Dawsen had allowed a man who was not her husband to hold and caress her, to breathe his desire across the bare flesh of her ear? The act was so wicked it raised goose bumps on Claire's neck to imagine the private, heated moment from fifty years past.

Judging by the date of the journal entry, her grandmother would have been in her early twenties at that time, and her Grandpa Dawsen would have been exiting his forties. Was their age difference the cause of her grandmother's attraction to another man? Claire was just a child when her grandfather died, and though he'd been rather plain and quiet, he'd seemed like a good man who hadn't deserved his wife's infidelity.

What on earth had compelled a warm-hearted, honorable woman like Marie Dawsen to have relations with a married man?

Had Abe taken liberties with her grandmother? Had he trampled her protests like Boyd Grayson had trampled Claire's earlier this morning? Had Abe pushed her grandmother into something she may not have wanted?

Lord knows Claire had tried to dissuade Boyd from such inappropriate behavior, but he'd been insistent and persuasive about doctoring her foot. His infringement on her person had been shocking. He'd frightened her with his nudging and controlling ways, embarrassed her with the liberties he'd taken. All she'd wanted was to get him out of her house. But the feel of his warm hands caressing her foot and ankle had made her shiver with need.

She never should have let him see her foot, let alone touch it. She'd been perfectly capable of treating her own wound. But she was so lonely, so desperate to connect with another human being, that she'd been unable to pull away from his touch.

Foolish, but true. Had her grandmother felt that way too?

The sound of laughter and a firm knock on her door startled Claire. She glanced at the clock above her mantel and realized the women were already arriving for the prayer meeting. She closed the diary and set it on a brass-trimmed tripod table beside her chair. When she opened the door, Desmona Edwards and four other women stood on her porch.

"I see we're the first to arrive," Desmona said, stepping into the foyer at Claire's bidding. "These are my daughters," she added, waving her wrinkled hand at four women of Claire's mother's age. "Elizabeth is my youngest daughter. Mary is my oldest then Beatrice and Virginia."

"Pleased to meet you, ladies," Claire said.

They all returned Claire's greeting. The youngest daughter, Elizabeth, who looked the oldest with her weary eyes and salt-and-pepper hair, shrank away from Claire's regard. Her visible discomfort surprised Claire, who glanced at Desmona.

"I'm afraid Elizabeth has never outgrown her shyness," Desmona said, exasperation in her voice.

Elizabeth's flushed cheeks elicited Claire's sympathy. "Are you married, Elizabeth?" she asked, hanging their coats in the closet then guiding the ladies into the parlor.

Elizabeth nodded, her eyes as bleak as if she were admitting to being an inmate in Hell. Suddenly Claire knew that it wasn't shyness making Elizabeth shrink away from people. It was fear. Women who were beaten didn't often make new friends. They typically pulled away from family and friends, and shut down their emotions to protect themselves.

Compassion rushed through Claire, but she warned herself not to get involved. She had her own troubles. She was finally free to build herself a safe new life. She would march for temperance to help women like Elizabeth, but she couldn't involve herself personally with anyone else's marriage problems.

With stiff-jointed slowness, Desmona lowered herself into the rocking chair Claire had just vacated. "Dreadfully cold this evening."

"It certainly is," Claire agreed, remembering how the bitter cold had permeated her bones earlier that afternoon when she and ninety-eight other women had trudged through the snow-covered streets to plead their case with the saloon owners. "Do you think Mr. Clark will allow us inside tomorrow?" she asked, irritated that the drug store owner had locked them out and refused to listen to their request to stop selling liquor.

"We have decided not to call on Mr. Clark tomorrow."

Desmona tugged her sweater around her hunched shoulders. "The men will pay him a visit to see if they can talk some sense into him."

"Let's pray they're successful." Claire looked out her window to see several women walking up the street toward her house. "The rest of the ladies are coming."

"Good to be prompt." Desmona glanced at the end table beside her chair and lifted her gray eyebrows in surprise. "What a beautiful book," she said, reaching for the journal on the table.

The thought of anyone reading her grandmother's diary made Claire's heart race. Especially after discovering her grandmother's inappropriate actions with Abe. If anyone learned of it, her grandmother's reputation would be sullied, and Claire would suffer as well.

"Is this your journal?" Desmona asked, tilting the leather-bound diary toward the light while admiring the gilded lettering.

"No." Claire stepped forward to retrieve the journal, but Desmona opened the cover.

"Oh. It's your grandmother's," she said, her eyes focusing inside.

"It's rather dry reading," Claire said, opening her hand as a request for Desmona to return the book.

Desmona ignored her and turned to the first incriminating page. "I've always wondered what one would write in a journal."

"Daily information mostly," Claire said, trying to distract Desmona from reading further. "She wrote about the weather and the neighbors and such."

"Really?" Desmona asked, but when she lifted her head, Claire could see that Desmona had read enough to know that she was lying. Her heart pounded as she faced the knowing look in Desmona's eyes. "I should love to read this when you're finished with it."

"I'm afraid I can't share something so personal." She boldly tugged the diary from Desmona's gnarled fingers. "It would breach my grandmother's privacy. I'm sure she expected to burn this long before she died."

Desmona's lips thinned. "Perhaps she should have."

Claire couldn't agree more. Why would anyone document something so unsavory? She tucked the book under her arm and went to the foyer. How stupid of her to have let Desmona open the diary. She put the book inside her desk, turned the key in the lock then slipped the key into her skirt pocket.

She opened the front door, and a stream of women flowed inside. After several minutes of holding her door open to the frigid weather, Claire's house was filled with rustling skirts and the smell of winter air mingled with lavender and rose powder.

Women crowded into every room and vied for a position in the doorways to see Mrs. Barker who was speaking in the foyer. They complained that they couldn't see her, or hear her, interrupting so often that Mrs. Barker finally raised her hand for silence.

She turned to Claire. "Would you mind if we moved our prayer meeting to the church?"

"Of course not," Claire said with relief. She had no idea how crowded her house would be, or how invaded she would feel having a hundred women milling through her home. She thought to support her cause and taunt Boyd Grayson at the same time, but she was the one who felt infringed upon.

The women poured out of her home and headed toward town. Desmona and her daughters exited last, and Claire felt a physical rush of relief when she stepped outside behind them, pulling her door closed.

She glanced across the street to the Pemberton Inn where Boyd Grayson stood on the front steps of his saloon. "Short meeting tonight?" he asked, his deep, sardonic voice carrying over to her.

She lifted her chin, irritated that her plan to annoy him had fallen through. "We're just getting started, Mr. Grayson. We'll be back tomorrow." She turned away from his knowing grin and ran straight into Desmona.

"Oh! Mrs. Edwards!" She caught Desmona's arm and steadied the old lady. "I'm so sorry."

"No harm done." Desmona shooed her daughters ahead of her then cautiously planted her walking stick as she picked her way down the rutted street. "Your grandmother was an interesting lady," she said. "I'm sorry I didn't know her better."

Claire's stomach tightened, her mind scrambling for a way to yank this bone from Desmona's teeth without provoking the woman. "Grandma was a grand storyteller. She filled my ears with stories about knights and princes and ordinary men who would move heaven and earth for their lady love. Her journal is filled with dozens of story ideas. I appreciate them because I grew up with her tales, but I doubt you would find the journal all that interesting."

"On the contrary. I was intrigued by her diary from the very first sentence."

Heat rushed up Claire's neck. Desmona didn't believe a word of her explanation. This old woman might look frail, but she smelled scandal, and wouldn't stop digging until her curiosity was satisfied.

"Do you think Mr. Harrison will stop selling liquor in his hotel?" she asked, deciding that an abrupt change of subject would effectively show Mrs. Edwards that she had no business asking questions about the diary.

"I presume so," Desmona said, watching her footing as she walked beside Claire. "If he's set on getting the deputy sheriff's position, his conscience will force him to stop."

"Does this mean that Sheriff Grayson will take our pledge, too?"

Desmona shook her head, making the tiny beads on her gray velour bonnet tremble. "He already holds the position of sheriff with little fear of losing it."

"Why should the sheriff be an exception?" Claire asked. "He should be one of the men setting an example for this town."

"He does. The Grayson boys are highly regarded by our menfolk. Each year those boys contribute a goodly amount of lumber for our local charity projects. The oldest boy, Radford, is a war hero. Kyle is a respected businessman who employs several of our townsmen. Sheriff Grayson does a fine job of keeping our town safe. He may visit the saloons on occasion, but he doesn't cause trouble or sell liquor." "His younger brother does. In that rum hole across the street from my home."

"A shame it is, too," Desmona said, huffing as they crossed the Common toward the church. "That boy is wasting his life in that saloon."

Claire couldn't agree more.

"I suppose he comes by it naturally though," Desmona said. "His father was tall and handsome and full of charm. Hal Grayson was a rascal, if an incredibly talented young man. My Addison wanted to hire him to build furniture for our store. I'd hoped the boy would take a shine to one of my girls, but Hal had other plans. He started up a sawmill and set his sights on Nancy Tremont. They had four boys who inherited his good looks and her energy. Boyd got Hal's talent and wild nature." Desmona stopped at the entrance to the church. "And that young man is as obstinate as his father was, and he isn't going to close his saloon just because we ask him to."

Claire's shoulders sagged. She'd sensed that Boyd wasn't a man who could be told what to do. He wasn't the sort of man who would bow to pressure from his neighbors. He seemed to be everything Desmona called him: obstinate, talented, and wild—an incredibly handsome man who was used to getting what he wanted. He was from a respectable family and had the protection of the sheriff.

How was she going to fight that?

Chapter Five

B oyd ordered a round of drinks for Duke and Kyle, who were sitting at the bar smoking cigars to celebrate the birth of Kyle's first child.

"You look awful," Boyd said.

Kyle passed him a cigar. "It's been a long day."

Boyd lit his cigar from one of the three gas lights in his bar. He anchored the cheroot between his teeth, struck a match, and drew until an orange glow traveled a quarter inch up the length. He braced his elbows on the bar and exhaled a ring of smoke that circled their heads. "Did Marshall Thomas give you and Amelia a rough time today?"

Kyle scraped his brown hair off his forehead. "Doc said a fourteen-hour birth is a blessing. Amelia delivered without a problem, but it sure wrung me out."

"Well, look on the bright side," Boyd said. "In about six weeks you and Amelia will be able to use those handcuffs you never gave back to Duke."

Duke's shout of laughter made Kyle grin. "You're never going to let me forget that, are you?"

"Not a chance."

If Boyd lived to be a hundred years old, he would never forget the night that Kyle, who'd been married for two weeks and hadn't yet consummated his marriage, had demanded Duke's handcuffs then bolted from the bar with a determined look on his face. Boyd suspected that Kyle had wanted the cuffs for himself, to ease Amelia's fear of him, but he'd never said and Boyd had never asked.

Kyle pulled another cigar from his pocket for Radford, who'd just entered the saloon. "I'll have to tell you about it sometime."

He would never give Boyd that kind of ammunition, but Boyd laughed, amazed at the change in his older brother. Just three years ago, Kyle had been a humorless, miserable man. His fiancée, Evelyn Tucker, had fallen in love with their oldest brother Radford, which had nearly destroyed their family. Then, barely six months after Kyle's broken engagement, Kyle was forced to marry Amelia Drake, their competitor's daughter. It seemed a miracle to Boyd that they all had ended up happy.

"What did I miss?" Radford asked as he stomped snow from his boots and straddled a barstool beside Kyle.

Boyd signaled Karlton to bring a mug for his brother. "Kyle is going to make a confession about his love life."

Kyle laughed. "My adventures consist of fighting for a place in bed between two spoiled cats and my wife's protruding belly. Your love life would be far more entertaining, Boyd."

Duke shot a wry look at Boyd. "When has *love* ever had anything to do with your affairs?"

A small ache started in Boyd's chest. He struggled not to show any outward sign of the emptiness that overwhelmed him at times. He would never fall in love. He wasn't worthy of it. He asked too much. And gave too little. He would spend his life with his crazy, mixed-breed mutt. All Sailor needed was regular meals and a good daily scratch behind his ears. Boyd didn't want anything more emotionally challenging than that.

Radford picked up the mug of ale that Karlton had just set in front of him. "Don't look so smug, little brother. You'll take the fall someday, and when you do, Kyle and I are going to enjoy every minute of it."

It would never happen, but Boyd didn't argue. He glanced at Duke and changed the subject. "Heard you got a new deputy today."

Duke nodded. "Levi Harrison signed the ladies' temperance pledge then accepted the position."

"He signed their pledge?" Boyd asked in disbelief, exchanging a disgusted look with Karlton.

"Said he had to if he wanted to become a lawman. The ladies pressured him to stop selling liquor in his hotel and set an example for the rest of us men."

Boyd rolled his eyes. "Next thing you know they'll be hounding you to sign their pledge."

"They already have."

"You won't do it, will you?" Karlton asked, butting into their conversation.

"I don't see any need to. I don't have an unquenchable thirst for alcohol, or a family I'm neglecting because of it. And I don't sell liquor." Duke shrugged. "Can't see how my stopping for an occasional mug hurts anyone or keeps me from doing my job."

"Neither can I, and I wouldn't let their nagging sway you," Boyd said. "Besides, the ladies will get tired of marching in this cold weather and give up this nonsense before long."

Kyle and Radford glanced at each other and chuckled. Radford rested his mug on his bent knee. "For being a blatant philanderer, Boyd, you don't know a thing about women. They don't give up until they get what they're after."

"Hogwash," Boyd retorted. "Five dollars says they last a week, maybe two at most."

Radford lifted his mug. "My money says they won't stop until they close every saloon in town, including yours."

"It will never happen." Boyd tapped his mug to Radford's. "I'm confident enough to double the wager."

"Count me in," Kyle said. "I'm with Radford though. Once a woman gets it in her head to do something or change something, there's no reasoning with them. They won't give up. They'll keep after you like a saw blade against a tree, scraping and cutting until you fall."

"Not if they fall first," Karlton said. "I'll triple the wager that the women quit before we give in."

Boyd looked at Duke. "What's your wager?"

"I'm staying out of this. I know how hardheaded you are, but those women are serious about their cause. They've gotten financial backing from a large group of men and they have the support of every church in town. They aren't going to back down any more than you are." Duke lowered his hands to his knees. "The saloon owners are irritated by the ladies' visits. The ladies are outraged by some of the owners' rude treatment of them. And they're all complaining to me."

"Maybe you should tell the ladies to stop marching," Karlton said, walking away.

"They have a right to march."

"Well, I have a license to sell liquor," Boyd argued.

"That's my point, Boyd. Both sides are entitled to do what they're doing." Duke lifted his mug and took a long drink before setting it on the bar. "This isn't my fight. All I can do is keep the peace and make sure nobody gets hurt."

"No one's asking you to choose sides." Boyd signaled for another round of drinks, but Karlton wasn't behind the bar. Assuming he was in the stockroom or relieving his bladder, Boyd got up and poured the drinks himself. He felt better behind the bar.

How ridiculous to think a band of women could close down several profitable saloons. Duke was just feeling pressured because of his job. Radford and Kyle were giving the temperance women too much credit because of their own experiences with their lovely but strong-willed wives.

The women could march and pray all they wanted, but it wouldn't change a thing. They couldn't vote. They couldn't revoke his license to sell liquor. They were wasting their time with all this foolishness.

Radford pushed his mug forward, but instead of ordering another, he stood up. "Good luck with your lady friends," he said, buttoning his coat.

"Where are you going?" Boyd asked.

"Home. I promised Rebecca and William a story before bed."

Boyd had always enjoyed his freedom, but sometimes he envied Radford. Three years ago Radford had come home from the war with his four-year-old daughter Rebecca, both of them emotionally wounded and hurting. Evelyn Tucker had loved and healed them and gave Radford a son a year after they married. They had found a deep happiness with each other, like Kyle had found with Amelia.

Like Duke would someday find with a woman of his own.

Like Boyd would never have.

"I'll walk you out," Kyle said, getting to his feet.

Boyd nodded to Karlton who was carrying in a fresh keg of beer from the stockroom. "I'll be back in a few minutes," he said then followed Kyle and Radford outside. He bade them goodnight then stood on the porch and watched them walk down Main Street. It wouldn't take them ten minutes to reach Radford's home and livery on Liberty Street. Kyle would have to travel five minutes farther to reach his home near their sawmill in Laona.

The night was cold, but Boyd breathed in the frigid air, wondering what it would be like to have a wife and a family. Marriage had changed his brothers. Radford wasn't so jumpy and tense anymore. Kyle had found his sense of humor again. Both of them seemed content and happy. But did the responsibility of having a family ever weigh them down?

A noise across the street snapped his attention to Claire's house. To his surprise, Claire stood on her porch with the door open, angling a paper toward the light from her foyer.

Recognizing a perfect opportunity to speak with her, he descended his steps with a jaunty gait. With any luck she'd taunt him with the success of getting Harrison to sign their pledge. That would be better than having her close her door in his face. It would give him time to talk his way inside.

The snow muffled his footsteps as he crossed the street to her house. She was so absorbed in whatever she was reading that he climbed the steps to her porch without disturbing her.

"That must be some interesting letter," he said.

She cried out and clasped the letter to her chest. Fear filled her eyes, and she panted as if she'd just run up West Hill.

"Are you all right?" he asked, shocked by her reaction.

"Go away." She inched her way inside.

"Wait a minute." He thrust out his hand to stop the door from closing. "What's wrong?"

"Go away or I'll... I'll get my gun."

"What?" He shook his head. "What's going on here?"

"You should know." She pushed on the door, but he braced his foot to keep it from closing. Her jaw clenched, and she glared at him. "Will you kindly remove yourself from my property?"

"Not until you tell me what's going on. I just scared the stuffing out of you, and for some reason you're treating me like a criminal."

"You sell liquor. You drink alcohol. You carouse in that rum hole all hours of the night without a thought or care for your neighbors' comfort. That, Mr. Grayson, is criminal. Now leave or I'll get Sheriff— I'll... I'll get my gun."

"Just because the sheriff is my brother doesn't mean I get special privileges, Claire. If you ask him to remove me from your property, he'll do it."

Her hands trembled, and she leaned her forehead against the edge of the oak door. She lifted her lashes to reveal dark, fear-filled eyes. "If you have a shred of decency, you'll leave as I've requested."

Sensing she was on the verge of tears, he stepped back. "The sheriff is across the street. I'll send him over."

"No." She dragged in a shaky breath. "I'll stop by his office tomorrow."

"Claire, what's going on?"

She glanced at the letter in her hand then lifted her chin and silently glared at him. "I don't know, but I intend to find out." She slammed the door in his face.

He heard her twist the key in the lock, and he turned away thoroughly confused. *What just happened here?* She was scared to death. Of him!

Chapter Six

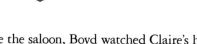

From his apartment above the saloon, Boyd watched Claire's house. Why were her lamps burning at two o'clock in the morning? No shadows or movement shifted across her windows, so she must be sleeping. But why with the lantern burning?

He and Duke had searched her yard, but hadn't found anything to warrant her fear. Duke had knocked and announced himself, but Claire wouldn't answer the door or even bother to look out the window.

So what had spooked her?

Boyd paced his apartment, glancing at her windows. Was she awake? Was she watching him, too? Or was she cowering in her house, afraid and alone?

The thought had him heading for the door, but he stopped in his kitchen and blew out a breath of frustration. Even if he went to check on her, she wouldn't answer the door. Worse, if he knocked on her door, it would just make her more scared, which was the last thing he wanted to do.

He would just have to wait until tomorrow.

With a sigh of fatigue, he headed to a small room off the parlor where he dabbled with his carvings. He'd boarded up the window that Claire's wild gunshot had shattered the previous weekend, but the room still felt chilly.

Sailor padded in behind him, sniffing and circling the life-size, partially carved statue that forever intrigued the dog.

"It makes me nervous too," Boyd said, scratching the dog's head. "What do you think? Will tonight be the night?" he asked, wondering if the day would ever come when he would resurrect his talent.

The dog wheezed and stared at him with adoring brown eyes.

"You have more faith than I do, but I'll give it a go." He surveyed a long narrow table that was covered with several curved carving knives, various-size chisels and gouges, shaving blocks, sanding paper, tubs of wax, cans of varnish, and other items he and his father had once used to carve furniture. He picked up a small carving knife and turned to the huge block of basswood sitting in the center of the room.

Claire's bullet had torn away a brick-sized chunk of wood from the upper portion of the statue. When Boyd had first discovered the damage, he'd felt as if the bullet had torn away a piece of his own flesh. But now, in this light, seeing the partially carved block of wood from a different perspective, the missing chunk of wood seemed... right somehow.

"Maybe that's my problem," he said, talking as naturally to his dog as he would to his own brothers. "Maybe I've been approaching this from the wrong direction." Boyd began shaving away the splintered edges where the bullet had struck the wood. He worked his knife in slow, methodical strokes, but his apprehension grew as the night deepened. He feared he would cut away too much, and despaired that he wouldn't know if he had.

His hands trembled and his face flushed with heat. This had been so easy once. There had been a time when he'd known the result of each knife stroke before he took it. Now, each curled wood shaving that fell to the floor filled him with anxiety because he was carving blind. He could no longer see the treasure the wood contained.

⋙⋘

Claire jerked awake with a gasp.

She clutched the gun on her lap and searched the shadows of her bedchamber. Nothing moved. No one panted in her ear and threatened her. No one clutched her throat and issued instructions. She was alone and unharmed. Heart pounding, she sank back into the wing chair with a trembling sigh of relief.

She couldn't live like this again.

She couldn't bear the sleepless nights, the gnawing fear, the watchfulness.

The heavy iron revolver pressed down on her thighs, but it didn't comfort her. She had no idea how to successfully use the gun. Her chances of being able to actually shoot anybody were slim, but she kept the revolver nestled in her lap.

It was the only protection she had if the man who left the threatening note on her door decided to visit her.

She slipped her hand into the pocket of her skirt and wrapped her fingers around the carving Boyd had given her. The note was in her pocket, too, but she had no need to pull it out and read it again. The threatening words had circled in her mind all night long.

A woman who lives alone shouldn't stir up trouble. Stop the marches or you'll have an unpleasant visitor.

She was too familiar with the instability of alcoholics to discount the note. Whoever wrote it, meant it.

Was it Boyd? Had he been waiting near her porch to purposely frighten her? He had as much to lose as anyone if the marches were successful. And if he hadn't written the note, who had?

She leaned her head back, sick with exhaustion. Her body begged for rest, but she didn't dare undress and climb into bed. She'd saved herself from Jack's rage on many occasions by running out of the house before he could grab her. She couldn't run for help if she was undressed.

Smarter to remain fully clothed and sitting in her grandmother's wing chair with the gun in her lap. In the morning she would march with the women then slip away to see the sheriff.

That was sensible. That's what she'd do. There was no need to panic.

Then why was she sitting shivering in fear with a revolver clenched in her hands?

Chapter Seven

Friday morning Claire slogged down Main Street through ankle-deep slush, shaking with cold and exhaustion. She longed to be safe in bed beneath her grandmother's thick comforter, sipping a cup of hot tea.

Instead, she spent an hour at church then tromped through the cold wind to visit Baldwin's Drug Store, the Taylor House, and three saloons. The proprietors all refused to sign the temperance pledge.

The women ended their march at Barker Common. Claire was shaking so badly from the cold and fatigue, she sank onto a park bench to rest before going to the sheriff's office. Elizabeth winced as she half-collapsed beside her.

"Are you all right?" Claire asked, her heart filling with compassion for the hurting woman. "I noticed you've been favoring your left side all morning."

Elizabeth's eyes misted and she gravely shook her head. "I'm not all right, but my mother is heading our directions and I don't want her to know the cause of my injury." She met Claire's eyes. "How did you know?"

"I was in your situation once," Claire said, realizing too late that she'd revealed her secret. She saw Desmona making her way toward them. "Maybe you should tell your parents. They might be able to help you."

Elizabeth shook her head. "My father is too old and unhealthy. I'm afraid the shock and worry would kill him. He thinks my husband is a good man. I don't want him to know about this."

Claire frowned. "A good man doesn't beat his wife."

"He's not all bad," Elizabeth said, repeating the same words Claire had once said about her own husband. "Ted works hard and provides well for us. He was a good father to our two girls."

"He didn't... bother your girls like this, did he?"

"No. He was good to them. They never knew we had problems."

Desmona was too near for them to continue the conversation, so Claire patted Elizabeth's hand and stood. "Take care of yourself," she whispered. Then she strode across the park toward the old academy building that housed the sheriff's office, before Desmona could corner her.

Sheriff Grayson sat at a scarred pine desk, elbows propped on either side of a stack of papers. One finger tapped the page he was reading, the other hand was braced on his forehead with his fingers stuck in his thick brown hair. He was handsome in a rough and rangy way, but clearly Boyd's brother.

The massive desk sat in the middle of a room the size of the connecting jail cell. Although the sheriff seemed comfortable in the tiny walled off space, she thought he would appear more at home in his family sawmill, wrestling logs and working alongside the massive horses that moved the timber. She was hesitant to disturb him, but couldn't leave without telling him about the note. She tapped on the doorframe.

"Sheriff Grayson?"

He looked up and smiled as if he'd seen her coming for miles and had just been waiting for her knock.

"Has another saloon owner locked you out?" he asked, referring to Don Clark, who had done just that on Wednesday.

"We didn't call on Mr. Clark today," she said. "We sent the men around yesterday, and decided this morning to adjourn our marches until Monday."

"Then you're either guilty of something or you've got a good-sized problem on your hands."

She stepped into the room. "This was tacked to my door last night." She handed him the note.

He leaned back in his chair and gestured for her to sit. As he read, his dark brows lowered. "Is this why you wouldn't answer your door?"

She nodded.

"Do you know who wrote this?"

"Maybe Don Clark. Maybe... I don't know. It could be anybody." She sighed, feeling weary to the bone. "Whoever wrote it obviously means to stop our marches."

He scowled. "Did you tell anyone about the note?"

"No." She met his eyes and knew he wasn't only referring to the women she marched with. He wanted to know if she'd accused any of the saloon owners. "I don't want to worry the ladies, or cast suspicion on any man without knowing who wrote it."

"I need to keep this." He laid the paper on the arrest warrant he'd been reading. "I'll question Don and the other saloon owners this afternoon."

"Will you question your brother too?" Despite her effort to maintain eye contact, his frown made her drop her gaze to her cold, clenched fingers.

"Do you think Boyd would do this?"

The sheriff's tone implied his brother would never do such a thing, but she could only shrug. She honestly didn't know what Boyd Grayson would do.

"Mrs. Ashier?"

She looked up to see sympathy in his eyes.

"I know you're frightened, but I'd stake my badge on my brother's innocence. He would never threaten a lady. In fact, when I tell him about this note, I'm going to have a hard time keeping him from hunting down the author."

"Why would he get involved?"

"Because he's the kind of man who protects those who can't protect themselves. When Boyd was ten he fought a boy twice his size because the boy had been picking on one of our friends. Kyle, Radford, and I had to restrain Boyd while the older boy ran home."

"You believe he's innocent then?"

"Yes." The sheriff leaned his wide shoulders back in his chair. "My brother is too hot-tempered to spend time writing a note, Mrs. Ashier. If he'd wanted to give you a warning, he'd have banged on your door and made sure you understood his message. But I'll question him along with the other saloon owners."

"Thank you," she said, but she wasn't ready to take the sheriff or Boyd Grayson at their word. She would watch and judge them by their actions.

She got to her feet and moved to the door. "Will you let me know when you find out who left the note?"

"Of course," he said, pushing his chair back. The room shrank when he stood, and she instinctively took a step back. "My deputy and I will be around this afternoon to check on you."

She nodded, but didn't leave. "Did you ask Levi Harrison to stop selling liquor at his hotel?"

His eyebrows lowered. "Why?"

"Because it was an honorable thing to do."

He sighed. "Don't accuse me of being noble, Mrs. Ashier. I acted out of self-preservation. I couldn't hire a rum seller as deputy when there are a hundred women in town who would scalp me for doing so."

"Despite your penchant for frequenting your brother's saloon, Sheriff Grayson, you just climbed a notch in my regard."

⸺⟨⊱ ⟨⊱⸺

Boyd slammed his empty mug on the bar, outraged. "Claire thinks *I* wrote the note?"

"Settle down," Duke said then finished telling him about the incident. "She's scared and doesn't know what to think."

Pat Lyons leaned his elbows on the bar beside them. "Who could be threatening her?"

"Any man in town." Karlton, who was four inches shorter than Pat, stood behind the bar drying a beer mug. "She's stirring up trouble with everybody."

"Unfortunately, that's true," Duke said. "When Mrs. Ashier started the temperance push, I decided to do a little digging into her past. It seems her husband died sucking river water. Apparently Claire was there but unable to save him."

Boyd's gut tightened. "Do you think someone from her past could have left the note?"

"I don't know. Mrs. Ashier suspects everyone, but thinks Don Clark might be responsible. I can't see Donny doing something like this though," Duke said. "I'm going to talk with him now, but I want you three to keep this information about Mrs. Ashier in strict confidence. She's pretty shaken up about it."

"She should be," Karlton said. "The saloon owners and our patrons aren't taking too kindly to being harassed by a nagging group of women."

"That doesn't give anyone the right to threaten those women."

"Didn't say it did, Sheriff." Karlton turned and thumped the mug down onto the back bar shelf, a handsomely carved unit backed with beveled mirrors.

Boyd clenched his fists to keep from swatting Karlton for being careless of the wood. It had taken him and his father six months to build and carve that back bar. It was the centerpiece of his establishment, a masterpiece of exquisitely figured mahogany combined with holly, flamed birch, and satinwood inlays, painstakingly joined together to showcase the wood and give the piece depth. And it had taken an entire day to mount the fifteen-foot unit behind the bar. It reflected the gas lighting and turned an otherwise ordinary saloon into a palace.

Boyd pushed away from the bar and grabbed his heavy coat off the rack behind him. "I'll go talk to Claire," he said, needing to get some air before he started barking at Karlton, or dwelling on the past.

"Don't do that," Duke said. "You'll only scare her. Just watch her house and see if she gets any visitors."

"Pat can do that. If she doesn't want to talk to me, I'll go with you to see Donny."

Duke stepped in front of him and blocked his exit. "Don may not have had anything to do with this, Boyd."

"I intend to verify that."

"That's my job."

"I'm the one Claire suspects. I have a right to clear my name."

With a lightning-quick flick of his hand, Duke snapped a handcuff around Boyd's wrist.

"What are you doing?"

Duke jerked the empty cuff up to eye level, pulling Boyd's bound wrist upward. "I'm making a point. You're not getting involved in this. Settle down or I'll finish the job."

Boyd gritted his teeth, hating that his brother was the sheriff. Experience told him that if he didn't back off, Duke wouldn't hesitate to haul him downtown to that tiny jail cell, a claustrophobic little room with a cot and a latrine. His brother was a good drinking partner when he wasn't wearing his badge, but he was hard-nosed when it came to upholding the law. No man got in the way of his duty. Not even a brother.

"Stay away from Don Clark," Duke said.

"Fine."

"Stay away from his store."

Boyd gritted his teeth.

"Stay away from his house—"

"All right." Boyd yanked his wrist. "Take this off me and get out of my saloon."

Duke uncuffed him. "Walk me out."

Boyd whistled for his dog then stepped outside into the frigid December air.

"I didn't want to say this in front of Pat or Karlton," Duke said, pulling the door closed, "but Jack Ashier died two months ago."

Chapter Eight

Claire was in the kitchen writing a letter to her sister when she heard a dog barking in her wood shed. She pushed away from the table then opened the door, glad to have some canine company for a while. Sailor stared up at her with bright eyes and a silly tongue-lolling grin that made her laugh.

"Did you come to beg table scraps again?" she asked, having fed him the past two days.

With a happy yip, Sailor bounded inside, nearly knocking her over in his rush to enter.

"Oh. You rascal" She turned to face the dog, her hands on her hips. "You are supposed to wait to be invited inside."

"Me, too?" asked a male voice from behind her.

Her heart careened into her ribs, and she whirled to find Boyd Grayson standing in the doorway with his arms full of firewood.

"I was supposed to fill your wood bins this morning, but I got delayed," he said, forcing her to step aside as he entered the kitchen.

"Oh, well, yes..." She gripped the doorknob and tried to catch her breath. "Thank you for remembering, but I... I've decided to do it myself."

"I can't let you do that." He dropped the pile of wood into the empty bin by her stove with a loud crash. She and the dog both jumped. "I made a promise to you."

"Thank you, but I've changed my mind," she said, opening the door wider to encourage him to leave. "I'd really rather do this myself."

"Why, Claire? Because you think I wrote that note?"

Heat rushed to her face.

"Duke told me you suspect me."

"I said you *could* have written it."

"How could you think that?"

"You're a saloon owner."

His brows lowered. "So?"

"You have as much to lose as anybody if our marches are successful."

"That doesn't mean anything, Claire. The person who wrote that note is a coward without morals."

She stepped away from him, afraid of the anger in his eyes. "Would you admit it if you had written it?"

His face darkened. "I don't threaten women. I don't commit cowardly acts. And I don't lie."

"How can I know that?" She lifted her chin and stared him in the eye. "Write a note for me."

"What?"

She released the door knob and rushed to the table. She took a pen from a crystal inkwell and thrust it at him. "Let your handwriting prove that you didn't write the note." She pushed a sheaf of paper in front of him.

His eyes flared with anger, but he bent over the table.

With bold, angry slashes, he wrote on the paper then tossed the pen down.

Claire studied the slant of his writing. The author of the original note had slanted the top of his letters to the left.

Boyd's slanted right. His script was bolder and more controlled than the script in the note she'd received.

But her heart stuttered as she read his scribbled words. *I'm not leaving until you stop questioning my integrity.*

She cursed herself for being foolish. Without her gun, there was no way to evict Boyd Grayson from her home. Why had she been so rash to challenge him? Had she wanted to believe him innocent because she was beginning to like and respect his brother? Because she suspected there was more to Boyd than the rakehell he seemed to be?

Sailor nosed her thigh, and she reached down to stroke his half-mast ears. "I'm sorry, Boyd. I didn't mean to insult you."

"Then you believe I'm innocent?" She didn't know what to believe, but couldn't voice the truth. "Your writing is different from the script on the note."

"I could have purposely changed my script—is that what you're thinking?"

Her fingers trembled as she pressed them to her nauseous stomach. "I don't know what to think."

He gaped at her. "Do you honestly believe I would hurt you?"

She didn't answer.

As he moved toward her, his shoulder collided with the edge of the door. Irritated, he elbowed it closed.

The loud slam made her recoil. She backed away from him, willing to agree with anything he said to get him out of her house. She didn't know him. She didn't know what he was capable of. A cruel, calculating man could be lurking behind his handsome face.

Tremors snaked through her stomach, and she struggled to keep her breathing even. "I... I don't want anyone in my house right now." She pointedly reached for the doorknob to show him out.

He clapped his hand over hers and trapped it. "I didn't threaten you."

She pulled away. "Then who did?"

He stepped around his dog, trapping her in a narrow space between his tall, hard body and the wall. "I don't know, but it wasn't me."

She tried to move past him, but he blocked her escape.

His nearness smothered her. Her chest jerked with quick, panicky breaths. Jack had stalked her like this, torturing her with his cat-and-mouse games. He'd always won.

And she'd always lost in the most humiliating and painful way possible.

As if the dog sensed her distress, he wheezed and pushed against her side, offering comfort, but effectively blocking her exit from one direction. The wall was at her back. Boyd was directly in front of her. The kitchen door, her only escape, was to her right.

To her shame a whimper of panic squeezed from her throat. She planted her palms against Boyd's chest and shoved him aside. She bolted for the door and yanked it open. The scuffle behind her sent ice through her veins as she sprinted into the woodshed.

A second later Boyd's strong arms clamped around her waist, and the sound of her own scream filled her ears. It was useless to fight. She knew that. But she fought anyway.

⊷⫶ ⫶⊶

"What the...?" Boyd stared in shock at the wild, gasping woman in his arms.

Her futile struggles and frightened whimpering wrung his heart.

She gasped and tried to wiggle out of his arms.

He tightened his grip. "I'm not going to hurt you. Shhhh... I won't hurt you, Claire." He kept his grip firm, holding her back against his chest as she struggled. "Easy. I'm not going to hurt you. Stop fighting me, and I'll let you go."

She stilled, but her chest jerked with every frightened breath she drew.

"I want to talk to you. That's all."

He felt the tension rippling through her stiff body.

"I'm only going to talk to you. Turn around and I'll answer any questions you want to ask."

Her shoulders slumped as if the fight had drained out of her. He loosened his arms, and she turned to face him.

Seeing her eyes glistening with tears tore a hole in his chest. He put some space between their bodies, but didn't release her. "I'm sorry I frightened you."

She raised wet, spiky lashes, and he saw real fear in her eyes.

"Ah, Claire. I'm sorry. I didn't write that note. Nothing could make me harm you. Nothing."

Doubt filled her eyes.

"No matter what the reason, I could never hurt a woman."

She shivered, her breath misting in the cold air as she exhaled.

The fragrant smell of cut wood filled the frigid shed.

Her waist felt firm and warm against his forearms. He wanted to pull her close, tuck her head beneath his chin and hold her until she stopped trembling. Instead, he loosened his grip and turned her toward the open kitchen door.

"Go inside. It's too cold out here," he said, guiding her into the house.

He closed the door behind them, allowing her to put the table between them.

With a sigh, he leaned against the door. "Claire, I value two things in life. My family. And my integrity. I swear I didn't write that note, and I would never, for any reason, harm you."

"Why do men need to order and push and boss us around?" she asked, her voice hoarse and unsteady.

"I don't know," he said, sorry that he'd used his superior strength against her. "Maybe we just want women to listen."

"I think you do it to intimidate us."

He sighed and scraped his hair out of his eyes. "I just wanted you to hear what I was saying. Selling liquor doesn't make me a woman-beater."

"I never suggested it did."

"But you think if I sell liquor, I'm capable of other reprehensible behavior."

"Every man is capable of bad behavior, whether he drinks or not."

"I agree. But I've never hit a woman and I never will. Despite my bad habits and faults, women seem to like my attention," he said, hoping a bit of humor would calm her.

"I don't."

"You're the first," he said honestly. "Every mother in town has pushed their little princess into my path, hoping one kiss from their sweet lips will turn me into a prince. But alas, no luck." He glanced down at Sailor, who was panting and nudging his thigh for attention. "I'm still a toad, and you're still a dog," he said, scratching the mutt's head. "But we have our honor and our integrity, don't we, boy? We don't steal, we don't drink our profits, and we don't hurt women." He glanced at Claire to make his point.

"I was afraid, and..." She shrugged, her face flushed. "I'm sorry."

"It's my fault. I didn't realize how frightened you were."

"Because you were too concerned with your wounded pride to notice."

"He nodded. He had been too abrupt and aggressive. "I'm sorry, Claire. It makes me crazy to have my integrity questioned," he said. "This is the first time I've lost control with a woman though." He grinned, hoping to bring some levity to the situation. "Usually it's the other way around."

Her jaw dropped.

He loved the flush on her face and knowing that his stupid comment had taken her mind off her fear. "You would think all that kissing and amorous attention would have worked some magic on me. But I guess this toad hasn't been kissed by the right woman."

"It was a frog," she said, her voice laced with disdain, "not a toad, that turned into a prince."

"Toad. Frog. What's the difference? The princess kissed the slimy thing and he became a prince."

"Not in the fairy tale I read. In the Brothers Grimm version, the princess threw the frog against the wall."

"*After* he'd slept in her bed for three nights," he countered, enjoying their turn of conversation.

"That's likely the reason she threw him against the wall."

He laughed at her retort, glad he'd succeeded in turning their conversation. "This toad would definitely respond better to a kiss."

"Then perhaps you should go find one of those many ladies who are willing to kiss you."

"Would you do it, Claire? Would you kiss me and turn me into a prince?"

The wariness settled back in her eyes, but she didn't bolt from the kitchen. "I kissed a man who looked like a prince, but he was a liar and a cheat. I've no desire to repeat the mistake."

"Is that why you prefer to remain a widow?"

Her eyes narrowed, and he knew he'd offended her sense of privacy.

He didn't care. She was too private, too defensive. Whatever she was hiding had left her shaken and wary. He wanted to know why she was living here in Fredonia when her family was in Buffalo. Why had Marie left her home to Claire instead of her own son?

"Why didn't you move back to your father's house when your husband... when you became a widow?"

"I prefer to live here."

"Many women would have returned to their father's protection rather than struggle to support themselves."

"Supporting myself wouldn't be a struggle if you would close your saloon. Nor would I need protection."

He couldn't argue her point. But he would never close his business. The best he could offer was a promise. "I'm at your service, if you should need me in any way."

"I need a thriving business, not a guardian."

"Just the same, I'm within shouting distance."

Her lips pursed. "I'm only too aware of that."

He smiled, longing to kiss her. "You know, you really ought to give this toad a chance."

Sadness filled her eyes. "I don't believe in fairy tales anymore," she said. Then she walked out of the kitchen, leaving Boyd with a new itch he couldn't scratch and a dog who was a better ladies' man that Boyd had ever been.

Chapter Nine

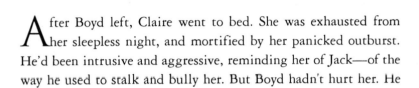

Afet Boyd left, Claire went to bed. She was exhausted from her sleepless night, and mortified by her panicked outburst. He'd been intrusive and aggressive, reminding her of Jack—of the way he used to stalk and bully her. But Boyd hadn't hurt her. He wasn't Jack.

Boyd wasn't the same type of man. She knew that intuitively. But he *had* intimidated her, and intentionally. If she spent more time with him, would his nudges and proposals turn into shoves and demands? Did all men shove when they couldn't get what they wanted?

She didn't want to believe that.

She couldn't.

Because part of her had needed the comfort of Boyd's arms. She needed the compassion he offered, needed to feel safe again. But his actions had confused her. How could she know when his arms would offer comfort and when they would seek to control her?

She buried her head beneath the pillow, and fought for sleep. When she woke up the next morning, her stomach was upset and her head groggy. She used her ill health as an excuse to turn away a boarder, but the truth was, she was afraid to have the man in her house. He was too quiet, too watchful, too... male.

Embarrassed by her fear, Claire hid inside all weekend.

She didn't want to cross paths with her too-handsome neighbor or the man who'd left that note on her door. She couldn't even bring herself to face the women at the temperance meeting on Sunday evening.

By Monday afternoon, four of her concerned fellow marchers knocked on her door.

"Thank goodness you're all right," Elizabeth said. "We heard about the warning note left on your door."

"I'm fine." Claire would have liked to invite Elizabeth inside, but Desmona was with her. After her offensive probing into her grandmother's journal, Claire couldn't bear to have the prying woman in her home again. And she couldn't afford to befriend Elizabeth or get involved in her problems. Claire had her own troubles to tend. She would march for Temperance to help women like Elizabeth, but that was all. That's all she could do.

"We noticed you weren't at the meeting last night," Desmona said.

"I've been unwell these past couple of days."

Desmona shivered in the cold wind, making Claire feel guilty for not inviting them inside. "Better that you didn't attend if you're ill."

"I'll make the meeting this evening," she promised, hoping it would send Desmona on her way.

"There won't be a prayer meeting tonight," Mrs. Cushing said. "We decided at our afternoon meeting to adjourn until Friday after Christmas."

"There was a meeting today?" Claire asked with dismay. How unforgivable for her to have missed two meetings when she'd been the one to summon Dr. Lewis to visit and start the march for temperance.

"There certainly was." Desmona puffed up with importance. "We wrote a pledge and formed our own Women's Temperance Union today." Her lips pursed, and deep grooves fanned above her upper lip. "I offered to be president, but Mrs. Barker wanted the position. Her sister-in-law is our vice-president, and Mrs. Barmore is our secretary. We are organized as a society now."

"That's wonderful news." It was, but it depressed Claire to have missed such an important meeting, all over a cowardly fit of nerves.

"Thank you for checking on me," she said to the small group of women. "I'll definitely be at our meeting on Friday."

Claire sighed in relief as she closed the door, but she felt incredibly lonely. How lovely it would have been to invite the ladies inside, to share a pot of tea and some conversation with someone. She hadn't been with friends since she was a girl, intruding on her sister's weekend entertainment.

The older neighbor girls used to call on her sister Lida every Saturday afternoon. The kitchen would smell like lavender powder and baking bread, and the room would ring with shrill laughter. Mother would smile and chastise them for being too loud, but Lida and her friends would giggle and gossip for two full hours while Claire—too young to be included in their circle—hovered in the background soaking up every exciting word.

The girls would scurry out when Claire's father came home for supper.

But that's when Claire's day came to life. For as far back as she could remember, her father would come inside, tug her straight blond hair and ask, "What trouble has my Claire gotten into today?" Claire would crawl onto his lap or leap into his arms and bask in his attention. When she got too old for holding, she would blush and giggle and dance around him until he would capture her and give her a bear hug. He'd kiss her on the forehead and tell her that he'd missed his girl.

The memory made her throat close. She hadn't seen or heard from her father since he'd disinherited her over four years ago.

She opened the desk and retrieved her grandmother's journal. She had vowed not to read about her grandmother's sordid affair, but the journal was the only link she had to her family.

The leather felt soft and warm beneath her fingertips as she carried it to the parlor. The fire had burned down to embers, and the room was cold... and empty.

The airy sound of the chimney made her think of Sailor and the dog's wheezy way of talking to her. She would gladly give her last seventeen dollars to see his lopsided smile and have the clumsy canine with his warm body, admiring eyes, and protective bark beside her for the evening.

She stirred the red coals and added a log to the fire then sat in the rocking chair.

Despite her disapproval of her grandmother's affair, she was curious about how it had happened, what had lured her grandmother into the situation.

This morning Abe asked me if I've ever been in love.

He shouldn't have asked a married woman such a question, but I answered him. I said no.

Claire settled into the rocker and angled the journal toward the lantern, her heart aching for her grandmother and the man she'd loved.

I have a deep, respectful affection for my husband, and it breaks my heart to have these feelings for another man. But for good or bad, my love for Abe is real. I've never experienced the excitement or passion I feel for Abe. I don't understand it. I'll never understand it, but one minute I was preparing lunch while Abe was building my cupboards, and the next instant we were staring across the room at each other with the shameful truth of our desire burning in our eyes. We didn't speak of our attraction, but the knowledge was as present in that room as we were.

My marriage is built on duty, kindness, and community. My moments with Abe are private, passionate, and as addictive as a drug. I cannot resist him.

God knows I've tried. He's tried. We both failed.

Abe owns my thoughts. He commands my desire.

He fills this hollow space inside me. I would cast everything aside for him. I would. But he will never ask me to do so.

Claire stroked her fingers over her grandmother's pain-filled words. No wonder her grandmother had been captured by moments of intense sadness.

Claire hadn't understood when she was a girl. But now, as a woman who had once longed for this kind of love and never experienced it, she knew how rare it was—how devastating it must be to find love and not be able to claim it.

Abe is tall and handsome in a dark, brooding sort of way. He's a private man, filled with passion and life and a sense of humor that he tries to hide. I see these things. I know him, this amazing, conflicted, lonely man who tries so hard to honor his vows. He says my smiles melt his resistance. I am ashamed to admit that I smile each time I see him. I should be sorry, I know, but if my soul must make restitution for grasping this breath of life, I'll gladly go to Hell.

Perhaps it was her grandmother's reference to Abe's passion and sense of humor that brought Boyd's image to mind, but Claire couldn't clear the vision from her head. Despite Boyd's flippant attitude, Claire sensed his conflict and loneliness. Maybe that's why she was drawn to him.

Foolish.

Simply foolish to even admit such a thing. She believed Boyd hadn't written the warning note, that he would never harm a woman as he adamantly claimed, but her judgment was terrible. She knew better than to trust her instincts.

Boyd Grayson couldn't be more unsuitable.

But the other man lurking in his shadow... *that* man intrigued her. *That* man might be honorable enough to close his saloon.

Tuesday afternoon Boyd propped his hands on his hips and stretched his back. He was glad to end his workday at Edward's furniture store. Each Tuesday, and sometimes on Friday, he and Matthew Sesslier, Addison Edward's grandson by marriage, taught Addison's hired help how to build and carve furniture.

Addison leaned on his walking stick, the wooden tip buried in an inch of wood shavings on the workshop floor. "You boys finished for the day?" he asked, looking like he'd just crawled out of bed. A drab gray sweater hung from his stooped thin shoulders, his white hair whipped into peaks above dark bushy eyebrows.

Boyd nodded to the old man who was still as sharp as his best carving knife. "We got a lot done today, Addison.

Your boys will be able to finish building that bedroom suite next week." Addison waved gnarled fingers. "Don't know why you won't carve the thing."

"I don't have the time, Addison. I've got a saloon to run and a sawmill to work."

"Bah. You're as stubborn as your father was." He turned and limped back into the store, leaving Boyd and Matthew grinning at each other.

"Your grandfather is a bit cantankerous today."

Matthew nodded. "He's like that when he doesn't get his own way. I wish you'd quit wasting your talent in that saloon and let him hire you."

It aggravated Boyd that Matthew thought he was wasting his talent. He no longer had any talent. "Are you upset that your wife is marching with those temperance women?" he asked, purposely changing the subject.

Matthew, a plain, quiet man Boyd had known since they were boys, dumped a shovelful of wood shavings into a barrel by the stove. "She believes it's the right thing to do, just as I believe you're wasting your talent." Matthew propped the shovel against the wall and dusted his hands on his denim trousers. "If you weren't a friend, I'd call you a fool."

"I've been called worse."

"I was serious."

"So was I." Boyd whistled to Sailor, who scrambled to his feet and paced between Boyd and the door.

"You're a natural craftsman, Boyd, and an exceptional teacher. Why are you using your hands to pour ale?"

Teaching wasn't doing. His apprentices used their own hands, found their own treasures in the wood. Anyone could instruct an avid pupil.

Besides, his best memories were at the Pemberton. Saloon-keeping was easier than the fatigue and fear he experienced each time he worked on the statue. He had lost his passion for carving when he buried his father.

He didn't want to talk about his lost talent or his shortcomings. He was tired and wanted a tall mug of ale to wash the wood dust from his throat. "Sailor! Get out of there," he said, scolding the dog for rooting in the bucket of wood shavings. "I'll see you next week," he said to Matthew then strolled out the door before Matthew could nag him further.

He walked up Main Street in the dark with Sailor trotting alongside him. The instant they neared Claire's house, Sailor bounded onto her front porch, yipping like a maniac. Light illuminated her windows, but there was no sign of activity outside or inside the house. Wondering why he hadn't seen her all weekend, Boyd climbed the porch steps and peered in the window to make sure nothing was amiss.

Sailor barked again, and Claire opened the door. Boyd ducked away from the window, hoping she wouldn't think he'd been peeping in at her.

But she didn't see him. Her gaze was focused on Sailor.

"Where have you been?" she asked, the light from her window casting a hazy glow across her face.

Sailor panted and wheezed and paced in front of the door like a smitten fool.

Claire laughed—a light, heartwarming sound that splashed over Boyd like sunshine. He'd never heard her true laugh. He'd never witnessed a full smile on her face. He'd never seen the real, unguarded Claire Ashier. Until now. And he liked what he saw.

She was magnificent.

"You're not coming in with those wet paws, mister. Go around back." She closed the door, not realizing that Boyd had been standing three feet away, falling in love with her.

In love?

In lust.

Interchangeable words that simply meant he desired to see more of the real Claire Ashier.

A lot more.

The cold wind cut through his jacket as he followed Sailor to the back of the house. He'd thought about Claire all weekend, about her irrational fear, about the way he'd frightened her last Friday afternoon. Four days had passed, and he still hadn't found a proper way to apologize. What could he say? *I'm sorry I let my wounded pride rule my head?*

Sailor barked and barreled through the open shed door.

Claire's laughter drifted outside. "Do you really think I would leave you out here in the cold?"

Boyd stepped into the small room.

A flash of fright crossed her face and she took a step back.

"I'll leave if you want me to," he said. He couldn't bear to frighten her.

Sailor pushed between her thigh and the door frame, scurrying into her kitchen as if he owned the place.

"I thought I'd fill your wood bins while Sailor tracks up your floor, but if you'd rather I didn't..." He left the sentence unfinished, waiting for her to decide.

Her lips parted, but she couldn't seem to make up her mind.

"I'm sorry, Claire. I didn't mean to frighten you the other day. I was insulted that you thought I could have written the note, but it was no reason to bully you." His breath sighed out in a frosty cloud and he slipped his hands into his coat pockets. "If I could erase my actions, I would."

She leaned her narrow shoulders against the door casing. "So would I."

He waited for her to say more, but she seemed as devoid of words as he was. Her honey-gold hair was uncovered and swept back in a loose clasp of some sort. He wanted to pull the clasp from her hair and let it spill across the shoulders of her brown and black checkered dress.

"The kitchen bin is... if you wouldn't mind, I haven't brought in any wood today." She flushed and lowered her lashes.

"Thank you, Claire."

She looked up in surprise.

"For liking my dog and for accepting my apology when you have every reason not to."

He turned away, giving her the opportunity to disappear inside while he filled his arms with wood. But when he turned back, she was still standing on the threshold.

"I'll manage the door for you," she said, opening it wide so he could step inside.

He did his job in silence. It was enough that she was allowing him into her home. He wouldn't press her for more.

Not today. But tomorrow... tomorrow he would start over and win her friendship in a gentler, more considerate manner.

"Would you like a cup of tea?" she asked, as he returned from carrying his final armful of firewood upstairs to one of the guest rooms.

Her offer surprised him, and he stopped mid-stride.

Sailor, who had been following him step for step, ran into the back of his legs.

Claire smiled, and called the dog to her side. His toenails clicked on the oak floor as he scrambled across the room and butted up against her.

Boyd shook his head at the dog. "Tea would be nice, if you're comfortable with your offer."

"Not completely," she said, "but I'll manage if you promise to behave yourself."

"I'll be a prince," Boyd promised with a smile.

To his surprise she smiled back. The flash of her white teeth and blue eyes made his hands itch to capture the image on canvas. But his talent wasn't painting. He had no talent anymore.

"Do you take sugar in your tea?" she asked, moving to the stove to retrieve the tea kettle.

"Only if you think I need sweetening."

Her lips tilted as she filled two cups. She glanced at him from the corner of her eye. "Have you considered signing our pledge by any chance?"

To realize she was offering him tea so that she could bend his ear about her temperance pledge was the most deflating setback he'd ever experienced with a woman.

But damn, if he didn't like her persistence.

He'd had enough easy conquests to know they were generally unfulfilling. This woman offered a challenge. A real challenge. She wasn't playing coy with him. Her agenda was to get him to sign their pledge and close his saloon.

Nothing more.

Well, he had an agenda, too, and it had nothing to do with making pledges. Feeling a tad mischievous, he accepted his tea with a nod of thanks. "You know, Claire, your home could earn you considerably more money as a saloon."

Her eyes widened and she gaped at him. He laughed and nearly spilled his tea.

She pursed her lips. "You promised to act like a prince and not a toad."

"I was merely drawing a comparison, to show you how ridiculous your question was."

"I suppose it was a ridiculous question." She sighed as if she'd expected his answer. "I was hoping you would understand what the saloon is costing the rest of us."

"I don't want my business to hinder yours, Claire. I'll do my best to control the noise."

"Thank you," she said, but he sensed her disappointment in him. And it bothered him.

Chapter Ten

Wednesday morning brought Christmas Eve, the second most depressing day of the year for Claire. Christmas Day would be the worst.

She buttered a piece of bread for breakfast and took it to the parlor where she kept her grandmother's diary. Reading was the only way she could escape the emptiness of her house.

An impatient yelping sounded outside on her front porch.

She smiled and set aside her plate. Her visitor wasn't a paying boarder, but he was the next best thing. Sailor.

When she opened the door, Sailor stood on her porch wearing a huge red ribbon around his neck and a wide canine grin.

"What's this?"

Sailor bounded into the foyer, wheezing and tracking a circle of wet paw prints on her parquet floor as he stared up at her.

She laughed and knelt to hug the silly dog. "You don't have to beg for my affection."

The dog let out a growly moan and pushed against her side, nearly knocking her over.

"Who put this bow around your neck?" she asked, holding him away from her to look at the red ribbon. A rolled up piece of paper was attached.

Her heart convulsed.

Oh, no. No. She rose to her feet. *Not another warning. Not today.*

Boyd wouldn't threaten her. He wouldn't. So who would have sent this note?

Any of Boyd's patrons on familiar terms with Sailor.

The dog tilted his head and stared at her as if trying to understand the sudden shift in her demeanor. Her fingers fumbled as she untied the ribbon from around the note and unrolled the parchment.

Merry Christmas, Claire.
Sailor and I would like to take you for a sleigh ride to celebrate the season. Say yes and I'll close my saloon for the night.
Boyd.

Her breath rushed out, and she sagged against the desk.

It wasn't a warning. It was an invitation. From Boyd.

She was nothing but a frightened goose!

Sailor nudged her knees with his nose, as if saying he needed an answer for his master.

She swallowed and tried to calm her erratic heartbeat, her palm against her chest. It wasn't a threat, she reassured herself.

Sailor barked twice, his front paws lifting off the floor.

"A gentleman doesn't rush a lady," she said, but she reached for a pen from her desk. She flattened the note on the desktop, prepared to write a short regret, but the last sentence caught her eye. "Say yes and I'll close my saloon for the night."

She grinned. He'd finally seduced her into saying yes to one of his proposals. His offer was too tempting to pass up.

What a blessing it would be to have no noise for one entire evening. Two, if she could finagle it. A smile bloomed on her face as she wrote her reply.

Dear Mr. Grayson,

Close your saloon Christmas Eve and Christmas night, and I will be ready in an hour.

She rolled the note, tied it to the ribbon then kissed Sailor's spotted head before sending him outside. He ran across the street and bounded up the saloon steps where Boyd was waiting.

She waved to her handsome neighbor, assuring herself she was only going with him to help the temperance cause. Getting out of her lonely house for a while would be an added benefit.

But an hour later, when Boyd pulled up in front of the house, her heart somersaulted. The white sleigh was decked with red ribbons and silver bells. Two handsome bay Morgans stood in full harness. Sailor—the silly darling—was perched on the floor in front of the seat, still wearing the huge red bow around his neck.

Boyd wore a heavy gray ulster, a Windsor-style plush cap, and a white smile that melted the last of her resistance. He hopped down from the sleigh, swept his cap off his head, and executed a ridiculous bow that made her laugh.

"The Pemberton Inn is officially closed for two evenings," he said, "which leaves me at your service for forty-eight hours."

She warned herself not to be drawn in by his flirting and his charm. Charm had nearly been the death of her before. She knew men like Boyd didn't change their bad habits. And women like her couldn't live with them.

He swept his gloved hand toward the sleigh, a Portland cutter with hickory knees, nickel-plated arm rails, and a springback seat with a green, broadcloth-upholstered spring cushion. "Your coach awaits, fair lady."

She laughed and trudged through the snow. "Where did you get this sleigh?" "My brother Radford and his wife Evelyn own a livery. Evelyn and my niece Rebecca decorated the sleigh for us."

"It's beautiful."

"I'll give your compliments to Evelyn and Rebecca." He lifted her into the sleigh, climbed aboard and sat beside her.

Sailor stuck his nose between their knees, wheezing and panting and begging for attention. Boyd wrapped his gloved fingers around Sailor's jaw and stared the dog in the eyes. "Other side, pal."

Claire opened her arms to the dog. "Don't let him bother you, Sailor. Come here and keep me warm. "

The mutt barreled onto the seat but lost his balance, his wet paws scratching at the cushion as he scrambled to stay in the sleigh. His clumsy, comical actions made her laugh.

"You are precious," she said, brushing his nose with her wool mitten. Sailor settled beside her and gazed up with his canine grin and adoring eyes.

Boyd laughed and nudged Sailor's jaw. "Where's your pride?"

The dog ignored him, his attention riveted on Claire. She laughed again and put her arm around the dog, pulling him close to her side. "There's nothing wrong with showing your emotions."

"To a point." Boyd opened a heavy lap robe and laid it over their legs. "But groveling is shameful."

"For the groveler perhaps—but it's flattering to the one on the receiving end." She lifted the robe and tucked it around Sailor. "You're just being honest in your affection, aren't you?"

Boyd shook his head. "He's making a fool of himself."

Claire kept her arm around the dog, loving his warmth and the feel of his heart beating against her side—and her success at putting Boyd off balance. "Where are we going?"

"It's a surprise." Boyd winked and lifted the reins. "We'll stay in town."

"Thank you."

His gaze lingered, his smile fading. "You're so beautiful," he said, his voice so intimate it sent a tickle swirling through her stomach. "I can't seem to keep my mind on anything but you."

Her face heated, but she refused to look away, to let him know how much his flirting affected her. She hadn't felt this wicked thrill zinging through her since she'd fallen head over heels for Jack. That "thrill" had led her straight into a cage.

But Boyd was only flirting with her. There was no need for nerves. Still, she couldn't shake the need for caution. "I only agreed to a sleigh ride."

"I understand. I guess open adoration only works for dogs."

"I guess so." She smiled.

He smiled back.

If he were a gentle shopkeeper, or a pastor, or a man without vice, she would welcome his flirtation as harmless, flattering, sincere. She would never marry, of course, not even one of those men, but she would enjoy their companionship.

"Are you warm enough?" he asked.

She nodded then looked away. Companionship wasn't in her future either. If a man wanted companionship, he took a wife. She would never be a wife. She would spend the rest of her days sharing her house with strangers, decent strangers—travelers, amiable people who left for other climes, troubled people for whom she could be a wayside, young lovers on a honeymoon starting out their married lives. All of them going somewhere. All of them but her. She bit her lip to stop the tumble of her thoughts.

Sailor yawned and flopped across her lap. She stroked his neck, wishing the clumsy mixed-breed mutt belonged to her.

"How long have you had Sailor?" she asked.

Boyd started the horses moving and pulled the sleigh onto the snow-packed street. "A year or so. Found him on my porch, drunk as a sailor, lapping up ale that was draining from a cracked barrel."

"How shameful."

"I thought so. He was only a puppy."

Claire rolled her eyes. "I meant it was shameful for you to leave alcohol lying about where an animal could drink it."

He chuckled. "It brought us together, gave Sailor a name and a home. What's so terrible about that?"

She couldn't argue his point so she scowled at him. "Your mother must have had her hands full with you."

"My mother adores me."

"Undoubtedly. But does she adore your choice of profession?"

He winced. "She would rather I work the sawmill."

"Why don't you? If I understand correctly, it belongs to you and your three brothers?"

Boyd slowed the sleigh and turned left onto Day Street near the center of town. "I've worked the sawmill since I was a boy," he said, steering the team around a small carriage parked on the side of the street. "I wanted a change."

"Do you ever think of going back?" she asked, sending up a prayer that he would announce his intentions to close his saloon and return to his family business.

"I'm happy working a few hours a week there. That's enough."

"Is it?"

He glanced at her, his expression quizzical. "Why wouldn't it be?"

"Because your brothers are there?"

"Kyle is the only one who works the mill full time. Duke and Radford and I work when we can."

He made a right turn at the intersection of Day and Lambert Streets where Claire had recently marched with her temperance friends. As Lambert Street angled hard left, Boyd veered right and entered Forest Hill Cemetery.

"Is there a reason you're taking me to a cemetery?" she asked, wondering what on earth he could be planning.

"Yes." He winked at her, but didn't say another word.

Huge, snow-covered maple trees and towering pines cast shadows across the narrow lanes that wound through the cemetery. Everything was buried in several inches of snow, but he seemed to know where he was going. The horses' shod feet kicked up a dusting of snow with each step, the bells on their harness tinkling with each shift of their majestic bodies, creating a light, rhythmic music that captivated Claire.

Boyd guided the sleigh on a winding path through the towering trees and leafless, snow-covered bushes, past squat, somber tombstones and tall monuments. Suddenly he brought the sleigh to a stop, his expression serene and oddly respectful. "I thought you might like to visit your grandparents today." He nodded toward two matching headstones on Claire's side of the sleigh.

Stunned, she glanced to her left and saw two gray stones side-by-side with her grandparents' names engraved on them. She'd never been here, but Boyd obviously had. He must have come earlier to clear the snow off the stones.

In the few weeks she'd been in Fredonia, she'd been so preoccupied with opening and managing her boardinghouse and the temperance marches that she hadn't yet visited her grandparents' graves. Her grandmother hadn't liked coming to the cemetery, and had never brought Claire here to visit her grandfather's grave. She'd wanted to remember her husband as a living man, not as a cold stone in a cemetery.

Claire had felt the same. Still, she should have visited the cemetery out of respect for her grandparents. Despite the demands of her new responsibilities, she knew she could have squeezed in a visit. Truth was, she hadn't been able to face the loss of her grandmother, or the reminder of burying Jack.

"I thought we could hang these on their stones," Boyd said. He lifted two fir wreathes out of a satchel at his feet and handed them to her. Tiny pinecones and elaborate gold bows decorated each wreath.

His thoughtfulness and generosity touched her.

"How did you know they were here?" she asked, keeping her eyes downcast so he couldn't see the moisture that was blurring her vision.

"I was a pallbearer for Marie."

She glanced up, surprised by his confession.

"Marie had lots of friends, you know."

She knew. The summer she'd spent with her grandmother had been filled with daily visitors. Still, it surprised her that her grandmother would have consorted with a saloon owner.

"I know what you're thinking." He smiled, and she felt a guilty flush burn her face. "We were good friends. I cared about your grandmother."

"Do you have any idea what happened... how she died?" The letter from her grandmother's lawyer hadn't explained the circumstances. He had just sent the deed with a note saying Claire now owned the house.

"She was beating me soundly in a game of poker when she slumped over the table."

"You were with her?"

"Yes." He caught Claire's hand and stopped her nervous fumbling with the wreath. "She didn't suffer. Whatever took her was fast and merciful."

"I didn't know she played poker." The instant the words left Claire's mouth she cringed. What a stupid thing to say. She could have expressed her heartbreak over her grandmother's death, or thanked Boyd for bringing her here, or... or any number of thoughts circling her mind, but no, she'd blurted out the most mundane and inappropriate comment of all.

"Marie loved playing cards. She was an ace player."

So was Claire, but she would never reveal the dirty little secret that had enabled her and Jack to eat.

"Pat and I played cards with your grandmother a couple evenings a week. We kept her wood bins stocked and she kept us fed." He released Claire's hand and braced a forearm over his knee. "I miss her. She treated me like her own son."

So that's why her grandmother had consorted with a saloon owner. She had missed her son. Boyd had filled that void in her life.

A void Claire had created by eloping with Jack while staying with her grandmother. Her father hadn't spoken to his mother since that day.

Her grandmother couldn't have known that Jack had a dark side. She would have only heard Claire's declaration of being in love with Jack Ashier.

Thank goodness she wasn't here to learn the truth. Jack had been a deeply conflicted and angry man. While living with him, Claire had been just as conflicted.

"Would you like to hang the wreaths now?" Boyd asked.

She nodded, glad to turn away from her thoughts.

Sailor sniffed the wreath and sneezed. She smiled and hugged the dog, knowing she needed him more than he would ever need her.

Boyd climbed out of the sleigh then helped her down. Her feet were barely on the ground when Sailor leapt off the seat and hit the back of her legs.

She fell against Boyd's hard body. Her face brushed the breast of his coat as his arms clamped around her waist to steady her. She smelled a mixture of wool and cologne, heard his breath near her ear, felt the warmth of his body seeping through the thick fabric of his coat.

Sailor tore off after a gray squirrel scampering back to its hole in an aging oak tree.

Boyd gazed down at her, an indulgent smile creeping across his lips. "Remind me to thank Sailor for this unexpected opportunity."

"Tell me you didn't train him to do that."

"I didn't. But I don't regret his recklessness."

Merciful heaven. Were all rakes blessed with such a heart-stopping smile?

Jack's smile had been practiced and purposeful, a tool or weapon to use at will. She'd sensed his insincerity, but he'd been too handsome, a master to her youthful naiveté.

She was older and wiser now, but the warmth in Boyd's smile and the mischief sparkling in his eyes made her feel young and full of foolish thoughts.

"What do you want for Christmas?" he asked, tightening his arms to keep her against him, his mouth only inches from hers.

"We are in a public cemetery."

"I don't mind," he said, ignoring her protest. "What do you want?"

Unwilling to let the rascal unnerve her, she met his eyes. "I want you to close your saloon," she said, being as flippant as he was prone to being.

"Done. Consider it closed tonight and tomorrow."

She laughed and swatted his arm. "I mean forever."

His smile faded, and he gazed down at her. "Nothing is forever, Claire."

She lowered her lashes. She knew that only too well.

He nudged her chin to make her look at him. "That wasn't supposed to make you sad."

"I'm not sad, I'm... cold." No, that wasn't true. She wasn't cold. She was empty. And lonely. Her sudden longing to stay in his arms scared her. She turned and lifted the wreaths off the seat. "Let's hang these before we freeze to death."

She'd barely known her grandfather, but she'd adored her grandmother. It wrenched her heart to think of her grandmother lying beneath the frigid snow and earth.

"I brought wire," Boyd said, pulling a small spool from his pocket. He gestured toward the wreaths in her hands. "It'll keep the wind from blowing them away." He pulled off his gloves and positioned the wreaths on the stones. His long, nimble fingers brushed Claire's mitten-covered hands as he twisted and bent the wire.

"What made you think of doing this?" she asked.

He glanced at her, his cheeks pink from the cold. "Family should be together during the holidays."

Nothing would make her happier than to spend time with her family, but that wasn't going to happen. Ever.

For the balance of her life, she would spend her holidays alone, or with strangers.

Boyd's strong artist's hands secured the second wreath then he sat back on his heels. "What do you think?"

His boyishly expectant expression melted her heart. "Thank you. This was... it was..." She cleared her throat, cursing herself for being so emotional. "You were kind to do this."

The smile in his eyes dimmed, and he gave her a small nod.

How miserly her thanks. How stingy her praise. He'd done something many men wouldn't think of doing, and all she could acknowledge was his kindness?

She reached out and clasped his hand. "Grandmother would be touched by your gesture," she added, unable to tell him how deeply he'd touched her own heart.

"Your grandmother talked about you often, Claire. She claimed you had a head full of dreams and that you would get hurt." Boyd held her gaze. "I think you did."

His bold comment embarrassed her. She stood and headed toward the sleigh.

He caught her hand and stopped her. "I know we're on opposite sides of this temperance issue, but it will never dictate the way I treat you. You're safe with me. If you ever need anything, you can trust me. I just wanted you to know that. "

His earnest declaration prodded her to believe him. She did believe him in the deepest part of her soul. But she'd believed Jack, too.

Still, her grandmother wouldn't have befriended Boyd if he wasn't a trustworthy man, would she?

"I'd like us to be friends," he said.

She hadn't had a friend since she was sixteen years old. But she could never be friends with a saloon owner. Especially the one who was ruining her business.

He nodded toward the sleigh. "I think Sailor's ready to leave."

The dog sat beside the sleigh, his tongue lolling from the side of his mouth while a dusting of snow melted on his nose. Claire smiled at the silly dog. "What have you been doing? You're covered with snow."

With a happy bark, he leapt forward and plowed into her knees, knocking her onto her backside in the snow. He dove onto her lap and licked her cheek then grabbed a mouthful of her skirt and tugged.

"Sailor! Get off of her, you ill-mannered maniac." Boyd pushed the dog aside and helped Claire to her feet. "Are you all right?"

"Just wet," she said, drying her cheek on her wool coat.

Boyd retrieved a clean handkerchief from his pocket.

"Did he rip your dress?"

She hoped not. She had too few as it was. Her grandmother's dresses were too small to be re-cut for her, so she'd salvaged material from several dresses to make five for herself. "No holes or tears," she said, brushing her hand over her skirt.

"Sailor. Come here and apologize," Boyd said.

The dog sat in the snow and tilted his head.

"Come here and tell Claire you're sorry." Boyd snapped his fingers and Sailor sprawled onto his stomach. "Apologize."

The dog lowered his nose to his paws and looked up at Claire with sad eyes.

"It's all right, Sailor." She couldn't bear the pathetic look in his eyes.

Sailor whimpered and inched forward on his belly until he was at Claire's feet. He put his paw over his eyes and let out a mournful howl that echoed through the cemetery.

She flinched. "That was definitely a vocal apology."

"Good boy, Sailor." Boyd stomped his foot on the snow.

Sailor scrambled to his feet and reared up on his hind legs. Each time Boyd thumped his foot, Sailor took a hop across the ground.

Amazed, Claire laughed at the dog's circus antics.

Boyd aimed his finger like a gun. "Bang!"

Sailor hit the snow in full body flop, his tongue lolling from his mouth as if he'd just been shot to death.

"What have you done to this poor dog?" she asked, her voice bubbling with laughter.

"We've educated him."

She was still laughing when she knelt down to hug the dog. "I forgive you," she said then jerked away to save herself another wet swipe of Sailor's tongue.

"Better stay clear," Boyd said, a gorgeous smile lighting his face. "He'll lick the paint off a post if given a chance."

"I believe it." She stood up, determined to get herself a dog just like the rascal sniffing her boots. "Do you know where I can get a dog? Like Sailor?"

Boyd shook his head. "There isn't another dog like him. He's been corrupted by living in a saloon and spending his time with drinking men." He gave her a sideways grin. "It takes a long time to acquire all his tricks and bad habits."

"I'm sure."

Their gazes held, but she didn't feel threatened or offended by his silent perusal. She felt alive for the first time in years.

And happy.

Her nightmare with Jack was over. She'd survived. She could have friends now. She could laugh again. She could move on now.

But what did moving on entail? Days spent catering to strangers? Nights spent alone in her bed? Uninspiring at best, dreadfully lonely at worst, but it was safe.

"Thank you," she said, turning away from his searching gaze. "We should head back." He couldn't know how much he'd given her today. She could never tell him.

Chapter Eleven

B oyd drove out of the cemetery, knowing he'd seen another side of Claire today. Despite being frightened and vulnerable, she was courageous and outspoken. She was fragile, yet there was an inner strength that held her together. She was wounded and hurting, but independent and proud. She was determined but not confident. A puzzle.

An enigma.

A challenge.

"How did you teach Sailor those tricks?" she asked, glancing up at him with her gorgeous blue eyes that made him want to kiss her until she forgot he was an unsuitable saloon owner.

"My patrons are responsible for his quirks. They teach him those bad habits when I'm not looking."

"Why don't I believe that?"

"Maybe because you're an intelligent lady?" he said, enjoying her unexpected playfulness.

"I'm intelligent enough to know when a man is trying to hoodwink me."

"All right. I confess. I taught Sailor most of his tricks." He slanted a repentant look her way. "A man gets bored living alone."

She pursed her lips, a habit she had when fighting a smile. "Perhaps you should move back home with your mother."

"Gads, no! Sailor would never survive the shock."

Her laughter bubbled out, and his heart lifted. "I think you are the one who couldn't manage the shock," she said. "You wouldn't be able to carouse and carry on all night."

"So that's what you're angling for. You want to move me back with my mother to get rid of me."

"Exactly."

Her eyes sparkled and her lips twitched, and Boyd was thoroughly bewitched.

He'd had romantic liaisons with all kinds of women, tall and beautiful, shy and pretty, tiny and cute, and one homely dear and tender lass who'd made him laugh and forget his troubles for a few weeks. He'd appreciated all of them, but not once had he found himself longing to spend time with a woman outside the bedroom.

Until now, because everything with Claire was different.

She stirred him up, kept him off balance. He sensed her attraction to him, and yet, he couldn't easily seduce her. More than that, He was giving her his best efforts, and not making any headway. Claire was forthright, and he respected that. She was outspoken, too, but he admired her ability to speak her mind and stand up for what she believed in.

He turned the sleigh onto Day Street. "Is your mother as outspoken as you are?" he asked.

"I doubt she's had an opinion of her own since marrying my father." She turned her face toward the park, but he'd seen the sudden sadness in her eyes.

"My mother always has an opinion," he said, purposely directing the conversation back to himself. "She's half your size and tougher than any man I've ever met." Claire pursed her lips and stroked Sailor's head. "I don't believe she would consider that a compliment."

"Well, it's true, My father wouldn't even argue with her."

"If your brothers are anything like you, I'm sure she had to be tough. Any mother with four boys has to be tough."

The light returned to Claire's eyes, and Boyd knew his shift in conversation had been the smart thing to do. For some reason, she didn't want to talk about her family.

"What about a mother with four girls?" he challenged.

"She had better be a lot tougher."

He turned onto Main Street, and decided to test the waters again. "Do you have any sisters?"

"One. Lida is three years older than me."

"Is she married?"

"Yes."

"Any children?" he asked, hoping she would talk about her family.

"Three that I'm aware of, but we were talking about your mother, weren't we?"

"We were," he said. He eased off the reins and let the horses have their head as they started up West Hill. He settled against the seat, intentionally tucking his shoulder against her own. "My mother is bossy, but she doesn't meddle. She speaks her mind, but doesn't offer advice. She's patient, but doesn't take any sass from me or my brothers. She's got a hug that will make you feel like a hundred dollar bill, and a right swing that will make your ears ring for days."

Claire laughed. "I'd love to meet her."

"Then come with me this evening."

"What?"

"We celebrate Christmas Eve at my mother's house. She'd enjoy meeting you. Come with me."

Claire gaped at him then let out a breathless laugh. "You're serious?"

"Yes." To his surprise, he really wanted her to come with him.

She pressed her hand to her breast. "Thank you, but I can't accept."

"Why not?"

"Because I would be intruding, and for so many other reasons I couldn't list them all."

"You won't be intruding. What other reasons?"

"You know why, Boyd. I shouldn't have even taken a sleigh ride with you."

"Why not?"

She sighed. "Because it's not in my best interest, or yours. We're enemies, remember?"

"No, we're not." He slowed the sleigh and looked at her. "We're friends now. We just happen to be standing on opposite sides of an issue."

"We can't be friends."

"We already are, Claire."

She huffed out a frosty breath. "We can't even agree on that issue," She stroked Sailor's head, which was resting on her lap. "I appreciate your invitation, and your kindness today, but I cannot be your friend." She met his eyes. "My grandmother may have had money to take care of herself, but I don't. I need boarders, and I won't get them as long as your saloon is open." She sighed. "I can't afford to be your friend."

"I guess this means you won't be inviting me in for hot cocoa like your grandmother used to do?"

She gave him a chastising look. "I can't."

"I understand," he said, but he wasn't about to give up. He pulled the sleigh up in front of her house and helped her out. Not wanting to push her too hard or too fast, he walked her to the door and said good-bye like a proper gentleman.

But the instant she closed the door, Boyd grinned and turned to Sailor. "The lady doesn't believe in fairy tales," he said. "But you and I are going to change her mind."

Claire hung her coat in the closet then went to the parlor to build up the fire. A movement outside drew her to the window. To her surprise, she saw Boyd in her yard rolling a huge snowball while Sailor tromped through the snow biting at snowflakes.

She knocked on the window and lifted her palms. "What are you doing?" she asked, even though he couldn't hear her through the glass.

He grinned and gave a jaunty wave then turned back to his project.

What the devil was he up to?

Curious, she stood at the window. He rolled the huge ball of snow to a spot a few feet from her window then packed snow around the bottom to hold it stationary.

Then, while she watched, he pulled out a knife of some sort and proceeded to sculpt the lumpy ball of snow into a snow castle.

He was so absorbed in the task, and she was so absorbed in watching, that an hour passed without her noticing. The mantel clock chimed six o'clock, and she shivered. She hadn't tended the fire and it was nearly out.

With regret, she left to stoke the fire in the kitchen. She put milk on to heat then returned to the parlor to build up the fire. By the time she glanced outside again, Boyd and Sailor were gone.

But the snow castle was glowing with light from a dozen tiny windows that reflected off the snow and turned her yard into a magical kingdom.

Breathless, she gazed at the shimmering masterpiece before her and felt her heart expand. "Oh, Boyd, you should be using this talent," she whispered to the empty room.

She whirled away from the window and dashed to the front door. Boyd and Sailor were climbing his steps when she stepped onto her porch.

"Mr. Grayson," she called then cringed at her unladylike shout.

Boyd turned in surprise. Sailor didn't wait for an invitation. He barked and bounded across the street as if he hadn't seen her all day.

She laughed and greeted the dog with a brisk rub on his head. She glanced at Boyd and waved him over.

While he crossed the street, she lavished Sailor with affection, her heart needing to express all that it held in the one safe way she could show it.

Boyd stopped at the bottom of her steps and looked up at her, his eyes questioning, his cheeks pink from the cold. "Do you need something?"

"Would you like to come in for hot cocoa?" She laughed at the surprise in his eyes. "I want to talk to you."

"We'll meet you in the back," he said then snapped his fingers for Sailor to follow.

Claire hurried to the kitchen and checked the milk on the stove. It was hot enough to make cocoa. She poured milk into two cups then opened the door for Boyd.

"Don't worry about your boots," she said, when he leaned down to remove them. "I'll wipe the floor when you leave."

He stood by the door while she stirred cocoa, sugar, and vanilla into the hot milk. "What made you change your mind about inviting me inside?"

She handed him a cup of cocoa. "That fabulous snow castle you built."

He winked at the dog. "She likes it."

Sailor wheezed and gave Boyd a wide canine grin.

She laughed. "I honestly think he understands every word you say to him."

"Of course he does," Boyd said, as if she should have known that.

"Why are you hiding in that saloon when you have such incredible talent?"

He scowled but didn't answer, so she knew she'd struck a chord.

"That castle is magnificent, Boyd. That carving you forced on me is a work of art. Why aren't you using your talent?"

"I thought you were going to throw the carving away." She pressed her hand against her skirt pocket, feeling the tiny piece of wood that had become her constant companion. "You're avoiding my question," she said.

"And you're avoiding mine."

She set her hot cup on the counter. "It was too beautiful to throw away."

"Thank you.

"Stop being evasive." She crossed her arms over her chest and scowled at him. "You are an artist, and yet you spend your time tending a saloon. Why?"

"Because I enjoy it."

She eyed him, sensing his answer was only half honest. "Does your mother know you're an artist?"

"I'm not an artist."

"Does she know about your talent for sculpting snow castles and carving roses in wood?"

He leaned against the door. "Yes, Claire. I've given her enough of my boyhood carvings to fill her house."

"How about the carvings you make now? Does she have any of those?"

He sipped his cocoa and studied her. "Why are you so interested in me all of a sudden?"

"I'm interested in your talent and why you're not using it."

A wry grin lifted his mouth. "Ah, I understand. You're hoping you can convince me to give up the saloon and pursue this talent of mine."

The idea thrilled her. No more saloon. No more noise.

No more worries.

"Sorry, Claire. I'm a saloon owner, not an artist," He leaned over and set his empty cup on the table. "Thanks for the cocoa."

"Wait. I wasn't trying to offend you," she said, moving toward him. "I just don't understand how you could possess such talent and not use it."

"I do use it. I build things for my saloon. I teach people how to carve furniture. I dabble with bits of wood when I'm bored. I have a piece of my handiwork in my pocket right now."

"Really? Can I see it?" she asked, wondering what treasure he was hiding.

He slipped his hand into his pocket then pulled it out and lifted the item above her head.

"What is it?" she asked, squinting up at his hand.

"Mistletoe."

He leaned down and kissed her, his firm lips still cool from his hour in the snow.

The thrill racing through her rooted her to the floorboards. Everything inside her dipped and swirled then exploded outward in a million fragments of sensation. She felt alive and vibrant, connected to another human being for the first time in years.

He cupped her chin and angled her mouth, nudging her lips open to deepen the kiss. The smell of fresh air clung to his hair and clothes, the taste of cocoa lingered on his tongue and mingled with the chocolate in her own mouth.

She savored the feel and taste of him even as she pushed him away. She wouldn't deny her attraction, nor the intense longing rushing through her. Both were real.

Too real.

And both were terrible mistakes.

He lifted his mouth an inch from hers, his eyes gazing into her own. "Merry Christmas," he whispered. "Sure you don't want to come to my mother's with me?"

She clutched the table for support and stared at him. "You purposely tricked me with that mistletoe."

"You deserved it."

How could she chastise him for his behavior when her own motives were suspect? He'd been a gentleman all day, thoughtful to the point of gallantry. She had been the one to use his talent to press him about closing his saloon.

No wonder he'd retaliated.

But to trick her into a kiss?

Kissing was so... It was so... intimate.

"You're impossible," she whispered.

"Impudent," he said.

He was beyond impudent. He was a rascal, a tease, as she well knew from her own experience. A philanderer, as he'd admitted. A rake.

But thoughtful and generous and kind. An artist who saw beauty in simple things, who made simple things into things of beauty.

A man with two faces.

No wonder she couldn't understand him.

He called Sailor away from the stove then opened the door. "I enjoyed the kiss, Claire." He winked and stepped outside, closing the door behind him.

She released a shaky breath and carried her cocoa to the parlor.

The little fire she was burning on Christmas Eve did not warm her at all. To her shame, she longed for the warmth of Boyd's arms.

"This man is trouble, Grandmother," she said, her whispered words lost in the empty parlor.

She wrapped an afghan around her shoulders and settled in to the rocking chair to read the journal.

Boyd was prying at her resistance, forcing her to pay attention to him, to see him and make space for him in her thoughts.

"Is that what Abe did to you, Grandmother? Did he make you notice him when you knew you shouldn't?"

She leaned her head against the back of the rocking chair, feeling half crazy. She was talking to herself, and thinking of a man who couldn't be a worse candidate for her affection. It was crazy to think about him.

But she did.

Time passed and the wind kicked up, and still she thought of Boyd.

His charm and wit challenged her to stay alert. But the tender, serious side of Boyd intrigued her and made her want a closer look.

Which image reflected the real man? The impudent rakehell, or the kind and thoughtful gentleman?

A loud banging on the door brought her to her feet with a squeak of fright. She clasped the journal to her pounding heart.

Whoever stood outside pounded again.

Half terrified, she hurried to the foyer and peeked out the small window beside the door.

To her utter shock, Anna—a woman Claire had met briefly while living with Jack in a crude rooming house near the docks—was standing on her porch.

"Dear God..." Claire clutched her reeling stomach, unable to open the door. Anna's husband was a monster, worse than Jack could have ever been.

"I need a place to stay." Anna pressed her hand to the glass, desperation in her eyes. "I saw the sign for your boardinghouse in the store window."

It would cost Claire too much to open the door.

"Larry's in j-jail," she said, her chin quivering from the cold. "He doesn't know I've left him."

The wind howled past the window, whipping Anna's cape around her, pelting her with snow. Claire's heart twisted, but she couldn't move.

"He won't come here. He doesn't know we were friends," Anna said.

They weren't friends. They'd spoken a few times during the two weeks they'd both lived in the squalid dockside apartments. They had recognized each other as being in the same inescapable situation, but they'd never talked about it.

They had talked about the approaching holidays. When Jack drowned, Anna had expressed her sympathy and her relief that Claire had a place to go.

Now Anna was here seeking refuge, bringing her dangerous life right to Claire's doorstep.

Anna's bare palm slid down the window, the hope in her eyes dying as she turned away. She pulled her cloak around her thin body and crossed the porch.

Compassion warred with self-preservation, as Claire watched Anna descend the steps. Where would she go? Where *could* she go? That was the question Claire had faced each time she'd thought about running from Jack.

The answer was the same for Anna. She couldn't go to her family because it was the first place Larry would look. Even if Claire had been welcome at her father's house, she wouldn't have put him in Jack's destructive path. Jack had been too sly and conniving. He would have found a way to win.

She'd been trapped with no place to go.

Just like Anna.

With a silent curse, Claire wrenched open the door. "Are you hurt, Anna?"

Anna turned toward the house, and her eyes filled with tears. "No. But I can't go home."

"Come inside then."

Anna brushed the tears from her eyes and climbed the steps. "Thank you," she whispered.

Claire closed the door behind them then slipped the journal into the desk.

"Larry's in jail for killing a man during a card game. He doesn't know I'm gone. I haven't told anyone about you, so he won't be a danger to us."

Claire wished she could believe that. Men like Larry had a way of finding their wives.

"I'll get us some hot tea," she said, guiding Anna into the parlor. "Make yourself comfortable."

When she returned, Anna was staring out the window at Boyd's shimmering snow castle. "How beautiful," the woman said, her voice filled with awe. "It looks so warm and inviting inside I want to live there."

Claire felt the same way each time she looked at it. "My neighbor Boyd Grayson built it this evening."

Anna regarded the castle as if deep in thought. "He's in love with you," she finally said.

Claire choked on her tea. Her sinuses burned, and she blinked her eyes to clear her tears.

Anna glanced at the shimmering castle then back at Claire. "He must be."

"Boyd Grayson doesn't know the meaning of the word. He's a rakehell who is trying to manipulate me."

"Any man who would build a magnificent snow castle and light it with a lantern, meant it as a gift." She gestured toward the castle. "This was a gift to you. Whatever his motivation, he gave you a part of himself today. You can see it."

Claire's stomach plunged and she sank down onto the sofa. What if Anna was right?

He had given her a gift today. He'd taken her to the cemetery to connect with her family then he'd built a fairy tale castle to make her feel less alone. Somehow he'd known that she needed a friend today.

He'd been that friend.

He'd given her a part of himself.

The castle was beautiful and luminous, a gift he'd made just for her.

How shameful that she'd never properly expressed her gratitude, that she had insisted on seeing him in a superficial light. There was much more to this man. He was artistic and giving, a light to those around him.

She definitely owed Boyd a thank you, but his saloon was stripping away her independence dollar by dollar, day by day, boarder by boarder. No matter how charmed she was by his gifts, she couldn't afford to overlook that.

But she felt torn between her need to thank him and her need to protect herself.

⚓

The walk to his mother's house was cold, but it gave Boyd time to think about Claire. He shocked her earlier with his bold kiss, but she hadn't been offended.

She'd liked it.

He'd loved it.

And he was going to kiss her again. Soon.

She would pretend that he'd taken advantage of her, that she was affronted by his forwardness, that she hadn't enjoyed the kiss. But she'd liked it. He'd kissed enough women to know when they were responding with passion. Claire had definitely responded. And definitely with passion.

The windows of his mother's house were brightly lit. The house would be filled with food and family and laughter.

He always enjoyed their celebrations, but tonight he felt an odd discomfort about attending.

Was it because Claire was alone?

He should have left Sailor with her instead of at the saloon. Both would have enjoyed the evening more.

Before he could consider turning back, the door opened and Duke stepped outside.

"Leaving already?" Boyd asked.

"Just getting the wine." Duke reached into the snow bank beside the door and plucked out a gallon jug of white wine. "Rebecca's in a snit that you're late."

"Is she now?" Their seven-year-old niece was all curls and attitude. And absolutely irresistible.

"She's lecturing Kyle about taking care of Ginger's litter of kittens."

"Then I'm going in to watch."

Duke chuckled and followed him inside.

The parlor was filled with his family, and the house smelled of cinnamon, roast turkey, and plum pudding.

Boyd had spent every Christmas Eve here with his mother and brothers, and eventually with their wives and children. Now Kyle's mother-in-law Victoria, who'd been widowed two years earlier, brought her suitor Jeb Kane to share the holiday with them. The sounds and smells were so familiar they were etched in Boyd's brain.

But this year something was missing.

It wasn't his father's absence. He'd been missing his father from the moment disease had started to cripple him, and long before it had killed him. This emptiness felt different. It was an ache in the center of his chest that left him longing for something of his own, something to fill the void inside him.

He stepped into the room, hoping to step away from the feeling that haunted him. "Merry Christmas," he said to everyone then swept his mother into a hug that lifted her off her feet.

She laughed and swatted his shoulder. "Don't think that will sweeten me up. It's been almost a week since you've been to see me."

"And I've been pining the whole time."

"The devil you have." She pushed him away, but her eyes sparkled with love. "You were so busy making eyes at Mrs. Ashier this morning, you nearly ran over me and Rebecca near the Common. Rebecca even shouted at you, but you drove right by us."

His glance shot across his brothers' grinning faces. The wretches were savoring every minute of his discomfort. Even Jeb was trying to hide a grin.

Heat 'burned his neck because he *had* been preoccupied with Claire. While she'd been sitting beside him, he hadn't cared who was strolling through town. It could have been the Union Army, and he wouldn't have noticed one of them.

"Rumor has it you're in love with the pretty widow," Evelyn said, the mischief in her eyes suggesting she enjoyed watching him squirm as much as his brothers did. Radford's wife had grown up as Boyd's neighbor, so the raven-haired beauty was more like a sister than a sister-in-law to him.

Like a true brother, he ignored her and spoke to his mother. "I didn't see you and Rebecca," he said, hoping they would all drop the subject.

"You didn't see me either," Duke added. "You nearly ran me over on Day Street."

"The devil I did."

"If it wasn't you in that decked out sleigh with the pretty widow then you've got a twin in town who can't manage a pair of horses."

Boyd scowled at Duke. Brothers could be such a pain in the ass sometimes.

"You and the lovely widow created quite a buzz in the park this morning," his mother said. "You two made a cozy picture in that fancy sleigh. Are you courting her?"

He was trying to court Claire, but wasn't about to discuss his situation with his too-eager family. Instead of answering, he winked at Rebecca. "Hey, sprite. I've got mistletoe in my pocket. Where's my kiss?"

Rebecca's face filled with joy, and she leapt off Kyle's lap.

"Did Mrs. Ashier like our sleigh?"

He groaned. "She loved it, Sprite."

"Why didn't you wave to me?" she demanded, her bottom lip full of attitude.

"Because I didn't see you." He swept her up in a twirling hug that made her squeal with laughter—and made his head spin. "Why are you picking on Uncle Kyle?" he asked, swinging the attention to his deserving brother. Let Kyle squirm a bit.

"He's gonna give Ginger's kittens away."

"Is that so?"

Rebecca nodded. "Aunt Amelia says she won't let him."

Boyd slanted a your-turn-to-squirm look at Kyle. "Looks like you're outnumbered."

He shrugged. "I plan to change that by giving away a few kittens."

Amelia wrinkled her nose at Kyle. "Would you want someone to give our baby away?"

"I might consider it if he doesn't start sleeping at night."

"You would not," she said with a laugh that flushed her cheeks and made Kyle grin.

"Ginger had five kittens," Rebecca said, tugging on Boyd's black bow tie. "She has two boys and three girls."

Kyle rolled his eyes. "Want one?"

"No thanks," Boyd said, but then he thought of Claire. "But I might know someone who does."

"Ask if they want five."

Amelia nudged Kyle in the ribs.

He grunted and chuckled. "All right. We'll keep one."

"Where's your mistletoe?" Rebecca asked.

Boyd pulled it out of his pocket, held it above his niece's head, and gave her a loud smack on her cheek. She giggled and he growled against her neck, making her squeal and squirm out of his arms. Laughing, he tucked the mistletoe back into his pocket and glanced down at his nephew, who was soaking something with drool. "What's William trying to eat?"

Rebecca squatted beside her brother. "His shoe," she said then giggled when her mother wrinkled her nose and removed the leather boot from William's mouth.

Radford wasn't concerned at all that his son was eating his shoe. Neither was Boyd. They had pilfered potatoes and rhubarb from their gardens and fruit from their orchards, scrubbed them clean on their dirty trousers, and they'd survived.

Boyd played with William until his giggles caused hiccups; then he introduced himself to his newest nephew, Marshall, who promptly spit up on the sleeve of Boyd's suit jacket. Rebecca climbed onto his lap and instigated a tickling match.

At last he sank into a chair, into the warm, welcoming bosom of his family, feeling at home... and yet, not at home.

The joking and light banter between them was the same, but something inside him was different this year.

The thought gnawed at him throughout the evening, distracting him by turns, poking him incessantly until finally, he wandered into the kitchen to snatch a second helping of pie. He reached for a plate, but ended up admiring the oak pie safe his father had made for his mother before Boyd was born. Boyd trailed his finger over a cluster of rosettes carved in the center of the safe door. Even his father's early work had the mark of a master craftsman.

"Beautiful, isn't it?" his mother said, entering the kitchen.

"Everything Dad made was beautiful."

"It certainly was," She stopped beside Boyd, but instead of cutting the pie, she stroked her hand over his back, a loving gesture she'd performed too many times to count, "What's bothering you?"

Years of experience had taught him not to try to skirt the question, His mother always knew when he was carrying a heartache or a problem, whether it was a lost puppy or a hurt ego.

"Guess I'm missing Dad more than usual this year."

"Me too," she admitted with the same deep sadness in her voice Boyd felt in his chest,

He looked down at his mother, the most loving, stable person in his life. She had loved him through his childish rages and shenanigans. She had comforted him a thousand times. She'd buried her disappointment when he left the mill and became a saloon keeper. He'd had many lovers, and though his mother had cautioned against it, she'd never manipulated his conscience to direct his decisions. She'd forgiven him everything, and loved him despite his many faults and failings. She'd even stood up against her fellow church members and refused to march against his saloon.

He'd taken it all for granted.

Regret welled up inside him as he pulled her into a hug. He kissed the top of her head, which barely reached his chin. "I'm sorry I've asked so much of you, Mother. I haven't meant to be selfish, but I know I have been."

She tipped her head back and gave him a long, hard look. "Of all my boys, you've been the least selfish. I don't know why you think otherwise. What's weighing on your mind tonight?"

"I haven't done enough for you. I've asked for too much and given too little."

"Boyd Benjamin, where did you get that fool-headed idea? You never ask me for anything."

"Maybe I should have." His lowered his arms and leaned against the sink. "I never asked what you wanted when Dad broke his hip. I only thought of my needs when I refused to hug him. I didn't know my refusal to accept his death would ask too much of you and Dad."

"Is that what this is about?" She sighed and laid her hand on the pie safe, her loving gaze studying him. "If it weren't for you, your father would have given up. After you stormed out of the house that day, refusing to let him quit fighting and give in to the disease, your father wept a river because he felt so loved."

"But he suffered so much after that."

Her frown lines disappeared, and her face grew serene. "That last year was one of our best," she said quietly. "We didn't waste a single moment. Because of you, we had time to prepare ourselves to be separated."

"I couldn't let him go," he confessed hoarsely.

A soft smile touched her lips. "He loved you with all his heart, Boyd. His last breath was a laugh over that little carving you left in the water closet for him."

Boyd couldn't recall anything from that day other than running out of the house with angry tears blurring his vision.

"You don't remember?" she asked with a surprised chuckle. "It was an extremely detailed carving of a nude woman. You'd left her standing on the sink basin as a joke for your father."

The memory rushed back like a dam bursting open. Boyd had whittled the statuette during the hours he'd spent at his father's bedside. He wouldn't tell his father what he was working on, only that it was a surprise for him. From the day they had mounted the back bar at the saloon and drunk their first ale together, Boyd had left his boyhood behind. He talked to his father about manly things like carving, receiving hours of instruction while sitting at his bedside.

They talked about timber costs and running their sawmill. And they had talked about women.

At fifteen, Boyd had been wild for them. His preoccupation amused his father to no end. So Boyd had whittled his youthful idea of the perfect woman, and left the big-breasted, full-hipped statuette on the water closet sink as a joke. He knew it would make his father laugh. And his father, who had grown frighteningly weak, had desperately needed a diversion from his pain.

His mother slipped her warm hand over his knuckles. "Your father died with that carving in his hand. I made sure it stayed in his hand when we buried him."

A torrent of grief rushed through Boyd and burned his insides.

"You didn't ask your father to fight his battle alone," she said, unaware of the battle Boyd was fighting with the emotions clogging his throat. "You were at his side every day, cheering him up, making him laugh, giving him a reason to keep living. You were his strength. And mine. You brought light to those dark hours, and your father died knowing he was loved—by me, by your brothers, but most of all by you. That's all any man can hope for. You've never asked for anything, Boyd. You've always been the one to give the most."

Her words made him hopeful that he would someday be able to view his past in a kinder light. He'd buried so many memories in the avalanche of grief.

"I wish I could have helped him."

"Me too," she said. "But I couldn't protect your father from that crippling disease any more then I could protect you boys from painful falls and hurtful comments. I could only love you and give you someone to hold on to when you were hurting. That's all anyone can do."

He nodded, knowing she was right, but wishing he could have done more for his parents.

She sighed and stroked her hand down his arm. "I think you have more on your mind than your father," she said, probing as only a mother could. "Duke suggested that you care a great deal for Mrs. Ashier. I think he may be right."

Boyd sighed. "Duke talks too much."

"Mrs. Ashier seems like a nice young lady."

"She is, Mother, but she's not for me. Or rather, I'm not for her."

"Why not? She seemed smitten with you this morning in the sleigh. And I've seen the looks you two exchange in church. What's the problem?"

"I'm a saloon owner. Claire can't see past that."

"My sight isn't what it used to be, but I know what I saw this morning. That girl wasn't looking at a saloon owner. She was looking at a man she desired."

Boyd rolled his eyes. Women saw romance in everything. He picked up the metal spatula and cut a slice of apple pie. "Want a piece?"

"No." She tugged his coat sleeve. "Come here."

He laid down the spatula and followed her to the kitchen door.

She pointed at Evelyn and Radford, who were side-by-side on the 'parlor sofa with a sleepy William and Rebecca flopped across their laps. "Look at your brothers," she said, her gesture encompassing Kyle and Amelia who had returned to the settee after supper. Kyle held his son with one arm, and his wife with the other, while joking with Amelia's mother and Jeb. "That's happiness and fulfillment." She nodded toward Duke, who sat alone in a wing chair sleeping like a well-fed bear." That's contentment." She faced Boyd, "I see loneliness in you, and it breaks my heart."

He sighed and guided her back into the kitchen. "I'm fine, Mother. I'm not lonely, I'm just pining for another piece of pie."

She swatted his arm. "Let me put some pudding and tarts in a basket for you to take home." A few minutes later she handed the basket to him.

"Gads, Mother, this was supposed to be pudding and tarts, not a feast for a family of twelve."

"You're too skinny. You need to get yourself a wife who will cook for you."

"I've got Sailor. Why would I need a wife?"

A wistful look filled her eyes. "Take another look in the parlor on your way out."

He did, and all he could think about on the way home was Claire. Would her presence have made a difference tonight? Would having Claire in his arms have warded off the loneliness his perceptive mother had noticed?

Of course it would have. His discomfort this evening wasn't a matter of him wanting Claire in his arms. The problem was that a saloon owner's arms would never be acceptable to Claire.

Chapter Twelve

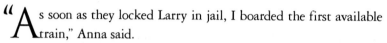

"As soon as they locked Larry in jail, I boarded the first available train," Anna said.

Claire's heart softened, and she stoked the parlor fireplace, knowing it would be a long time before bed. Anna needed a friend to talk to and a safe place to rest for a while. Claire understood. She was in the same place only a short time ago.

They talked through the evening, feeling safe and warm beside the fireplace.

Until someone knocked on the door.

Claire gasped and jerked upright in her chair. Anna leapt to her feet and they stared at each other in fear.

"It can't be Larry," she said, but the terror in her eyes made Claire's heartbeat accelerate.

Who else could it be? No decent human being would call on someone at ten o'clock in the evening.

Anna followed her to the foyer. Claire—peeked out the window, but it had grown too frosty to see through clearly. She only knew there was a man at her door.

She took her revolver from the closet then dangled it behind her skirt, praying she wouldn't accidentally shoot herself in the leg. Her first encounter with Boyd had revealed her dreadful lack of skill with the gun.

Claire signaled for Anna to stay hidden behind the door then she unlocked it and pulled it open two tiny inches. To her surprise, Boyd

Grayson stood on her porch holding a huge wicker basket that emitted the delicious aroma of turkey and plum pudding.

"Are you hungry?" he asked, boldly stepping into her foyer without being invited inside.

"What are you doing here?" she asked, relieved that it wasn't Larry barging into her home.

"Delivering a basket of goodies from my mother."

"It's ten o'clock."

"I'm always hungry at this time of night." He held the basket out to her. "My mother packed enough for a family of twelve."

"Thank you, but I can't accept this." She slipped her hand into her pocket and closed her fingers around the carving he'd given her. "I appreciate the gesture, but you know how I feel about accepting gifts from you."

"It's not a gift from me. It's a gesture of kindness during the holiday. My mother will be disappointed to know her hard work went into the garbage."

Claire couldn't refuse without feeling rude and unappreciative. "Well... thank you. Would you put it on the desk?" she asked, unable to take the basket from him because of the revolver she was hiding at her side.

He leaned forward to set it on the desk, but spotted Anna hiding behind the door. His eyes narrowed, and he glanced at Claire. "I'm sorry, I didn't know you were entertaining."

"Anna's my... guest tonight." She closed the door against the biting cold. "This is Anna Levens, a friend of mine."

He took in Anna's appearance and greeted her with a nod, but his eyes cut back to Claire. "Are you ladies in need of anything?"

He knew. Somehow he knew that Anna was taking refuge with her. His power of intuition and his gentle inquiry touched Claire.

"I can take a room here tonight, if you like."

"No. Thank you for offering," she said, warmed by his concern. "Anna and I will be fine. We have a basket of delicious-smelling food to eat, a fire to warm us, and I have my gun to keep us safe." She lifted the revolver to show him.

He clamped his hand over the barrel and angled it away from his chest. "You really need to get rid of this thing before you shoot yourself—or someone else."

"It's the only protection I have."

"In your hands, this gun can be more harm than good." His fingers circled her wrist, and he nodded at the revolver. "Let go."

She sighed and released her grip on the gun.

He opened the chamber of the revolver, and his eyes glinted with disapproval. "This is loaded!"

"I know."

"You could have blown a hole in my chest."

"Nonsense. I wasn't even aiming at you."

"That is what terrifies me."

Wariness settled in Anna's eyes as she backed against the desk. "I'll put the basket in the kitchen," she said then grasped the handle and rushed to the kitchen.

Boyd sighed. "Looks like you both need protecting."

Claire straightened her shoulders. "We'll be fine." She held out her hand, palm up. "Please return my gun."

"I'd rather not."

"If you don't, I'll report it stolen and tell your brother that you took it."

"Claire, I'm genuinely afraid that you're going to wound yourself with this weapon."

"Nonsense. I keep it in the closet."

"You have no idea how to handle it. Nor do you know how to aim it."

"Well, I won't have to do either as long as I'm not threatened again."

He sighed. "Are we back to that note again?"

His look stung her conscience. "No. I believe you about the note."

"Honestly?"

She nodded. She really did.

"Thank you. That's the best gift I've been given tonight." His gaze shifted to her mouth. "Unless you'd care to top it with a kiss."

Her heart leapt and she stepped away from him. "You'd better not have that mistletoe in your pocket."

His lips quirked, but he shook his head. "It wouldn't work a second time." He nodded toward the closet. "Is that where you keep your gun?"

"Put it on the back corner shelf." She opened the closet door and he put the gun away.

When he turned back, he was wearing a frown. "I assume Anna is running from someone?"

"Yes, her husband. He's in jail for killing a man. The problem is, Anna doesn't know how long he'll be there."

"And you took her in knowing this?"

"What was I supposed to do? She had nowhere else to go."

He opened his mouth then gave her an understanding nod. "If he should show up, do not confront him."

"I have my gun."

"Which you do not know how to use." He placed a finger across her lips to stop her argument. "Come get me. Don't argue with him. Don't try to protect Anna. Slip out the back and come get me immediately. Understand?"

She nodded.

"I mean it, Claire. If the man killed someone, he could be deadly to you or Anna."

A rush of fear made her nauseous, and she pressed her hand to her churning stomach.

"I'm right across the street. Just let me know if you need me."

"Thank you," she said, suddenly wishing she wouldn't have been so quick to decline his offer of taking a room.

He cupped her jaw and studied her so intently, a flush of weakness stole through her body. "Every time I look at you, I want to kiss you."

Her stomach dipped. No wonder women swooned at his feet.

He stood so close, looked so handsome, smelled so good, she couldn't help being attracted to him. But it was more than his handsome face and warm charm that drew her. She was touched by his natural inclination to protect her and Anna. He would protect anybody in danger. He couldn't help himself. The honorable man in him wouldn't allow him to turn a blind eye, to ignore a person in need. Why hadn't she seen that before?

Her heart begged her to forget that he owned a saloon and was unsuitable for her. But she couldn't. No matter what his heroic impulses, or how handsome and seductive he was, he wasn't the man for her. No man was for her.

"Thank you for the sleigh ride and the visit to the cemetery." She peeked at him from beneath her lashes. "It meant a lot to me."

"I was glad to do it."

"It was kind of your mother to send the basket of food. Please thank her for me. Anna and I will enjoy every morsel, I'm sure."

"I'll tell her." He reached for the doorknob to let himself out. "Lock your doors tonight."

"Boyd?"

He hesitated with his hand on the door handle.

"The castle is magnificent," she blurted, unable to let him leave without telling him how much the gift meant to her.

A soft smile crept across his lips, "So are you, Claire."

He stepped outside and pulled the door closed behind him.

She locked up then peered out the frosted window, finding herself in a wonderful, harrowing new danger.

Boyd was the magnificent one, bringing her the basket of holiday cheer, promising to defend her against the dangers in her life. But he didn't realize that he was the biggest danger of all. He was tempting her to take a risk with a man... completely unsuitable for her.

Chapter Thirteen

The basket Boyd left was filled with food. Claire and Anna wrapped the turkey and dressing, and put them in the shed for the night. Then they sat at the table drinking tea, eating plum pudding and talking.

Claire told Anna about her temperance marches and the good she was trying to accomplish in her new town.

Anna's eyes widened with respect. "Someday I hope to be as brave as you."

"I'm not brave at all, Anna. I'm just trying to survive, and help other women like us." She laid her fork on the table. "Do you think Larry killed that man?" she asked, needing to know what she was up against.

Anna's lashes lowered, but she gave a weary nod. "I saw him do it. Larry was in a high stakes card game, but another man won. Larry claimed the man cheated. They fought, and Larry shot him. As soon as the sheriff took Larry to jail, I packed my bag and left. I was too terrified to stay." She sighed and looked at Claire, her brown eyes bleak. "You're lucky you're a widow." Claire sat in shocked silence.

"Oh!" Anna slapped her hand over her mouth as horror filled her eyes. "I'm so sorry. I didn't mean that the way it sounded."

Of course she hadn't. Claire wouldn't have wished Jack dead either, but she was glad to be free of him. Not that she could ever confess that, or the truth about how he died.

"I'm sorry, Claire. I just... I'm scared." Her eyes misted and she averted her face. "Living with Larry was like living with a volcano. I was always waiting and watching to see when he was going to erupt."

"I know." Claire covered Anna's shaking hand with her own. "I know." She'd existed in the same state of anxiety while living with Jack.

"He'll kill me if he finds me. That's why I can't go home to my family."

Claire understood. There was little Anna could do about her situation. She could return to her husband and endure the violence. Or she could hide.

"How did you meet Larry?" she asked.

"My hat blew off in town, and Larry retrieved it for me. He wouldn't return it until I promised to take a drive with him," Anna sighed. "I thought his teasing was romantic. I didn't know it was laced with meanness. All I'd wanted was an honorable man to love, a small home to keep, and lots of laughter, That wasn't so much to ask, was it?" she asked, her eyes dark with pain.

"No," Claire assured her. "It's far less than I wanted." She smiled, hoping to lighten Anna's heart. "I wanted the full fairy tale. I wanted the prince, the castle, and everything that came with it."

"I wish you could have it all."

"You too, Anna."

"I don't even know what a good man is like," Anna said. "I honestly don't know anymore."

"I suppose integrity would be at the top of the list," Claire said.

"And honor."

"He should be kind and show tenderness."

"Definitely," Anna said. "And he should have a sense of humor."

"I'd stir in a good dose of intelligence."

"And add a big helping of romance."

Claire smiled. "It wouldn't hurt if he was handsome."

"And wealthy."

They both smiled for the first time all evening.

Anna pressed her hand to her chest. "And he absolutely must make you swoon in the bedroom."

Laughter slipped from Claire before she could cover her mouth. Anna's outspokenness shocked her, but it was honest and freeing. It was wonderful to have someone to talk with, who understood how a simple, unguarded conversation could unshackle a person.

Suddenly, Claire was glad that Anna was sitting in her kitchen. "You're welcome to stay, Anna. We can run my boardinghouse together. We'll close down the saloons, build up our business, and live like two old women who have earned the right to speak and live as they wish."

"What a lovely idea." Anna's smile brightened the room. "Imagine the outrageous things we could get away with."

"Life would be amusing, wouldn't it?"

The haunted look stole back into Anna's eyes. "I couldn't imagine a life like that. To feel safe again, to have a friend, and to speak without fear. It really would be a fairy tale."

"It shouldn't be."

"I know." Her eyes misted. "You have no idea how much your friendship means to me."

"Yes, I do," Claire said, for she'd been without a friend for years.

They spent Christmas Day working on a quilt Claire had just started. In the evening they made a small supper from the basket of food Boyd had brought Christmas Eve. Then they relaxed in the parlor, talking and dreaming about the life they would lead if they were wealthy men. They pounded their delicate fists on the coffee table and agreed that a woman was entitled to more say in her marriage and in controlling her own life.

"We have a right to vote," Claire said, her indignant voice ringing through the parlor.

"And a right to live without fear," Anna added. "We are human beings. We should not be considered our husbands' property."

They spouted their dissatisfactions all Christmas evening and picked up again Friday morning, only stopping their diatribe when two men came to Claire's door wanting to rent her best two rooms. They were young businessmen who would need the rooms until Tuesday.

Claire's spirits lifted knowing she would have some income for the week. She and Anna went to the temperance meeting then marched to the saloons. The sound of one hundred women singing hymns filled Claire with renewed purpose. But when she marched into Boyd's saloon, and was greeted by his burly, disgruntled bartender, his cold glare made Claire glad that they would be adjourning their marches until Tuesday. As soon as Mrs. Barker pleaded their case to the unresponsive wretch, they filed out.

All Claire wanted was to get home to her warm kitchen and drink a hot cup of tea, but Desmona caught her arm and stopped her in the street. "Do introduce us to this lovely lady," she said, nodding toward Anna.

Claire made brief introductions between Anna and Desmona's three daughters who were with her. "Where is Elizabeth?" she asked, to shift the attention away from Anna.

Desmona humped her shoulders against the cold wind. "She took to her bed last night saying every bone in her body ached."

Claire exchanged a look with Anna and knew they were both wondering if it was illness or a beating that had driven Elizabeth to bed.

Guilt smote Claire for not doing more to help Elizabeth. But other than taking Elizabeth into her home, which she simply couldn't afford to do, what help could she offer? Elizabeth would have to find the courage to ask her family for help.

—◦— ◦—

On Saturday morning Boyd arrived to fill Claire's wood bins. He came inside in a heavy barn jacket, a gray wool cap, and work boots. Claire thought he'd never looked more handsome.

"Please tell your mother how much we enjoyed the food," she said. "I'm returning her basket with some tea cakes I made last night. You're welcome to eat a few."

Boyd took the basket and peeked inside. "They smell great. I'll eat a couple for lunch."

"Didn't you pack a sandwich?"

He shook his head, his cheeks flushed with cold. "Never do. I'm usually too busy to eat. I'll wait until I get home."

"You need to eat, especially when it's so cold out. I'll fix a sandwich for you to take along."

"The tea cakes will be plenty."

She ignored him and began slicing bread. "I have some of your mother's turkey left."

He leaned his shoulder against the door. "You are stubborn, you know that?"

"'Determined' is the word I prefer. Will the turkey be all right?"

He gave her a warm smile and watched her make his sandwich. "I think you're beginning to care about me, Claire."

"I'm returning your mother's kindness is all. She fed me. I'm feeding you."

"Then you don't care about me?"

She closed his sandwich, wrapped it, and handed it to him. "Of course I care about you. You're the man who fills my wood bins. I'll feed you to make sure you keep your strength."

He laughed and tucked the sandwich in the basket. "I'm touched."

She smiled, and realized she was enjoying their exchange. "We'll be eating the last of your mother's leftovers tonight. You're welcome to come for supper if you like."

"Thank you, but I have another engagement this evening." His smile faded, and he glanced behind her. "Has Anna heard from her husband?"

"No," she said, oddly disappointed that Boyd had turned down her invitation. She hadn't meant to invite him to supper, but now that she had, and he'd declined, the evening stretched ahead of her with little appeal. "As far as we know, Larry is still in jail."

He nodded and opened the door. "I would suggest that Anna stay inside until Duke confirms that her husband is locked up."

"If the sheriff can find out, it would be a huge relief to both of us."

"I'll let you know as soon as he gets the telegram."

"Thank you," she said. "And thanks for filling my bins."

He lifted the basket and gave it a small shake. "I think I got the best bargain, but you're welcome. Let me know if you or Anna need anything."

She locked the door behind him then watched him cut through her snow-covered yard as he headed toward his family sawmill. She secretly hoped he'd stop back, but he didn't.

She prepared a hearty lunch for her male guests, but scowled when they gulped it down then crossed the street to Boyd's saloon. By Saturday evening she and Anna were feeling imprisoned in the house.

"We need to get out for a while, Anna."

"Where can we go?"

"How about the cantata at Union Hall?" There was so little left in Claire's money bag, it no longer mattered what she spent it on.

Anna's face lit up. "It would be a lovely diversion."

"Exactly. Let's get dressed so we can go early." She turned toward the stairs, but Anna caught her hand.

"I can't go." Her face flushed. "I don't have any money."

"I assumed that, Anna. I'll pay our admission."

"No."

"You can pay me back when your situation changes."

"It won't change."

"You can't know that." Claire hadn't believed her situation would change either, but it had. She was still poor and worried about money, but she had her freedom. "We need some recreation and pleasure, Anna. Come on." She hooked her arm around Anna's waist and drew the woman toward the stairs. "Let's pretend we're rich, independent women going out for an evening. We'll go to the cantata and forget about everything that makes us unhappy."

"That would be men." Anna smiled and started up the stairs. "I suppose we are entitled to one night of enjoyment, aren't we?"

"Absolutely. "

"All right then. We'll go, but I intend to return your kindness when I'm able to do so."

"You can do that right now." Claire stopped in the hallway. "Dress my hair for me and we'll be even. I loathe doing it."

"Really?"

"Really."

Anna followed Claire to her bedchamber dressing table.

Thirty minutes later Anna pressed her palms together, her face beaming with excitement as she eyed the waterfall of ringlets cascading down the back of Claire's head and shoulders. "I have just the thing to complement your hair."

She hurried out of the room then returned carrying a hair comb with a cluster of blue sapphires on it.

"My grandfather gave this to me, but the sapphires get lost against my brown hair. I told Larry I lost it so he wouldn't sell it, but I've kept it hidden in my reticule."

"I can't wear this, Anna."

"Sure you can."

"It's too expensive. I couldn't bear it if I lost it."

"You won't lose it."

"Your grandfather gave this to you."

"He won't be at the cantata."

Claire laughed. "That's not the point and you know it."

"Let me do this," Anna said, her voice earnest. "Please. It looks beautiful in your hair and it makes me feel good to share something so special with you."

This was all Anna could offer, the only gift she could freely give. Claire's eyes misted. "This is... thank you, Anna. I'm honored to wear it."

Anna stepped away from the dressing table and peeked in Claire's closet. "Wear this blue velvet gown. It'll look gorgeous with the sapphires."

"All right, but you must borrow a dress from me." Claire dug through the closet and retrieved an emerald poplin and silk gown that had belonged to her grandmother. Her grandmother had worn it once each year the day after Thanksgiving. She'd never told Claire why the gown was special, but she'd kept it cleaned and protected for over fifty years. When Claire had found it in the closet, she'd considered using the sicilienne material to make her own gown, but hadn't been able to ruin her grandmother's favorite dress.

"It's not the current fashion," she said, "but if we add a flounce crinoline petticoat it may suffice."

"It's lovely as it is." Anna caught the soft fabric between her fingers and slowly drew her hands down the length of the skirt. A wide band of black velvet adorned the hem, and inserts of black velvet graced each side of the skirt, ending in two points. "I've never owned something so beautiful."

"My grandmother called it her magic dress. I don't know why, but maybe it'll bring you some magic tonight."

Anna sighed. "I could certainly use it."

"It should fit you. My grandmother was tiny like you."

"It'll fit. I can tell just by looking." She clasped it to her bosom. "Are you sure you want me to wear it?"

"Positive." Claire sensed that her grandmother would approve of Anna wearing her special gown. Claire's own dress was more current, but not elaborate in style. The tunic was made of sapphire-blue velvet, with matching pomponnette velvet for the skirt.

Anna dressed her own hair then they helped each other into their gowns. When Anna pulled on the emerald-colored dress, Claire stared at her.

"I can see why my grandmother called that her magic dress. You're beautiful, Anna."

Anna's eyes misted and she smoothed her palms down the bodice. "I can almost feel pretty again."

The bruises on Anna's arms were covered by the long fitted sleeves, but a hint of yellow still rode her cheekbone where Claire suspected Larry had struck her. No woman with such bruises could feel beautiful; Claire knew that firsthand. To see Anna take such pleasure in wearing the gown filled Claire's heart with both joy and pain. Anna was beautiful. She shouldn't need a dress to make her feel that way.

"You are pretty, Anna. And you deserve to wear beautiful dresses and go out for an enjoyable evening'." Claire curtsied to her friend, hoping to lighten the evening. "Let's dance our way to the cantata."

A tender smile tipped Anna's lips.

"Come along." Claire fanned her skirt and twirled in a circle. Dipping and swaying, she swept into the hallway and descended the stairs.

Anna followed her into the foyer.

"We can dance down Main Street," Claire said, taking their coats from the closet.

Anna finally laughed.

Claire's heart lifted. As hard as her life with Jack had been, she had survived without too many scars. Anna's situation was far more painful because Larry was still alive.

Claire handed Anna's coat to her. "Let's pretend we are rich, independent women tonight. We can do or say anything we like."

"Let's do it." Anna buttoned her coat and waltzed onto the porch with forced gaiety.

They left the house and chatted all the way to Union Hall.

Claire paid their admission and reminded herself not to think about her last eight dollars. She could worry about her desperate circumstances tomorrow. Tonight she wanted to escape her past and her present, to exist in a place of safety and joy.

Chapter Fourteen

Claire and Anna hung their coats then headed into the main room of the hall. Floor-to-ceiling arched windows dressed with garnet-colored velvet draperies lined the north and south walls. A massive, gas lit chandelier hung from the ceiling, illuminating the room and casting a warm yellow glow on the crowd gathered below.

The excitement of the evening was palpable in the air, and Claire breathed it in. She was so thankful not to be spending another evening alone in her boardinghouse. The cavernous hall hummed with excited chatter and the rustling of evening gowns.

Anna tapped Claire's elbow. "Our neighbor has spotted you." She gestured to a small cluster of men and ladies standing less than ten feet away.

Claire looked straight into Boyd Grayson's seductive eyes. A hint of a smile lifted his lips, and he nodded his head.

She returned his silent greeting, but noticed a female hand tucked in the crook of his elbow.

Her gaze shifted up to a tantalizing bare shoulder and a delicate, exotic face. The woman's hair was piled high on her head in a mass of ebony curls that spilled down her neck to her shoulder blades. She smiled at one of the men beside her, and the sharp claw of jealousy clutched Claire's chest. The woman was beyond beautiful.

An odd sickness filled her stomach, and she dropped her gaze to her clasped hands. So what if Boyd was with a lady. Despite the woman's beauty, she was probably just one of many for him. Beautiful women flocked to men like Boyd. Like Jack. Claire had given up trying to compete with those ladies long ago.

She wouldn't deny that she was attracted to her handsome neighbor, but she was smart enough to ignore it.

Boyd lifted his hand and beckoned her and Anna to join him and his group of friends. Claire didn't want to meet the pretty lady on Boyd's arm, but she forced herself to move forward.

Boyd clasped Anna's hands. "You're breathtaking, Anna. Marry me," he joked.

She glanced at Claire. "This really is a magic dress."

Claire smiled, glad that Anna hadn't flinched away from Boyd's gentle teasing.

"How are you, Anna?" he asked, concern replacing his flirtatious smile.

"Fine," she said quietly. "Claire is good medicine for me."

"I'm sure." He reached out and caught Claire's hand. "I'm glad to see you out this evening."

The woman he was standing with turned and eyed Claire with open curiosity.

"This is Anna Levens and my neighbor Claire Ashier. Ladies, this is Martha Newmaine from Buffalo."

Martha shot a sidelong glance at Boyd then greeted Anna, but her gaze lingered on Claire. "Are you the lady who started the movement to close the saloons?"

"Dr. Lewis did that, but I'm doing my best to help him succeed."

To her surprise, Miss Newmaine smiled. "I've heard that your... efforts are upsetting the saloon owners." She turned her beautiful brown eyes toward Boyd, a teasing smile on her face. "Are you going to close your saloon for her?"

A lazy grin touched his lips. "I'm afraid not. I wouldn't even do it for you, darling."

Her smile widened and she rubbed the sleeve of his suit coat. "What if I threaten to spill our secret?"

"Then I'll return you to Buffalo."

She laughed and turned back to Claire. "I'm not ready to take a train home just yet, so I'm afraid you'll have to fight this battle on your own."

"On the contrary, Miss Newmaine. There are over three hundred of us working for temperance in our community. We'll succeed."

Martha flashed a stunning smile at Boyd. "If that's the case, you'll have to come to Buffalo to open a saloon."

Unwilling to witness their flirtation, Claire nodded to Martha and Boyd. "If you'll excuse us, the cantata is about to begin," she said.

"I'll escort you ladies to your seats," Boyd suggested, capturing Claire's hand. He tucked it into the crook of his elbow then glanced at Martha. "I'll be right back for you." She nodded, and he gave his other elbow to Anna, who took it willingly.

Claire tried to pull away, but he drew his elbow against his side, trapping her fingers against his ribs. He tipped his head and put his mouth near her ear. "You're stunning tonight."

"So is your companion, Mr. Grayson."

"She is magnificent, isn't she?"

She was, but Claire was too shocked by his blatant admission, and her own hurt reaction, to answer.

"I'm surprised to see you and Anna here," he went on.

She found it more surprising to see him here, and with that gorgeous female hanging on his arm, but she said nothing. She didn't want to talk to him. She didn't want another word with the charming, self-satisfied flirt. Because every word hurt.

He stopped and guided her into the row where Anna had quickly seated herself. Claire sat in the end seat beside her. She breathed a sigh of relief when Boyd left, but to her irritation, he guided Martha into the seats directly across the row. He sat in the end chair and nodded to Claire who was sitting a mere three feet away from him.

To avoid looking at him, she turned and engaged Anna in conversation, hoping their chatting would calm both of them.

Suddenly, forty people gathered at the front of the hall. Their joyful singing filled the room and flowed through Claire. She closed her eyes and listened with her whole being, letting the song lift her. This was worth her precious money.

The solo singer Estella came on stage, singing with such power and beauty, Claire was mesmerized by the performance. Estella hosted a make-believe party, and invited the male singers. To entertain the ladies, the men battled with pretend snowballs, which made Claire think of her childhood and of the unfettered joy she had once felt romping in the snow with her sister and friends.

The talented group of singers and their performance captivated her.

Estella's true love William, defeated Jenkins, the man who was planning to propose to Estella. Watching Jenkins try to win Estella's affection made Claire and the audience laugh.

Later, when Estella and William slipped away to express their love for one another, Claire's heart felt achingly empty. Despite her hoydenish ways as a young girl, she'd dreamed of a dashing prince who would fall in love with her. She imagined him to be tall with dark hair and sparkling eyes that promised passion. He would be her strength and her weakness, her lover and her friend, her slayer of dragons. He would enjoy her too-forward manner, and laugh at her dry sense of humor. Their days would be filled with sunshine and laughter, their nights with whispers and passion.

The young girl in her still believed that man existed, still hoped that he could rescue her from living a scared, dull life.

But the woman in her knew it was a fairy tale, a dream, and that any joy in her life would be of her own making.

As the cantata was ending, William and Estella came upon Jenkins, who, not succeeding in gaining Estella's heart, concluded to marry Araminta, one of the singers. The audience smiled and sighed with satisfaction as forty voices rose in a good night chorus to finish the performance.

Claire slipped her hand into her pocket and squeezed the little carving in her palm. She listened to the singers' beautiful voices while she dreamed of love, of a more youthful and hopeful time of her life. What if Jack had been kind, if he'd really loved her? Would she, like her grandmother and Estella, still feel drawn to another man? Would she still feel drawn to Boyd Grayson, or would she be content as Jack's wife?

The gas stage-lighting cast a glow across the audience's upturned faces. Claire glanced at Boyd, but he wasn't watching the performance. He was looking at her.

Warmth surged through her chest, and she clenched her hand around the carving. Why was he looking at her when Martha was sitting beside him?

His face was half in shadow, and his eyes were dark, but she saw his lips lift in a smile—for her. There was no one else in the shadowed room he could be smiling at.

With his dark coloring and handsome face, Boyd could be the prince she'd once imagined. But the prince she imagined would never have taken her to a cemetery on Christmas Eve. Of all the unromantic things in the world to do, Boyd had chosen the one thing that had touched her the deepest. Somehow he was finding every way possible to wrench open her heart. He was giving her gifts she couldn't refuse, making her laugh when she wanted to cry, filling her lonely house with his and Sailor's silly antics.

What she had once felt for Jack in the earliest days couldn't come close to all the ways Boyd had already touched her heart with his smile, his charm, his silly dog, and his art.

She was older and wiser now. She understood the difference between real life and make-believe. But she wondered what her life would have been like if she'd met Boyd instead of Jack.

"Beautiful," Anna said with a sigh, rising to her feet with the rest of the audience and clapping vigorously.

Claire shook her head and got to her feet. She was still an idle dreamer. Boyd was with Martha. When Martha returned to Buffalo, Boyd would find another beautiful lady to cling to his arm.

Desmona Edwards was looking straight at Anna. Claire moved forward to shield her friend from the gossip. Desmona was too nosy. She would ask too many questions. Anna needed peace and privacy, not an interrogation from the prying old crone.

They moved into the congested aisle ahead of Boyd and Martha. They couldn't hurry because of the crowd filling the hall, but Claire felt Boyd's tall body shifting behind hers. She imagined him looking at her while he held Martha's hand in the crook of his elbow.

Some men did that. Jack had. Those men held one woman on their arm and ogled others.

Jack's arm had been reserved for her, but every woman in the crowd had been his. He'd admired them, winked at them, cast lascivious gazes that made them giggle. He was tall and golden and gorgeous.

Claire had believed she would feel proud on his arm. She'd felt like a ball and chain.

Boyd touched her arm and stopped her. "Beebe's Saloon was loud earlier, so pay attention on your way home."

Claire thrilled to his unexpected touch, and immediately called herself a fool. He only wanted to caution her to be careful. He wasn't flirting with her. He was simply being considerate.

She nodded to Martha. "Good-bye, Miss Newmaine. Perhaps we'll meet again."

"I'm sure we'll see each other soon, Mrs. Ashier." The woman turned to Anna. "That dress is lovely on you."

"It's a magic dress," Anna said again, with wistful smile that made Claire's heart ache.

They chatted and shivered all the way home. Inside, they took off their coats, made tea, and carried their cups to the parlor.

"What was your favorite part?" Anna asked, as Claire knelt to stoke the fire.

"When William confessed his love for Estella," she said. "What was your favorite part?"

"I couldn't possibly choose." Anna released a dreamy sigh. "I loved every minute. It was wonderful to escape life for a while. Thank you for taking me. And thank you for letting me wear this dress."

"I'm glad you enjoyed yourself."

"I did," Anna said. "Did you?"

"Of course."

"I thought you might have been uncomfortable with Boyd watching you all evening."

Claire brushed her hands across her skirt. "He wasn't watching me."

"He most certainly was! His eyes barely left your face during the whole performance."

"Nonsense. Martha had his full attention."

"No, Claire. You did." Anna sighed. "That man is definitely attracted to you."

"Twaddle." She flapped her hand and sat in the rocker. "Boyd Grayson is attracted to every woman."

"That's not true. All women are attracted to him, but few of them can get his attention. Believe me, you've got his full attention."

"Only because he's playing games with me, hoping I'll stop marching and badgering him to close his saloon. This is sport for him, Anna."

Anna sipped her tea in silence, but her downcast eyes reflected her disagreement.

"Why would Boyd bother with me when he has women like Martha swooning at his feet?" Claire asked

"Because you're beautiful, and because you aren't swooning at his feet."

"Then he's pestering me because he sees me as a challenge?"

"Possibly." Anna lowered her cup. "Although I think he's genuinely attracted to you. He can't keep his eyes off you."

"That's because he's a rake."

Anna leaned back on the sofa. "Rake or not, that man is smitten."

Bosh. Ridiculous. Utter nonsense. Boyd Grayson was smitten with Martha. Even now he was probably seducing the lovely woman

The thought pierced Claire's heart with such pain, she shoved the image from her mind and took a large gulp of tea. The hot liquid scorched her throat and made her eyes water. Served her right for being such a ninny.

How on earth had she let that reprobate sneak beneath her guard?

It was that carving. That little gift from him had been the beginning of her downfall. The exquisite piece of art had elicited her curiosity about the man. From the first, she'd been awed by his talent and attracted to his good looks. But it was the way he tended her injured foot, the way he loved his dog, the way he built that astonishing snow castle just for her, that had touched her heart.

And now he was probably making love to Martha.

Had he given Martha one of his carvings?

Were they laughing and flirting with each other? Or were they whispering and touching and... doing all the things that lovers did when they were alone in their bedchamber? The thought of him loving Martha carved a chunk out of Claire's heart.

How had she allowed herself to have feelings for Boyd?

How could she be so utterly pathetic?

Anna yawned and stretched like a cat. "I'm exhausted and relaxed and truly happy for the first time in ages. If you don't mind, I'm going to go to bed before I start dwelling on my life again."

"Good idea." Claire placed her teacup on the stand beside her then followed Anna from the room.

Her gentleman boarders opened the front door and entered the foyer holding large goblets of whiskey-colored liquid and laughing uproariously.

"Ah, our lovely hostess," said the taller of the two men.

"Good evening, Mr. Carver. Mr. Hosington," Claire said, exchanging a wary glance with Anna.

"George and I were hoping to see you ladies this evening," Mr. Carver said in a too friendly manner.

"Why?" Claire asked then cursed herself for allowing her suspicion be so obvious. "Was there something you gentleman needed?"

"Just your company. Join us," he said, gesturing toward the parlor with his glass.

Anna backed toward the stairs, and Claire gave her a discrete nod. "It's been a long day for the both of us," Claire said. "We'll bid you gentleman a good night."

"Don't spoil the evening, ladies." Mr. Carver stepped forward and captured Claire's hand. "Stay," he said earnestly, the whiskey on his breath assaulting her nose. "Let us enjoy your company for a while."

Claire retracted her hand. "I provide a room and meals, Mr. Carver. Not companionship. Goodnight, gentlemen!" She turned to head upstairs, but Mr. Carver caught her shoulder and forced her back toward him.

"How much?"

She frowned. "How much for what?"

"Your companionship."

The insult burned through Claire and ignited her fury, but she remained outwardly calm.

"Don't play coy, Mrs. Ashier. The bartender next door told us about your extra amenities. We're willing to pay you ladies," he said.

Anna gasped, but Claire forced herself not to slap the man's face. Without uttering a word, she walked to the closet, opened the door, and pulled out her revolver. She turned and pointed it at Mr. Carver.

"Get your bags and get out."

Mr. Carver scowled. "How dare you point a gun at me."

Claire shifted the nose of the barrel toward his chest. "Anna, go upstairs and gather their bags for them." Anna hurried upstairs.

"This is ridiculous," Mr. Carver said, exchanging a glance with Mr. Hosington, who seemed as upset and uncomfortable with the situation as Claire was. "You can't toss us out at this time of the evening."

"The Taylor House is just down the street by the Common. I'm sure they can put you up for the duration of your stay."

Anna hurried down the stairs clutching two large valises. Clothing spilled from the bags and fell onto the floor as she plunked the bags at Mr. Carver's feet.

"Take your bags and leave," Claire said, keeping the revolver pointed at the man.

"Fine." Mr. Carver reached down, stuffed his clothing into the bag, and picked up the valise. "You probably wouldn't have been worth my money anyhow." He stormed out the door, leaving Mr. Hosington to gather up his bag and mumble a brief apology before he followed his nasty friend outside.

Anna locked the door, and Claire put the gun back on the shelf in the closet. "Remind me not to rent to men who drink liquor," she said.

"You shouldn't rent to any men," Anna said, her quavering voice revealing her upset.

"I'd rather not, but I have to." Claire sighed and hooked her arm around Anna's waist, turning her toward the stairs.

"Let's try to forget this insult and remember how much we enjoyed the cantata this evening."

Lord, her life was becoming a mess. She had men propositioning her like a common harlot. She was attracted to an unsuitable man who served liquor to men like Mr. Carver, and she had taken Anna and her dangerous situation into her home. Claire had lost her common sense for certain. She had only just freed herself from a tyrant. She didn't have the strength or the will to face men like Mr. Carver or a devil like Anna's husband.

But she couldn't stop taking in boarders any more than she could send Anna away, not when she needed the money and Anna so desperately needed an ally. Besides, she genuinely liked the woman. Their relationship was the closest Claire had come to having a friend in years.

Whatever the cost, Claire had to find the courage to open her door to strangers and to help Anna.

"Maybe I'll dream about the cantata tonight," Anna said, heading upstairs.

"That's a grand idea." Claire followed Anna, hoping she could think about the cantata too. Or lose herself in her grandmother's journal. Anything that would turn her mind from thinking about those wretched intoxicated men or about Boyd spending the night with the beautiful and exotic Martha.

She and Anna helped each other out of their dresses and bade each other goodnight. Claire slipped into her nightrail and a heavy velvet housedress then took her grandmother's journal and crept back downstairs to the parlor.

Claire was glad Anna had enjoyed herself at the cantata; she was entitled to a bit of enjoyment, and it pleased Claire to have had a share in giving her some pleasure. She hoped Larry would spend the rest of his wretched life in jail, because Anna wouldn't find happiness otherwise. A man like Larry would not let his wife go. Anna was his possession, and the only thing keeping Anna safe were the locked bars of a jail cell.

Weary, Claire settled into the rocking chair, feeling she was engaged in an unending battle. First it was her own battle with Jack. Now it was Anna's battle with Larry, and her own battle to keep the boardinghouse open.

Her father had called her rash and reckless from the time she'd begun to walk. She had stumbled into life with wide-eyed wonder, grabbing and grasping at anything that promised excitement. She'd taken dozens of foolish risks in her life: climbing the highest trees, slipping into the elephants' tent at the circus, running off with the first dashing rakehell to cross her path. How foolish she'd been. How incredibly poor her judgment.

With her history, was it any wonder she was putting her own safety on the line for Anna? Was it any wonder she was attracted to Boyd Grayson?

She sighed and opened the journal. She didn't want to think about her faults, or about what Boyd and Miss Newmaine were likely doing at that very minute.

But in the glow of her parlor fireplace, Claire imagined his naked shoulders flexing in the shadows, his dark head dipping to kiss Martha's lush mouth, her slender neck, her full breasts...

He would be a good lover. Instinct told her that. He would be slow and purposeful, as exacting in his lovemaking as he was in his carving. His eyes would sparkle, and he would kiss and tease and make Martha feel like the most special woman in the world.

But tomorrow he would flirt with the first woman to cross his path.

Jack had.

He introduced Claire to the intimacy shared between a man and woman. He gave her pleasure but reveled in the power of controlling her response. She shared her heart and her body with Jack, had forgiven him so many offenses during their lovemaking, but it hadn't been enough for him.

For Jack, the novelty had worn off in months. He moved on to new women and more exciting challenges.

He never understood how deeply it hurt her knowing he was warming other women's beds, that he desired them while still making love to her. He said a wife didn't question her husband, and as his drinking grew worse, she learned not to question.

But memories carved a ravine through her heart as she sat alone in her parlor. She didn't want to think about Jack or lovemaking or the feeling of helplessness that washed over her each time her mind slipped into the past. The pain of his betrayal had scarred her. His unstable personality had left her wary and afraid.

Here in the safety and solitude of her home, she could finally face the truth. Jack had shattered her dreams along with her heart. His violent temper and cruel comments had wounded her, but his tearful apologies and solemn promises hurt her the most. He had given her hope where there was none. He made her believe he could become the man she needed him to be.

After beating her, he would storm out of the house. Within an hour he would be back, repentant and begging her forgiveness. It sickened him to lose control of his temper. The decent and sincere side of Jack's nature struggled to assert itself against the cruel drunkard who was ruling him. But his need for alcohol was too strong, his will too weak, and it destroyed both of them.

Jack hadn't just left her scared. He left her empty and aching, unable to trust or believe in love. He silenced that youthful, hopeful part of her, and that was the worst sin of all.

Claire's chest tightened, but she refused to weep any more tears for Jack or herself. She'd cried a river of them during her marriage. It was time to move beyond her loss and sorrow.

But she hurt too much tonight, felt too lonely to see any joy in her future. Watching Boyd and Martha together had been painful. She wanted love and passion in her life. But she needed safety.

She opened the journal, wanting to understand her grandmother's affair and why two seemingly honorable people had lost their way. Maybe her grandmother's story would help her understand her own confusing feelings about life and love.

I begged Abe not to leave me. I was beyond pride. I was desperate. I couldn't lose him. I couldn't face each day without his smile, without the stolen moments that kept us alive. I needed Abe and I begged him not to end our affair. He asked me to meet him the next day in our special place.

I left early in the morning after Joseph had gone to work. I walked down Barry Road then ducked into a stand of trees. From there I picked my way to the far edges of the fields, praying nobody would see me. I climbed down a creek bank where I was hidden from view. Then I followed the creek until I saw Abe sitting beneath a stand of leafy maple trees.

We were hidden there, far away from prying eyes. I longed to run to him, to rush into his arms and never let him go. But it was August, and I was flushed with heat. I stopped on the opposite side of the creek and dipped my hands into the cool water. Abe watched me wash my warm cheeks and cool my heated neck. I unbuttoned my bodice and trickled water between my breasts.

He stepped into the water and walked toward me, his eyes dark and intense. I knew we would cross that last threshold today, but I couldn't turn away, couldn't deny either of us our one moment in time.

He stopped before me, but didn't speak. He didn't need to. I could read the love and desire in his eyes.

I released another button.

Abe took off his wet boots.

I opened my gown, and he slid it off my shoulders.

We made love beneath the maples in a bed of fragrant summer grass and clover. Our emotions overflowed and we wept because there was too much to express. We loved deeply and desperately, believing our first time would be our last time.

Abe held me against him and told me he'd fallen in love with me the first time he'd seen me in my kitchen.

It was the day after Thanksgiving and I was wearing my new green dress when I offered him a sandwich for lunch.

He wasn't hungry, but he'd said yes because he couldn't bear for me to leave the room.

Despite its heavy fabric, I wore the same dress the next time I met Abe in the meadow. Skin to skin, we savored each other, capturing tiny details with each second that slipped by.

I can still picture Abe's eyes that afternoon, as blue as the sky above us. His shirt was a worn and faded green like the grass we were lying on. His cheeks were sunburned and he needed to shave. The skin on his shoulders felt smooth beneath my palms, his hip muscles flexing beneath my hands as he loved me. Oh, how he loved me, this man of my heart.

Claire closed the book with a snap. Her stomach felt tight, and an ache throbbed deep in her heart. She wanted love and passion... a man who would love and cherish her as much as Abe had loved her grandmother. The journal was proof that love existed.

But that depth of love required immense trust—something she was no longer capable of.

She was alone in her boardinghouse with a woman who reminded her that it was safer to live a lonely life. There were too many men like Jack and Larry in the world. With her poor judgment, she would be more likely to find another Jack rather than an Abe.

Sighing, Claire took the journal upstairs and shoved it beneath her mattress. Delving into her grandmother's feelings for the man she loved was making Claire long for more fulfillment in her own life.

A woman was entitled to miss her marriage bed. But it was inconvenient and scary business she did not need to get involved with. She needed to forget about her grandmother's affair, and to control her own pathetic yearnings.

But when she slipped beneath her heavy comforter, the ache of loneliness slipped in with her. It wasn't Jack she was longing for, though, or the prince of her girlhood dreams. It was that man in the shadow of Boyd Grayson's reckless smile that made her yearn to be touched and kissed and loved.

Chapter Fifteen

Anna attended the temperance meetings and marches with Claire, but they shied away from Desmona Edwards, who was relentless in her questions about Anna. She even called on them at home under the guise of discussing temperance business. But Claire suspected the woman was digging for something.

Claire raised a debate about state licensing for liquor sales, and suggested pleading their case with the government agency who issued the liquor licenses. Her idea was roundly applauded, as were her convictions that a woman should have a rightful say in her life and the management of her home. Temperance was only the beginning of her fight for liberation.

Claire and Anna worked the ladies into such a frenzy, their singing shook the rafters on Tuesday morning as they marched into Don Beebe's Saloon. He refused to close his tavern for New Year's Eve, or sign their pledge, but the women moved on with a sense of purpose.

The proprietor of Taylor House locked them out.

Mr. Smeizer barred the doors to his saloon too.

They entered Boyd's saloon without a problem, but his short, rude bartender was the only person in the bar. He was chucking wood into the stove, and when he turned to look at them, Claire gasped.

His eye was grotesquely swollen and bruised, and his lip was puffed out like he had a fat plug of tobacco stuffed between his lower teeth and lip.

"There's no one here to pester, ladies, so go on home," he said, banging the stove door closed.

"We'd like to talk with Mr. Grayson, please," Mrs. Barker said courteously in the face of his rude greeting.

"He's busy. Now, go on. You women have no right to come in here and put your nose in our business." He clasped Mrs. Barker's elbow and nudged her toward the door. "Get back to your kitchens and children." He nudged Mrs. Cushing along behind Mrs. Barker.

But when he reached for Claire, she slapped his hands away. She suspected he was the cur who had told Mr. Carver that she offered private amenities for a fee, but she couldn't confront the wretched man without embarrassing herself and starting gossip that could hurt her business.

"We have a right to protest the sale of liquor and to protect our homes," she said.

"Well, you don't have a right to swarm in here and interrupt me every day." Karlton grabbed her by the shoulders and forced her toward the door. "Get out."

"Karlton!" Boyd's reprimanding voice cracked through the room as he stepped from a small room near the back of the bar. "That's enough. These women have every right to come here and speak their minds."

"I have a right to speak my mind, too," Karlton said, releasing Claire with a small shove, "Especially when they're sticking their noses in my business,"

"You don't have a right to manhandle them."

"They're just trying to find a way to control their husbands and get their hands into his money pouch."

Several women gasped at the insult.

"Excuse us a moment, ladies." Boyd pulled Karlton aside, wondering what had riled a man who was usually in control of himself. "What is wrong with you?"

"I can't lose any more money because of these harpies," he said. "I've got debts to pay."

"Is that what your bruised eye is all about?" Boyd asked.

Karlton didn't answer.

"Your debt isn't their concern."

"My mother is going to lose her house if my liquor sales drop any lower. I've already had some trouble making payments."

"Then why have you been gambling?" Boyd shook his head and lowered his voice. "No wonder you're in trouble, Karlton. You've been making wagers every night."

"I'm trying to get caught up."

"You aren't going to do it by gambling." Boyd glanced at Claire and the group of women who were growing restless waiting for him. "I'll give you an extra night of tending bar, but quit gambling, and lay off these women. They can come here as often as they like. You got that?"

Anger flared in Karlton's eyes, but he nodded.

Boyd turned back to the ladies, expecting a scowl from Claire, but her eyes registered concern.

When Mrs. Barker asked him to close his saloon tomorrow for New Year's Eve, he apologized and said he couldn't close on his busiest night of the year.

Claire scowled.

Not one of the rum holes would close for the holiday.

Undaunted, the women resumed marching. Claire and Anna returned home after one long, cold jaunt, but when they entered the foyer, they stopped in stunned disbelief.

"Oh, Lord," Anna whispered, her gaze taking in the open desk drawers that had obviously been ransacked.

Claire couldn't utter a word as she hurried to her bedchamber. Her chifforobe had been gone through as well, but her precious eight dollars were still there.

"What could they have been looking for?" Anna asked, shaking her head at the obvious trespassing someone had done.

Claire didn't know, but it terrified her to know someone had been in her house, had gone through her few personal possessions.

"Do you have any valuables?" Anna asked.

"I have one necklace that I'm wearing, and exactly eight dollars to my name," she said, her voice trembling with fear and anger. "Whoever went through the house must have been gravely disappointed."

"Who could have done such a thing?" Anna asked, her voice filled with sympathy.

A thunderous pounding on the front door jolted them.

"Open the door, Anna!"

Anna gasped and pressed a hand to her stomach. "Oh, my..."

Claire's blood turned ice cold. It was Larry.

"I know you're in there, Anna. Now open this door."

"He'll pound it down," Anna said, her voice quaking.

"Let's slip out the back and go for the sheriff."

Anna's gaze darted through the bedroom as if seeking a hiding place, "He didn't know about you. How could he have found me?"

"Let's hurry out the back."

She shook her head. "He knows that trick. We won't get by him."

"I have a gun. Maybe we can scare him away."

"You'll have to pull the trigger or he'll kill both of us."

Could she shoot Larry? She froze in indecision. Maybe. No. No, she couldn't. But how would she get rid of him? She couldn't endure another violent man like Jack, like the man outside shouting obscenities. Her only protection was her gun. But she couldn't bring herself to shoot any living thing, no matter how dangerous.

Her mind whirled as she and Anna hurried downstairs to the foyer. She would get the gun and make a run for Boyd's saloon. He'd know what to do, how to handle Larry.

The door burst open with a splintering crash. Larry appeared.
Anna screamed.

Claire's knees turned to water.

Larry backhanded Anna across the face so hard it drove her head into the wall panels. "Stupid woman! Do you think I'd sit in a stinking cell and not have someone keep an eye on you?" He jerked Anna onto the porch. "Gary followed you right to the door of your little hideout."

Tears leaked from Anna's eyes, but she didn't utter a sound as he dragged her out and across the porch.

Claire followed them outside, her entire body shaking with fear. And fury. "Mr. Levens! Please don't do this."

He stuck his finger in Claire's face. "You mind your business, lady, or you'll find out what sort of man you're dealing with,"

She knew what sort of man she was dealing with, and it terrified her. She shrank from him, worried about her own safety, but terrified for Anna. "You're hurting my friend."

He caught Anna's chin and jerked her face up. "You have a friend, Anna? How charming."

"Mr. Levens, please—"

He glared at Claire. "If you stick your nose in my business again, I'll break it." He turned to leave, jerking Anna's arm so hard she fell to her knees.

Claire reached out to help her stand. Larry slammed his palms into Claire's chest so hard it shoved her against the wall of the house. The impact knocked the breath out of her.

Black dots danced through her vision, and pain radiated outward from her spine. She heard a shout from across the street then the sound of feet thumping across the snow-covered road.

A second later, Boyd Grayson vaulted her porch steps with a murderous rage blazing in his eyes. He grabbed two fistfuls of Larry's coat and drove him into the wall beside her. The house shuddered, and Claire sagged away from the men. "If you've hurt either of these women, I'm going to break your arms, mister."

Larry swung his fist into Boyd's side just as Sheriff Grayson mounted the steps. Several patrons from Boyd's bar stood in the street watching.

"What's the problem here?" the sheriff asked, helping Anna to her feet. He was tall like Boyd, but broader and thicker-limbed, a virtual bull of a man. Larry stood a good three inches shorter than Boyd and the sheriff, but he looked like a wild dog with his fur up and his teeth bared.

"I came to get my wife," he said, shoving Boyd away from him.

"You ladies go inside," the sheriff said, but Claire and Anna were rooted by fear.

Boyd stood firm and unyielding, like the sturdy wood columns on her porch. Power emanated from his tall, solid body as he glared at Larry. "Anna doesn't want to go with you."

"She'll go if I tell her to."

Boyd's patrons crowded around the porch.

"This isn't your business, Sheriff. It's between me and my wife."

"You're trespassing on Mrs. Ashier's property," the sheriff said. "That makes it my business." He slapped a handcuff around Larry's wrist.

"What are you doing?" Larry demanded.

"I have a warrant on my desk requesting your return to Pittsburgh. "

Larry wrenched his arm away and swung his cuffed wrist at the sheriff. The sheriff sidestepped the flailing metal and shot his fist up under Larry's guard. The blow snapped Larry's head back, but instead of buckling his knees, it enraged the man. He fought like he was fighting for his life, but Boyd and the sheriff out-muscled him. With an enraged growl, he lunged for Anna.

The sheriff grabbed Larry's wrists and dragged his arms behind his back. Boyd helped his brother take Larry to the floor. The sheriff pinned him with a knee in his back and finished snapping the cuffs on him.

All three men were covered in snow when the sheriff hauled Larry to his feet.

Steam left his nose in angry bursts as he glared at Anna. "I'll be back." He gritted his teeth as the sheriff and Boyd nudged him down the steps and marched him toward town.

When they returned thirty minutes later, Claire and Anna were huddled near the kitchen stove, trying to shed the chill and fear that had left them both shaking. Anna was holding a snow pack to her cheek.

"Are you ladies all right?" the sheriff asked.

Claire nodded, but she knew Boyd could see through her bravado.

The sheriff's keen eyes studied Anna, as if checking for injuries. "Larry won't be bothering you again," he said. "I'm taking him back to Pittsburgh tomorrow where he'll be tried for the murder of two men."

"Two?" Claire cut her eyes to Anna.

Anna lowered her lashes. "Larry shot the deputy sheriff when the man tried to take him to jail," she said, her voice quavering.

Claire sighed, wondering how much worse the situation could get. "I'm afraid I have another problem, Sheriff. Someone ransacked my house this afternoon while Anna and I were marching."

"Why didn't you come get me?" Boyd asked, his scowl full of concern.

The sheriff frowned and followed her into the foyer. "Was anything stolen?"

"Not that I can tell, but as you see," she said, gesturing to the papers spilling from the open desk drawers, "I haven't put things in order yet."

She took Boyd and the sheriff through the house to show them the extent of the intrusion then returned to the foyer.

"What were they looking for?" the sheriff asked.

"I have no idea," she said, feeling exhausted. "I have no valuables, and they didn't take my money."

The sheriff scanned her desk with a distant look on his face that suggested he was taking in the whole of her house, thinking, mulling over the possibilities of who had done it and why.

Boyd eyed the door and splintered frame. "I'll get some wood and tools to fix this," he said, wrenching open the door before bolting into the cold.

"What's the trouble between you and Larry?" the sheriff asked Anna.

She lowered her hand and sighed. "I didn't want to stay in our apartment alone while he was in jail."

Claire bit her tongue. She understood Anna's hesitation to pour out her troubles to the sheriff, but who else was going to help her? Larry had made it painfully clear that Claire would pay a high price if she continued to shelter Anna. They had no choice but to ask the sheriff for help.

Anna may be too frightened to reveal the ugly truth about her brute of a husband, but Claire wasn't. "Larry is a violent man," Claire said. "He has hurt Anna, and could easily kill her the next time he beats her. Believe me, there's always a next time, Sheriff."

Sympathy filled his eyes. "I don't condone Larry's treatment of you, Anna, but by law, a husband has the right to bring his wife home if he chooses."

Claire slapped her palm on the desktop with a loud crack. "*No law should force a woman to stay with a man who beats her.*" She clenched her fists, suddenly furious enough to march to the jail and hit Larry over the head with a liquor bottle. "Anna cannot go back to that bully. If he dares darken my door again, I'll... I'll shoot him." Speaking the words felt wonderfully freeing, but inside, Claire trembled with doubt. She could never defend herself against a violent man like Larry.

She'd been defenseless in the face of Jack's rage. Larry terrified her. Boyd's anger had frightened her too. If he ever turned that rage on a woman, the damage would be worlds worse than Jack had ever inflicted. Yet, Boyd's strength had saved her and Anna this evening. He'd protected her.

"You ladies stay inside tonight. Your marches have upset a lot of men, especially this week with your push to get their licenses revoked. Someone has broken into your home, and it may not have been Larry. I'm going to rent a room from you tonight so I can keep an eye on things."

She exchanged a glance with Anna, who looked relieved. Having the sheriff under her roof would allow Claire to sleep better too. "That would be generous of you, Sheriff. I'll make up the blue room for you, but you certainly won't be paying for it."

"Generous of you, too, Mrs. Ashier. I'll have my deputy keep an eye on Larry tonight. I'll be back later this evening."

The instant he stepped outside, Anna burst into tears, "Larry will find a way to come back here. He will. And he'll kill me next time."

⊶⊷

After Boyd finished repairing Claire's door, he went to the kitchen, needing to be certain the women were both unharmed. "Where's Anna?"

"In bed with a snow pack on her shoulder." Claire crossed to the stove.

Boyd could see that her gait was stiff and she favored her left side. Anger surged through him and he ached to avenge the insults Larry had inflicted on the women. "Why did you put yourself in the middle of this mess with Anna?"

She stared at him as if he'd gone daft. "How could I not? I couldn't turn her away any more than you could stop from interceding when Larry was dragging her off the porch."

"It's different for a man to step into a dangerous situation like that. It's foolish for you to put yourself in jeopardy."

"Foolish?" She planted her hands on her hips and winced as if it pained her. "What is foolish about giving a beaten woman a safe place to stay? What is foolish about trying to help a friend?"

"Claire," he said, trying to reason with her, "you can't save Anna. She must have family who can help her."

"She's ashamed to tell her family about Larry."

"What's to be ashamed of? Larry is the one with the shameful behavior."

"No woman wants to admit that her husband beats her, and that she made a dreadful mistake marrying him."

"Anna's life is more important than her pride."

"Of course it is, but if Anna goes to her family for help, they'll have to defend her. She's afraid that Larry will hurt them."

"What about your safety? Why didn't she consider that when she led Larry to your door?"

"She had no idea that Larry would have her followed. He didn't know me. Anna thought we'd both be safe here."

"Well, you're not."

"I know."

"You need to send her to her family, Claire."

"I can't."

He clenched his teeth to bite off his curse. "You're getting involved in a situation that is going to get you hurt. Or worse. Dead."

"I know exactly what the danger is. That's why I'm giving Anna a place to stay. If I don't, it's quite possible she'll end up dead."

Boyd froze. How could she know the danger unless... He pinched the bridge of his nose, sickened by the thought, furious with the situation and Claire's stubbornness. "I'd like to talk with Anna tomorrow."

"I won't change my mind about letting her stay here."

"Well, I'm afraid Larry, or one of those men you're irritating with your temperance nonsense, will try to change it for you."

He stepped outside and slammed the door, his body shaking with fury. The woman was just begging for trouble. She had just tangled with a murderer. She could have been killed!

Worry tightened Boyd's chest, and he knew he was in trouble. He cared too much for Claire, had gotten in too deep to walk away from her and her crazy life.

Chapter Sixteen

At five o'clock Tuesday morning, Claire wrapped her heavy velvet robe around herself and crept down to the kitchen. Shivering, she opened the thick iron door of the stove and quietly built up the fire, wanting to have the kitchen heated and coffee on before the sheriff or Anna got up.

It was the least she could do in return for the sheriff's kindness. He came in late last evening while she and Anna were getting ready for bed. He apologized for keeping her waiting then checked the doors and went to bed.

The aroma of fresh coffee wafted from the percolating pot, and she huddled close to the stove, loving the quiet morning and the homey feel of her grandmother's kitchen.

But she no longer felt safe here.

How long would Larry stay in jail this time? Knowing he could beat on her door at any moment terrified her. Boyd was right. Even if Duke planned to transport him to Pittsburgh for trial and incarceration, Larry wasn't going to give up and go away. She'd lain awake most of the night imagining every horrible possibility. What if he broke out of jail again and came back when the sheriff and Boyd weren't here?

She moved closer to the stove, regretting the dreadful mess she'd gotten into. How she longed to return to the safe, solitary life she'd begun building before Anna came seeking sanctuary. But that life hadn't included her new friendship with Anna, and Anna's desperate need.

She couldn't ask Anna to leave.

If her financial situation didn't improve, though, she and Anna might find themselves on the street. Without a paying boarder soon, she wouldn't be able to afford wood for her stove, or coffee for her breakfast.

The crackling fire and the percolating coffee soothed her. She would face each day as it came, and do what she must to survive. Pray to God she would never have to sell her grandmother's house; it was the first and only home she'd known in many long years.

The hurried tread of feet on the oak floor startled her. She expected to see Anna rushing into the kitchen, but to her astonishment, Sheriff Grayson stepped through the doorway, revolver drawn, eyes squinted against the lantern light illuminating the room.

He wore ankle-length cotton drawers and nothing else.

Over six feet of nearly naked male stood before her. She was so transfixed with the muscles shifting in his bare chest and arms, she could barely speak. "G-good morning, Sheriff." His eyes widened, and he spun to face her. "I beg your pardon," he said, his voice gruff from sleep. "I heard a noise down here and thought someone was forcing the door."

He was so apologetic that she couldn't stop her smile. "That would explain the gun."

He lowered his revolver to his side. "Excuse me." He started to back out of the kitchen, but a thump from the woodshed snared his attention.

He took two steps toward the door, and it swung open.

Boyd stepped inside, jostling an armload of wood. Confusion marred his handsome face, but when he saw Claire standing by the stove in her robe, he nearly dropped his armload of wood. His eyes registered her state of undress then flew to his brother, who was still standing in his drawers. "What is going on?"

The sheriff glanced at Claire then back at Boyd. "We were about to have coffee," he said nonchalantly.

She opened her mouth to correct Boyd's obvious assumption, but the sheriff winked, as if warning her to let him do the talking.

Seemingly unconcerned, the sheriff crossed his arms over his wide chest and braced his bare feet on the floor like a sailor on rough water. His chest and arms were small mountains of muscle and hair, his stomach tapered and flat, his legs long and solid-looking in his snug drawers. The sheriff was a gorgeous man, and he would have been the sensible choice, but he wasn't Boyd. Leave it to her to be attracted to the wrong brother.

Boyd's snort of disgust told her he'd caught her staring at his brother.

"Shut the door," Duke said. "You're letting in the cold."

Boyd shoved the door with his foot and just missed slamming it on Sailor's tail as the dog squeezed inside. Tension sparked from every inch of him. Claire feared he was going to attack his brother. She glanced at Duke to see why he wasn't trying to clear up Boyd's suspicions, but he reached down to scratch Sailor's ears.

"How you doing, clumsy?"

He was purposely driving Boyd crazy. She would have never imagined the sheriff like this, but here in her kitchen, he wasn't a lawman. He was a brother. Duke was playing games and taunting his sibling and making her like him even more.

The light of humor in the sheriff's eyes delighted her. In that moment, she sensed the two of them becoming friends. She understood quite clearly what thoughts Boyd was having that put the ferocious scowl on his face, but she wasn't offended. She loved making him wonder about the situation, about her. He deserved it after flaunting Martha on his arm at the cantata.

Boyd dumped the wood into the kitchen bin, but Claire was watching Duke, whose wide shoulders were shaking with silent laughter.

She pursed her lips to hide her smile.

Murder filled Boyd's eyes when he stood to face his brother. "Why are you standing in Claire's kitchen half dressed?"

Duke shrugged. "Because I wanted a cup of coffee?"

Boyd gritted his teeth and took a step forward, but Sailor started barking like they were under attack.

"It's all right," Duke said to the dog. He glanced at Boyd and burst out laughing. "Calm down, hothead. I took a room last night to make sure nothing happened."

Boyd glanced between them, his fists clenched. "That doesn't explain why you're standing in her kitchen in your drawers."

Anna rushed into the kitchen, her eyes brimming with worry. "What the devil is—oh, my..." Her eyes widened as her gaze swept the perfect form of Sheriff Grayson.

Boyd's face grew as purple as Anna's house robe, and he glared at his brother. "Get some clothes on and let's take a walk."

Unperturbed by Anna's perusal and Boyd's ire, Duke chuckled and left the room.

⋙⋘

When his brother was dressed, Boyd followed Duke out of Claire's house, wondering what was between him and Claire.

"She's one gorgeous lady." Duke's smug grin made Boyd want to rearrange his brother's teeth.

"You're doing a fine job of irritating me this morning."

Duke threw his head back and laughed. "I knew it." He chuckled again and ignored Boyd's scowl. "You've finally met your downfall, little brother. Radford and Kyle are going to love this."

"It's nothing more than my usual romance."

"We'll see." Duke headed across the Common. He chuckled three more times before Boyd elbowed him in the side.

"I want you to deputize me."

"I have a deputy."

"I'm serious, Duke. Deputize me, and I'll take a room at Claire's."

Duke halted in the middle of the Common. "Now why would you want to do that?"

"To keep Claire from getting hurt."

"And to seduce the lovely widow into your bed perhaps?"

Boyd clenched his jaw. "If we weren't in the Common, I'd pound you for that."

"I have a duty to protect those women. I'm not going to put a fox in the hen house to keep out a bear."

"All right, I care about her. For some reason Claire feels a need to help Anna. She's fool-headed and too stubborn to listen to reason."

"Claire seems like a smart lady. Maybe she just doesn't agree with your reasoning."

Boyd jammed his cold hands into his coat pockets. "She's gotten herself into a mess with this temperance nonsense, and now she's refusing to send Anna home to her family."

"What does that have to do with you?"

"My patrons are grumbling that they're tired of the women nagging us each day. I'm afraid someone is going to cause trouble. Deputize me, and I'll look out for Claire and Anna. You and Levi have all you can handle without doing guard duty with those crazy women."

"Bad idea." Duke resumed walking. Boyd kept pace, his irritation rising to a dangerous level.

"Whoever nailed that note to Claire's door two weeks ago sounds like they aren't toying with her. Those stubborn, idiotic women need someone who can save them from their own foolishness."

"You sound worried."

"I am." Boyd huffed out a frosty breath and stomped through the snow. "Claire has a loaded gun in her closet that she thinks will protect her, but she'll probably put a bullet in herself before shooting anyone else. If I stay there, I can try to talk sense into both of them. And if they won't listen, at least I'll be there if anything happens."

Duke entered the building that housed his office. "If you can convince Claire to let you take a room, I'll deputize you."

"Deputize me, and I'll convince her."

Duke took a badge out of his desk drawer. "I'm only doing this because I have to take Levens back to Pittsburgh. I'll be back Friday. If I hear one complaint," he said, "or find out you're taking advantage of Claire in any way, I'll yank this badge off your chest so fast your head will spin."

"If you insult my integrity one more time you won't have a head. I'll knock it off your shoulders."

Duke laughed and handed Boyd the badge. "Glad we understand each other."

Chapter Seventeen

———————◆———————

B oyd picked up his valise and carried it downstairs to his crowded
saloon. "Come on, Sailor." The dog scurried out from under the
billiard table and trotted to Boyd's side.

On the way out of the saloon, Boyd nodded to Pat, knowing
his friend and former owner of the saloon was more than capable of
running it for a few nights. Karlton would be there to help out too.

Boyd drew in a lungful of bracing winter air as he crossed the
street to Claire's house. He went around to the back door and knocked.

"Who's there?" she asked without opening up.

Sailor gave a shrill bark. Boyd rubbed the dog's head.

"Thanks," he whispered.

When Claire opened the door, Sailor barreled inside. She turned
to scold the dog, and Boyd followed Sailor's lead by stepping inside. He
sat his valise on the oak floor and nodded to Anna who was drying her
hands on a red checkered apron tied around her slim waist.

She nodded to Boyd then leaned down to pet Sailor. "Good
evening, mister." She ruffled the dog's ears. "How did you know we
were missing you?"

Sailor wheezed then trotted to Claire. He pushed against her legs
until she smiled and stroked his head. "What mischief are you up to
this evening?"

"He came to rent a room," Boyd said, deciding to dive in rather
than test the water. He nudged his valise with the toe of his boot. "I
brought his bag."

Claire frowned at the valise.

Boyd pulled his deputy's badge from his pocket. "My brother's out of town until Friday. He deputized me to stay here and guard you lovely ladies."

Her frown deepened.

"That means I need to rent a room."

Claire glanced at Anna then returned her scowling gaze to Boyd. "I see no humor in this." She opened the door and nodded for him to leave.

"I've been dispatched here by the sheriff."

"Bother that. He's your brother, and somehow you've convinced him to give you a badge. There can only be one reason you want a room in my boardinghouse when you have your own apartment not fifty feet from here."

He pushed the door closed and braced his palm against it. "I have a badge that makes it official, Claire."

She shook her head, but it wasn't fear filling her eyes. It was something else—worry or discomfort, but not exactly fear. "You can't stay here."

"I have to. My brother has entrusted me to keep you ladies safe until he returns from Pittsburgh."

She lifted her chin. "Then you can sleep in the shed."

He loved her spunk.

"Excuse us for a moment," Anna said. She caught Claire's elbow and nudged her out of the kitchen.

Boyd heard the murmur of Anna's voice then Claire's voice raised in dispute then Anna's soothing murmur again. Then it was quiet. Deadly quiet.

Even Sailor stopped pacing and panting and cocked his ears, listening to the sudden silence.

The sound of a defeated sigh made Boyd grin. He knew that sigh. Claire did that just before she accepted the inevitable.

The two women came back to the kitchen, Anna looking a little nervous, Claire frowning. "It will cost you three dollars a week," Claire said.

"Fine."

"I serve breakfast at five-thirty, lunch at noon, and supper at six o'clock. If you're not present I'll assume you're eating elsewhere."

"Fine."

"You're free to use the downstairs rooms and the upstairs bath, but all other rooms except the one you're sleeping in are private."

"Fine."

She gave a stiff nod. "Dry your boots, and I'll show you to your room."

He removed his boots and picked up his valise.

She glanced at his stocking-clad feet, and her face flushed.

He followed her across the kitchen and up the stairs, grinning to himself. If seeing him in stocking feet flustered her, she was in for some jolting moments over the next few days.

Her skirt swayed with each step she climbed, making his hands itch to cup her hips and pull her against him. Ignorant of his thoughts, she strode up the hall and opened the door to a corner room. Two tall windows gave him a view of Main Street—and his saloon.

Perfect. He could keep an eye on things there too.

His attention lingered on the large sleigh bed. He pictured Claire lying across the mattress, her hair spilling around her shoulders, her mouth parted and her arms open to receive him. Lust pushed through his groin and the ache nearly made him groan.

She fluffed the bed pillows. "How long will you need the room?"

"Until my brother and I think you and Anna are safe without one of us here."

"I'm sure we'll be fine."

"I think Larry proved that it doesn't take much for a man to punch through a window or break in a door."

Her face blanched and she turned away. "The bath is your first door to the right," she said, stepping around him to straighten the drapes on his window. "This is my best, and warmest, room, but if you should need another quilt, I keep one on the top closet shelf." She took a handkerchief from her pocket and dusted the stand beside his bed. "I wasn't expecting a guest tonight."

"Claire." He touched her hand and stopped her nervous fidgeting. "Why are you afraid of me?"

"I'm not."

"You are," he said, knowing it was the truth. It hurt that she still felt she couldn't trust him.

She tucked her handkerchief in her pocket and moved toward the door. "If I were afraid of you, I wouldn't allow you in my house."

"Then you must be afraid of yourself, because you are intentionally avoiding me."

"Don't be ridiculous."

"You are, Claire. You're fidgeting like a schoolgirl. Either you're afraid me, or you dislike me."

"I'm not afraid of you. And I don't dislike you. I dislike your lifestyle and your obvious attempts at seduction."

"My attempts at seduction?" He laughed and brushed his fingers across the soft underside of her jaw. "It is you who are seducing me."

Her eyes widened, but she boldly met his stare. "If I were seducing you, Boyd Grayson, you would know it."

⊷ ⊶

Downstairs, a few minutes later, Sailor met Claire in the foyer, acting so pleased to see her that she released an airy laugh.

"You are just like your master," she said, brushing her fingers over his tilted ears. "Far too obvious in your affections."

She went to the music room where Anna was playing the piano. Anna glanced up, her cheek as purple as a grape from Larry's brutal fist, but she seemed serene.

"It feels wonderful to play again," she said.

Claire listened for a minute, but she was too tense from her exchange with Boyd to relax. "It's a terrible idea for him to stay here," she said, interrupting the song Anna was playing.

"He's a paying boarder," the woman said without missing a note.

"He's a reprobate, and I shouldn't have allowed you to talk me into renting to him."

"Well, he's the one who's causing you to lose business. It's only fair that he make restitution." Anna continued playing, but switched to a soothing ballad.

Claire leaned against the piano and closed her eyes, letting the music flow through her, striving for a calm she couldn't quite manage. She loved Chopin.

"May I join you?"

The sound of Boyd's voice startled her and sent her pulse racing.

"Of course." Anna started to leave the bench, but Boyd stopped her with a light touch on her arm.

"Stay and play a duet with me," he said, paging through the sheet music on the Piano. "Ah, here it is. Claire's grandmother and I used to play this Bach piece together."

After a slight hesitation, Anna sat beside him on the bench. Boyd laid his long fingers on the keys and began playing Aria from Suite in D.

"That's beautiful," Anna said with admiration. She studied the sheet music and joined in playing the duet.

Claire stewed. She'd given Anna refuge, understood and supported the woman at her own detriment. She couldn't bear to have Boyd win Anna's affections so easily. Or worse yet, to have Anna win his.

When the song ended, he winked at Anna. "May I?" he asked, gesturing to the piano.

"Of course." She slid off the bench and stood beside Claire.

Boyd ran his fingers up the keys and back down then started a lively tune that made Anna tap her toe. Claire was beginning to get caught up in the rhythm when he started to sing.

I once had a lover with gorgeous blond hair, but the lady was so ornery, I called her Cold Claire.

Anna's eyes widened, but Claire gasped. She wasn't cold. She wasn't! Boyd grinned and kept singing.

She taunted and teased, while I begged and pleased, but the lady didn't dare, so I called her Cold Claire.

He ran his fingers up the keys then back for another verse.

She pouted so pretty and scowled so sweet, I would have been honored to rub the lady's feet.

So smitten was I, that I knew I should die, if I didn't get a kiss from her sweet lips.

Anna ducked her head, but Claire knew her traitorous friend found Boyd's song humorous. She wanted to slam the piano cover on Boyd's nimble fingers, but decided it would be more satisfying to put the rascal in his place.

He finished the naughty song and flashed a grin so full of mischief that she felt her knees weaken.

"May I?" she asked, gesturing to the piano in the same manner he'd used with Anna.

Instead of leaving the bench, he slid over and offered her half. Unwilling to let him unnerve her, Claire settled herself beside him and placed her fingers on the cool ivory keys.

He smelled wonderful—a woodsy sort of smell mingled with a hint of cologne. Had he worked the sawmill today? Or had he been carving another piece of art before coming here? Although he wasn't touching her, she felt his solidness beside her as clearly as if he were flush against her.

Inhaling, she straightened her shoulders and focused on the keys. With every ounce of bravado she could muster, she began singing a temperance song, "Lips That Touch Whiskey Must Never Touch Mine." It was a sad song about a woman losing her lover to alcohol. He'd promised to reform, but she'd trusted in vain, his pledge broken time and again. The song was reminiscent of her own life, and Claire sang it with conviction.

By the time she finished, Boyd was silent. "Touché," he said. His handsome face, only inches from hers, was filled with respect and admiration. "You have a lovely voice, Claire." His dark lashes lowered as his gaze dropped to her mouth. "And lovely lips that should never touch whiskey," he teased, but his voice was too intimate to be taken lightly.

Claire heard the swish of a skirt as Anna slipped out of the music room. Blast her. How could her friend desert her? Claire wanted to call Anna back, to leap off the bench and follow, but Boyd clasped her hand.

"I'm sorry if I offended you earlier."

Heaven help her. She couldn't look into his handsome face and keep her wits about her. She stared at the keys on the piano. "I don't like your games."

"I wasn't playing with you. I meant every word I said." He rubbed his thumb over her knuckles. "I think you're afraid to be near me, and that bothers me. I won't hurt you."

She glanced up, but he wasn't smiling. He was gazing directly into her eyes, his own dark and serious. "I'm not afraid," she said, but she was, and his half-smile said he knew the truth.

She tugged her hand free, but he hooked his arm around her waist and kept her on the bench with him.

"Stay a minute," he said, but it was a gentle request. He removed his hand from her waist, and she felt a thrill race through her. She hadn't been touched so intimately since before Jack died.

And never so tenderly.

Her knees bumped his, and she slid back an inch. "Where did you learn that naughty song?"

"I made it up."

"You did not."

"I did." He smiled. "You inspire me."

"Are you playing with me because I'm a widow?"

He stroked his hand up her forearm. "I like you," he said, curling his fingers around her arm. "I'm attracted to you." He gave her a gentle squeeze as his gaze roved her face. "I'd like to kiss you again."

Her breath whooshed out, and she stared at him. Common sense told her to lift her bottom off the bench and get out of the room, but the reckless girl in her stayed and waited in breathless anticipation.

"You tell me when you're ready." He got to his feet and gave her a courteous nod. "I'll close Sailor in the kitchen for the night. Sleep well, Claire."

Chapter Eighteen

E mbarrassed by her wanton feelings, Claire bade Boyd a good night and rushed to the safety of her bedchamber. She would talk to Sheriff Grayson as soon as he returned. Whatever it took, she was going to convince him that she and Anna were safe alone in the house. Maybe Boyd would let Sailor stay with her. A dog would offer some protection. And she still had her gun.

Whatever happened, she had to get Boyd out of her house.

He was too handsome. Too persuasive. Too tempting.

Despite her promise to never marry again, her body still responded to a man's touch. It still yearned and ached to be held. She couldn't help it. She'd enjoyed the early months of sharing her marriage bed with Jack.

With a sigh, Claire sank into the wing chair with her grandmother's journal. Heaven knew she could use a diversion or some words of wisdom.

Abe danced with me!

For three dreadful hours we stood mere feet from each other, dancing with our spouses, pretending our hearts weren't aching with the need to hold each other.

Abe talked with my husband about our kitchen. He would finish it this week. He would have no reason to return. He would no longer drink coffee in my house, no longer look up to see me watching him, no longer lay down his tools and pull me into his arms.

I couldn't bear the thought. I turned away to hide my tears. Abe slipped his hand into mine and led me onto the dance floor. He said friends are allowed to dance with each other.

But we're so much more than friends. It'll show, I thought. Still, I could not end our dance. I could not withdraw my hand from the warmth of his grip. He squeezed my hand. I squeezed back. My husband was only feet from us. My actions horrified me, but I was helpless to stop the secret communication with Abe. He said this would be our first and last dance. My eyes filled and I nodded. He whispered to be strong, to appreciate the moment, to live it fully and keep it alive in my memory. I swallowed my tears and looked at that beautiful man.

His eyes were dark with pain, but filled with love. For me. Everything he couldn't say was there. I closed my eyes and inhaled his scent. He smelled of forest and soap and man.

Abe. Oh, Abe...

The song was ending. Our hands clasped in desperation. Our bodies betrayed us and moved close, brushing each other, aching, longing, begging to embrace. "Smile," he whispered, but I could not. If I blinked, my tears would have spilled over my lashes. I couldn't release my breath, fearing I would sob. If I had dared to look at him again, I would have begged him not to leave me.

I held all that emotion inside, dying as the music faded and he released my hand.

Her grandmother's pain was so real, Claire's eyes misted.

The affair had been wrong. They'd known that. Claire knew that. But what about the love? How could it be wrong? How could something so true and unwavering be wrong? The timing was wrong. The circumstance was wrong. But not the love. The love was real.

The fire crackled in the fireplace, but Claire felt chilled. No one should know this depth of heartache. Jack had hurt her innumerous ways and broken her heart when he smashed her dream of love, but her pain couldn't compare to what her grandmother had endured. To love and be loved so deeply, and to be denied that love had to be the most painful thing in the world.

Her grandmother's words broke Claire's heart and made her lonely. She felt a deep need to be held and comforted.

Tucking the journal beneath her arm, she picked up her lantern and tiptoed to the door. The hall was empty, so she slipped downstairs and hurried to the kitchen. "Hello, dear," she whispered as she knelt by Sailor. "How about some company?"

The dog wheezed and licked her cheek.

"Oh, yuck." She wiped her cheek with her sleeve. "That really wasn't necessary. Come on." She pulled a chair next to the stove, welcoming the warmth as she sat. Sailor sat beside her and put his head in her lap. Claire stroked his soft fur and began to read again.

Several pages of the journal were filled with accounts of stolen moments between Abe and her grandmother: a chance meeting at Brown & Shepherd's store, a secret letter tucked into Abe's coat pocket while she passed him on the street, a private glance shared at church. Even the tiniest of things had momentous significance. Those morsels sustained them when they couldn't steal away to be with each other.

It seemed impossible to Claire that the two lovers could have been happy, but a deep joy resonated in her grandmother's words.

Abe's wit is bone-dry, but the darling man never ceases to make me laugh. He tells me outrageous stories about his patrons that I can hardly believe, but he assures me they're true. When we're alone, we talk about the meaning of life, and why we share this forbidden love. After many conversations, we have given up trying to understand. Some things are beyond comprehension or explanation. We've accepted that pain will accompany the joy and love we share.

Abe and I shared a private glance in church this morning, but as I looked away, I noticed his wife watching me, her eyes filled with hatred and heartache. She knew.

I could bear her hatred, but my darling Abe had to live with that resentment and anger.

I left church believing Abe would cancel his visit to repair a hinge on my cupboard door. But he arrived on schedule. I told him my suspicions. He assured me I was wrong, that nothing had changed. I wanted so desperately to believe him, but to my despair, I was right.

Abe's wife confronted us in my parlor where Abe had kissed me only minutes before. She asked if I knew the definition of honor. I asked if she knew the meaning of love. She confessed that she did not. I cannot credit my emotions in that moment, but it shamed me to feel relief rather than pity, to know that I alone owned Abe's affection.

I was forced to bid him farewell with a brief, guarded glance, to try to express the depth of love in my heart with the mere meeting of our eyes.

If only I could hold him one last time, hear his heartbeat beneath my ear, have one final moment of feeling alive, but all I have left of my beloved is this child in my womb.

Abe, my darling, I'm going to have your baby.

Claire clapped a hand over her mouth and stared at the date of the journal entry. It couldn't be true.

Her father had been born... No. No! It wasn't possible.

But the truth was right there on the page in her grandmother's own script.

Abe had sired her father.

It was entirely believable. For whatever reason, her grandmother hadn't gotten pregnant before or after giving birth to Claire's father.

Claire's hands shook as she turned the page, but the rest of the journal was blank. Had their story ended there? Did she ever see Abe again? Did she ever tell him about his child?

Tears flooded her eyes, for her grandmother and Abe, and for Abe's wife who had also suffered. Her grandfather had been betrayed, too, but he probably never realized that his wife loved Abe, that his son was sired by another man.

A man who might still be alive.

Claire's heart leapt with hope. What if Abe was alive? Would he want to meet her? Would he admit the affair and privately acknowledge her, or would he pretend his love for her grandmother never existed?

The kitchen door opened, and Boyd stared at her. "Gads, Claire. I thought someone was prowling around down here."

She ducked her head, trying to hide the fact that she was crying. "It's just me."

"Is something wrong?" He crossed the room and knelt beside her chair. "Are you all right?"

She nodded. "I'm fine."

"When a woman cries, she is not fine."

"I'm just reading something sad and... it's nothing, really. I'm fine."

He tilted his head to see the cover of the book. "What is it?"

"A journal." She wiped her eyes with the back of her hand, but her tears wouldn't stop. "You can go back to bed."

"I'm not leaving you crying in the kitchen alone."

She sighed, knowing he wouldn't give up, and she was glad because she didn't want to be alone right now. She needed a friend.

He stroked his hand over her fist that was clenched on top of the journal. "Trust me, Claire. Tell me what's hurting you."

His tender inquiry brought a fresh rush of tears to her eyes that had nothing to do with the journal. Claire hadn't felt any tenderness in so long, she'd forgotten how good the gentle stroke of a man's hand could feel.

"Why are you sad?" he asked.

She sniffed and wiped her face, deciding to trust Boyd with the truth about her grandmother, if not about herself.

He had cared about her grandmother enough to cart her wood and carry her coffin, it wouldn't make sense for him to do anything to tarnish her memory now.

"I'm reading my grandmother's journal," she said.

"I hope she didn't divulge how often she beat me at poker."

Claire smiled, glad for Boyd's humor, which brought some levity to the moment. "She wrote about her affair."

His dark eyebrows lifted in surprise.

"My grandmother had a lover," she said then let Boyd read the first page of the journal.

He let out a low whistle. In the few weeks she'd known him, it was the first time she'd ever seen Boyd truly shocked. "I would never have guessed Marie was involved with someone."

"Her affair took place fifty years ago. I think it ended a short time later, long before you or I were born."

He sat back on his heels. "I wonder who Abe was."

"According to this," she said, lifting the journal, "he's my grandfather. My grandmother's last entry said she was carrying Abe's child. Judging from the date of her entry, that child would have been my father."

Boyd blew out an astonished breath and stood. "Do you think your father knows?"

She shrugged, because she didn't know and because she couldn't ask her father. "Do you know any men with the first or last name of Abraham?"

"You think Abe is still alive?"

"I don't know. Most likely, no, but I... I hope so." She more than hoped, she prayed he was alive. He would be the only family she had left. He could finish the story about his affair with her grandmother. Maybe he would even want to share a secret friendship with her.

"Is this why your father quit speaking to his mother?"

"No." She rose from the chair and laid the journal on the counter beside the sink. "I broke their relationship when I eloped with Jack. Grandmother sided with me,"

Boyd's eyebrows lowered. "You must have loved him a great deal to have eloped with him."

She had, but she turned away from Boyd's intense regard and pulled her chair back to the table. "Jack was handsome and charming, everything a naive girl could want. He was also an angry young man with an addiction to alcohol, which is why I'd like to leave my past in the past."

"We all would, Claire. Unfortunately, the past has a way of hanging around."

It certainly did, and that's why she shouldn't have told Boyd about Jack. She didn't want any man to know too much about her, to have power over her. And she didn't want his pity.

But it wasn't pity she saw in Boyd's eyes. It was concern and compassion. And it elicited a fierce need in Claire to share her secrets and fears and heartaches with him. But she couldn't. Ever. So she fled from the kitchen before she could divulge her whole sordid history.

Chapter Nineteen

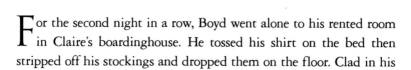

For the second night in a row, Boyd went alone to his rented room in Claire's boardinghouse. He tossed his shirt on the bed then stripped off his stockings and dropped them on the floor. Clad in his trousers, he pulled the chair toward the fireplace in the front corner of the room.

Retrieving a small chunk of wood from his pocket, he began whittling, glancing out the window on occasion to watch his saloon.

The house grew quiet, and he imagined Claire nestled in her big bed. Did she miss her husband? Did she miss their lovemaking? If so, what had she meant when she said, "I know exactly what the danger is." Did Jack beat her?

The crackle of the fire and an occasional creak of the joists beneath the floor sounded inside. Outside, the din of music and voices flowed from his saloon. Some of the conversations were so loud he could hear what the men were saying.

If it was this loud with the windows closed and snow muffling the streets, he could well imagine how loud it would be in the summer months with the windows open and the men conversing on the porch.

This was why Claire was complaining.

This was why she hated his saloon.

This was why she continued to march to his saloon day after day.

Shame stole over him, and he lowered his hands to his lap. How late did the noise keep her awake at night?

He'd slept above his saloon while it was open, but on those rare occasions he'd been so exhausted he could have slept through a battle.

Tonight, though, he wasn't exhausted, nor was he drinking. He was wide awake. And embarrassed.

The minutes dragged, and the noise escalated outside.

His neighbors must hate him.

Claire's grandmother had never complained about the noise, but it must have bothered her. To think he'd caused Marie sleepless nights gnawed at his conscience. He never meant to be inconsiderate of his neighbors.

Yet, while he sympathized with Claire and the rest, he couldn't close his saloon.

Maybe he could close earlier. The neighbors would be happy, but his patrons would give him fits. It wouldn't take long for his regular patrons to shift their loyalty to a bar where they wouldn't be pushed out the door halfway through the night.

Boyd shaved the piece of wood in his hands as his mind turned the situation in numerous directions, mulling over ideas, but finding no solution. He grew so absorbed with the problem that the loud shouting outside startled him. It was coming from his saloon.

He pulled on his shirt and lunged across the room. He had to stop the noise before it woke the neighborhood.

He heard the other bedroom doors open as he dashed down the hall. "Stay up here," he said then raced down the stairs. He was going to clobber those Carson brothers if they were fighting again.

But it wasn't the Carson brothers who were causing the ruckus. It was Zeke Farzin, an obnoxious drunk who'd been thrown out of Boyd's saloon on several occasions. Apparently Karlton was attempting to toss him out, but Zeke wasn't inclined to leave.

Furious, Boyd marched barefoot into the snow-covered street and hauled Zeke away from Karlton. "What are you doing back here?"

Zeke swung his arms out. "Get away from me."

Sailor barreled outside, barking and growling as he lunged toward Zeke.

"Off!" Boyd commanded. Sailor halted three feet away, his teeth bared, hackles raised, growling with such fury it sent a chill down Boyd's spine.

Zeke glared at the dog then shifted his black eyes toward the porch. "Well, would you look at that," he said, glancing at Claire, who stood on the porch in her house robe. "I didn't realize this temperance bitch was your mistress."

Claire gasped in outrage, and Boyd buried his fist in Zeke's gut.

"Apologize to the lady," Boyd demanded.

"Sorry," Zeke said through gritted teeth.

Boyd pushed him toward town. "Get out of here, and don't patronize my saloon again."

Zeke staggered toward town, but pointed a finger at Claire. "You're itching for trouble, lady."

Boyd let him go but turned to Pat and Karlton who were standing with several patrons. "Shut down for the night."

Pat and Karlton exchanged a glance then went inside. The men grumbled, but Boyd told them to leave. As his patrons made their way home or to the next open saloon, he let his heart slow and his anger ebb.

The freezing snow finally drove him inside. Sailor followed him in, and Boyd closed the door. Claire was waiting in the foyer. Anna was standing on the stair landing, her eyes huge with fear.

"It was just a drunk," he said.

She sank onto the steps and rested her head against the spindle railing. "I thought it might be Larry."

Sailor bounded up the steps and licked her ear.

She sobbed and hugged the dog. "Thank you, Sailor. I needed that."

With an angry tug, Claire cinched her house robe around her waist, but she couldn't stop shivering. The foyer was cold, and she was shaking with fury. That wretched saloon should be closed permanently.

She moved to the foot of the stairs. "Since we're all awake; let's make some hot cocoa and try to forget about this." Not that she would or could.

Anna pulled herself to her feet. "Thank you, but I think I'll just go back to bed," she said. She turned and slowly climbed the stairs, her body visibly shaking.

Claire turned to Boyd. "This is what your saloon does to a woman like Anna."

"Or a woman like you?" he asked.

She headed toward her kitchen. "That man scared us half to death."

"I'm sorry about that."

She sighed and faced him. "Will you have some cocoa.?"

"I need to dry my feet first."

She glanced down at his red feet and gasped. "You must be freezing. Come to the kitchen and I'll get a pan of warm water for you."

"A towel would be enough."

"Nonsense, your feet are red as beets. Come on," she said, heading toward the kitchen with Sailor at her heels.

"Claire, my feet are fine," he said, trailing behind her. "They're just cold and wet."

"You'll be lucky if you don't catch your death from this." She lit the lantern on the kitchen table then hurried to the stove where she kept a tea kettle and a pan full of water.

Her hands shook so badly she could barely handle the kettle. She slopped hot water into an empty pan then used the small hand pump on her sink to add cold water. She tested it with her fingers, added a touch more cold water then carried the pan to the table. "Sit down.

He cupped her shoulders and held her still. "I'm fine."

"Well, I'm not." Dash it all, her eyes were welling up. She pulled away and put the pan on the floor. "Soak your feet while I make the cocoa."

He sighed and sat down, which was a good thing, because if he hadn't, she would have dropped the pan onto the table and thrown herself into his arms. She desperately needed a hug, and to feel safe for a moment. Being jolted awake by loud cursing had spiraled her straight back into her nightmare past with Jack.

Sailor stuck his nose out from beneath the table and sniffed the pan of water.

"You won't like it," Boyd said. The dog licked the warm water then sneezed and backed away. "I told you," he said, casting a grin at Claire.

She turned away to put a distance between herself and Boyd that she needed but did not want.

His shirt was unbuttoned and hanging open, revealing a chest sculpted with muscles and covered with shiny dark hair. She'd seen her husband's naked chest more often than she cared to remember, but Jack had been blond like her, his chest nearly hairless.

She couldn't bear having Boyd here, tempting her, but she was glad he'd insisted on staying. What if it had been Larry shouting outside? What if he found a way to get out of jail again? What if he sent one of his nasty friends to bring Anna home? What good would her gun have been if she couldn't pull the trigger?

It would have been no good at all. She or Anna could be dead right now.

The realization sent a shiver down her spine. She couldn't bear living in fear again. She couldn't. She took two cups from the cupboard and banged them onto the counter.

"Claire, there's no danger now. You can relax."

She huffed out an angry breath.

"There's no need to be upset."

"No?" She stirred cocoa and sugar into two cups of hot milk. "A drunkard threatened me and called me a whore tonight. Why should that upset me?"

"Technically, Zeke called you my mistress."

"I fail to see the difference."

"A whore takes all offers. A mistress has one lover."

Like her grandmother. She had loved Abe. Had that made her Abe's mistress, or just a woman who'd fallen in love with the wrong man? Oh, bother, love was far too complicated.

"I'm sorry." She carried the cups to the table. "I've grown cynical about men and their motives, but that doesn't give me the right to be nasty to you."

Their eyes met, his dark and long-lashed. Her attention shifted to his chest and that ebony hair that shone in the lantern light. Their eyes met again, and a hint of a smile touched his mouth, as if he wanted her to know that he felt the attraction too. She flushed and looked away. She stared at the brown liquid in her cup, nowhere near as appealing as Boyd's chest but much safer.

And much smarter.

Her hastily thrown on wrapper was as indecent as his unbuttoned shirt. Could he tell that her breasts were bare and unbound beneath her nightrail and wrapper? The cotton fabric brushed her peaked nipples, sending heat up her neck. She angled her knees, purposely turning her shoulder to him.

He pointed to the pan of water. "I think my hallux is turning into a prune."

She glanced down and saw his big toe sticking out of the water. Despite her embarrassment, she smiled, remembering the first time he sat in her kitchen. Only it was her hallux that had been damaged that day. "I'll get you a towel." She patted Sailor's head as she stood.

When she came back to the table, Boyd looked up at her with adoring eyes. "Would you dry my feet?"

She tossed the towel in his face. "Do you ever stop flirting?"

He laughed and lifted his feet out of the water.

While he dried them, she propped her hands on her hips. "Do you ever have a serious conversation? Do you even know how?"

He tossed his towel onto the floor and stood in front of her. "I'm serious about protecting you," he said, his voice resolute. "No one is going to hurt you again."

Again? Her breath lodged in her chest and she stared at him. How much did he know about her past? "You're too tense, Claire." To her shock, he shrugged his shirt off his shoulders. It slid down his arms and over his hands, landing on the floor behind him.

Her gaze dropped to his beautiful, bare chest then bounced back to his handsome face. "What are you doing?"

"Letting you see what you've been peeking at for the last half hour."

"I was not peeking at your chest."

He leaned down and pressed a soft kiss to her mouth. "You were peeking." Before she could protest, he sank into his chair and pulled her onto his lap. She gasped, but he put his finger over her mouth. His eyes, only inches from hers, were sparkling with humor. "You have to stop taking everything so seriously."

Being held in his arms, feeling his bare torso against her wasn't serious?

His hard, warm thighs felt sturdy enough to hold her for hours. His muscled arms circled her waist, but she felt protected rather than trapped. The beat of his heart vibrated his chest, and she felt a mad urge to curl against him, to lay her head on his bare shoulder and take refuge for a while.

His long, sooty lashes lowered as he kissed her. The deep, molten kiss sent a river of heat coursing through her body.

She clenched her fist, needing to move, wanting to stay. His arms offered heaven and hell, sin and salvation, safety and danger.

And passion.

Without her stays and corset, she had no barrier against him, nothing to stop his hands from touching her.

But he didn't touch her. He drew away, his eyes dark with desire. "You'd better go up to bed now."

She studied the crescent shape of his black eyebrows, the perfect line of his nose, the enticing contour of his lips, and knew she didn't want to leave. All that waited upstairs was an empty bed and an empty life.

She'd rather run her palms over his gorgeous body, feel the weight of him pressing her into her mattress, kiss him until they were both mindless with need, until they couldn't turn back. She didn't want to return to her empty life. She wanted to stay right here in the safe circle of his arms, feeling passionate and alive.

Two huge dog paws plunked down on her stomach and knocked the air from her lungs. She gasped and glanced down to see Sailor staring up at her with an indignant canine squint.

It was as if her own mother were standing in her kitchen wearing that scornful look. The reality of what she was doing struck her like a slap on the head. She was sprawled across Boyd's lap, kissing him like the mistress Zeke had accused her of being. Worse yet, Boyd was a paying boarder.

He was here on business for the sheriff no less.

Sailor plopped his head on her thighs, wheezing with excitement, his tail whipping behind him as he begged for her attention. She rubbed his head and silently thanked him for interrupting what would have been a terrible mistake.

Boyd lifted the dog's jaw and stared at him. "You are really starting to irritate me."

Sailor wheezed and burrowed against Claire's side. Despite the tension between them, she smiled.

Boyd smiled, too. It was a soft, sincere smile. "I guess it's obvious that we're both fond of you."

She slipped off his lap before she could think about kissing him senseless. "I'll take Sailor up with me, unless you'd rather he stay in the kitchen."

"Sailor would never forgive me if I denied him your company." Boyd got to his feet, bringing himself, and his tempting chest within inches of her. "You know, this is the first time I've ever been envious of a dog." He winked and stole a brief kiss before strolling out of the kitchen. It left her heart pounding and her brain spinning with rash, reckless thoughts of following him upstairs to his bed.

Chapter Twenty

"Look at 'em," Gus Wriensler said to the sheriff, jabbing his finger toward Claire and the women gathered around her. "They're like a bunch of wasps, swarming into my saloon, buzzing about us men like we're all worthless swine. A man's got a right to have a nip when he feels the need. And I got a license to sell liquor. "

"You don't have a right to point your gun at unarmed women. Keep it put up, or I'll take it."

"Then keep 'em out of my saloon!"

Duke turned toward the women. "Ladies, give Mr. Wriensler some time to mull over your message."

"I ain't mulling over nothing."

The sheriff scowled at Gus. "Would you prefer to have these ladies on your doorstep every day trying to bring you around to their way of thinking?"

"Hell no."

"Then I'd suggest you agree to consider their message and send them word once you've reached a decision."

"I already know what I—" Gus clamped his mouth shut, his eyes registering the meaning behind Duke's words. "All right then. But you keep 'em off my doorstep while I'm making up my mind."

Every woman there knew that the minute Gus closed his door he would forget they'd ever been there. Claire saw the disappointment in their faces, knew that some of the women would lose hope and consider the battle lost. But she wasn't going to let one rude bar owner stall her mission or the dreams of thousands of women across America. "Sheriff Grayson?" she called.

He had stopped to see her and Anna last night, assuring them that Larry was locked up, and that his friends had been warned to stay away.

The sheriff gave her a nod of greeting. "Good afternoon, Mrs. Ashier."

"It is *not* a good afternoon when a man points a gun at you.

"Then get off my property," Gus said.

She ignored him and spoke to the sheriff. "It's apparent to all of us that Mr. Wriensler has no intention of considering our message. Each of us has pledged to march for temperance until we've stopped the sale of all intoxicating beverages. I believe I speak for all of us when I say we will not turn our heads simply to appease Mr. Wriensler."

The ladies' voices rose in agreement.

"I've pledged to visit everyone who is violating our mission," she went on, looking straight at Gus Wriensler. "No gun or vulgar threat is going to stop us from doing what we believe is right." They couldn't allow it to stop them, or nothing would ever change.

The ladies cheered, and Gus glared at Duke. "Get this herd of cattle off my property," he said, his face crimson with anger.

Gus argued, and the ladies protested until the sheriff finally fired his pistol in the air. Everyone gaped at him in the ringing silence.

"Thank you," he said, his voice admirably calm. "Now, here's the way it's going to be. You ladies stay clear of Mr. Wriensler's saloon for a while. And Gus, you keep your gun put up or you'll spend a week as my guest." Gus's roar mingled with the ladies' disappointed protests, but the sheriff ignored all of them. He pushed Gus inside the bar and slammed the door then spread his arms and turned the women away from the saloon. "There's plenty of other places to do your work. Start there."

Claire followed the disheartened women to the Common. She felt helpless. She had no idea how to convince a man like Gus Wriensler to close his bar.

Desmona lifted her hand for silence then addressed the ladies. "Gus Wriensler is only part of our problem. There is speculation that some of us are becoming too friendly with the saloon owners," she said, shooting a meaningful glance at Claire and Anna.

Elizabeth, who was standing beside Desmona, gasped at her mother's malicious accusation. For Elizabeth's sake Claire refused to show any anger or embarrassment. Deciding to turn the tables on the pushy witch, she linked her arm with Desmona's elbow and faced the crowd of fellow marchers. "I'm the guilty party," she said without preamble. "I'm spending time with Boyd Grayson because I'm working on a surprise." Not a lie exactly. She was spending time with Boyd. And she was hoping to surprise everyone by stopping his liquor sales.

She let the ladies gather close then raised her voice to be heard. "We need to find the Achilles' heel of these saloon owners," she said. "Who influences them? Who has power over them? Who can hurt or help them? For one man it might be his banker. For another man it might be his mother. It's our job to find that person and recruit them to help us clean up the town. How better to discover that information, or influence these men, than by befriending them?"

Admiration filled Elizabeth's eyes, and she gave Claire a small nod of support.

The ladies considered for a minute then a buzz of excitement rippled through the crowd. Suddenly a babble of voices filled the Common.

Claire signaled for Anna to sneak away from the crowd. The instant her friend was safely heading up Main Street, Claire thrust Desmona into a group of chatting women then slipped through the mass of bodies and hurried home herself.

Inside her foyer, she closed the door and leaned against it with a huge sigh of relief. Anna was waiting for her.

"How did you get away from that witch so quickly?"

"I dumped her in the middle of a debate over who was more influential to Gus Wriensler, his wife or his mother."

Anna sighed. "I feel sorry for her daughters. It must be awful having a mother like Desmona. Elizabeth seems wary of her."

"Elizabeth is wary of her mother learning the truth about her marriage."

Anna shook her head in sympathy. "So tell me, what's this big surprise you're planning?"

"I don't have clue," Claire said, feeling slightly nauseous. "I made it up so I could get us away from her. But I'll think of something."

Admiration filled Anna's face, and she gave Claire a shy hug. "You are a smart and wonderful friend."

Tenderness filled Claire's heart, because she understood what it cost Anna to give her that gesture of warm affection.

Anna lowered her lashes as if embarrassed, but a sharp knock on the door made them both leap back in fright.

Dreading the possible danger lurking outside, Claire peeked out the window. A handsome young couple stood on the porch, the man clutching a valise, the lady holding an infant in her arms. The man waved, and Claire ducked back in embarrassment. What a frightened ninny she was becoming.

She opened the door and gave them her friendliest smile.

"We saw your sign in Brown & Shepherd's window," he said. "We're moving to the area and need to rent a room until we can find ourselves a home."

Chapter Twenty-one

"Come on, Sailor."

Claire stood in the foyer in her boots and coat, trying to get the dog away from the foot of the stairs. He'd been standing by the newel post growling for ten minutes, staring upstairs at the room she'd rented to Mr. and Mrs. Ormand.

The dog had been fine all afternoon while Claire had visited with the Ormands. He had sniffed the baby's blanket and tiny fingers then flopped down beside Claire's rocking chair while she rocked the baby. She'd held the precious child so Mrs. Ormand could enjoy a cup of tea, but the instant she had given the baby back to Mrs. Ormand, Sailor's hackles lifted.

For some unfathomable reason, he didn't like Mrs. Ormand taking the child. He seemed protective of the baby, as if the child belonged to Claire. In her heart, Claire wished it did.

It was early evening, but the Ormands were exhausted from two days of traveling and in dire need of rest. They wouldn't get any sleep, though, if Claire didn't get Sailor out of the house.

She nudged him outside and closed the door behind them." What's wrong with you?"

He wheezed and planted his right paw on the porch floor, as if making a statement.

"I had to give her back," she said, shooing him down the steps. But she already missed the warm, welcome weight of the baby nestled against her breast.

She waited on her porch, thinking Sailor would run to the saloon, but he sat down in the middle of the road and looked at her, as if waiting for her to catch up.

She waved her hand toward the saloon. "Go on. I can't take you inside."

Sailor didn't budge.

"Oh, bother." It was bitter cold outside, and she had to make sure Sailor was safely inside with Boyd before she could return to her cup of tea. She descended the steps, and Sailor bounded to his feet, and ran to the back of the saloon.

Claire tromped through the snow and found him sitting in front of a wide door. She inched it open and peered into what looked like a small, dimly lit storeroom filled with liquor bottles, kegs of ale, and other supplies. She considered shooing Sailor inside, but what if Boyd didn't discover the dog? The thought of Sailor being trapped in the cold room all night made her reconsider. She stepped inside.

Sailor bounded in after her then crossed to another door and nosed it open. The sound of the tavern spilled out as Sailor slipped into the other room.

"Where'd you come from?" she heard a man say then a mixture of noise assaulted her ears.

From her position, she could see a narrow strip of the bar area. Boyd was talking with three men who were discussing spring planting. Two men sat at the bar sketching something on a large paper, debating the merits of brick versus wood to build a shelter. Despite the early hour, a man in the far corner of the room was playing a lively song on the piano, and several patrons surrounded the bar. She wrinkled her nose at the cigar smoke and the smell of ale.

The crack of billiard balls riveted her attention. She slipped her hand over the doorknob and leaned forward to peer through the opening. Half the billiard table was visible to her. Two men stood with long sticks in their hands, eyeing the table with intense concentration.

So, this was what they did here.

Somehow, it didn't look as evil as she'd imagined. Despite Jack's penchant for drinking, he'd never taken her to a saloon. He'd held private card games in their apartments and used her as a decoy. If he couldn't win using her as a distraction, he would push her to the table and force her to play. She loathed those nights. Especially if she lost.

But the view before her didn't inspire fear or disgust. It made her curious. Much of the noise was a result of having so many men in one place at one time with several active conversations going on at once. The piano added another layer of sound, as did the clacking sounds of the billiard balls. But taken individually, none of it seemed overtly rude or intrusive as it sounded from across the street.

No wonder Boyd couldn't understand her complaint.

Suddenly, the knob beneath her hand turned, and the door wrenched farther open with a violent tug. She stumbled forward and fell against a bear of a man not much taller than herself. He locked his fingers around her arms and yanked her against him.

"Why are you snooping around our storeroom?"

It was Boyd's nasty bartender, Karlton.

"Is spying a new tactic for you ladies?" He jerked her arms, sending a spear of pain through her left elbow. "What were you looking for?"

"N-nothing."

"Karlton!" Boyd's voice cut across the room. "Let her go."

Karlton's vise-like fingers bruised her flesh. "I'm fed up with these women meddling in my business."

"I said, release her." Boyd strode across the room.

Karlton didn't obey. He wrenched her arm upward and pinned her between the hard wall and his heavy body. "You'd better back off, lady, and stop the marches."

"Karlton!" Boyd's eyes were fierce as he yanked the man away from her.

Karlton elbowed Boyd and grabbed the front of Claire's coat. "Stay out of my business or you're going to be sorry."

Boyd grabbed Karlton's shirtfront and shoved him against the bar, his face red with fury. "Don't ever handle her like that again."

"This lady is costing me money. I have accounts to settle!"

"That's not her problem."

"She was sneaking around the storeroom." Karlton glared at her. "What were you looking for?"

The saloon became silent and every man stared at her with suspicion. She struggled to hold back tears of mortification and pain.

Boyd shoved Karlton away and turned to face her. "What are you doing here?"

She lifted her chin and glared at him. "I was bringing Sailor back because he's bothering my new boarders." Not caring if he believed her or not, she turned and bolted into the storeroom.

Boyd followed her and pulled the door closed. "Are you hurt?" he asked, his face too shadowed for her to see it clearly.

"How can you employ an offensive brute like him?" she asked, gesturing toward the bar.

"I had no idea he'd do a thing like that." He caught her wrists and gave them a light squeeze. "Don't lump us all in the same mold," he said. "Ninety-nine percent of the men in that room would rather cut off their own hand than hurt a woman."

She rubbed her elbow. "Why do I always seem to find the one percent?"

"Because you provoke every man you meet." He shook his head and released her wrists. "Karlton's angry, Claire. He distributes liquor to all the saloons you've been marching on. Your temperance cause is threatening his livelihood."

"That doesn't give him a right to physically accost me."

"No, it doesn't," he said. His voice was filled with regret. "I'm sorry he hurt you."

"You won't need to stay with Anna and me tonight. Mr. Ormand will be there."

"Is he capable of dealing with a man like Larry Levens?"

The young man seemed capable, although he was probably too exhausted for her to depend on. "I have my gun if he's not." She pushed the door open and stepped outside.

Boyd followed and halted her with a gentle tug on her hand. "I don't mind staying, Claire."

"I don't want you there." And that was that.

At Claire's cold look, Boyd let her go. Miserable, he watched her walk off. He couldn't undo the damage Karlton's hands had inflicted, but he could make sure it never happened again.

Silence greeted him when he stepped back into his saloon. The men were waiting to see what he would do. The image of Karlton wrenching Claire's arms fueled the fire in his gut, but he shoved his fists into his pockets. Pounding Karlton wouldn't fix anything.

He strode to the bar and faced his part-time bartender. "You're fired."

Anger flashed in Karlton's eyes. "She was sneaking in the back door to spy on us!"

"She was bringing Sailor back."

"So she says. We lost six regulars this week. Eight if you count the Carson brothers who signed the widow's pledge yesterday. I've lost ten percent of my sales this week with Maynard's and Corbie's canceling their liquor orders. I can't afford to lose that money. I think she was here to cause trouble."

"So do I," said Peter Garven, a regular patron at the saloon. Others nodded in agreement.

"I don't care why she was here," Boyd said. "I won't tolerate any man abusing a lady in my presence."

"Those women you're protecting are killing our business one man at a time," Karlton said. "They've even petitioned to have our liquor license revoked."

"No one is going to take my license," Boyd said, but he didn't feel as certain as he sounded. If the women could convince drunks like the Carson brothers to sign their pledge, who knew what trouble they could cause.

"Somebody's got to stop this nonsense before it goes any further," Karlton insisted. Several patrons seconded his argument.

"I'm sick of seeing that sea of bonnets every time I sit down for an ale," Peter said. "We need to put a stop to this nonsense."

"But not the way Karlton handled Mrs. Ashier," Boyd countered, still itching to make the man pay for hurting Claire. He pulled several bills from the till and handed them to Karlton. "You're no longer welcome in my saloon," He faced his patrons and raised his voice. "That goes for anyone who manhandles a woman."

The patrons complained, and Karlton slammed the cupboard so hard the back bar shuddered. Boyd clenched his fists to keep from closing his hands around the man's throat. Everyone who frequented Boyd's bar knew how much he cherished it. He'd built and carved the back bar with his father. They'd watched him polish the wood and clean the mirrors religiously each week for the past two years. It was the shining jewel that lifted his saloon above the ordinary. It was his pride and joy, and no one abused it without facing his wrath.

Karlton stormed out the front door, leaving behind a bar full of irritated men. Boyd took a long drink of his ale, wondering how to handle a situation that was growing so ugly. He needed to make Claire understand the mess she was creating, but she would see him as a disgruntled saloon owner, not as a friend. Talking with her wouldn't make a bit of difference.

But he had to do something before she marched herself straight into trouble.

He needed to distract her somehow. He needed to make the temperance cause less personal to her.

If she wasn't suffering directly from the saloons, she would have less reason to close them down. She would have less reason to consider him the enemy.

If he could divert Claire's attention away from her ridiculous temperance cause then maybe the other ladies would lose steam and quit marching. If Claire wasn't bothered by the noise from his saloon all week, maybe she would be more forgiving on the weekends. If her business improved, she might have less cause to want to close his saloon. And she might also have more reason to spend time with him.

⚓

Claire was sitting in the parlor with Anna, working on a quilt, when she heard the back door open. She tensed and looked up to see where she'd left the fireplace poker.

Before she could leave her chair, Boyd entered the parlor. His cheeks were flushed from the cold. His dark hair glistened with melting snowflakes. "How are you feeling?"

She lowered her lashes, not wanting him to see the truth. Karlton had hurt her with his strong hands, and embarrassed her in front of a bar full of men. "Why are you here?"

"To make sure you're all right. Where are your boarders?"

"They're sleeping." His dark brows winged upward. "It's just after supper. Rather early, isn't it?"

"They were tired from traveling. I'm trying to keep the house quiet for them, so please go back to the saloon." Though Boyd hadn't accosted her in any way, she was irritated by his refusal to see the reality of their situation.

Instead of making a cryptic remark, he braced his shoulder against the archway between the parlor and foyer.

"How would you ladies like to get out of the house and go ice skating with me?"

She stared at him, wondering if she'd heard him correctly. "How can you even ask after what just happened at your saloon?"

"I'm trying to apologize for what Karlton did."

"It should have never happened."

"I agree. That's why I fired him."

She was speechless—and touched. He'd protected her. He'd fired Karlton.

"Go skating with me, and I'll close the saloon tonight."

She exchanged a glance with Anna, who laid the quilt square in her lap. "You haven't had an outing since the cantata. You should go. What harm will it do to get out for the evening? Especially if Boyd's willing to close the saloon."

With the saloon closed, she wouldn't have to worry about the Ormands being disturbed. And if she got out of the house, she wouldn't have to listen to their occasional noises that told her they were definitely not sleeping.

Maybe while she was with Boyd, she could convince him to close down completely. Maybe she and Anna could break down his resistance while spending time with him. Wouldn't that be a surprise for the temperance ladies?

She straightened in her chair. It would be the perfect surprise.

With renewed purpose, she gave Boyd a decisive nod. "All right. Let me find my grandmother's old skates for Anna," she said, informing him that they wouldn't be going alone.

"I'll close the saloon while you ladies get dressed."

Twenty minutes later the three of them were bundled in heavy coats, walking down Main Street, their feet keeping time with the clacking blades of the skates that were slung over Boyd's shoulder. As they chatted, the heaviness of the day slowly lifted from Claire's shoulders. Why shouldn't she enjoy herself? She was entitled to an evening out. What harm was there in skating? Anna was with her. Boyd would act a gentleman in public.

The thought of closing his saloon made her smile.

"I'd give a night's earnings to know what brought that look to your face," he said, his voice intimate and teasing.

"You just did."

A sardonic grin lifted his lips. "I guess I did."

She inched away, unwilling to let him turn their outing into a romantic event. She wasn't fully recovered from the kiss he'd given her in the kitchen.

She glanced at Anna to include her in the conversation. "The first time I tried skating, I couldn't move my feet without falling. I cried until Lida took pity on me and towed me around the pond with her neck scarf."

"You're lucky your sister was so nice," Anna said. My siblings would have left me standing there all night."

Claire stopped and stared at Anna. "I didn't realize you had siblings."

"Four brothers and three sisters."

Claire exchanged a look with Boyd and knew what a family man like him must be thinking. He and his brothers worked together and helped one another. Anna's siblings should be helping her out, not Claire. She shook her head, warning him not to ask questions.

He gave her a discrete nod. "As soon as my brothers and I learned to skate," he said, "we were out to kill each other. Whoever was still standing or not bleeding by the end of the night was the winner."

"Sounds dreadful." After being manhandled by Karlton, Claire's bones ached just thinking about the roughhousing that must have gone on.

"Those were some of the best times of my life," Boyd said, his eyes filled with a warmth that made her want to move closer.

But Claire warned herself to keep her distance.

"Why did Duke chose a profession of upholding the law, while you chose to own a saloon?" she asked.

"I craved more excitement than being a lawman."

"Chasing criminals isn't exciting?"

"It's irritating, and I don't have the patience for it. Duke has always been a peacemaker. I was the troublemaker."

"You still are in this neighborhood."

His snort, and Anna's chuckle, made Claire smile.

"What are your other brothers like?" she asked.

He tilted his head and studied her. "Why all the questions?"

"I'm curious about your family."

"There's not much to know. Radford is the oldest. He fought in the war, became a hero then came home and stole my brother Kyle's fiancée."

She pursed her lips. "Are you intending to make Radford look bad to make yourself look better?"

"No, I just gave you the short version of the truth."

"That must have been a difficult time for your mother," she said, hoping to lead their conversation in another direction. She wanted to know more about this lady who'd raised four well-respected sons.

"My mother stayed out of it, but yes, it was a rough time for everybody, especially Radford and Kyle. They're both married now, and their wives are having babies."

"Is Kyle spontaneous like you?"

"Gads no!" he said with a laugh. "He's methodical and practical to the point of boorishness. I can't work with him for more than an hour before I want to cuff him on the head and wake him up. And I drive him crazy."

"I'm sure," she said wryly. "Despite your similarities to Duke then, you sound quite different from your other brothers."

His smile faded and his eyes darkened. "I'm not at all like them."

Claire exchanged a glanced with Anna, both women realizing she'd stepped over some invisible line and trespassed on personal territory.

They walked the last few yards in silence.

A five-inch board rail surrounded a huge sheet of ice that covered much of the east park. Wooden posts with suspended lanterns glowed throughout the Common and shimmered across the ice. People chatted as they crossed the park or circled the rink. Children raced across the ice, shrieking with laughter. Two old men sat on a bench playing harmonicas for the lovers who couldn't see anything but each other.

Boyd guided them toward an empty bench, but as soon as Claire was seated, he knelt and tugged off her boot.

She jerked her foot back. "I don't need assistance."

Boyd winked at Anna. "I'll help you next, as soon as this irritating woman sticks her foot in this skate." He cupped his hand around Claire's toes.

"What are you doing?" she asked, glancing around to see if anyone was watching.

"Warming your toes. They're freezing."

Boyd slipped the boot over Claire's foot and laced it tight up to her ankle. He slipped the other boot on without any teasing. She waited while he helped Anna on with her skates then she hurried to the rink.

"We should have waited for him to put on his skates," Anna said, following Claire onto the ice.

"He'll catch up with us."

"I know you didn't believe me the first time I said it, but that man is in love with you."

"Nonsense. He just likes to irritate me."

"He does more than irritate you."

She wanted to deny it, but her feet wouldn't let her. Her left foot was achingly cold. But her right foot, the one Boyd had caressed with his warm hand, was nestled comfortably in her skate.

"Why not enjoy his attention?" Anna suggested as they slowed to avoid the people in front of them. "What harm can come from ice skating?"

And maybe Anna was right.

Boyd was a saloon owner—the man responsible for her failing business—but he had also been her protector this evening when Karlton had hurt her. He wasn't the same kind of man as Jack, or Larry, or Karlton—he was of an altogether higher caliber. It wasn't fair to lump him, or other honorable men, into the same category.

As long as she kept alert to his intention, she could avoid getting hurt. And maybe she could find a way to bring Boyd around to her way of thinking about whiskey and saloons.

Her legs were just warming up to the side-sliding rhythm when Boyd skated past. He pivoted in front of her and skated backwards.

"Would you ladies like an escort?"

Her heart hitched. His grin was irresistibly boyish and charming. Already she was in trouble, and the evening had just begun.

"You two go ahead," Anna said. "I need to tighten the laces on my skates."

He held out his hand to Claire. "Want to see how fast we can go?"

She could see by his lifted eyebrow that he was challenging her. "Why not?" she said with a saucy lift of her chin.

He pivoted with ease and skated beside her. "This won't hurt your arm, will it?"

She slipped her hand into the crook of his elbow. "I'm fine."

"It should have never happened, Claire." His voice was filled with apology and concern.

Karlton's mauling was nothing compared to what she'd experienced with Jack, but it had obviously upset Boyd enough to fire the man. "Does Karlton have a wife?"

"No."

"That is something to be thankful for. I can only imagine how horrible he'd be after a night of drinking."

"He doesn't drink." She glanced up in surprise, and he nodded. "It's true. I've never seen him touch a drop of ale or liquor in the two years I've known him." He steered her around a couple of children clowning with each other. "Karlton is a staunch businessman out to make his fortune. That's why all this temperance nonsense has him so upset."

"It's not nonsense."

"Let's not argue. In fact, let's not talk about the subject at all." He tucked her arm more firmly against his side. Their bodies shifted into a synchronized rhythm as they skated in silence. Their breath formed frosty funnels as they circled the rink.

Men and women greeted Boyd with warm smiles as they passed. Even the women who marched with Claire gave him friendly nods. This was his town, she realized. He belonged here. These people were his friends and neighbors. His family was well respected, and despite Boyd's choice of owning a saloon, so was he.

Suddenly, Claire saw Boyd as a playful boy, a beloved son, a respected man, instead of a saloon owner. He was all of those things, and more.

"You're too deep in thought for skating," he said. "It terrifies me that you're cooking up a plot to ruin me."

She smiled. "Nothing so sinister."

"Then let's make our evening more festive." He nudged her toward a group of people who were forming a circle. He caught Anna's hand and pulled her into the ring with them. Then he linked hands with Claire. A man to her left clasped her other hand, forming an unbroken circle. Suddenly, the group of people began to skate to the right. As they increased their speed, their arms stretched out. Claire was pulled along by Boyd as the people circled faster and faster. The women shrieked, the men laughed, but Boyd never took his eyes off her face. His teeth flashed white in the lantern light, his deep laughter spilling over her, warming her.

Her own laughter bubbled out and she clung to his strong hand, enjoying the wild ride and the sounds of laughter around her. Several of the ladies begged to stop, but the men merely slowed and forced the circle in the opposite direction. The women shrieked and protested then laughed as easily as Claire did. She felt young in that moment.

When the crazy circling finally stopped, Anna skated away with a group of ladies who were still gasping and laughing. Claire clung to Boyd's arm and begged him to take her to a bench until she stopped swaying.

"I'll keep you upright," he said, and slipped his arm around her back.

Instinct made her stiffen, but she was too off balance to pull away. They rounded the rink twice before her head cleared, but by then she'd grown to like the feel of his arm against her back.

"Are you going to be chastised by your lady friends for consorting with the enemy?" he asked, his eyes sparkling with humor.

"Not once I've told them I'm helping our cause by wearing down your resistance."

"Is that what you're doing?"

"Of course."

He laughed and tightened his arm, drawing her against his side. "Then let's see how persuasive you can be."

Instead of wiggling away, she boldly met his eyes. "Please close your saloon, Mr. Grayson."

He smiled down at her, and she felt as if she were spinning in that crazy circle again, dizzy and half-scared but unable to let go.

"Spend the evening with me tomorrow, and I'll close the saloon for the night," he said.

"I don't believe you." She tried to slow down, but he held her tight and pulled her along with him.

"I will, but only if you spend the evening with me."

"Doing what?"

"Anything. Whatever you like."

"That's all it will take to get you to close it?"

"Yes."

"I won't spend the time alone with you."

"I'm not asking you to."

Her face heated for unfairly assuming the worst. She averted her eyes. "Why is spending time with me worth closing your saloon?"

"I like your company."

She glanced up, doubting his sincerity. "Forgive me if I suspect another motive."

"All right. It's because you like to debate topics with me."

"No, I don't."

He tossed his head back and laughed.

Her face burned as several people glanced over. She'd do most anything to shut down his saloon, but she wouldn't risk her reputation. She needed to do business in this town. "Are you intentionally trying to cause a scandal?"

"No, but I won't mind if it happens." He was looking at her with those gorgeous eyes that made her knees weak. He pulled her closer to him. "I'm a bachelor. I have a right to flirt with a pretty lady."

"Then you should have brought Martha skating."

"I'm afraid she had to go back home."

"Well, if you're looking to flirt then you'd better go to Buffalo."

He slowed their pace and studied her. "Are you only with me tonight to further your temperance cause?"

The hurt in his eyes shamed her. The truth was, she liked his company and his roguish sense of humor. Too much. If not for her business needs, she could easily fall for his seduction.

But she did have a boardinghouse and a serious reason for caution with Boyd. His saloon was hurting her business. He could easily hurt her.

She averted her face. "This isn't the place for this conversation."

"Then let's go someplace more private," he said quietly. "My saloon is empty. We could talk there."

They could, but they wouldn't. "You underestimate my intelligence. We wouldn't talk if we were alone in your saloon."

"We wouldn't?" The mischief in his eyes was so flirtatious, she wanted to stay in his arms all night.

"You're incredibly tempting to a lonely woman," she boldly admitted. "But you would romance me, thrill me then crush me." She released his arm and drifted a few inches away. "I can't afford the price of the ride."

Chapter Twenty-two

Sub-zero temperatures made mid-January so brutal that the temperance marches were cancelled for the week. Claire spent much of her time near the stove and purposely avoided Boyd, but to her dismay, she thought about him constantly.

She and Anna kept busy with charity work, and spent their evenings with the Ormands and their precious daughter Emily.

They resumed their marches on Monday, and spent Monday evening in the parlor, watching Mrs. Ormand tease the baby into a bubbly smile. Claire's heart melted when the infant's pink lips pursed and her chubby arms flailed above her blond head.

Her own baby would have been just over a year old, had Claire not miscarried in her second month. When she lost the baby, Jack had gone into a rage and a four-day drunk. Claire had spiraled into a dark and angry depression.

The loud whack of her door knocker startled her so badly that she jumped from her chair with a gasp. She exchanged a glance with Anna, and they went to the foyer together.

When Claire peeked out the window, her heartache eased and gladness filled her. She opened the door. Boyd's cheeks were shiny from a recent scrubbing. His hair was combed back, showing the angles and contours of his handsome face—a face she missed far too much. As much as it shamed her to admit it, she missed his sense of humor, his playful teasing and flirting.

"I heard the news about Willard Lewis closing his saloon," he said. "You ladies must be thrilled with your success."

"We are," she said proudly. Willard Lewis had heeded their plea to close his saloon. Mr. Baldwin, the druggist, had followed suit and pledged in writing that he would no longer sell intoxicating beverages in his store. Both men agreed to help the women further their good work.

Boyd's saloon had remained open every night but Sunday.

"You ladies are becoming regular news in The Censor. They reported that Washington, Ohio shut down all liquor sales in just one week, which I find hard to believe."

"Dr. Lewis confirmed it," she said. "Liquor licenses will be voted on by the legislature soon."

"I'm impressed."

She was, too. They still had several saloons to close, but they were finally making real progress. "You're welcome to join us in the parlor," she said, wanting his company and the levity he usually brought to the evening.

"I was hoping you would invite me in before I froze to death."

"You're dressed too warmly to freeze." She waited while he shrugged off his heavy wool ulster then took it from him and hung it in the closet.

He winked at Anna. "I think she's beginning to like me."

To Claire's shock, the woman slipped her hand into the crook of Boyd's elbow. "Stop baiting her and come help me with my chess game. Claire is annihilating me."

"I admire the concentration the game takes," he said, "but it's too tame for my blood."

Claire's heart warmed as she followed them to the parlor, understanding that this was Anna's way of working through her fear one small step at a time. Anna needed to relax, to lower her guard, to learn how to socialize again.

She evidently trusted Boyd to help her do that.

Boyd greeted Mr. and Mrs. Ormand then sat on the sofa and watched Anna and Claire finish their chess match.

Mr. Ormand, who looked like a boy beside Boyd's worldly confidence, gave an exaggerated yawn and got to his feet. "The baby is fussy this evening, and I'm dreadfully tired of a sudden. The wife and I will bid you all goodnight." His wife clutched their infant to her bosom and climbed the stairs behind him.

Anna and Claire exchanged a grin. The baby hadn't fussed once. Mr. Ormand was just eager to get his wife into bed.

"Would you mind if we switched to cards?" Anna asked.

"Of course not." Claire had never cared for chess. It felt too cat-and-mouse to her, too much like the games Jack had played. She swept the pieces into a felt bag and laid them on the playing board. "Would you care to play a hand of poker?" she asked, with a pointed glance at Boyd.

He raised his eyebrows. "Isn't that a bit immoral for you ladies?"

"Not if you don't tell."

He grinned. "I'll let you ladies decide what the wagers will be."

"It had better be something small," Anna said, "because I don't know how to play."

"If you win, we won't march on your saloon for a day," Claire said. "If we win, you close for a night."

He arched a superior eyebrow. "Are you certain you want to make that wager?"

"Why wouldn't I?" she asked, hoping she looked innocently naive.

"Won't your lady friends be upset when you tell them why you aren't marching on my saloon tomorrow?"

She merely shrugged, not about to debate the issue and divulge how much she knew about the game. She retrieved a deck of cards from the drawer in the sturdy oak coffee table. "Would you like me to deal?"

He leaned back on the sofa. "By all means. Ladies first."

An hour later he stared at her in open admiration. "Did your grandmother teach you how to play?"

She shook her head. Claire had learned the art of playing from Jack and his acquaintances. "Will you keep your promise and close the saloon tomorrow?"

He frowned. "I honor my wagers, Claire."

"Excuse me," Anna said, getting to her feet. "I'll make some tea."

The instant she left the parlor, Claire sighed. "Why do I always seem to be insulting you?"

"Because I'm a saloon owner. Because you pigheadedly hold some bigoted notions of what a saloon owner must be, and you can't see me separate from my profession."

His words rang true. As long as he ran a saloon she would have difficulty seeing him as anything but a reprobate. But hadn't he proved himself a gentleman on many occasions? Didn't he defend her and Anna against harm numerous times?

He moved to sit on the coffee table, angling his body to face her. "This temperance business is getting out of hand."

"So is the drinking in this town."

He braced his forearms on his knees, bringing his face closer to hers. "Most of my patrons are good, hardworking men who don't deserve to be harassed."

"When you serve only those decent, hardworking men, I'll stop trying to shut you down."

"This isn't a game. You're stirring up serious trouble. The saloon owners and their patrons are furious that Lewis shut down, and that you ladies are meddling with their right to sell liquor. "

She bristled. "I wonder how those men would feel if they were women and had no rights."

"You ladies are worming your way into every part of our lives. You're talking to our bankers and our patrons, and even our mothers!"

"What do you want me to do?"

"Use some common sense," he said with exasperation. "Your house has been ransacked. Karlton manhandled you because you're meddling with his livelihood. What else needs to happen before you stop this nonsense?"

She'd seen him angry before, but this was the first time it was directed at her. Oddly enough, she wasn't afraid of him. She liked his earnestness even more than his charm. "Is your anger supposed to stop me from doing what I believe is right?"

"Yes." He slapped his thighs and stood up. "I'm trying to tell you that there are a lot of angry men out there who've had enough of your meddling. They're raising a ruckus in the saloons. They aren't going to sit back and be gentlemen about this much longer."

Worry snaked through her. All it would take was one man to drink too much, to get too aggressive, and she could be facing another terrifying situation. But if she stopped marching, all the work would be for naught. She thought about women like Anna and Elizabeth and knew she couldn't quit.

He sighed. "This isn't the time to dig in your heels."

"I'm not digging in. I'm... thinking." How could she proceed with her work and keep herself, and the women she marched with, safe?

Agitated, she rose to her feet just as the picture window behind her exploded with a sickening crash. Pain burst in her shoulder as she doubled forward in a shower of glass.

Boyd's heart convulsed as he threw his arms around Claire and pulled her to the glass-littered floor. Anna raced into the room, her eyes wide with fright.

"Dear, God," she said, her voice breathless as she knelt on the floor beside them.

Boyd sat up, his heart thundering as he helped Claire to her knees. "Are you hurt?" he asked, praying she'd only cried out in alarm and not pain.

She clutched her shoulder. "Something hit me," she said, her voice tight.

Blood seeped between her fingers, and his gut clenched. A brick lay not three feet from her on the glass-speckled carpet.

Anna pulled the gown off Claire's shoulder then glanced at Boyd. "You'd better get the doctor."

"What happened?" Claire asked, shivering in the frigid wind that was blowing through the window.

"Someone threw a brick." He stood and helped her to her feet. He guided the women into the foyer where Mr. Ormand was standing in his nightshirt in shocked silence.

"Stay out of the parlor," Boyd said to them then turned to Claire's boarder. "Do you know how to use a gun?"

"Y-yes," the man said, bobbing his head.

Boyd yanked open the closest door and grabbed the revolver. He checked to see that it was loaded then handed it to Mr. Ormand. "Shoot anybody who tries to enter the house without Claire's approval."

Mr. Ormand took the gun, but his hands were shaking so badly he could barely hang on to it.

"I'm going to run for the sheriff and the doctor. You three wait in the kitchen until I get back."

As if his legs turned to butter, Mr. Ormand sank down onto the stairs. "I'll stay here," he said, his face ashen, his hands shaking. "My wife and daughter are upstairs."

Boyd guided Anna and Claire into the kitchen. "I'll send the boys over to cover the window." He jerked his boots on. Then, with a last look at Claire, he rushed outside.

He sent Pat for the doctor and the sheriff then scoured the area around Claire's house to see if he could track the culprit's footprints. The prints led back to the street, which was a churned up mess. Within minutes, there were so many men moving around her house that he gave up and went back inside.

Anna put a makeshift bandage on Claire's shoulder.

"There's a gouge there, but it isn't as bad as I thought," she said. She handed a note to Boyd. "This was attached to the brick."

When he read the note, fury pulsed through him for the lowlife who would attack a woman, and for Claire, who was being so hardheaded and careless.

"This is what I'm talking about," he said, his voice grating with anger as he shook the note at her. "The person who wrote this is serious about stopping your marches."

"That was obvious when the brick sailed through my window," Claire retorted.

"That brick could have been a bullet, Claire."

She rose to her feet, her eyes flashing. "I'm fighting for something I believe in, and no one, especially a coward throwing bricks through my window, is going to stop me."

"No. They're just going to kill you."

Her jaw clenched and she glared at him. "Then teach me how to shoot my revolver. It appears I'm going to need to protect myself better."

"Why not just stop the marches and let things calm down a bit?"

"Because we're finally making progress. No matter what happens, I'll keep marching until every last saloon in this town shuts down."

"If this is just about your business," he said, "I'll give you money."

Indignation burned a hot path up her neck and face. "This is about women like Anna who should be home sleeping in her own bed without the fear of being beaten to death. It's about men like Larry who use alcohol to fuel their bad behavior. The only people who seem to care about money are you saloon owners," she said then stormed from the kitchen.

Furious, Boyd bolted after her and caught up in the dining room. He grabbed her arm and spun her to face him. To his shock, she cried out and raised her arm as if to block a blow. The way she cowered against the wall pierced his heart. This woman knew what nightmares were made of.

His anger dissolved, and his chest constricted with sadness. He wanted to pull her into his arms, to hold and comfort and promise to keep her safe, but he sensed it would be the wrong thing to do. She was too shaken and wary to let him touch her.

He backed away and lowered his hands to his side. "Who hurt you? Was it Jack?" he asked quietly.

She averted her face, peering through the window into the darkness.

"Talk to me, Claire. I'll understand."

She squeezed her eyes closed.

Watching her struggle to keep her composure rent his heart.

"At least let me hold you."

A breathy sob slipped through her lips, and she clapped her hand to her mouth.

"Claire..."

She turned into his arms, and buried her face against his chest. He stroked her back, feeling the hard trembling in her body. "I'm sorry." His throat grew hot, and his chest ached, and all he wanted to do was take her pain away. "What did he do to you? You can trust me. You know that."

"He did what many drunkards do," she said. "He drank too much. He gambled away his money. He said vile things, and he beat me."

Which gave her several reasons to hate Boyd's saloon. Not only was the noise hurting her business, it had to be a constant reminder of Jack's drinking problem. She sniffed and wiped her eyes.

"Jack was smart and handsome, but he gambled away any success he might have had. That made him angry. Drinking made it worse."

"Why did you marry him?"

She raised her eyes, as if surprised by his comment. "I was in love with him."

Jealousy and compassion tore him in opposite directions. He wanted to tell her that Jack Ashier was no good and hadn't deserved her love. But the compassionate side of him wanted to hold her until her heartache went away.

"Jack was the man of my dreams," she said, as if she needed to explain. "He thought I was the answer to all his problems until my father disowned me without a dowry."

"Your father didn't like Jack?" he asked.

"No," she said wearily. "Daddy insisted I annul my marriage. His partner in his steel mill had suggested that a disreputable man like Jack might make demands on my father that would infringe on their business."

"Like what? Blackmail?"

She shrugged and stepped away. "I don't know. But when I refused to let Daddy annul my marriage, he vowed to disown me. I was young and naive. I turned my back on him and left with Jack."

The despair in her eyes wrenched Boyd's chest. "You loved your father," he said.

"Very much," she said softly. "When I was young, I imagined my father to be a strong, tall tree. I would swing from his arms like they were branches. His laugh was like a boom of thunder that shook the house and made Mama chastise us for roughhousing inside." A bereft sadness dulled her eyes. "One day we both realized that I was too old to swing on his arms, that I was no longer his little girl. That's when he arranged my marriage to his partner's son."

She looked up, her face filled with sorrow. "It was our first serious disagreement. I left the next morning for my grandmother's house without speaking a word to him."

"That's when you met Jack?"

She nodded. "I eloped with him two weeks later. You know the rest of the story. I haven't spoken to my parents since." Her nostrils flared, but she bit her lip and lowered her face. "A hundred times I wanted to write to my father and tell him I was sorry, that I loved him and missed him. I'd have crawled back to him on my knees, but I was afraid Jack would try to take advantage of Daddy, or find a way to manipulate him. I couldn't be responsible for causing my father any more pain, so I lied in my letters and said I was happy with Jack. I've hurt Daddy so deeply, he could never forgive me."

Boyd slipped his arms around her and rubbed her back, wishing he could rub away her pain, that he could protect her from heartache. "I don't want to see you hurt again, he said. "That's why I want you to stop marching. I'm afraid for you."

"I need to finish this."

"Why?" he asked, struggling to hide his irritation.

"Because it's the right thing to do. Because last winter I did something I'll never forgive myself for." She pulled a handkerchief from her pocket, stepped away from him, and wiped her eyes. "We had a bad storm that covered the trees and streets and houses with ice. I heard a cat crying at our door, but I was afraid to let it in because Jack had been drinking, and he hated cats."

Boyd didn't know why she was talking about a cat, but he let her talk.

"I'll never know if the cat found refuge, or if it froze to death because I was too frightened to take it in. I was a coward that night, and I regret it."

"You probably saved the cat's life by chasing it away."

She shook her head as if she'd failed to do the decent thing and protect the cat.

"That's why I can't walk away from this," she said. "I can't be a coward. I need to do the right thing this time."

He understood. But he didn't like her decision. Not at all. "I'll teach you how to shoot your gun tomorrow afternoon," he said. Because he didn't know what else to do to keep her safe.

"Thank you," she said, but the deafening sound of hammers pounding against the house startled a gasp from her.

Boyd's heart leapt and he bit back a curse. He was doomed to be forever on guard around her, looking out for bricks and bullets.

"Good heavens," she said. "I forgot all about Mr. and Mrs. Ormand." She wiped her eyes again and babbled about being a poor hostess, and that the Ormands would probably leave first thing in the morning because of this fiasco.

"Claire." He caught her hands but kept his grip loose enough for her to pull away. "The Ormands are fine. Anna's cleaning up the parlor. Your window is being taken care of. You can take a minute to pull yourself together."

"I'm beginning to think that isn't possible," she whispered. Then she hurried from the room.

Boyd followed her to the foyer where Mr. Ormand was still sitting on the stairs with the revolver clenched in his hands.

"We won't be needing the gun now," Boyd said, taking the revolver from the young man. He clasped Mr. Ormand's bony shoulder. "Good thing nobody tried to force their way inside."

"I'd have blown a hole right through them." Despite his bravado, Mr. Ormand's legs seemed a tad shaky as he climbed the stairs and returned to the room with his frightened wife and child.

Boyd put the gun in the closet and turned to Claire. "I'm going to help the boys board up the window." He lifted his hand and brushed his knuckles over her soft cheek. "You know, cats are exceptional at finding shelter. I'd wager my saloon that your stray found a warm place to sleep that night."

Her tremulous smile brought a deep and satisfying warmth to his heart.

Chapter Twenty-three

The next morning, Boyd ordered a pane of glass for Claire's parlor window and also the window above his saloon that he'd been remiss in fixing. Then he headed to Edwards's Furniture store. All he could think about was Claire.

When he had stopped to check on her this morning, she assured him that her shoulder was fine and that she would be ready for their shooting lesson when he returned this afternoon. But it was frigid outside. Her shoulder must be stiff and sore. It might be best not to push her recovery, but he felt an urgent need for her to know how to handle her gun. After last night, there was no doubt she was in danger.

Because the woman was foolishly stubborn, determined to do herself in over a hopeless cause.

He tripped on the threshold to the store and stumbled inside. Addison's showroom was empty, but the sound of angry voices caught his attention.

He peeked inside the large but unpretentious office where Addison was standing beside a mammoth oak desk. The old man leaned on his walking stick, his white hair mussed, his face red with anger as he waved his hand at his grandson Matthew. "I don't care what they're threatening. This is my store and I'll operate as I please."

"They will place their orders with our competitors if we continue to support these men," Matthew said.

"Then let them." Addison's wrinkled jaw clenched and he turned away. When he spied Boyd standing in the doorway, his eyes filled with sympathy.

"What's going on?" Boyd asked, sensing the argument had something to do with him.

"Nothing important." Addison flapped a hand as if dismissing the conversation. "You boys get to work."

With a sigh, Matthew headed to the workshop at the back of the store.

Boyd followed. "What's going on, Matthew?"

The man stopped and shoved his hands into his pockets, his face grim. "The ladies are boycotting our store because of what happened at Mrs. Ashier's house last night."

"Why? Addison didn't throw that brick through her window."

"I know, but the women refuse to patronize any business that employs men who imbibe alcoholic beverages."

Boyd smirked with disdain. "That's preposterous. They don't know who threw the brick. And Addison's own wife is marching with those women."

"I know. Addison is outraged with Desmona. He refuses to let her, or her temperance friends, dictate how he runs his business."

"Good for him."

Matthew frowned. "Mrs. Clarke stopped in this morning to cancel her order for that bedroom suite we were working on. Emil Cushing came in to say he wouldn't be needing that hutch for his wife. Mrs. Barnes showed up ten minutes later to cancel her order for her dressing table." Matthew began rolling his shirt sleeves up his forearms. "I signed their pledge this morning."

A niggling dread crept up Boyd's neck.

"I had to." Matthew took his apron from a hook by the shop door and tied it on. "Addison can't afford this. He's too old to battle over the principle of a situation he hasn't created or condoned. I'm going to ask the men who are working here to sign the pledge."

Boyd's gut tightened, but he gave Matthew a nod of acceptance. "I understand." Matthew was doing what he felt was necessary to keep Addison's business from suffering. Boyd respected that. But he sure didn't respect Matthew's kowtowing to a bunch of harpies. The women had gone too far. They'd crossed the line of fairness. Addison had nothing to do with this fight.

And it *was* becoming a fight.

Matthew held out Boyd's apron. "Will you stay?" he asked, but he was really asking Boyd to lie down and give up everything he'd worked for.

He shook his head. "Sorry, Matthew."

Boyd left the store without speaking to Addison. What could he say to him? Your grandson is spineless? Matthew was an honest, hardworking man. He was doing what he felt was right. That was no reason to malign his character.

But Boyd wouldn't lie down and let a group of overzealous women dictate his life.

<hr />

It was freezing outside, but Claire was glad to escape the house. The Ormands had decided to stay despite the incident. She was relieved not to lose her tiny income, but the constant tension that radiated between the Ormands was unbearable. They couldn't spend ten minutes in their bedchamber without their intimate murmurs drifting into the hallway. Baby Emily was certain to have a sibling before long.

"Where's Sailor?" she asked as she climbed into the carriage Boyd had brought for her.

"Home. I didn't want him running around while we're shooting." He pulled onto Main Street, took a quick right turn onto Chestnut then a quick left turn onto Barry Road. "Did you know that your lady friends are boycotting Addison Edward's furniture store?"

She frowned. "Why would they do that?"

"Because I'm a saloon owner and they don't want men like me instructing his help."

"That's ridiculous. We never discussed boycotting other businesses. "

"Well, your friends apparently decided to do so after hearing about your window being shattered last night."

She tried to contemplate the impact such a boycott might have, but her mind kept returning to last night, and how Boyd had held her against him in a comforting embrace when she'd confessed about Jack.

"I don't like what's happening, Claire. Addison Edwards hasn't done anything to deserve this boycott."

The boycott might be an effective way to separate the liquor sellers and drinkers from the community, but it felt wrong. Their crusade wasn't supposed to punish the local business owners. It was supposed to unite the community, not divide it. It was supposed to encourage the saloon owners and their patrons to become upstanding citizens, to do good for the community.

Boycotting wasn't the answer in this situation. It was wrong. Boyd should be free to employ his talent at Edwards's Furniture store regardless of his position on temperance. His work at Edwards's had nothing to do with her temperance cause.

But if it pushed him to close his saloon, perhaps she should bite her tongue. It could serve her purpose—and, more important, it might force Boyd to realize his potential.

That wasn't for her to decide, though. She shivered and tucked the lap robe around her legs.

"If you're not feeling well, I can take you back home," he said, glancing at her shoulder.

"I'm fine." She sighed. "I'm sorry about the boycott. Anna and I will talk to the ladies at our next meeting."

He nodded but didn't comment.

She studied his handsome profile, wishing she knew him better. "Other than running a saloon and keeping your neighbors awake all night, what is your purpose in life? Is there anything you are willing to invest yourself in?"

"My purpose is to enjoy life."

"I want to enjoy life, too," she said, "but I also want to contribute to my community. I want to improve the lives of women and children who need help." She wanted to connect with that other, more serious man inside him. "What's most important to you?"

"To live my life on my terms."

"That's all?" she asked.

"That's enough. Some men are as in love with vice as others are with virtue."

"Unarguably true," she said. "But after talking with you last night, I'm sensing you want more than your saloon has to offer. Why aren't you using your talent? Why don't you fill your hours with creative endeavors and spend your time with people you love? Don't you ever get lonely living by yourself?"

He stared at her with suspicion in his eyes. "Are you perchance angling for a husband?"

She reared back against the seat, sending a spear of pain through her shoulder. "Of course not!"

He lifted one eyebrow, as if challenging her statement.

"Never," she said. She would never marry again.

Irritated with him, and with her sore shoulder, she scowled. "I was trying to have an intelligent conversation with you, but I'm convinced it's impossible."

His chuckle drove her irritation a notch higher. She averted her face and let the biting wind cool her ire.

"Claire." He covered her mitten-shrouded hands with his palm. "Why are you always so serious?"

"I'm not."

"You are." He gave her a coaxing smile. "What do you say we call a truce and simply enjoy the day. No talk of temperance or boycotts or the purpose of life. Imagine that I'm your friend and we're on a grand adventure."

"In the dead of winter?"

"Pretend we're Eskimos."

She laughed. "With your imagination you should consider writing a book."

"There you go again, attaching a purpose to everything."

"I wasn't..." She sighed in acknowledgment. "All right, I was. But you have wonderful ideas and—"

He cupped his hand over her mouth. "If you say one more word, I'm going to kiss you until you can't remember your name."

She bit his finger.

He yelped and jerked his hand away.

"That was a warning."

"I'm trembling in fear." He winked and pulled the carriage to the side of the rutted road. "Ready for your lesson?"

"Not particularly."

He sighed dramatically. "Poor Cold Claire. She has no sense of adventure."

She lifted her mitten-covered fist to his nose, but he laughed and leapt out of the carriage.

"You shouldn't tease me when you're about to put a revolver in my hands," she warned.

"Who said I was teasing?" He looked up at her, his cheeks flushed from the cold, his eyes sparkling with humor. He raised his arms. "Come on. I don't want to keep you out in the cold too long."

He helped her out then led her into a wide field surrounded by dense woods of maple, beech, oak, and conifer trees.

"Step in my tracks if you can," he said, leading her several yards into the field. "I want to move away from the horses."

She followed slowly, struggling to stay upright in the knee-deep snow.

"Wait here." He walked a long distance away before dropping a wooden keg on the snow.

"Don't tell me that's our target."

He grinned and headed toward her. "I thought you'd be delighted to blow holes in one of my kegs."

She propped her fist on her hip. "I thought we weren't going to talk about temperance."

"Did I say anything about temperance?"

She stuck her tongue out at him and pulled off her mittens.

He took the revolver out of his pocket and slipped it into her hand. "Step over here and I'll help you aim the first shot or two."

Fear rushed through her as she clenched the loathsome piece of frigid steel. "I'd rather that you shoot it first," she said, thrusting the gun back at him. A horrendous explosion blasted through the air, wrenching her arm and blowing a spray of snow in all directions.

Boyd locked his hands around the gun and angled it away from his legs. "Claire, honest to Pete, you terrify me."

The shock on his face wasn't humorous in the least, but a sense of hysteria snaked through her and made her snort.

"You could have shot my foot off."

"I... I just wanted to give the gun back to you," she said, her voice shaking from fear and laughter.

He blew out a breath. "I'm beginning to think this was a dumb idea."

"You told me not to be so serious."

"That didn't mean I wanted you to shoot me."

She grinned. "I'll try not to."

"Then release your grip." She let go, and he took the gun away from her. "Your first lesson is how to hold a gun."

He spent several minutes explaining how the revolver worked, how to handle and load it safely, and how to aim and shoot. Finally, he turned her toward their target and stood behind her. "Raise the revolver, and sight the target."

She lifted the gun with both hands, but it hurt her injured shoulder. "It's too heavy."

He moved behind her and put his arms around her. He cupped his hands beneath hers and lifted the gun to her eye level. "Can you see the target?"

"I could see it from home," she said, staring at the fat brown keg squatting in the middle of the white field.

"I meant through the sights."

"Oh. You mean those pointy little things that are getting in my way?"

"Wiseacre." He nipped her earlobe with his teeth.

She jerked away and the gun exploded, kicking her back against him.

"Claire..."

"Don't blame me!" She tipped her head to see him. "You bit me!"

"I did not. That was a nibble."

"Whatever. Your horseplay caused me to pull the trigger."

He rubbed the end of his cold nose against her ear. "Maybe we should forget about shooting the gun."

"Maybe I should use you as a target."

"Vicious woman."

"Reprobate."

"Guilty." He kissed her neck.

She longed to turn and kiss him, to savor his touch, his mouth, but she drew away because it was safer than where they were headed. "If we're going to shoot this thing, kindly remove your finger from behind the trigger."

His chuckle warmed her. "Just protecting myself."

"Let's get this over with."

He acquiesced without argument and helped her steady the revolver. "Sight it at the center of the keg."

She aimed and fired, but the shot missed the target. "I can't do this. It nearly knocks me over when it fires."

"Spread your feet, keep one slightly behind the other, and lock your elbows."

Maneuvering in the deep snow was nearly impossible, but she managed to steady herself.

"I'm going to brace you with my body," he said, fitting his chest and hips against her.

"If I don't hit that target, Mr. Grayson, I'm going to know this was a ploy."

He laughed and nudged her hands up. "Come on, before you freeze to death. You're shaking."

"I'm exhausted. This gun weighs more than I do."

"Quit stalling."

She pulled the trigger and hit the top of the keg. "Good, but aim a little lower next time to allow for the concussion."

His instructions came on warm breaths of air that caressed her ear and made her shiver. It would be so easy to turn around and kiss him. Maybe she should. Maybe she should admit her attraction and... no... no it would be foolish to give him that power. He was already bending her to his will. But it felt divine to be held against him. It would be heaven to be kissed and caressed and...

She pulled the trigger, the successive blasts shattering her fantasy and clearing her mind as she emptied the revolver.

"Good job." He gave her a light hug and let her lower her arms. "That wasn't so bad, was it?"

"Aside from getting my ear bitten, my fingers frozen, and my shoulder dislocated, it was a grand adventure."

He leaned around her shoulder and gave her a playful, lusty kiss on the cheek that connected with a loud smack. "Feel better?"

"You've obviously forgotten that I'm holding a weapon."

"The gun is empty, darling."

"Yes, but it's heavy enough to knock out a bull."

He laughed and guided her back to the carriage. "Honestly, you have no sense of adventure." He was teasing her, but she sensed the truth behind his words. Her childhood had been filled with adventure, but she hadn't embraced her sense of daring since eloping with Jack. Maybe that's why she faced each day as something to get through, instead of seeing it as the opportunity she'd once believed it to be.

She climbed into the carriage and felt a deep sadness well up in her as he drove them back toward town.

"It worries me when you're so quiet."

"I'm just cold," she said, but a sense of loss pervaded her body. What had happened to the half-wild, willful girl, who'd tested her parents' patience on a daily basis? Her antics had made them laugh and chastise her by turns, but their house had been full of horseplay and laughter.

Boyd pulled the carriage to a stop in front of her house, and anxiety filled her. She didn't want to be alone. She didn't want to hear the gasps and whispers of other people making love.

"Would you like some hot cocoa or tea?" she asked, craving his company

He climbed out of the carriage then helped her out. "I've got to return the carriage to Radford and Evelyn's livery then take care of a few things at the saloon."

"Don't tell me you're opening tonight. I won that poker game, Boyd. You promised to close."

"I intend to. But I need to feed Sailor and clean the bar." He handed the revolver back to her. "I'll stop by later to check on you and Anna."

She clenched her mittens around the heavy gun, resisting the urge to beg him to come inside.

"Thank you for the lesson."

"Thank you for not shooting my foot off." She smiled, realizing how much Boyd brightened her days, how he never ceased to bring a smile to her face.

"I'll see you later," he said then jogged back to the carriage.

As he drove off down Main Street, she stood on the porch wondering when she'd begun to consider having an affair with him.

Chapter Twenty-four

"Sailor! Leave that alone." Boyd pushed the dog away from the spilled glass of whiskey then reached for a rag.

The dog circled back for another lick.

"Don't whine to me if you end up sick."

Sailor sniffed the floorboards then flopped down by the door, staring at Boyd with accusing eyes.

"Life is like that, pal." Boyd washed his hands at the sink then poured himself another whiskey.

He leaned against the bar and studied the smooth curves and graceful valleys his father had carved in the ornate shelving unit. It was a master's work. The mark of a great man's passion.

Boyd knew each ridge and gully, each scroll and crest that transformed the natural pieces of mahogany, birch, and holly into a one of a kind masterpiece. He knew each section that his own knife had carved, where his father had guided his hand, where he'd boldly displayed his own talent.

They carved, sanded, and varnished the piece together.

Boyd spent each minute at his father's side, watching, learning, testing, proving himself. Some nights they worked shoulder-to-shoulder in focused silence. Other nights Boyd and his father exchanged light banter or clowned and laughed, while challenging each other to a higher level of expertise.

Boyd expected to spend his life like that, sharing his days with his brothers at their sawmill and his evenings working beside his father in their wood shop.

But his father had grown too crippled to work.

Then he'd broken his hip.

A year later, he was dead.

Boyd traced his fingers over the furrowed wood. How many hours had he spent examining the mirrored shelf, the last project he and his father had worked on together? How many times had his chest cramped with grief? With regret?

How many times had he avoided his image in this mirror?

A shadow shifted across the glass, and Claire's reflection looked back at him, but he didn't turn around. She wouldn't be there. Her image was a frequent visitor in his mind. To see her face, or her fleeting smile, was nothing new.

"Can you see your future in that mirror?" she asked.

Sailor leapt to his feet with a happy bark, and Boyd spun to face her.

She scratched Sailor's head, but looked at Boyd. "You said I had no sense of adventure. Maybe you're right. I want to understand. About you. About this." Her gesture encompassed the saloon. "Show me what this is all about."

He was far from drunk, and yet her request baffled him.

To his surprise, she moved forward and picked up the bottle of whiskey. "Show me what the attraction is to drinking alcohol, and to spending time in a saloon." She held the bottle out to him. "I assume you drink this from a glass?"

He took the whiskey from her, mildly horrified at the thought of a woman like Claire enjoying hard liquor. "Why the sudden interest?"

"Maybe I haven't considered both sides of this issue fairly." Sincerity filled her voice. "I want to understand who you are. I want to understand why you and other men choose this life."

How could he explain when he didn't know the answer himself?

He put the whiskey bottle back on the shelf then shooed Sailor away from the bar. The dog flopped down on his bed beneath the billiard table.

"You shouldn't have left the house alone. I'll take you home."

"Anna knows I'm here." She pressed her hands to his chest to stop him from stepping around her. "I'm not leaving until I experience a night in a saloon."

He laughed. "Don't be ridiculous."

Her chin shot up and she glared at him. "Don't insult me. I've made my position on intemperance specific and clear, but you've never shown me one reason to support your view. Show me now." She retrieved the whiskey bottle and held it out to him. "Convince me to stop marching for temperance. "

Her eyes sparkled with challenge. He'd rather kiss her than drink whiskey, but she was so sincere in her quest that he couldn't turn her away.

He exchanged the whiskey for a jug of wine. "What do you want to know?" he asked, filling two glasses.

"What do you do here? What do you talk about? What attracts men to alcohol? Why do you like being here?"

He handed her a glass. "This could take a while."

"I've got all night." To his shock, she lifted her glass and drained it. Her face pruned, her eyes squinted, and her body quivered in reaction.

He burst into laughter. "You were supposed to sip that."

She clutched her stomach and leaned against the bar. "I wish I would have."

He laughed again and gestured for her to follow him. "Come on." He took the bottle of wine, rounded the bar, and nodded for her to sit beside him. "Relax. That's what most men come here to do."

She took off her coat and laid it over the bar then perched her perfectly rounded bottom on the edge of a barstool.

"They can relax in their parlors with their families," she said.

He filled their glasses then braced his elbow on the bar.

"When a man sits in his parlor, he thinks of all the unfinished chores he should be doing, or the attention he should be giving his wife and children, or the neighbor he should be helping. When he sits in a saloon, he doesn't have his family or his fields to remind him of his duties and obligations."

"That's exactly why I'm fighting to close these places," She lowered her half empty glass to the bar. "His family needs him at home, or in the fields, or anyplace that supports them. Your saloon merely tempts him away from his commitments."

"That's not true."

"It is." She finished her drink then reached for the wine bottle.

He grabbed the neck and stopped her. "If you don't want to be sick, I would suggest you pass."

"I'm perfectly capable of drinking wine with you."

"I agree, but not at my pace, and definitely not double my pace."

"I didn't come here for a lecture. I'm here to learn about this life. I intend to experience all the sin and vice your saloon has to offer."

"Darling, you couldn't sustain the shock."

Something dark flickered in her eyes. "You have no idea what I can endure."

It dawned on him that he wasn't talking to a virgin, but rather an experienced widow, who understood the layers of their conversation. She was daring him to treat her as his equal, to test her intelligence and grit.

"Are you certain you can handle the education, Claire?"

"Quite." She tugged on the bottle. "Go ahead and indulge all your bad habits. You can pretend I'm a man for the evening."

The wine had gone straight to her head. It must have. Even during his worst drunk he couldn't mistake her for a man.

But she was interesting with her guard down and her dander up. The scruples and secrets she used as a shield had been washed away by her first glass of wine. It would be interesting to see what another few ounces would wash away.

He took the bottle from her then filled her glass. "Sip that one," he instructed then placed the bottle out of her reach. She teetered on her chair, and he frowned. "Sit back and put your feet on that rail." He pointed to a brass rail attached to the bar, eight inches off the floor.

She slid back on the stool and propped her feet on the rail. "That's a definite improvement. Now, if the rail were heated, I could be quite content to sit here and warm my feet for a spell.

"Only a woman would think of something like that." He patted his thigh. "Lean back and put your feet up here."

She glanced at him. "Now you're being ridiculous."

"I'm just offering to warm your feet. There's no one here to tell you it's improper. Now put them up here—unless you've changed your mind about sin and vice and want me to take you home."

She hesitated then lifted her chin and swung her knees toward him. "I'm staying."

He slid his chair back to allow her to stretch out her legs. She put her feet in his lap but eyed him warily while he unlaced her boots and pulled them off. He dropped her boots on the floor then slipped his palms over her cold feet.

"Mmmm... that's good." Her eyes widened. "I mean, the wine is good."

He grinned. "Of course."

"I was trying to make a point." Her brow furrowed as if she were searching for the thread of their conversation.

He nearly laughed, but bit his lip. "We were talking about why the men come to my saloon."

"Right." She sloshed the burgundy wine in her glass. "So why do they?"

"For camaraderie."

"Oh..."

Her shivery moan sent blood singing through his veins. He wanted to kiss her. He wanted to start nibbling at her slender ankles and kiss all the way up her sleek, long legs until he reached the apex of her thighs. And then...

"Those men can find companionship at home with their wives," she said, her chin lifted in challenge.

"What?"

"Those men should give their wives more credit."

"Oh. Right." Now he was fighting to keep his mind on subject. "My saloon isn't meant to draw men away from their families or responsibilities, Claire. They also come here to seek information to help with their crops and businesses."

She frowned. "Do you expect me to believe that?"

"It's true. Some men want to play a game or two of billiards after sweating in a factory all day." He shrugged. "They come to saloons for all sorts of reasons."

"Why do they come to your saloon?" She glanced around the room then looked at him. "The bar is beautiful, but I can't believe they come for the decor. What draws them here?" His gut reaction was to swing the conversation to another topic like making love, but he could sense her sincerity, her honest desire to understand what this place meant to him and his patrons. And she was starting to relax. The tension had drained from her shoulders, and the frown lines between her eyebrows had dissolved. She probably didn't even realize she was flexing her feet beneath his fingers or emitting small sighs that were boiling his blood. "It's a refuge to most of us." He watched her intently to see if she would scoff.

"From what?" she asked, her expression openly curious.

"Responsibility, I guess." He struggled silently for a way to explain. "Men carry a financial burden on their backs all day. In hard times, it's heavy. Sometimes a man just needs a place where he can blow off steam before it builds into something ugly."

"We have a place. Or... we will soon. We've been raising money for a public parlor where men can go instead of... here."

How ridiculous. What man would want to frequent a place like that? Boyd wouldn't. Perhaps the men who'd signed the temperance pledge would use the room. But why? For what?

She lowered her lashes as if she knew the idea was ridiculous and that it would never replace the saloons. "We're thinking of providing food and a place to read or play games." She peeked from beneath her golden lashes. "The men could meet women there, too."

Women? Any sane, unmarried man would jump at the opportunity to meet women in a social setting like that. If the women got behind this, their public parlor just might work. But not for long. Once the boys met the available girls, and married, they would head right back to his saloon.

He smiled because she seemed so hopeful, and he didn't have the heart to tell her it wouldn't work. "I'm sure the men will appreciate having an option."

"It's not meant to be an option."

"I see. Well, I guess I'll have to work harder to convince you to stop trying to close my saloon." He gave her toes a light squeeze. He had to get his hands off her before he slid them up her legs and gave her all the sin and vice she could handle. "Let's see if you have the daring to learn how to play billiards."

She toasted him with her glass then took a healthy swallow. "This is really quite lovely." She slid off the barstool in a rather loose-jointed manner then swung her glass toward the billiard table. "Lead on."

"Would you like some help with your boots?"

She pressed her palm to the front of her dress. Her toes peeped out from beneath the heavy blueberry-colored velvet. "I think I'll leave them off. This seems like the perfect opportunity to let my hair down."

He grinned. "Claire, darling, I'm really beginning to like you."

She returned his smile, warm and open. "Our friendship is rather... unexpected, isn't it?"

They were more than friends, but it was enough for the time being.

Sailor scrambled from beneath the table and butted his nose against her legs. She knelt and hugged his spotted head to her cheek. "The Ormands have found a house and will be leaving in the morning, so you can come visit me again."

"That will improve his life—and mine—considerably," Boyd said. "Sailor's been irritating me all day."

"Good for you, Sailor." She giggled and kissed the dog's head. "I need all the help I can get." The dog stretched and gave a huge tongue-curling yawn that made her laugh.

Boyd watched her play with his dog, enjoying her new, uninhibited side. Sailor wheezed and pushed against her, making her wobble. Boyd caught her elbow and pulled her to her feet.

"You've ruined my dog," he said.

"I'm just teaching him how to treat a lady."

"That was supposed to be my job."

"Sailor's better for my intervention." Claire finished her wine then licked her lips and grinned up at him. "After that first swallow it goes down easy. Should I get the bottle?"

"Absolutely not." He handed her a billiard stick. "You won't be able to play if you drink too much."

"I feel fine. In fact, better than ever." She spread her arms and winced. "Well, almost fine."

He nodded toward her shoulder. "Is it causing you much pain?"

"Surprisingly, no. It is sore, and ugly, but the doctor says it should heal quickly." She set her glass on the edge of the table and pointed her stick at a corner pocket. "Do we just whack the balls into those holes?"

"Sort of." He moved her glass to the shelf that ran the length of the west wall. "You hit this cue ball into one of those balls to direct it into a pocket. Like this," he said, leaning over the table.

Years of playing made the move fluid, but he tried to slow it down for Claire's sake. The cue ball sent the nine ball in a forty-five degree angle where it dropped into the pocket with a thunk.

She studied the table, her eyes wide with wonder. "You weren't even aiming in that direction."

He showed her how to direct the balls. "We'll play fifteen-ball. The object is to sink the highest numbered balls in any of those six pockets. The first person to reach sixty-one points wins."

"Can I hit one?"

"Of course. Take several shots until you get the feel of it."

On her first shot, her stick lifted out of her fingers.

"Hold it like this." He took the stick and demonstrated for her then handed it back.

She adjusted her grip, but her aim was bad.

"Stay there." He placed his hand on her back to keep her bent over the table. Two thoughts raced through his mind as he stared at her rounded behind, but he chose the safer course of action and put his arms around her shoulders. "I'm going to show you how to eye this up."

To his surprise, she didn't tense up or pull away. With a happy yip, Sailor nosed up against them.

"Not this time, pal. Go lie down." Boyd nudged him away with his knee. Sailor trotted to the stove and flopped down with a huff.

"Keep the stick loose in your grip," Boyd said, turning back to his lesson with an eagerness that shamed him.

"Like this?" Claire sawed the stick between her slender fingers, driving him mad, making him cap his hand over hers. Her hands felt cool, but her hip burned hot against his thigh.

He gulped a breath and focused on the table. "Imagine a straight line from that corner pocket through the center of that green ball." He touched the tip of her stick to the ball. "You want the cue ball to hit this ball right here."

"All right." She drew the stick back with a quick jerk, but he stopped her hand.

"The motion should be smooth most of the time." He moved the stick across her fingers in a slow arc, cursing his train of thought that circled his roguish mind on one track. Her beautiful body. In his bed. "Easy," he said, speaking to both himself and Claire. "Like this."

She turned her head, putting her face within inches of his. "Like a bow across violin strings." The wine brought a pink flush to her cheeks and made her eyes sparkle.

"I've never thought about it that way," he said, battling the urge to kiss her. "But it has merit."

"It's like an art."

She was art. Graceful, glowing, beautiful. He wanted to smooth his palms over the peaks and valleys of her body, to learn her shape, to feel the grain of muscle and tendon along her bones, the texture of her skin. He wanted to tighten his arms around her and taste the skin where her neck and shoulder met, let her scent fill his nostrils like fresh-cut pine.

"Can I try it now?" she asked.

He forced himself to step back. "Line it up before you shoot."

She squinted at the ball, drew her stick back then pushed it forward with an admirably smooth stroke. The second ball hit the edge of the pocket and rolled back onto the table.

Her eyebrows lowered in concentration as she lined up another shot. Five minutes or more passed while she pushed the ball around the table, giving Boyd time to tamp down his wayward thoughts. Finally, she sank it in the corner pocket.

"I did it." Her eyes were filled with such surprised delight, he laughed. Sailor raised his head and gave her a wide grin.

"Stay," Boyd ordered, knowing the dog was on the brink of lunging to his feet to plaster Claire with affection. He didn't blame the dog. He wanted to plaster her with affection too.

"Can I shoot another one?" she asked.

"Of course." He nodded toward the table. "Hit a few more then we'll play a game."

He watched while she bent over the table, maneuvering her graceful body to accommodate her sore shoulder, moving the stick to make a shot. She missed often, but wouldn't give up until she'd sunk the ball. What she lacked in skill, she made up for with determination. He could watch her for hours.

After she'd dropped the last ball, she stood up and braced her hand on the table. "I'm ready." she said, giving him a bright, self-assured smile.

He bit his lip to stop his grin. Her slight imbalance made it obvious she was feeling the wine, but she was trying to hide it by bracing her hip against the table.

He was ready too, but not for a game of billiards. To distract himself, he walked to the bar, retrieved the jug of wine then filled their glasses. "Highest score wins, so aim for the highest-numbered balls."

She raised her glass in a mock salute. "What are we wagering?"

He'd like to wager her into his bed, but he doubted she would appreciate his suggestion. He scoured his mind for something that wouldn't chase her across the street to her sad boardinghouse. Nothing but undressing her came to mind. "I can't think of anything."

She set her glass on the shelf. "If I lose, I'll bake a pie for you. If you lose, you have to show me some of your carvings."

He chalked his stick and moved to the table. "That's an awfully tame wager for a lady who wants to indulge in all the sin and vice my saloon has to offer."

As he'd expected, her chin lifted, but the move unbalanced her. She gripped the edge of the table and stared up at him. "Name a fitting wager then."

"A kiss."

Her gaze dropped to his mouth.

"Or something less threatening if you don't have the nerve," he teased.

Her gaze snapped back to his. "All right. But it must be a totally improper kiss."

Oh, she was amusing. "How improper?"

"Sinful. The kind of kiss you would give a woman while... in private."

The stick slipped through his hand and hit the floor.

"Or something less threatening if you don't have the nerve," she said, the challenge so thick in her voice it made him snicker.

She reached for her glass, but he caught her hand. She wasn't slurring her words, but she'd lost the crispness of her speech. He didn't want her to be too drunk to remember the kiss. Because he was going to get one.

"Save that for after the game." He turned her toward the table then scooped his stick off the floor. "I'll break then you can shoot."

He bent over the table, but stopped in surprise when he realized his hands were shaking. The sight stunned him. Only three events in his life had made him tremble. Carrying his father's coffin had been one of them. Pulling his brother Kyle from a burning building was another.

The third was the battle he waged each time he worked on the statue.

Never had he trembled with need for a woman.

Now his body quaked and he ached to touch Claire, to kiss her and convince her to go upstairs with him. To his bed. To make love.

"What's wrong?" she asked.

He stepped away from the table and blew out a breath. This was ridiculous. It was... unnerving.

He forced himself to calm down, to focus on the game, to stop acting like a schoolboy. But his hands still shook, and he did a bad job of breaking the billiard balls.

"My turn?" she asked, her look so innocent and trusting that he felt the urge to warn her to run, to get away from him before he devoured her.

She missed her shot, but didn't pout or ask for another chance. In fact, she insisted that they play by the rules.

"It's grown rather warm in here, don't you think?" She pressed her palms to her flushed face.

He had an inferno roaring inside him, but her comment surprised him. He had let the fire die down, and had worried it might be getting too cool for her. "I can open a window."

"I can't risk being seen."

He grinned. "I suppose this would be difficult to explain to your lady friends."

"Can you imagine their faces if they saw me drinking wine and playing billiards?" She giggled and clapped a hand over her mouth, her gorgeous blue eyes sparkling with laughter.

"I'd pay a small fortune to see that."

Laughter bubbled out between her fingers. She lowered her hand, revealing a wide white smile. It was the first time he'd noticed that one front tooth was slightly ahead of the other. It was barely noticeable, but something about the slight imperfection warmed him and made him want to hug her.

"Wouldn't it be gay to do something naughty like that then wind back time so nobody would know what you've done?" she asked.

The implications of what she was suggesting astonished him. He planted the stick on the floor, waiting to hear what she might say next. "What naughty thing would you do if you wouldn't be found out?"

She lowered her lashes. "I can't tell you."

"Why not? You're trusting me not to tell anyone about your visit tonight."

"True."

"Well then, you can trust me to keep your secret."

She seemed to consider for a moment then she gave him an impish smile "I'd go swimming without any clothes on."

He gasped in mock horror and stumbled against the billiard table. She burst into laughter, deepening the flush in her cheeks, but took his teasing in good humor.

"What would you do?" she asked.

He lifted his hand to stroke her warm, beautiful face. "I'd make love to you."

Her breath whooshed out and her eyes widened.

"I've shocked you," he said, but he had also shocked himself. As much as he wanted her, she was not the sort of woman to have an affair. He knew that.

She gripped the table and looked up at him, her blue eyes wide. He liked that she was so aware of him, that she felt his desire for her.

"I should be used to your teasing," she whispered.

"You're no innocent, Claire." He stroked his thumb across her jaw, enjoying the flare of passion in her eyes. "You know I wasn't teasing." He enjoyed the blush that flooded her cheeks. "Shall we finish our game?"

At her nervous nod, he stooped down to eye up his shot. A tiny pearl button dropped onto the felt tabletop in front of him. He glanced up and stopped breathing.

Claire was unbuttoning the bodice of her dress.

Chapter Twenty-five

Claire tugged at the neckline of her dress. *Sakes alive*! She was burning up. She released several buttons then fanned her bare neck and chest. She had to cool down, sober up, regain her common sense. Her body had turned traitor, craving and yearning and leading her astray.

Boyd was purposely testing her, as he had from the moment they met. She knew that, and had even grown to like matching her will against his—but tonight, he was too tempting.

Looking at him made her want to throw propriety out the window. He was bent over the table, bracing himself on one hand, the billiard stick forgotten in the other as he stared at her.

"What are you doing?" he asked, his voice oddly strained.

Glancing down, she realized her bodice was gaping open. She was showing her body, revealing herself to him as boldly as a tavern wench. She'd been desperate for air, but suddenly Claire understood she needed more than air in her lungs. She needed freedom. Living with Jack had suffocated her. Her fear had suffocated her. She needed to breathe and gulp and gasp, to sing and dance and laugh. She needed to *live*.

She hadn't meant to tempt Boyd, had only meant to cool her flushed face, but now that he'd seen her partially exposed, she was sure she wasn't imagining the hunger in his eyes. Something wild whispered through her, daring her to shed the harness of propriety, to embrace her freedom and this gorgeous man for one glorious evening.

No one will know.

Her pulse throbbed beneath her fingers, reminding her she was alive, that risk was part of living, that tonight might be her only chance at passion. Needing to bolster her courage, she picked up her glass of wine.

He lowered his billiard stick. "Are we changing games?" he asked, his voice low and unsteady.

Yes. She had changed the game. And she liked it. She liked the idea of seducing him. Especially in his own saloon.

The idea was so wildly out of character for her, and so wonderfully ironic, she giggled.

"You'd better not drink the rest of that." He reached for her wine glass, but she stepped away from him.

The movement felt odd, like she was no longer solid, but rather a wave of water rolling across the floor.

She gratefully sank onto the piano bench. "Are you afraid of me, Boyd?"

"I'm afraid *for* you."

His genuine look of concern touched her. Underneath his flippant and charming manner, he was a sincere, and even honorable, man.

She set her wine glass on top of the piano. "I'm fine. I just want to play a song for you."

He braced his elbow beside her glass. "I thought we were playing billiards."

She waved a hand. "We'll get back to that." Her vision blurred as she looked down. Maybe she wasn't fine. She blinked and squinted at the black and white keys. "How about a temperance song?"

"No thanks."

The disdain in his voice made her laugh. "I was joking. I'm going to make up a song for you." Thankfully, her fingers functioned better than her brain, and she managed to play a verse of Cold Claire.

"I know that song."

"Not my version." She grinned up at him while naughty words—new words, wild words—flitted through her mind.

"I can hardly wait to hear this." He gestured for her to begin. "Show me how much nerve you have."

She lifted her chin and stroked the keys with authority.

The sound reverberated through the room as she began to sing.

I know a man who's impudent and bold.
He claims he's a prince, but I suspect he's a toad.

"Charming," he drawled, his voice rich with irony as a grin broke across his face.

She laughed and missed her next verse. "Oops." She lifted her fingers from the keys then started over.

He is handsome and charming and a little too bold, but there's something
I like about that naughty toad.

His face scrunched as if he'd bitten into a lemon. "Your lyrics are awful." She burst into laughter, and her hands slipped off the keys. "I know, but I enjoyed making them up. Play a song with me."

He sat and began the Moonlight Sonata.

"Oh, how lovely. My mother used to play this song." Her heart sang with memories of being ten years old and dancing with her father in their parlor.

She lay her palm on the piano, feeling the vibrations radiate up her arm. The music moved through her, and she ached to be held, to be touched, to be loved.

"This is so beautiful," she whispered.

"So are you, Claire."

Her breath hitched and he stopped playing.

"Dance with me." He pulled her to her feet and slipped his arms around her waist. "Hum your favorite song, and I'll do my best to keep time."

She smiled and started humming a verse of "Cold Claire."

He laughed and tightened his arms around her. "You should drink more often."

"I do feel rather friendly tonight."

"Is that bad?"

"I don't know."

She lowered her head to his shoulder, hanging onto him as their bodies swayed in the silence. "This doesn't feel bad."

"It isn't bad." His strong fingers played down the muscles of her back as if he were stroking piano keys, sending delicious shivers down her spine.

She remembered this rush of excitement in her blood.

She remembered love.

Fitting herself against him, she burrowed her nose into the crook of his neck. He smelled of soap and bay rum cologne, and warm skin, his own particular smell. "You smell so good, I'm tempted to bite your neck."

He gazed down at her. "You're a silly but amazing lady."

She was. In his arms, she was everything he claimed her to be. They were amazing together.

She felt the unmistakable plunge of her hair falling down her back, and knew he'd somehow pulled her pins free. His full, tempting lips tugged up at one corner, like he was too pleased with himself for words. "You said you were going to let your hair down."

She had let her hair down, hadn't she? She'd swallowed three glasses of wine, shed her boots, unbuttoned her gown, and played a bawdy song on his piano. If that didn't constitute letting her hair down, what did?

"It's just us, Claire. You can relax with me."

"That could be dangerous," she said softly. Couldn't he tell? She knew exactly how dangerous it was to relax with a man. But she wasn't afraid. She liked being touched by Boyd Grayson, charmer, rake, reprobate. She loved being caressed and held tight, deliciously tight, against his tall, hard body.

A small, rational corner of her brain cried out to be careful. He was a man, a strong man, a violent man when angered, a man who had loved many women. She had loved one man, a strong, violent man, who had tried to break her body and had broken her heart.

Lord, her brain was reeling. She was at the edge again, the very edge of loving a new man, her second man, a man she did not fully know.

Would he change without warning? Would he hurt her? Would he hit her? Would he mock her, punish her, desert her? Would he make her wish she was dead? That he too was dead?

She'd almost wished for death, hers and Jack's, at one point, but she survived. She was alive. And falling in love again.

Oh, how her head spun.

Boyd was a man of experience. She'd shared her bed with Jack and no one else, not ever. Early on, she enjoyed it, but then her bed had become one more cage she couldn't escape.

The tremor passing through her wasn't fear though. It was desire, sharp and intense. It was passion, hot and wild and demanding.

And what was wrong with desire?

She couldn't get pregnant. Why shouldn't she experience desire and passion? Why couldn't Boyd be her Abe? He was perfect for the position. He desired her, but surely didn't want the bonds of marriage. He wouldn't hurt her. He wouldn't cage her.

He would be content with passion.

He would keep their secret.

She could have one night of passion without selling her soul.

Excitement shook her as he pulled her closer to him. "Are you cold?" he asked, his voice low and husky.

"No." She was hot with need—her need, his need. Heat radiated from his body and burned through to hers. She lifted her hand and touched her fingers to his mouth.

He inhaled sharply and his eyes darkened. She looked into those eyes and saw her freedom.

He lowered his head and kissed her, eyes open, letting her see his need, the way she was shaking his control. Not an ounce of resistance resided in her as he pulled her against him. She felt weightless and giddy, reckless and wild, and oh, wonderfully free.

Nothing could possibly compare to the feeling of his arms around her, the heat and hardness of his body against hers, the slow, probing of his tongue in her mouth.

It was shocking.

It was sinful.

It was worse and better than anywhere she'd ever been.

And so unbelievably fulfilling.

The loneliness and pain and isolation that had cloaked her life fell away. Her thoughts and anxieties turned to vapor and vanished on her breath. What a blessing to be free of that voice in her head, to simply *feel*.

Warmth surged through her as she fit her hips more tightly to his groin. A raspy groan rumbled his chest, thrilling her, encouraging her.

No one would know.

And she would never tell.

In the pleasant haze, he broke away. She kissed his neck and licked his earlobe. His breath rushed out, and he buried his face in her hair.

No one would know.

She wanted to be free of her dress, free of everything that kept her from being skin to skin with him, but he gripped her arms and set her away from him.

"I'm taking you home," he said, but his voice was hoarse, and his body did not make a move in the direction of her boardinghouse.

"We haven't finished our billiard game," she said, not caring a whit. This new game was much more exciting.

"We'll finish it in the morning," he said firmly, but his unsteady voice gave him away. She'd turned the tables on him, and now *he* was fighting the temptation she was dangling in his face.

"It's my shot. Are you afraid I'll win?"

He sighed against her ear, his breath spiraling hot sensations all the way down between her legs. Perversely, he leaned back and gestured to the table "Go ahead."

She sauntered over, swaying her hips the provocative way Jack's lady friends used to do. The enhanced motion tested her balance, but she kept her head high and steadied herself by bracing her hand on the table edge.

She picked up her stick and eyed up her shot.

"Claire?" She glanced up.

Boyd stood beside the table, feet spread, arms akimbo, wearing a grin only the man's lover could understand.

Was she to be his next lover?

She wanted to be, Heaven forgive her.

He nodded toward the ball she was aiming at. She blinked, trying to focus on the bright red object against the dark green felt.

"You need to shoot the ball with the higher number to gain enough points to win." He pointed to the black ball near the corner pocket. "You need to sink that one."

"Oh." She flushed at her mistake. "I knew that. I was just... I was making sure I wouldn't touch your ball."

He barked a laugh then bit his lip.

Suddenly, she realized how he might have taken her comment, and she bit her own lip to keep from smiling. But she was past blushing now. She was committed to her night of sin, to opening the door of the safe little cage she'd been hiding in.

He leaned down and braced his hands on the edge of the table. They were tan and manly beneath his white shirt cuffs, and she imagined how good it would feel to have them roam her body, squeeze her breasts, cup her hips and... touch her lower.

Her breath gasped out as if he'd stroked the cradle of her thighs. She couldn't play this game with him a minute longer! And how could he? Was he feeling this same glorious rush of longing that was pounding through her body?

"You'd better sink enough balls to win, Claire. If you don't, you're going to owe me a kiss, because I won't miss my shot."

She was willing to owe him a lot more than a kiss, but how could she if he wouldn't ask?

"I'll move away if I'm distracting you."

She didn't want him to move away. She wanted him to pull her into his arms and kiss her until morning. Her stomach fluttered as she angled her tortured body over the table. "It's not necessary. A child could make this shot." The ball was lined up for a direct shot into the corner pocket.

She drew the stick back, feeling the wood slide between her fingers. Would Boyd's back and hips feel smooth like that?

Ignore him! Think about the shot.

She squinted, but her head felt light. Was it the wine? Was that why she was pulsing with desire for the man leaning against the table? Or was she finally being honest with herself for the first time in her life? Could she risk a bit of safety for a taste of passion?

Yes.

She wanted a lover.

She wanted *Boyd* to be her lover.

She laid the stick on the table without taking her shot. "I need to check my shoulder. May I use your water closet?"

Concern filled his eyes. "Would you rather I took you home?"

"I'd like to finish our game," she said, hoping she was convincing. If she had her way, they wouldn't finish the billiard game tonight.

He clasped her elbow and turned her toward a staircase that led to the second floor. "We'll need to go upstairs. Trust me. You don't want to use the water closet down here."

Sailor leapt to his feet, but Boyd waved him back before the dog could follow them.

Upstairs, he closed his apartment door behind them. "Wait here while I light a lantern."

He struck a match, and the little blaze lit up his handsome face, giving him a golden, princely glow, marking all the angles she coveted to touch—that she *would* touch. Slowly the room around them filled with light.

The kitchen walls were painted a warm buff color and topped with ornamental moldings and walnut wainscoting that matched the sideboard and cupboards. A small four-plate cookstove sat in the corner, and a tea table with two Windsor bow-back armchairs bordered a tall window. A small corner hutch, devoid of dishes, completed the kitchen furnishings. Clean and spare, the room was somehow welcoming.

This was his home, the place where he took off his mask. Being in his private space was like being inside his skin, and her stomach fluttered with excitement. Would she finally see the intimate, secret side of him tonight?

He picked up the lantern and guided her out of the kitchen.

The parlor was a dark, manly-looking room with pine wallboards painted forest green. Sturdy hickory armchairs and a camel-back sofa were upholstered in a green damask fabric. But the red carpet with a saucy green and yellow pattern made her head spin.

She shifted her gaze to the dark mahogany mantel above the fireplace, and tried to remember how many glasses of wine she had.

Oblivious to her spinning head, Boyd set the lantern on a hickory coffee table then lit another lantern at the end of the sofa. "The water closet is in there." He nodded toward a door off the parlor. "Take one of the lanterns with you."

She fumbled with the tiny buttons that closed the bodice of her velvet dress. "My fingers don't seem to want to cooperate. Would you help me remove my corsage?"

Wariness stole into his eyes, but he moved to stand in front of her. She lowered her arms to her side, giving him access to the tiny pearl buttons, to herself.

His artist's hands were nimble, but too efficient, as if he didn't trust himself to be near her. After he opened the buttons along her bodice and wrists, she turned her back to him, pretending a modesty she didn't feel. He peeled the fabric over her shoulders then cupped his palms over her bare, upper arms. Gooseflesh speckled her skin as he drew his warm hands down her arms, pushing the soft material to her wrists.

His warm breath caressed her neck.

She longed to lean back in his arms, but he tugged the sleeves over her hands and stepped away. He draped the top section of her dress over the arm of the sofa. "There's a mirror above the basin," he said, his voice low and gritty.

Until now, she had considered honor a virtue, but the vein of integrity keeping him from making love to her was becoming a major obstacle to her plan of seducing him. How could he act so deliberate and controlled? Was he so used to undressing women that it didn't arouse his ardor?

She ducked into the spacious, and surprisingly clean, water closet. The instant she closed the door, she set the lantern on the cabinet and pressed her hand to her pounding heart. He couldn't be rejecting her. He had just told her he wanted her. He'd said he wanted to make love to her. And he'd flirted with her shamelessly almost from the moment they met. Was he waiting for a sign from her? She asked him to unbutton her dress. What more of an invitation did he need?

The mirror flashed her own conflicted expression back at her. She leaned toward the glass and peeked at the one-inch gash marking the crest of her shoulder. The slash of dark red blemished her skin, but it wasn't that bad, and it wasn't bleeding, thank goodness.

What if he changed his mind? She was as committed and as ready as she would ever be. She couldn't lose this opportunity. Somehow, she must force him to see her, to forget everything but her for this one night.

She turned away and unbuttoned the waist of her skirt and petticoats. They fell to the floor in a puddle of lace and velvet. She stepped free of the yards of fabric then bent down to remove her stockings.

The room tilted.

She braced her hand on the basin stand to steady herself. Was she drunk? Was that why she was peeling off her clothes in Boyd's water closet? Suddenly, her actions seemed illogical, reckless, irresponsible, absurd. What was she thinking?

Boyd wasn't Abe—and Claire wasn't her grandmother. She was a lonely widow who'd had too much wine. She would regret this tomorrow. She... oh, Lord, that wasn't true.

She must do this. *She must!* If she turned coward now, she would never forgive herself for passing up her one chance for a grand passion. She would never be free if she didn't exorcize Jack from her memory and embrace a new man, a new life—her *own* life.

It had to be tonight.

She rolled down her stockings, stripped them off her feet, and dropped them on the floor in a wrinkled heap.

Years of depending on herself allowed her to struggle out of her corset. It fell to the floor with the rest of her garments, and she took her first full breath since dressing that morning.

Shivering, she stood in her chemise and lace drawers, suddenly afraid of how Boyd would see her, how he would react to her outrageous behavior.

Would he find her too wanton?

Of course he would. How could he not?

But would he reject her for her wantonness?

She was dressed in her unmentionables, and bent on seducing him. What else could her behavior be called but wanton?

Daring.

Stupid.

Adventurous.

A gamble.

Back and forth her mind rushed, questioning and weighing the rewards and repercussions of her actions until she clenched her fists to her temples. Her racing heart could not endure this a moment longer. For better or for worse, she was going out there. She would storm his senses before he could think, before the serious, noble side of him demanded he act with honor. She wanted the charmer, the rake, the man who had been seducing her for weeks. *That* man would make love to her.

With her stomach cartwheeling, she wrenched open the door and stepped into the parlor.

———

Boyd looked up from the carving he'd been fiddling with. Before him stood Claire Ashier, the widow he wanted to seduce, the woman he wanted to protect. She was ethereal and glowing in her lacy white chemise and drawers. Silky, golden hair draped her narrow shoulders and breasts, lifting and falling with each panting breath from her parted lips. Her stormy blue eyes, filled with questions and doubts, were fixed on him.

"What the..." He cleared the squeak from his voice, but could barely force words from his tight throat. "What are you doing?"

She crossed the carpet and sat beside him on the sofa. "I'm ready to give you that sinful kiss," she whispered.

His knife and wood carving fell to the floor.

"Tonight," she said. "If you want me."

If he wanted her? Manic laughter welled up inside him. He wanted her so much he was shaking like a schoolboy in a brothel. He wanted her from the first time he'd seen her standing on her porch. That evening she tried to scare him by pointing her revolver at him, but she only intrigued him. Tonight, though, he knew real danger. Her bare skin and lacy garments were a weapon he couldn't defend himself against. Her nearly naked body was a lure from which he could not turn away.

She angled her body toward him, her long, bare, incredibly gorgeous legs stretched out beside his. "Do you want me?"

He wanted to devour her.

He gripped her arms and held her away from him. "Any man alive would want you."

"I don't want any man. I want you."

He could hardly believe this was the same Claire who mere weeks ago had refused to let him touch her foot. "I shouldn't have allowed you to drink so much wine."

"You didn't allow me to do anything," she said. "I'm capable of making my own decisions, and I've decided I want you."

She leaned forward and kissed him, fusing their mouths together with such heat, his mind reeled like a runaway tire hoop. She lifted her knee across his lap, fitting herself more tightly against him, killing him, killing his willpower, killing every thought but those of her.

He roamed his hands over her body, sculpting her rounded bottom beneath his palms, pulling her around to straddle his hips, promising himself he would stop soon.

He kissed her tenderly. She took the kiss deeper, pushing him to respond until his breath came in gasps against her cheek.

She arched her neck, offering her smooth white throat to his mouth. He tasted her, sucked and kissed and nibbled until she lifted his palm to her breast.

He groaned, believing he'd betrayed her with the wine. "We need to stop."

"We don't." She tugged her chemise up over her waist, over the full globes of her creamy taut breasts, over her head until she had fully bared her torso.

She was beyond beautiful, surpassing every dream he'd ever had. Hunger gnawed at him as he looked at her. She was no virgin. She knew what she was doing, what she was asking for.

"My imagination didn't do you justice." He stroked his thumbs across the hardened peaks of her dusty brown nipples, knowing he should stop, that she deserved more than a tumble on his sofa. She'd been hurt by her husband. He didn't want to add to her heartache.

She threaded her fingers in his hair and kissed his neck, her tongue swirling over his skin.

He needed to get her out of his arms, out of his house.

She raised her head, her eyes glassy from the wine, or passion, or both. Which gave him pause, which lured him on.

"Make love to me," she whispered.

She rocked her hips against his groin and sent his heartbeat ricocheting through his chest like a bullet in a canyon.

His body melted then hardened.

Her face was flushed and her hair flowed across her shoulders in waves of gold. She was too perfect. She had no idea what she was doing to him, of the inferno raging inside. He gripped her wrists to stop her from unbuttoning his shirt. "I'm burning, Claire. It's going to consume both of us if we don't stop."

"Let it burn," she said, her eyes fierce, her breath hot against his jaw. "Let our passion scorch the walls."

"I can't. I don't have anything to protect you from getting pregnant."

"I can't conceive." She rolled her hips against him, sending a stream of heat burning through his groin.

He gritted his teeth, shaking from the battle raging between his desire and his conscience. He gripped her arms and forced her to look at him. "Are you certain?"

"Yes." She covered his mouth with her own, pressed her bare breasts into his palms. Like an insistent wind, she curled around him, caressing him, bending him to her will until a groan of surrender tore free and he pulled her down beside him on the sofa.

Desire rolled through Boyd, boiling his blood, melting his will, burning away his resistance.

Claire moaned into his mouth as he moved his fingers over her, slipped them inside her drawers, stroking her until she was as wild and greedy as he felt. She fumbled with the buttons on his trousers, caressing his hardness where it strained against the cotton fabric. She freed him then closed her fingers around his turgid heat.

He groaned low in his throat, knowing he was lost, knowing she'd just sealed their fate. He gripped her hand and stopped her before she pushed him over the edge.

He reared back on his knees and shoved his trousers down over his hips. She untied her drawers, and he pulled them down her long legs and over her bare feet.

"Make love to me," she whispered.

He slid between her white thighs, entering her with a groan, satisfying the wrenching need pounding through his body. She gasped and lifted her hips, pressing her breasts against his chest.

"Oh, Boyd..." She arched her throat to his seeking mouth.

He kissed her neck, her breasts, her mouth as he rolled his hips between her thighs. She clutched his shoulders and cried out with her release.

He felt contractions shake her body. She tightened her legs around his hips, pulling him deeper, driving him to a shattering climax. But in the hard rush of his release, he regretted taking something so intimate from her. His body shuddered. His conscience shuddered. He'd been unbearably selfish.

The caress of her warm palms sliding beneath his shirt and up his bare back made him sorry he'd been so quick. He raised up on his elbows and saw a soft, satisfied smile on her swollen mouth. She'd enjoyed it, but he could have given her so much more. He'd let himself get carried away, had let his demanding body set the pace.

She tugged the back of his shirt. "Why don't you take this off?"

Her request surprised him. He'd expected her to grow shy and want to go home.

"It's not fair that I'm the only one who is completely exposed," she said, shaming him for yanking his drawers down like an unfeeling cad.

He rolled to her side. "I'll get your garments for you."

She hooked her arms around his neck. "Do you want me to leave?"

He wanted to keep her in his arms, beneath him or on top of him, all night. Every night. And that scared him. He couldn't tell her that, so he said nothing.

Her smile faded. "Are you disappointed?" she asked, insecurity bleeding back into her eyes.

Only in himself.

He stroked her cheek, the feel of her soft skin making him regret his hastiness. He'd needed her so badly, but had missed so much. "I hadn't planned for this to happen."

"Does that mean you're sorry?"

"Not in the way you think. I've wanted to make love with you since I met you. But I shouldn't have taken advantage of the situation."

"I came to you in my undergarments. How can you think you took advantage of something I was freely offering? I wanted this, Boyd." Her lashes settled lower, seductively lower, over her gorgeous eyes. "I'd like more."

So would he. More than she could ever know. "Are you certain you can't get pregnant?"

A deep sadness stole into her eyes, smothering the starlight he'd been admiring. She nodded and withdrew her arms from around his neck. "I had a bad miscarriage almost two years ago. The doctor said I'll never conceive again."

The desolation in her voice broke his jealously guarded heart wide open. He had brothers who had children. He had a niece and two nephews he adored. Deep in his soul, he hurt for her, felt her loss, understood her heartache.

Words were useless at times, and this was one of those times. He drew her against him. She came willingly, letting him hold her for a long, long time in his silent apartment, the two of them listening to the mantel clock ticking toward dawn.

He'd lain on his sofa hundreds of times, a few of those times with a woman, but never with this tenderness in his heart. He felt protective of Claire. He wanted to shield her from her own memories, from all the hurts she'd suffered, kiss away her tears, and fill her life with joy.

But he suspected the only way to offer comfort was to share her grief. He kissed the top of her head that she'd nestled beneath his chin. "Did Jack cause your miscarriage?"

⊷⊶

Claire drew back and met his eyes. "No," she said, understanding why Boyd was asking. "Jack wanted our baby. My body just wasn't fit enough to nurture a child."

Boyd's dark eyebrows tweaked inward, his gaze sweeping over her healthy body as if questioning how it could be true.

"I wasn't in the best of health at the time," she said, answering his unspoken question. Two years of fear, scant meals, and Jack's rages had taken a toll on her body. She shivered, glad that Jack, and that whole wretched existence, was behind her. "It's chilly in here. I'm thinking your bed would be far more comfortable," she said, praying he would understand her desperate need to be held for a while.

Long lashes half concealed his honey-brown eyes as he studied her. Finally, without a word, he pulled away and stood beside the couch. He hitched his trousers up over his hips and buttoned them.

Claire reached for her drawers, accepting his silence as a rejection.

"I'll take you in," he said. He bent down and slipped his arms beneath her. To her surprise, he cradled her body against his chest and carried her through a door off the parlor. He lowered her feet to a plush carpet beside a huge four-poster bed then turned back a thick quilt. She slipped between linens that smelled freshly laundered, and he tucked the bedding around her shivering body. "I'll build up the fire," he said then left the room.

She lay in the dark, hearing the rattle of the stove door and the thump of wood being chucked inside. Seconds later, the sound of water splashing told her he was in the water closet washing up. She relaxed back into the thick pillows. Her mind was still a little fuzzy, but she was nowhere near as confused as she'd been before making love with Boyd. In fact, she felt an amazing sense of peace.

She'd taken a risk—and a lover.

She'd opened the cage.

Boyd entered the bedchamber with a lantern and sat it on the stand beside the bed. He stood with a white towel hooked around his neck, his lean, hard torso completely bare. Dark hair fanned across his chest and over muscle and sinew that gleamed with drops of water he hadn't toweled dry. His wet, slicked-back hair shone like onyx in the lantern light, emphasizing the shadowy fringe of his eyebrows and lashes... and those dark eyes that made her burn.

The force of his gaze tightened her stomach muscles.

He brushed his knuckles across her cheek. "I want to make love to you the way you deserve to be made love to."

Of all the things he might have said to her in that moment, none could have filled her with more confidence or joy. She turned back the bedding to welcome him, her lover.

Muscles shifted across his shoulders and tapered, naked back as he bent to lower the lantern wick. The room turned golden, his skin bronze. Unabashedly, she watched him shuck his trousers and drawers.

She'd seen Jack's body through peeks and glimpses, the young girl in her too shy, the experienced woman too intimidated to openly appraise him. But she wasn't shy or afraid tonight. The woman in her took a good, long look at the man she was inviting into bed, into her heart, into her life.

Boyd was impressive in every way.

He slipped beneath the covers and reached for her. She moved into his arms, coveting the warmth radiating from his hard body. The tangy smell of soap clung to his neck and chest where she nestled her head.

"What a surprise you are," he said, a tinge of awe in his voice.

She smiled against his chest, enjoying the rumble of his voice beneath her ear, enjoying his approval. She'd surprised herself too. "It pays to be daring at times," she said, recognizing the truth of her words.

"How daring do you feel now?" She lifted her head, expecting to see humor in his eyes.

She saw banked fire instead.

He scraped his blunt fingernails across her scalp, sending a delicious shiver through her as he slipped his fingers into her hair. "I want to touch you all night, starting right here." He drew his thumb over her lips. "And give you so much pleasure you beg me to stop."

She'd never begged, but when he rolled her to her back and kissed and nibbled and stroked her until she was mindless and gasping, she considered it.

And he hadn't even touched her below the neck.

"Roll onto your stomach," he said near her ear. A wicked thrill zipped through her, stealing her ability to speak. She hesitated, unsure what he was asking.

He kissed her neck. "Trust me."

She would. Oh, she would. She rolled onto her stomach, trusting that whatever he did to her would be heaven.

He sat up and spanned her back with his talented artist's hands, moving his warm palms over her skin with slow, fanning strokes that made her moan. The tips of his fingers dragged across her skin, leaving behind a trail of gooseflesh that made her shiver with pleasure.

His hands were magic, melting away the tension in her neck, her shoulders, her hips, and lower as he drew his hands down the length of her legs in long, gentle strokes.

She moaned.

And sighed,

And moaned again. "This is sinful," she said, her body so relaxed she could barely force out the words.

"I learned how to do this from a Chinese lady a few years ago."

"For a worldly man, you've missed an important lesson. You're not supposed to talk about other women at a time like this."

"Not even if she's old enough to be my great-grandmother, and our relationship was platonic?"

She arched her eyebrow. "That may give you some leeway."

He slid his thumbs along her arch and around the ball of her foot, pushing up beneath her toes. She moaned, unable not to.

"I like making you moan."

"This is taxing, but I can bear it a bit longer."

He laughed and kissed the arch of her foot. "Tell me when it becomes too much for you."

She smiled into his feather pillow, basking in the feel of his hands caressing her body. The depth of his kindness and the pleasure he was giving her were beyond anything she'd ever experienced. So was the feeling of his lips kissing a leisurely trail up the backs of her legs. She gasped when he nipped the flesh on her bottom.

"Turn over," he said, his voice ragged, his request gentle.

Her heart pounded as she rolled to her back, exposing herself to him.

He sat on his knees above her, appreciation shining in his eyes as he stroked his hands up her body. "You are an artist's dream. Your legs and curves and smile are a work of art." He leaned down and kissed her lips. "You're perfect." He kissed her breasts. "Enchanting." He kissed her navel. "Ravishing."

He kissed her—where she'd never been kissed before.

She gasped from the shock and the avalanche of pleasure rushing through her. She threaded her fingers into his hair, intending to make him stop, but she couldn't. Within seconds, she was moaning to the point of embarrassment, and praying he would never stop.

As if he sensed her racing toward the edge, he rose above her and stretched out on top of her. The weight of his body pressing her into the mattress thrilled her. She shifted her knees and he settled his hips between her thighs.

She smoothed her palms over his back, loving the feel of his hard body, the crisp hair on his legs that brushed her inner thighs as he pushed inside her.

She released a deep, satisfied sigh. "I've never been touched this way."

He nibbled at her lips. "You should always be touched like this."

"I'm available tomorrow evening."

A smile tilted his mouth, but she saw more than his handsome face. She saw the other, more serious man looking back at her.

She lifted her hips, making him groan and bury his face in her hair. She flattened her palms across his smooth, tapered back, savoring the feel of him, the weight of his body shifting and pressing into hers.

She would never get enough of him, this playful, serious man who was kissing her senseless and stealing her heart.

How would she manage to love him for only one night?

His kisses grew deeper, his thrusts firmer, until they were both half-crazed, gasping and clinging and squeezing—and then she was there: leaping from the peak of the mountain they'd been climbing, hurtling into turbulent currents that shuddered through her body, twisting and spinning her out of control. She cried out, grasping at his sturdy shoulders as he lunged hard and followed her into the vast blue sky.

She soared away on the wind, gloriously, wonderfully free.

⋘⊱⊰⋙

As Boyd's heartbeat calmed, he watched Claire's breathing slow, and her lashes flutter as she drifted into sleep. She lay on her back, her body flush with his, her hair splashed across his pillow like rays of sunshine.

He'd always prided himself on maintaining control of himself both physically and emotionally, but this woman, this vulnerable widow, had shaken his control and moved him beyond his wildest imaginings.

Her daring had stunned and impressed him. Her lusty, playful participation in lovemaking had thrilled him. Her confessions had torn his heart out. What man could touch her soft skin without wanting to give her pleasure? How could this energetic, passionate woman be too unhealthy to carry a child?

He stroked her silky hair, knowing he could make love to her a million nights and not get enough of her. Even now, he yearned to wake her with a kiss.

He held her in his arms for hours, stroking her hair, watching her sandy lashes twitch against her creamy skin, knowing he was completely and utterly trapped by his need for her.

It surprised and scared him.

But he couldn't let her get hurt again. She'd suffered too much already. She was a beautiful, giving woman trying to do good in the world. He didn't agree with her methods, but he admired her for standing up for what she believed in. He would stand beside her. He would protect her in the only way he could.

Chapter Twenty-six

"Are you awake?"

Boyd's warm breath caressed Claire's temple, and she snuggled against him, loving the feel of his warm skin against hers. "No."

He chuckled and ran his hand over her bare hip. "Then I'll have to find a creative way to wake you up."

Her skin thrilled to his warm palm as he skimmed his hand over her body. She leaned her forehead against his collarbone, reveling in the smell of him and the hint of soap that lingered on his skin. She rubbed her cheek against his chest, basking in the softness of his springy chest hair.

She'd come to his saloon in hopes of understanding him better. But she'd found herself last night. She'd unlocked the cage. She was free—blessedly, wonderfully free.

She'd taken a lover.

And what a lover he was, with those artist's hands that sculpted her body with a tender persuasion, and those honey-brown eyes that drank her in with every glance.

She wanted more.

"I think I'm waking up," she said, her voice muffled in his chest hair as she nibbled his small hard nipple with her lips.

He traced her curves and slid his hand down to cup her bottom. "I want to talk to you before I take you home."

"Why talk?" she asked, brazenly sliding her hand down his hard stomach and into the thatch of dark hair at his groin.

"Ummm..." He nuzzled her ear and fit his naked body against hers. "Who said anything about talking?"

She lifted her face and kissed his gorgeous mouth, wanting more, wanting it all.

He gave her everything she wanted and more—so much more that she couldn't contain her fierce desire for him. She kissed his firm lips and stroked his hard, muscular body, sliding her skin over his, pressing her breasts to his hungry mouth, clamping her legs around his hips and taking him with her when she cried out in a shattering climax.

They clung to each other, their skin damp, their chests pounding, their breathing ragged.

"Stay with me tonight," she said, lifting her hips and squeezing her legs around his thighs.

"I'll stay with you every night." He kissed her then gazed down with the heat of their lovemaking still in his eyes. "Marry me."

She waited for his teasing wink to let her know he was playing with her, but his eyes were earnest.

"Marry me, Claire."

"You're jesting."

"I'm serious. Dead serious. Seriously serious."

She stared at him. "You can't be. I mean, we don't need to marry. You can stay at my boardinghouse. Or I can come here. No one has to know about our... private moments."

He brushed her hair off her face. "What if the doctor was wrong? What if you can get pregnant?"

"I can't."

"Circumstances change. Doctors make mistakes."

"The doctor wasn't wrong." Jack had taken her to bed several times after her miscarriage and she had remained barren. Still, a flicker of hope burned in her heart. What if the doctor *was* wrong? What if someday she could have a child?

"It doesn't matter to me." Boyd cupped her breast. "I want *you*."

"I want you too," she admitted, because she did want him. She wanted him in her bed, in her life—but not as her keeper. She had too much to lose if she married. She would lose her property, her boardinghouse, and her independence. Her husband would take ownership of everything, including her.

She couldn't lose her freedom again, especially now that she had passion in her life.

"I can't," she said, and the light in his eyes receded. She cupped his strong jaw and drew her thumb across his chin.

"Your proposal is noble, Boyd, but unnecessary. I want to spend my private time with you. This can be the beginning for us, for all the exciting things we can share when we're alone," she said. "No one needs to know about this."

"I'll know about it. And you deserve better."

She slid her feet down the backs of his hard calves and rubbed her toes against his heels. "What's better than this?"

"Marriage. Honesty. Safety for you. Take my name and let me keep you safe," he insisted. "No one in this town would dare to harm my wife."

"Oh, Boyd, you can protect me, but you'll own me. How safe is that?"

His head jerked back as if she'd slapped him, a wounded look in his eyes.

"Don't be offended. Please," she said, rubbing her palms over his back. "Taking you as my lover has set me free. We can have this every night without being married."

She needed his touch, his kiss, the feel of his naked body against hers. He was a tender, considerate, and passionate lover. During the night, she'd fallen asleep in his arms with a sense of contentment she'd never before experienced. But she could make love with Boyd without locking herself back in a cage.

He rolled off her and lay on his back, his forearm draped across his forehead. "It's not right for you, Claire."

His simple statement touched her. Boyd was a tender and honorable man, and so handsome she could barely look without wanting to make love to him. But she wouldn't marry him.

Ever.

Not even if he was professing his love, which he wasn't.

She propped up on her elbow and looked down at him. "You're letting our attraction lead you into a marriage proposal that isn't necessary."

He lifted his arm, his dark eyebrows slashing downward. "You think I'm proposing simply because I like making love with you?"

She shrugged because his frown warned her not to say yes. "I'm saying that things will change for us. After the newness of my marriage to Jack wore off, I became a responsibility to him. One he resented."

"Do you honestly think I'd be that cold and callous?"

"No. You wouldn't be that cruel." She knew that. His changes would be more subtle. "But after a year or so, you'd lose interest in me. You would change." And she would be trapped.

He tossed the covers back.

"Where are you going?" she asked, watching him climb out of the warm, rumpled bed.

"To get dressed so I can take you home."

She reached out and caught his wrist. "Don't be angry."

"I'm not *angry*, Claire. I'm insulted that you would compare me to a man like Jack."

"I'm sorry. I didn't mean to insult you."

"Well, you did," He wrenched away and reached for his trousers. He sat on the edge of the bed and shoved one foot into his pant leg then stopped to look at her. "You're willing to share my bed but not my life. Does that mean you don't trust me? Or does it mean you don't care enough to marry me?"

"Oh, Boyd." She got to her knees and cupped his face — a face she adored, a man who touched the most vulnerable part of her heart. "This isn't about you at all," she said. "It's about me. I'm not the woman you think I am."

"You're stubborn and determined. You care about people and champion causes to help them. You love your family. You take in strays. What else is there to know?"

She gulped, knowing she needed to tell Boyd the truth, but dreading his reaction. "I let my husband drown."

As if he'd been gut-punched, Boyd sagged away and stared at her.

"I was in the river with Jack when he drowned." She raked her hair out of her eyes then pulled the quilt around her shoulders. "We were living in a ramshackle room near the docks in Pittsburgh. I'd just received the deed to my grandmother's house, and Jack wanted it. I knew he'd gamble it away, so I ran out of the apartment and refused to tell him where I'd hidden it."

The bedroom was chilly, but it was her memory of that terrifying night that made her shiver.

"We argued then we fought—physically, I mean,"

Boyd's brow furrowed and his fists clenched around the trousers he was still gripping.

"Jack hit me with the back of his hand like usual, but I refused to tell him where I hid the deed. So he slugged me with his fist."

"No, Claire..."

The memory of her husband, whom she'd given herself to body and soul, striking her without the slightest sign of regret, made her eyes mist.

"The second time Jack hit me, our feet got tangled up and we plunged into the river." A tremor shook her stomach, but she forced herself to finish the story. "He pulled me under the water, and I thought he was trying to drown me. I kicked away from him and swam to shore,"

"Which sounds intelligent to me," Boyd said, his earlier look of irritation replaced with one of concern.

"But Jack couldn't swim," she replied, regret and shame poking at her conscience. "I knew that, but I swam away anyhow."

Boyd squeezed her hand and she met his eyes. "He beat you. He would have killed you. You know that."

She nodded, acknowledging the heartbreaking truth. Her own husband would have killed her.

"Come here," Boyd said softly, pulling her over to straddle his lap. She went willingly into his arms, seeking solace and safety from the horror of watching Jack drown.

"I'm not a good person," she said. "That's why you shouldn't ask me to marry you."

He grinned. "I've been meaning to bring that to your attention. You've not only destroyed my desire to remain a bachelor, you've stolen my dog and completely ruined him as a saloon hound." A small laugh escaped her, because Boyd was good and true, trying to bring humor to the mess she'd made of her life. But an instant later that little spark went out and hot tears filled her eyes. She was confused and scared.

"I can't marry you," she whispered. "I can't."

He rubbed her back, patient and kind. "What you're saying is that you don't trust me enough to marry me," he said. His tone was guarded, despite the warm caress of his hands.

"I don't trust myself," she said, and she didn't. She made too many bad choices and wrong decisions. "I'll never marry again, Boyd. I can't,"

His hands on her back paused, and she knew she'd hurt him, and had maybe even made her worst decision yet. But how could protecting her independence be wrong? Marriage was a cage, love a trap, and trust merely an illusion.

Only passion was real. Boyd's naked flesh pressing against the peaks of her breasts was real. Her desire for him was real. She would show him the difference, and make him want the passion.

⊷ ⊷

Claire leaned against her kitchen counter, clutching a cup of strong coffee in her hands, hoping it would ease her headache. Boyd had turned away her last attempt at lovemaking. He'd been gentle but firm in denying her, cordial but silent as he helped her dress and walked her home. She'd rejected his marriage proposal. He'd rejected her offer of an affair. Her need for self-preservation wouldn't allow her to change her mind. His integrity wouldn't let him change his.

Sailor pushed against her legs, wheezing and begging for her attention.

"Yes, you're staying with me for a few days," she said, rubbing his knobby head. When Boyd had walked her home, he asked her to keep Sailor while he went to Buffalo. She'd agreed immediately, loving the idea of having the silly dog in her home, and hoping her gesture would thaw the coolness shrouding Boyd.

Only after he left her foyer had his words struck a nerve. He was going to Buffalo?

And Anna was going to Pittsburgh this morning with Sheriff Grayson to testify at Larry's trial.

"Claire?"

She looked up to see Anna setting her valise by the door.

Sailor scurried across the room and sniffed the woman's small bag.

Anna stroked Sailor's ears, but eyed Claire. "Are you all right?" she asked with concern.

Claire nodded. Anna knew she'd been with Boyd all night, and must suspect how they had spent the time. "Are you sure you want to do this?" Claire asked, fearing her friend was making a deadly mistake.

"I saw Larry kill that man. I can't pretend I didn't." She sank into a chair and rubbed Sailor's back. "Everyone, including me, will be safer if I can help keep Larry in jail."

"But what if he finds a way to get out of jail like he did last time?" Claire asked. "He'll hate you for testifying against him."

"He hates me already." Anna's shoulders drooped. "If he gets out of jail, he's going to find me and hurt me. He's going to hurt other people too. I talked with the sheriff, and he agrees that I should do everything I can to make sure Larry stays in prison."

Even though Anna was going to Pittsburgh to testify against her husband under Sheriff Grayson's protection, the bold move unnerved Claire. Larry was mean to the bone. If he ever got free, he would come after Anna. And if Anna was living here, Claire feared that Boyd's shooting lesson wouldn't be enough for her to protect them.

"The sheriff is going to take me to see my family after we go to Pittsburgh. If you prefer, I can stay there. As long as Larry's locked up, I should be safe with my family."

Claire admired Anna's courage, and was glad she would be able to see her family again. But from the tiny hints Anna had dropped about her parents and siblings, they hadn't exactly stood by her when she needed them.

"I'd be lost without you, Anna." Claire crossed the kitchen and gave her a hug. "Stay safe and hurry back."

Anna returned the hug. "Thank you."

"How long will you be away?"

"I don't know," Anna answered, but despite her apprehension over testifying against Larry, she seemed excited about seeing her family for the first time in several years. Claire felt a little envious. Anna would be seeing her family. Boyd was heading to Buffalo, probably to see the unfairly beautiful Martha. Claire was stuck in her empty boardinghouse alone.

Chapter Twenty-seven

"I have two boarders for you," Elizabeth began, standing at Claire's front door with two elderly women. "This is my mother-in-law Mildred," she said, her gaze locked on Claire in silent desperation as if trying to convey a secret message. "And this is her sister Maude. They've come to visit Ted and me for a couple of weeks, but I'm afraid they'll catch their deaths from the frigid drafts blowing through the walls of my daughters' old bedrooms. I'm hoping you have a couple of rooms where they'll be warm and comfortable during their stay."

With an understanding nod to Elizabeth, Claire drew the women into the foyer. "I have the perfect rooms for you ladies," she said. Elizabeth followed them inside, her relief easing the strain lines around her mouth. Claire intuitively understood that Elizabeth wanted to present a happy home to her mother-in-law, and that two weeks of living together would reveal too much.

Claire and Elizabeth carried the ladies' valises upstairs to their rooms. Mildred loved the blue room with its calming blue carpet and draperies. Maude preferred the room with the lavender decor and the large cherry bed with the white lace canopy. Both women decided to settle in and take a nap before going to Elizabeth's house for supper.

Downstairs in the foyer, Elizabeth stopped and quietly thanked Claire for providing the rooms, offering to pay in advance.

"You're doing me a favor, Elizabeth. You can pay at the end of each week, if that's all right."

Elizabeth was more than agreeable. "I'll come for them at five o'clock," she said then slipped outside.

Mildred and Maude were lovely old ladies, and they loved their rooms in Claire's boardinghouse, but like many of Claire's guests, they hated the noise from Boyd's saloon. Claire complained to the deputy, Levi Harrison, but the noise continued. By the fourth morning, Mildred and Maude refused to spend another night listening to the racket. Claire couldn't blame them, but knew this would put Elizabeth in an uncomfortable situation if the ladies moved in with her. To spare Elizabeth, and to make a point to Boyd Grayson, Claire had Levi put the ladies up in his two best rooms at his hotel—at Boyd's expense.

It was time that Boyd faced up to the damage his wretched saloon was causing.

After she'd settled the ladies at the Harrison Hotel, Claire trudged through the rutted streets of town. Eight more days and it would be February, a month closer to spring, and hopefully a month closer to shutting down the saloons.

The temperance marches gained considerable ground during the week.

Bench warrants were served on two billiard rooms for selling liquor without a license; the tables were taken down and the owners fined. The Randolph Board of Excise published notice in the *Fredonia Censor* that all dealer licenses might be revoked. Two more saloon owners, and one drug store owner, agreed to stop selling liquor.

Claire was pleased with the success, but her life was unbearably empty with Anna and Boyd gone. She was upset with him over the noise from his saloon, but she missed him. Boyd had hired his friend Pat to cart her wood and run his bar then he'd taken the first train to Buffalo—as if he couldn't wait to get away from her.

Would a man propose marriage to a woman then run to another woman if he was rejected? She didn't want to believe that. She missed

Boyd. She missed his friendship. She wanted him to shut down his noisy saloon and be her lover. If only for a few weeks, it would be a glorious escape from her lonely life.

He didn't want an affair. With her.

She gave Boyd her passion—and her heart. She thought that would be enough. But he wanted ownership, all or nothing.

Her freedom wasn't for sale at any price. It couldn't be.

The icy wind stung her cheeks, and the sign above A. B. Edwards's furniture store blurred as she entered the building. She lifted her chin, refusing to feel sorry for herself.

She was through living in half measure. Perhaps she'd been impulsive and bold when she slipped into Boyd's saloon—and into his bed—but she didn't regret their night of passion. She had loved it. She wanted other nights with him, more passion and lovemaking.

But she was afraid Boyd was sharing those nights and passion with Martha.

She closed the door against the cold day, refusing to dwell on her mistakes and losses. She had business to take care of, an apology to make. She moved forward with purpose, but hadn't taken three steps into the show room when she slammed to a stop. A sense of the familiar swept through her.

Her mind whirled as she stepped back outside to look at the sign above the door. "A. B. Edwards Furniture."

Was Abe a name her grandmother had chosen at random? Was it a shortened version of Abraham? Or did it stand for the initials of the man her grandmother had loved so deeply?

Claire's heart thundered with excitement and possibility as she reentered the store. Could A. B. Edwards be *Abe*?

A man not much older than herself offered to assist her, but she asked to see the owner. Minutes later, an elderly man with white hair and vivid blue eyes walked to the counter where she was waiting.

"If you're here to cancel an order or fill my ears with that temperance nonsense, you can leave now."

His gruff greeting made her nerves jangle with anxiety. "Actually, Mr. Edwards, I came to apologize for the boycott. Would it be possible for us to speak in private?"

He nodded then headed into an office a few feet away. After closing the door behind them, he hooked his hands over the top of his walking stick and openly scrutinized her.

"You look familiar."

"I'm Claire Ashier. I believe you knew my grandmother Marie Dawsen."

His fingers tightened on the head of his walking stick. "I built her kitchen cupboards fifty years ago," he said, his voice melancholy. "You have Marie's smile."

Hearing the longing in his voice, and knowing he'd built her grandmother's cupboards, told Claire all she needed to know. This frail, white-haired old man had to be Abe. Her grandmother's lover. Her grandfather.

She said a small prayer that she wasn't making a mistake, that she was doing the right thing. "Mr. Edwards, I came to apologize for the boycott that's taking place, but I think I may have something more important to talk to you about."

His bushy eyebrows lifted in question, but he remained silent.

"Is there any reason my grandmother would have mentioned you in her journal?"

His face blanched, and his walking stick fell to the floor with a loud clack. He sagged against the desk and gripped the edge with his gnarled hands. "Marie kept a journal?"

The desperate hope in his eyes wrung Claire's heart. "Her entries are dated fifty years ago."

"Don't you dare judge her," he said, his voice so fierce and protective that she could have hugged the old man.

"There is nothing to judge, Mr. Edwards. What I read was a beautiful tribute to a very special time in her life."

His eyes welled with tears and he ducked his head.

Seeing his struggle made her own eyes mist. She wouldn't tell him that she was his granddaughter. Not now. The shock would be too much for him.

"Would you permit me to read Marie's journal?" he asked, lifting his head. Moisture rimmed his eyes, and he looked ready to beg her. "It would be a great kindness to an old man."

"Of course, Mr. Edwards. But to protect her privacy, I have to ask you to read it in my home."

He pushed to his feet, so unsteady that Claire retrieved his walking stick from the floor for him. He caught her hand in a surprisingly tight grip. "Can I go with you now?"

An air of desperation surrounded him, as if he were afraid he wouldn't live long enough to read the words his lover had written.

"I don't have a carriage to offer you a ride."

"I can walk up the hill."

She doubted it, but couldn't insult him by saying so. "If you are certain."

He nodded.

"All right then, we can go together."

It took ten minutes for him to dress in his boots, coat, gloves, and hat, but his eyes glowed with anticipation when he said good-bye to his grandson and walked out of the store.

Claire held his arm and kept her pace slow as they made their way up the hill. She apologized for the boycott that hurt his business, and promised to talk to his wife and the other ladies about stopping it. He waved away her apology, but she suspected his mind was preoccupied with memories of his long lost lover.

He was trembling so violently when they reached the house, she insisted he leave his boots on. She settled him in a comfortable wing chair in the west parlor with a hot cup of tea and an afghan. He put up with her fussing without comment, but when she handed the leather journal to him, his hands shook so badly he dropped it in his lap.

"I'll leave you alone while you read," she said, but he barely acknowledged her as she slipped out of the room.

She tidied the east parlor where her window was still boarded up because the pane of glass hadn't come in yet then took the back hall to the dining room. From there, she peeked into the west parlor to make sure Mr. Edwards was all right.

He sat with the journal angled toward the lamp, his face a collage of joy and sorrow as he read.

She left the door ajar and went to the kitchen to bake tea cakes for the morning. Though she presently had no guests, she had to be prepared at all times. While she did her numerous chores, she kept glancing toward the dining room, worrying that she was leaving Addison alone too long then worrying that she would interrupt him too soon if she went to check on him.

Finally, she tiptoed to the dining room and peeked into the parlor.

Addison Edwards—Abe—was holding the journal to his thin chest, his wrinkled mouth open as he wept with deep, grief-filled sobs.

Claire's heart wrenched with sympathy, and she slipped back into the kitchen. She hadn't known that passion could be poisonous, that it could rush through your veins with a thrilling but deadly intent.

But Abe's torment attested to that. The poor man was dying a thousand deaths as he wept alone in the chair.

She felt the urge to go to him, but waited a half hour before returning to the dining room. Mr. Edwards was calmer, but tears still streaked his face as he thumbed through the Journal. She hesitated near the door, unsure if she should disturb him.

He closed the journal and held it against his heart. His eyes shut and he leaned his head against the chair back.

She would have left him to his memories, but it was growing late and she had no idea how to get him home.

"Mr. Edwards?" she called softly, not wanting to startle him by sailing into the room unannounced.

He turned his head and gave her the most peaceful smile she'd ever seen on a person. "Come here, granddaughter." He held out his hand.

Her heart filled with hope as she rushed forward and knelt beside his chair. He closed his fingers around hers. "You can't know the gift you've given me." His voice was hoarse and edged with emotion. "Marie never told me I had a son."

"Then you talked to her after you... after her last journal entry?" she asked, hoping they found a way to be together. She could no longer bring herself to condemn them or their love for one another. They didn't mean to fall in love or have an affair. They were just two lonely souls who found each other too late, and risked their own heartbreak to share passion.

Sadness filled his eyes and he shook his head. "Only to greet each other. We couldn't have said a word more without resurrecting our relationship."

To think of Abe and her grandmother denying their love for five decades while living only minutes from each other was unbearably sad. "That's heartbreaking."

He nodded, and his eyes said the heartbreak was greater than she'd imagined.

"Does your father know about me?" he asked.

"No. I... I haven't told him about the journal." She couldn't bring herself to admit that her father had disowned her. "He has very blue eyes, like you."

Sadness cut deep ravines in Addison Edwards' face. "I watched Bennett grow up and never once suspected he was my son. I would have never believed Marie wouldn't keep something so important from me."

"What would you have done if she told you she was going to have your child?"

He sighed and leaned his head against the chair back. "Probably something foolish."

"I believe that's why she never told you, Mr. Edwards."

He rubbed his hand over the soft leather cover of the journal, as if to thank his lover for sparing them more irreparable mistakes.

"You're welcome to come back and read the journal whenever you like."

"Thank you," he said. "I might."

Something in his tone told her he wouldn't read it again, that he was at peace now and had no need to revisit the past.

"I'm sorry, but I have no way to take you home."

He waved his hand. "I can walk to Spring Street. In fact, I'd better get home before Desmona starts fretting."

Claire flattened her hand across her suddenly nauseous stomach. "Your wife knows about the journal."

The light dimmed in his eyes. "She does?"

"She saw it during a temperance meeting. She only read the first page, but I'm certain she understood what the diary contained. I had no idea that you were Abe... that Desmona was... oh, how careless I've been."

He squeezed her hand. "You've done nothing wrong. Desmona knew about my affair long before she poked her nose in this journal. There's nothing for you to fret over." He patted her hand. "Help me up so I can get home before she comes looking for me. I don't want to bring trouble to your doorstep."

She helped him stand, but as soon as he had his walking stick in hand, he put his arm around her and gave her a hug. "Thank you for giving an old man back his youth. I'm honored by your trust in me."

"How could I not trust a man my grandmother loved so deeply?"

"I'd like nothing more than to openly acknowledge you as my granddaughter, but I have four daughters and a slew of grandchildren to consider."

"I understand. I shared the journal with you because I believed Grandmother would have wanted me to, and because I felt it was the right thing to do. I'm not looking for anything more than this," she said, kissing his wrinkled cheek. "I'm proud to know you, too, Mr. Edwards."

When she drew away, his eyes were moist, but she suspected it was tears of happiness and peace. "I'd prefer you call me Abe. Or Addison. Or Grandfather."

She took his coat from the closet. "How about Grandfather in private, Mr. Edwards in public?"

"That pleases me." He pulled on his coat then wrinkled his brow at her. "Are you going out this evening?"

"Yes." She buttoned her heavy coat then linked their arms. "I can't give you up just yet, so I'm walking you home."

He argued, but she insisted, until finally they both laughed and walked out the door arm in arm.

They walked slowly, but Addison was huffing and trembling so badly by the time they reached his house on Spring Street, Claire walked him right to his front stoop. Desmona met them at the door, scowl lines an inch deep between her gray eyebrows.

Claire was immensely grateful that she was free of the stifling prison of marriage. She would live with the loneliness and the longing that nagged her. She had learned that she could welcome a night of passion without shame. And why not? She was a grown woman, a widow who had risked her life to win her freedom. Boyd Grayson wasn't the only man in town.

But he was the only man she wanted. And he was in Buffalo.

Chapter Twenty-eight

For the fourth day in a row, Boyd banged on the door of the huge white mansion with stately pillars. To his relief, a lanky man with graying hair and brilliant blue eyes answered his knock.

"Is Bennett Dawsen at home?" Boyd asked.

"You're addressing him," the man said in an imperious voice.

Boyd ignored Dawsen's arrogance, and held out his hand. He'd been waiting for Claire's family to return home from wherever they'd been. "I'm Boyd Grayson, a friend of Claire's. We need to talk."

Bennett Dawsen invited him inside, and introduced him to Claire's mother, a fashionably dressed lady with dark hair and regal features. But Boyd was too worried about Claire to be overly cordial to her mother or impressed by the opulent house.

Claire was treading into a dangerous situation, and he just wanted to get back to Fredonia and make sure she was all right.

If only she would have agreed to marry him.

He thought she would have wanted to. Every woman he ever romanced had angled for marriage. They wanted him. They wanted security. They wanted too much. He never considered proposing to a single one of them. Not once. Not until he made love to Claire. Not until he realized that his name could protect her, that he could keep her safe, that he could make love to her every night.

He wanted desperately to marry her.

But she wanted an affair. For the first time in his life, Boyd received the same proposition he'd given to countless women over the years, and it stung his conscience. He never realized how callous he'd been.

"I'll leave you gentlemen to your business," Mrs. Dawsen said then quietly left the room. She was pretty, but darker and shorter than Claire.

"If you're a friend of my daughter's," Bennett said, "then you must know we aren't in communication with each other."

"You'd better change that, Bennett, if you want to keep your daughter alive."

"What's happened?" Bennett's face paled. The starch left his rigid body, and he sank into an overstuffed armchair.

"Claire has been lying to you, or rather Lida, about her life with Jack." Boyd repeated what Claire had told him about her marriage to Jack and about Jack's death. "She said she would have come back to you on her knees, Bennett, but she was afraid Jack would find a way to hurt you. She stayed away to protect you. Now she thinks it's too late, that you hate her."

"How could she think that?" Bennett asked, his voice filled with pain.

"How could she not? You disowned her without a penny or even a wish for luck."

Claire's father was every bit the arrogant rich man Boyd had imagined, yet Bennett Dawsen loved his daughter. When Boyd told him about the temperance marches and the danger Claire was putting herself in, Bennett insisted on taking the first train back to Fredonia.

"You need to talk some sense into your daughter," Boyd said later that day as they crossed the Common in Fredonia. "I'm overhearing some nasty grumbling from my patrons." He told Bennett about some of the conversations he'd overheard in his saloon, and that the other saloon owners were reporting the same unrest from their patrons. "I'm afraid these men are going to start retaliating. I've tried to explain this to Claire, but she insists on marching."

"Impulsive chit." Bennett shook his head. "She's been rash and reckless from the cradle."

"She's certainly reckless. She and her friends are agitating every drinking man in town, and the liquor salesmen are furious over their lost income."

"I don't blame them. They depend on those sales."

"I'm afraid they care more about their sales than being gentlemen. They're too greedy, and that scares me."

Bennett kept stride with Boyd without exerting himself. "Wanting to make money doesn't make one greedy. Desire can drive our ambition and help us achieve great things. Greed is when that desire gets out of control."

Boyd cut his eyes to Bennett's chiseled face. "Greed can also cause a man to disown his own daughter.

"I offered Claire the chance to stay," Bennett retorted. Boyd saw it as the confidence and arrogance of a wealthy man. "She chose to go with that wretch Jack Ashier instead."

"You gave her terms she couldn't live with," Boyd explained firmly. "Jack isn't the only man who has hurt Claire." Boyd slowed his pace, needing to speak his mind before reaching her door. "Jack was an abusive son of a bitch. But you didn't help. You tore Claire's heart out when you disowned her."

Bennett jerked to a stop and glared at him. Boyd didn't blink. He was prepared to go as many rounds as necessary with this man to get him to own up to the mistakes he'd made with Claire and with his mother.

"Claire may have survived her mistake with Jack, but it's very possible this temperance nonsense could get her hurt. You need to talk to her, Bennett."

"I tried to do that four years ago, but Claire was too hardheaded to listen."

"Make her listen. You're her father. Your daughter thinks you hung the moon. She needs you in her life, and she needs your common sense to keep her from making another dangerous mistake. If you're going to worry about being right, or about protecting your pride rather than your daughter then stay away from her. Because if you hurt her again, I swear I'll break your neck."

Bennett's nostrils flared, but he didn't say a word. He faced Boyd man-to-man, eye-to-eye, seeming to study and measure him. Boyd stood unflinching and let him look.

He didn't care if Bennett approved of him. All he cared about was keeping Claire safe.

What began as an amused chuckle in Bennett's throat grew into a robust laugh that forced his head back and echoed across the Common. "Where were you when Claire was eloping with that wastrel Jack Ashier ?" he asked, slapping his hand over Boyd's shoulder.

"Making my own mistakes, I'm sure."

⸺◁─▷⸺

Sailor's presence was a mixed blessing. The dog kept her company, but every time he curled against her, Claire thought of Boyd doing the same to Martha Newmaine.

Why else would he have gone to Buffalo?

Why else would his travel plans be uncertain?

Maybe he was considering Miss Newmaine's suggestion to open a saloon in Buffalo. Maybe he was simply enjoying himself too much to return. He'd been gone five days, and it was killing her to think of him in Martha's arms.

"What's bothering you?" Addison asked, lowering his hand of playing cards. "You look positively heartbroken."

She was. Her life was empty without Boyd. Only weeks ago she would have given her last nineteen dollars to shut down his noisy saloon and get rid of the rakehell, but now, "despite being two dollars away from broke because of his saloon, she missed him so desperately it hurt. The irony made her want to laugh and weep at the same time.

She had given him her heart. Every aching inch of it. She wanted him to be her lover, but he wasn't her lover. He was a rake who was in Buffalo with another woman. He was a handsome man, bent on seducing her. She'd known that. And yet, she had fallen in love with him anyhow.

How pathetic.

How stupid.

How typical of her.

"Do you want to call the game?" Addison said.

"Would you mind?" she asked, knowing she couldn't keep her mind on it. She was at a crossroads with Boyd, and she didn't know which way to go.

"Of course not." The old man tossed his cards onto the sofa cushion between them. "Truth is, I'd rather pester you with more questions."

Since Addison had read the journal, he'd visited each day, asking about Claire and her father and Marie. "What do you want to know?"

"Why you're pining over that young fella across the street, for one thing," he said, a teasing twinkle in his eye.

Claire adored her grandfather, and thoroughly enjoyed his company, but on this cold, dreary day, her heart ached too deeply to appreciate his teasing. She longed for Boyd, needed him, missed him so deeply she wanted to curl up in bed and sleep until he got back.

The knock on the door made Sailor yelp and scramble to his feet. Claire's heart leapt, and she followed the dog to the foyer, praying it was Boyd who was knocking.

Would he stay for a while? Would he allow their friendship to continue? Would he finally close his saloon and give her business a chance to flourish? Or was he only here to take Sailor?

When she opened the door, she gasped in shock.

Her father stood on the porch, a tall, imposing man with silver sideburns and salt and pepper hair, handsome despite the telltale signs of age in his face. The blue eyes that had once looked at her with pride were filled with sadness.

"Why didn't you tell me about Jack?" he asked, his strong voice wobbling. To her shock, he stepped into the foyer and pulled her into his arms with a gentleness and compassion she hadn't felt in a very long time.

After so many years of missing him, Claire burst into tears. She clung to his broad shoulders as he rocked her and let her cry like the little girl she'd left behind so many years before.

"Oh, Daddy. I'm so sorry."

"I didn't know you were unhappy," he said, his voice gruff. "Lida said your letters were filled with joy."

"They were." Claire sniffled and wiped her eyes. "I couldn't tell anyone the truth." She searched her pocket for a handkerchief, but came up empty-handed. "I'm sorry I broke your relationship with Grandmother. I'll regret it for the rest of my life."

He retrieved a crisp monogrammed handkerchief from his jacket pocket and handed it to her. "Your grandmother acted irresponsibly. I trusted her to chaperone you and keep you safe. Instead, she let you run off with a wastrel and ruin your life. How can I forgive her for that?"

She'd forgotten how unrelenting he could be, how stubborn and unforgiving. She slipped his damp handkerchief into her pocket then curled her fingers around the carving, needing Boyd's comforting presence. "What brought you here?" she asked, feeling the distance grow between them.

"Your young man paid me a visit."

She looked at him in confusion. "What young man?"

"Your suitor. Mr. Grayson. He's a bold rapscallion, but I rather like him. He told me I'd better take care of business with my daughter before she got herself into trouble again. "

She stared in disbelief. No one told her father what to do, not even his business partner.

"I believe that boy would have spoken as frankly to our good President Grant without batting a lash."

She didn't doubt it. Boyd was like her father in that way. "I'm sure he didn't mean to insult you, Daddy."

"That boy meant every word he said. He suggested I've been acting like a pompous ass. I'm afraid there's some truth to that." He caught her hands and squeezed them. "Why didn't you tell Lida you were unhappy?"

"What good would it have done?"

"I would have brought you home."

"You disowned me. You told me I was no longer your daughter." Tears flooded her eyes and spilled over her lashes. "You stopped loving me."

"Never." Regret filled his eyes, and he pulled her back into his arms. "I never stopped loving you. I only wanted what was best for you, sweetheart. I'm sorry I hurt you."

She could barely believe that her father was standing in her parlor, hugging her and apologizing for hurting her. But more unbelievable was that Boyd had gone to Buffalo to confront her wealthy, powerful father.

Chapter Twenty-nine

Claire waited three days for Boyd to come by her house, but he didn't set foot on her porch. He'd answered her note with his own note of apology, and he'd paid the bill at the Harrison Hotel, and reimbursed her lost income without complaint. But the saloon remained open and Boyd stayed away. He hadn't been in the bar during Claire's marches. Claire and her temperance friends had pleaded their case with his bartender, Pat, who promised to give Boyd their message.

Sailor ambled between their houses like a nomad, eating like a king, sleeping wherever he flopped down, and returning to the noise and excitement of Boyd's bar each night.

She spent her time at the temperance meetings and marches, or with Addison and her father, watching them play chess and talk about politics. She hadn't worked up the nerve to tell her father about the journal or Addison yet. Addison was leaving the timing up to her, but he obviously wasn't about to miss the opportunity to spend time with his son.

Claire left them to their chess game and went outside. The rhythmic chopping of an axe came from behind the Pemberton Inn. She crossed the street, hoping it was Boyd splitting wood.

Her spirits lifted when she saw Sailor pawing through a pile of firewood, and they lifted higher when she saw Boyd raising a long-handled axe above his head. He brought it down with a smooth stroke that split a fat stump in half. She stopped and watched, admiring

Boyd's strength and precision, the ease at which he worked. Sailor was too busy sniffing and digging in the chunks of wood to notice her.

The dog and the man captivated her. After Boyd split a stump, Sailor would clamp his teeth around one of the chunks and carry it to the mounting pile as if he knew exactly what to do. Claire smiled at the silly dog, wondering how long it had taken Boyd to train him.

Her attention swung back to Boyd, and her heart melted. Somehow he had gotten her hardheaded, stubborn father to forgive her, and even more surprising, to get on a train to come see her. Because of Boyd, she was slowly reuniting with her father, and hopefully would renew her relationship with the rest of her family in the spring.

She waited until Boyd had finished splitting a stump then crossed the yard. The instant Sailor spotted her, he tore across the crusty snow and lavished her with wheezy attention.

Boyd looked up as if expecting to see Pat rounding the corner. His nonchalant expression changed to surprise. He rested the axe head on a huge stump he'd been using as a chopping block, and watched her walk toward him, his gaze sweeping her from her eyebrows to her ankles.

She liked that he was looking. It gave her the confidence to lift up on her toes and brush a kiss across his lips. "Were you planning to avoid me forever?" she asked, easing down onto her heels but not away from him.

"I wasn't avoiding you. I've been working."

"Sailor says you've been avoiding me," she said, hoping to tease a smile from him.

Not a flicker of humor touched his face. His lips didn't quirk, his eyes didn't crinkle, he just stood stiff and unyielding in front of her. How could he be so cool? Had Martha reclaimed his full attention already?

Desperate to keep his affection for herself, Claire boldly placed her palm against his heart, feeling the scratchy wool of his coat, wishing she were touching the smooth skin and springy hair on his chest. "Would you be interested in having a visitor late this evening?"

He frowned and stepped away from her. "If you can't trust me enough to marry me then you shouldn't be inviting me into your bed. It's insulting."

She gasped as if he'd struck her. "You could have simply said no."

"I don't want to have an affair with you, Claire."

She never considered that an experienced man like Boyd might be insulted by her proposal. Of course, she'd never imagined that she would be proposing something so illicit.

What had happened to her morals? What had happened to her desire for a simple and safe life? From the minute she first met Boyd he'd sent her into a spin, and now she couldn't tell north from south, or right from wrong, because with Boyd, it all felt right.

"Why are you here?" he asked, his coolness cutting into her but reminding her why she refused to marry again. Right now she was free to walk away from his displeasure. If she married him, she would spend each day of her life striving to please him.

She pushed her hands into her coat pockets and backed away from him, from another mistake. "I wanted to thank you for bringing my father to Fredonia."

"He should have come on his own." Boyd yanked his axe from the stump.

"I shouldn't have turned my back on him."

He nodded, as if to agree with her. "Step back," he said then raised the axe above his head.

"Daddy wants me to move home with him."

Crack! The chunk of wood split in two. "Perhaps you should go." Boyd's jaw clenched, and he kicked a thick piece of wood away from his feet. "You wouldn't have to worry about your income if you lived with your parents."

"I'd go berserk within hours," she said truthfully. "Until this week, I didn't realize that Daddy and I are so much alike."

"I knew it the minute I met him." He swung the axe and it connected with a hard crack against a piece of oak. "You are both too hardheaded for your own good."

"Exactly," she said, agreeing with him because it was the truth. She was every bit her father's daughter and she knew it. "Daddy and I would be at each other's throats if I lived with him."

He stopped and propped the axe on his cutting stump, cupping his hand over the top of the handle. "Does that mean you two aren't getting along?"

"We're doing as well as we can under the circumstances. Daddy is used to giving orders. I've gotten used to living my own life. That causes friction. But we love each other and are happy to be reunited." She slipped her hand over Boyd's cold knuckles, wanting to connect with the tender side of him. Even if she couldn't have him as her lover, she wanted him as her friend. "Thank you for bringing him back to me."

He shrugged as if it were nothing.

Yet, despite his present coolness, his thoughtfulness in visiting her father meant everything to Claire. "You must have had a devil of a time convincing Daddy to come here. Is that why you were gone so long?" she asked, wanting to know if he spent the time haggling with her father, or if he'd spent it with Martha.

"When your father heard that you were putting yourself in danger, he insisted on taking the first train to Fredonia."

Her stomach grew queasy. If her father had immediately agreed to come back with Boyd, what had kept Boyd in Buffalo so long? More important, why did Boyd tell her father about her temperance work?

Her father had nagged her relentlessly since he'd arrived. She avoided the subject and talked about her mother and sister, but Bennett kept swinging their conversations back to her temperance work.

Suddenly, Boyd's motivation in visiting her father seemed suspect. "Why did you tell Daddy about my marching?"

"I'm worried about you."

"Are you worried about *me*? Or your business?"

He scowled. "How can you ask such a ridiculous question?"

"It doesn't seem ridiculous, especially since Daddy has been nagging me all week to stop my temperance work."

With a snort of disgust, Boyd turned and split another hunk of oak.

"Did you ask Daddy to talk me out of marching?"

"I was hoping your father could reason with you."

A wrenching pain gripped her stomach. She once suggested to her fellow marchers that they find each saloon owner's weakness. Boyd had turned the tables on her. He found her most vulnerable spot and exploited it. "How could you do that?" she asked.

"How could I not?" He slammed the axe into the wood then whirled to face her. "You've been deaf to my warnings. You refuse to stop marching. And you won't marry me. What else was I supposed to do?"

"Nothing," she spat. "Exactly nothing. You have no right to meddle with my life."

"You're meddling with mine."

"I'm trying to do something good in our town."

"So am I," he said just as adamantly. "I'm trying to keep an overzealous woman from getting hurt or killed."

"I am *not* overzealous."

"Your father thinks you are, and so do I." The wind flipped his hair into his eyes, and he shoved it back with an angry swipe of his fingers. "Claire, your father supported saloons long before he met me. He told me he's a member at several clubs in Buffalo. Of course he's going to disagree with your temperance efforts."

And Boyd would have suspected that and found a way to enlist her father's help. Her father was a man's man. He liked his whiskey and cigars. He liked Boyd. Of course he would give him support.

Her throat closed, and she curled her fingers into her palms, digging her nails into her skin. Focusing on the pain there instead of the pain in her heart was the only way she could squeak out her next words. "You brought my father here for your own purpose."

"I brought him here because you needed him, and because we both want to keep you safe." "Bosh," she said. "You asked me to marry you because you wanted to control my actions and decisions. When I rejected your proposal, you sought my father's help. Now that Daddy's here, he wants to control my life too."

"You can't believe that."

She laughed and sobbed at the same time, because she did believe it. She had become friends and lovers with Boyd during this war, but this battle had gone to him.

"I'll never learn," she whispered, and turned away before he could see her tears.

"You want to forget the past, Claire? Then quit living it." He caught her sleeve and pulled her around to face him, his eyes flashing. "I'm not Jack, damn it." He threw down his axe and stormed into the saloon through the back door.

Chapter Thirty

After her argument with Boyd, Claire's relationship with her father grew more awkward. It was clear to her that she was no longer his little girl. She'd lost her innocence. Her father was no longer that tall tree with outstretched limbs that offered her refuge; he was a man with faults that troubled her and opinions she didn't agree with.

They spent a tense afternoon together while several men from the hardware store installed a huge pane of glass in her parlor window. When it was finished, Claire built a hearty fire in the fireplace to warm the room and chase the chill from her bones. After too many minutes of silence, she scrounged up the nerve to tell her father about the journal and her grandmother's affair with Abe.

Her father was horrified.

Appalled.

And angry.

He condemned his mother's actions and refused to read the journal. He didn't want to know about her infidelity, or the name of the man who had sired him.

Claire met Addison in the foyer and quietly told him about her father's reaction. Addison was disappointed, but he went to the parlor to visit with his hardheaded, narrow-minded son. The two men spent a good part of the afternoon playing chess and discussing the pleasures of good whiskey and fine cigars.

Claire sighed and went to the kitchen. Were sin and vice the only things men thought, or cared about?

She prepared a roast chicken and chestnut stuffing for her father, who would be leaving for Buffalo the next morning, and for Addison, who wanted to spend the last evening with Claire and her father. The kitchen felt cozy and warm from the oven, and the aroma of baked chicken and stuffing lent a festive air to the evening.

They had just finished eating when someone banged on the front door. Sailor tore through the house with a yelp of excitement. Claire followed more sedately, but each step of the way she wondered if it was Boyd.

To her shock, Desmona stepped into the foyer.

Her red-rimmed eyes were full of anger. "I should like to speak to my husband," she demanded, her voice ringing through the foyer.

Addison hobbled in and leaned on his walking stick, wearily patient. "What are you doing here, Desmona?"

"That is the question I've come to ask you." Her lips thinned. "Have you lost your good sense, Addison? If the gossips see you here, there will be no end to the scandal."

"Nonsense. I'm visiting friends."

Sailor sniffed Desmona's hand muff, and she gave him an irritable nudge. She thrust a gnarled finger in Claire's direction. "This girl is trouble. Just like her grandmother."

"Go on, Sailor," Claire said, shooing the dog into the parlor.

"What's going on here?" Claire's father's imperious voice boomed through the foyer as he strode in and stopped beside Claire.

Desmona's eyes darkened with hatred as her gaze swept him. Her lip curled and she turned to Addison. "I'm not going to let this girl and her father ruin our family name, or steal our daughters' inheritance because of a book that chronicles your unsavory behavior."

Addison's bushy eyebrows beetled above his angry blue eyes. "What are you talking about?"

Desmona ignored him and spoke to Claire. "Where's the journal?"

Suddenly, everything came clear to Claire. "You were the one who broke into my home. You were looking for the diary, weren't you, Mrs. Edwards?"

Desmona lifted her chin. "Where is it?"

Her brazen demand outraged Claire. How dare the woman push into her home and demand something so personal? Claire turned to Addison. "Your wife is obviously distressed, Mr. Edwards. Perhaps you should take her home."

"I'm not leaving without that diary," Desmona insisted.

"Is she referring to your grandmother's journal?" Claire's father asked.

Claire couldn't think of a worse way to tell her father the truth, but she couldn't avoid it. She nodded.

His forehead furrowed. "Why would she care about that?" he asked. But in the next instant, his eyebrows lifted and he stared at Addison.

The two men resembled each other so much with their lanky builds and sapphire blue eyes, Claire was surprised her father hadn't realized before now. He sagged against her desk, utterly flummoxed by the revelation.

"I see the cat is out of the bag," Desmona said, irritation grating in her voice. To Claire's utter astonishment, Desmona pulled a revolver out of her hand muff and pointed it at Claire's stomach. "Where is it?"

"What are you doing?" Addison asked in shock.

Desmona ignored him and jabbed the nose of the gun into Claire's gut. "Get that diary."

"How dare you accost my daughter!" Her father's outraged voice boomed through the foyer. He shifted his stance, but Desmona drew back the hammer on the revolver.

"Stay back, Mr. Dawsen."

Addison teetered on his cane. "For pity's sake, Desmona,"

"Get your coat, Addison. We're leaving." She glared at Claire. "Where's the journal?"

Claire straightened her shoulders, unwilling to take one more step in fear. She refused to be pushed, prodded, or pounded ever again.

Her father touched her elbow. "Go get the diary, sweetheart." He was telling her to run, but she wouldn't leave the fate of the people she loved in the hands of this crazy old lady.

"No, Daddy." An odd calm stole over her as she stared into Desmona's manic eyes. "You have no right to my grandmother's personal life."

"I have a right to protect my family and my reputation. Believe me, I'll shoot you to do so."

Desmona was dead serious.

"No one knows about the journal, Mrs. Edwards."

"And I intend to make certain they never do." She waved the gun toward the desk. "Get the diary."

In that brief moment of distraction, Addison stepped forward and planted himself between Desmona's gun and Claire's body. Claire's father shoved her toward the parlor, but she stopped in the doorway, refusing to leave her grandfather to defend her.

Addison spread his arms, baring his chest to Desmona's revolver. "If you're going to shoot anyone, shoot me. I'm the one at fault. Not Claire."

His wife's hands trembled as she gripped the revolver tighter. "She has the journal, and I want it destroyed."

"That won't change what happened," he said.

"It will keep your unsavory behavior from ever being known."

His blue eyes turned into oceans of pain and sadness. "What difference will that make? *You'll* still know. You'll still hate me like you've hated me for forty-nine years."

"It will protect our girls and our grandchildren. They shouldn't have to suffer gossip or shame over your licentious behavior with another woman."

"Neither should you," he said. His thin shoulders stooped with defeat. Surprise whisked across her face. "I cheated you out of a good marriage, Desmona. I regret my infidelity. But my biggest regret is that I crushed the sweetness in you and turned you into a bitter woman."

"Bitter?" Her chin snapped up and her nostrils flared. "I was wronged. You fell in love with another woman and broke my heart, Addison."

"I ended the affair with Marie the day you found us in her parlor. From that moment on, I behaved with decency and respect toward you."

"Is that supposed to make your betrayal acceptable?" She glared at him. "Where was your decency and respect when you broke our marriage vows?"

He lowered his head, looking so abashed and ashamed that Claire's heart wrenched with pity.

He cleared his throat, but his voice came out a choked whisper. "I was lost, Desmona. I admit it. I wronged you. I've spent forty-nine years trying to make amends, but you've put up barriers at every turn. And now I realize I don't even know you. The woman I married would never point a gun in hatred at a decent human being who has never harmed her in any way."

Desmona's mouth fell open.

"Whatever happened to that beautiful, giving woman I married?" he asked, his voice thick with regret.

The anger drained from her face, leaving only desolation.

"I'm sorry I did this to you," Addison went on. "I'm sorry I snuffed out the stars that used to be in your eyes."

"Addison, you fool, it's too late for an apology," she said, her voice cracking with emotion. Tears shimmered in her eyes.

"Is it?" he asked. "Or is it just too difficult for you to forgive me?"

"How can I forgive you?" Her lips trembled and tears welled up and rolled over her lower lashes. "You loved another woman."

"And I loved you."

"No, you didn't." She shook her head and lowered the gun to her side, tears filling the grooves of her wrinkled cheeks. "You never loved me."

Addison slipped the gun from her hand and passed it to Claire's father. "Come here, Desmona." He pulled her unyielding body against him and rubbed her hunched shoulders. "I loved you when I married you," he whispered against her gray hair.

An anguished sob erupted from Desmona's throat, and she buried her face in Addison's chest.

"I'm sorry." He stroked her back. "I'm responsible for all of this."

Desmona's gnarled fingers clutched his gray sweater, and her shoulders shook with sobs.

Claire's throat filled with tears, but she couldn't turn away.

"We've got a few years ahead of us," Addison went on, his voice wobbling with emotion. "Let's spend it in peace."

Desmona wept too hard to answer.

Addison eased her away and tipped her chin up. Tears made her eyes red and puffy, but Addison looked at her as if she were the young woman he'd married. "If you can forgive me, we might still enjoy the time we have left."

A breathy sob flared her nostrils, and she pressed her brown-spotted hand to her mouth.

"Will you let me walk you home?" he asked, but Claire knew he was asking for more, that he was asking Desmona's whole forgiveness.

Desmona closed her eyes and gave a small nod of assent.

Claire exchanged a sympathetic look with her father then turned and went to the parlor fireplace where Sailor was lounging. She could hear Desmona sobbing and Addison quietly consoling her.

"You are going to be the death of me," her father said from behind her then he turned her toward him and pulled her into a crushing embrace.

He was trembling.

Her strong, tall father was trembling.

She clung to him, loving the starchy smell of his shirt and the hard pounding of his heart that affirmed his presence in her life. How had she ever walked away from him?

"I want you to come home with me," he said.

"I know." She hugged him. "I'll come for a visit in the spring."

He looked down at her with displeasure. "I meant for you to move home."

"This is my home, Daddy."

"Then stop marching."

"This business with the Edwardses has nothing to do with my temperance marches. It was about grandmother's journal"

"I don't care if it's a temperance march, a journal, or a cur like Jack Ashier that puts you in danger. I don't want you involved in anything that will hurt you!"

"Oh, Daddy..." She squeezed his neck then leaned back. "I love you."

He sighed and fit her against his chest again. "You give new meaning to the word troublesome."

She smiled and smoothed her palm over his firm shoulder. "I'm sorry you found out about your father this way."

"I assume Addison has known about this?"

She nodded. "He was thrilled when he found out about you, and he has asked a million, questions about you since."

Her father was silent for a minute then released a long sigh. "If you won't come home, and you won't quit marching, maybe you should rethink Boyd Grayson's marriage proposal"

Her heart somersaulted, and she jerked back to stare at her father.

"He told me he asked you. He told me you refused. But he's still willing. More than willing, if my guess is worth anything."

She had no idea how to respond. Why did Boyd tell her father about his proposal?

"He's a good man, Claire. I would welcome him as my son-in-law. "

That's why. Boyd had wanted her father's blessing.

She pulled from her father's arms and knelt beside Sailor, who was nudging her legs to get her attention. "I don't want to marry again," she said, stroking the soft fur on Sailor's neck.

"Why not? Mr. Grayson thinks you care for him, and it's obvious he cares for you."

"He wants to own me, Daddy."

"Bosh. You insult my intelligence, Claire."

"Then why did he go to Buffalo to get you? I'll tell you why," she said, her heart aching. "He wants you to convince me to stop marching. He's trying to keep me from shutting down his saloon. He was serving his own interests when he asked me to marry him. And he was serving his interest when he went to visit you in Buffalo."

She heard the front door close, and knew Addison and Desmona were taking their first steps back home, and hopefully steps toward healing a rift they'd endured for decades.

"A man like Boyd Grayson doesn't ask a woman to marry him because he wants to control her decisions," her father insisted. "That boy loves you. He brought me here because he knew we loved and needed each other, and because he is sincerely worried about your safety."

Claire sighed and bent to add a log to the fire. "I like not having to answer to anyone. I like being in charge of my life."

"Is it more important to you than sharing your life with a man you love?"

"Yes." She dusted her hands on her skirt and stood. "Yes, Daddy, it is." It had to be.

He shook his head. "You're as confused about love as you are about your temperance marches that aren't doing a bit of good. It's all nonsense, Claire. He shook his head in disgust. "If your independence is that important to you then I'll transfer your dowry money into an account for you. Believe me, you can live comfortably without taking boarders."

"Oh, Daddy, I don't want your money."

"As long as you insist on living an independent life, I insist on giving you the means to do so. His jaw clenched. "If Jack Ashier were still alive, I'd kill the bastard."

The fury in his voice shocked her.

"He ruined you. For that offense, I would gladly kill him." Red-faced, her father stormed out of the house.

Claire rushed to the foyer window and saw him cross the street, no doubt to nurse his anger with a manly glass of good whiskey at Boyd's still operating saloon.

She stood by the window, listening to the revelry next door, wishing she had a place to go and a friend to talk to. Was her father right about the temperance marches being a waste of time? She rubbed her temples to ease the ache behind her eyes. Maybe they weren't helping anyone. Elizabeth's situation hadn't changed at all. Anna's life wouldn't change as long as she was married to Larry. And truthfully, Claire's own marriage to Jack would have been abusive even if the saloons had been closed down. Jack would have made his own liquor, and had at times. So what was the point? What was she trying to accomplish by marching? She wanted to protect women like herself and Anna and Elizabeth, but all she was doing was antagonizing every man in town.

And questioning an honorable man's integrity.

She leaned her forehead against the frigid window pane, suspecting that her father was right about the temperance marches, and about Boyd's intentions. She was sorry she'd judged Boyd unfairly.

But most of all, she was sorry that her father was right about her, that Jack had ruined her ability to trust.

Chapter Thirty-one

B oyd lowered his axe and pulled a handkerchief out of his pocket. He blew his nose and cursed the wind that cut a chill path through the yard at the depot.

"You sick?" Kyle asked, stopping his team of Percherons in the middle of the yard where Boyd was whacking the bark off a maple log. Frosty clouds of air blew from the horses' nostrils and spun away on the wind.

Boyd wasn't sick. He was all twisted up inside, true, but it was nothing a doctor could cure. He stuffed the handkerchief back in his pocket and picked up his axe. "Remember that talk we had out here right after you married Amelia?"

"How could I forget?" his brother said. "It was one of your shining moments."

"Well, it's your turn to give me some advice. How do you change a lady's mind about something?"

"You think I know?" Kyle tipped his head back and laughed. Several of the lumberyard crew members paused in their labor to look. "Boyd, if there's a way to do that, I'd sure like to know."

"How do you get Amelia to change her mind when she's set on something?"

"I don't."

"She supports everything you want to do with the mills."

"That doesn't mean she always agrees with my decisions," Kyle said. "We each speak our mind then find a compromise. Easy in theory. Difficult in practice. "

"What if you had to change her mind?"

"I'd get on my knees and beg."

"I'm serious, Kyle." He felt foolish asking for advice, but he was desperate enough to suffer his brother's ribbing. "I need to change Claire's mind about pursuing this temperance issue before she gets herself killed. One of the ladies found a rattlesnake in her kitchen yesterday."

"At this time of year? I find that hard to believe."

Boyd shrugged. "That's what I heard. And I don't want something like that to happen to Claire."

"Well, well, well. I believe Duke was right," Kyle said, looking surprised. He gave a grin that made Boyd want to smack him. "The lovely widow has gotten her claws into you. It's going to be fun watching you try to shake loose." He grabbed Boyd by the shoulders with mock talons.

"Get away from me." Boyd jabbed Kyle in the stomach with the handle of his axe.

Kyle grew serious. "You're the expert at seducing women. Use that to change Claire's mind."

He'd tried, but Claire had turned the tables on him. She wanted him in her bed and nothing else. He asked her to marry him. He brought her father to Fredonia to see her. Her father had given her such a large sum of money, the town was still gossiping about her good fortune. Not one proposal had swayed her in the least.

"Our roving sheriff returns," Kyle said, jerking his chin toward Duke, who was crossing the yard toward them. "You coming to work today?" he yelled.

"For a couple of hours," Duke hollered back, closing the distance rapidly.

When he stopped beside them, Boyd dug the deputy's badge out of his coat pocket. He kept it with him to keep it safe, and also because he feared he might need it. But now that Duke was back, he would let his brother and Levi handle the mounting unease in town.

"Did Anna testify?" he asked, handing the badge to Duke.

Duke nodded. "She was scared stiff, but she did it. If they don't hang him, Larry is going to spend his life in jail. It took a lot of courage for Anna to testify against that bastard." His brother handed the badge back. "I could use an extra deputy right now."

Boyd fingered the silver star. "If the ladies find out you have a saloon owner as your deputy, they'll run you out of town."

"It's because of those ladies that I need another deputy," he replied. "Everyone's in an uproar. What's been going on while I've been away?"

Boyd told him that his patrons were furious with the saloon closings, the ladies' boycotts, and their continued visits to all working bars. "I warned Claire that she and her friends need to ease off for a while, but she refuses."

Duke scowled and scratched his head beneath his wool cap. "Maybe you should keep that room at her boardinghouse for a while."

He couldn't stay a night in her house without climbing into her bed. He was too weak. He wanted her too much. "I can't" he said. "Ask Levi to stay."

Duke arched an eyebrow.

"I'm too busy with my saloon right now." He held the badge out. "I don't have time to play deputy.""This isn't a game," Duke said. "Keep the badge. And when you're not too busy with your saloon, peek across the street to make sure those ladies are doing all right. Levi and I will stop by when we can."

Boyd nodded, but he was afraid that watching wouldn't be enough. If men would throw a brick through Claire's widow and sneak a poisonous snake into another woman's kitchen, who knew what they would do next?

It unnerved Boyd, not knowing how nasty the fight would get. Even if he closed his saloon, Claire would continue to march until all the saloons closed. That would never happen. Don Beebe and the Taylor brothers would never stop selling liquor. Claire and the others were fighting a losing battle—and it was going to get someone killed.

Chapter Thirty-two

The first week of February buried everything in a mountain of snow—the roads, the fields, and Claire's porch. She and Anna took turns shoveling. Tonight, unfortunately, was Claire's turn. She pushed a shovelful of snow off the end of the porch and cursed the winter weather.

Too bad her father wasn't still here. His arms and back were far more suited to this heavy work. Anna had offered to shovel, claiming she enjoyed it, that it was soothing to her, but Claire couldn't allow Anna to do all the work.

Anna had returned from Pittsburgh just before the storm dumped five feet of beautiful but freezing snow on their town. Claire was relieved to have the woman back safely, but Anna seemed saddened and changed by the trip. Testifying against Larry had been an emotional trial.

Claire was proud of her friend for taking the hard stand and being courageous in the face of danger. Despite her melancholy, Anna could build a new life for herself. Like Claire had done.

Or had tried to do.

Since Boyd stopped calling on her, the routine of her life seemed thankless and demanding. Her house was empty without the sound of his voice filling its cavernous rooms. Her bed was cold without his compelling touch, without his warm body curled against hers. Her days were dark and lonely without the challenge and surprise he brought to each moment, without the light and laughter that was such a natural part of him.

Claire shivered and chided herself for not shoveling earlier, when it had been still light enough to see what she was doing. The short days were just one more reason she loathed winter. Everything felt frozen—her hands, her world, her life.

She wanted Anna's courage.

She wanted her father's confidence and conviction.

She wanted Addison's wisdom.

And she wanted Boyd's ability to enjoy life.

How had she lost so much of herself? Even her father had noticed. He'd said she wasn't his bright-eyed Claire anymore, that she had grown wary and distrusting. Addison alluded to the same thing when he'd come to apologize for the incident with Desmona. He'd suggested that Claire was as entrenched in her views as his wife was, and that he was afraid for both of them because he knew their stubborn convictions wouldn't have allowed either of them to back down during the confrontation.

Claire didn't want to be like Desmona.

She didn't. But she feared Addison was right. She'd become so cautious and set in her ways that she'd become narrow minded and unwilling to change. Why couldn't she just admit that the temperance marches weren't helping stop men from beating their wives? Why couldn't she admit that she may be wrong about closing the saloon? Because she was afraid that changing her mind might cause more harm. That's why she couldn't accept Boyd's proposal. She was afraid of making another mistake that would trap her in a cage she couldn't escape. How could she change that? How could she stop being afraid?

She hated being afraid. She stabbed her shovel into a drift in the corner of her porch, angry with Jack for lying to her, angry with herself for believing his lies.

Even now she felt afraid. The tingling sensation crawling down her spine wasn't from the cold. It was from remembering the cold look in Jack's eyes the night he drowned. She'd been powerless against him. He'd hurt her, and she hadn't been able to stop him.

She grunted and pushed another shovelful of snow over the edge of the porch. How she wished she possessed a man's strength. How daring and adventurous she could be. How easily she could fetch and carry without straining herself. How freeing it would be to be able to defend herself against a man like Larry.

The thought of Anna's husband brought on another shiver, and the feeling of being watched caught her off guard. Her heartbeat jumped to double-time as she scanned the winter darkness.

Was she imagining things? Would she spend her life flinching at noises and searching the darkness for danger?

No. No, she would *not* live a scared life any longer. She pushed another load of snow off the porch with a vicious shove. She would stop being afraid. And she would stop flinching at shadows.

"Good evening, Mrs. Ashier," said a raspy male voice from the foot of her steps.

Claire gasped in fright and clutched the shovel handle to her pounding chest.

"I'm so glad to finally catch you alone."

The man's hat was angled too low for her to see his face, but his voice sent jolts of alarm pulsing through her. She hadn't been imagining danger. This was real. Her gut knew the difference between the threat of violence and the promise of injury. This man's voice and stance said he was here to hurt her.

She inched toward the door.

"Don't rush away. I want to talk to you," he said mildly, but his intent was clear in his bunched fists. He climbed her steps.

Trying to gain a momentary advantage, she swung her shovel into his knees then lunged for the door. She wrenched the knob with desperation, but the man shoved her from behind, and followed her into the dark foyer. She'd left a candle burning, but the light was negligible as she whirled to face the man.

She saw him then, and remembered the pain Karlton had inflicted the night he dragged her out of the storeroom in Boyd's saloon. She took a step back. "What do you want Karlton?"

He grabbed the front of her coat and yanked her against him. "I heard your father made a respectable deposit in your bank account. I came to collect the money you've caused me to lose because of those marches."

She groped behind her for the closet door. If she could get her gun, maybe she could force him to leave. But all she felt was a gaping space. Had she left the door open? Or was she too far away to reach the door?

"You ignored my note."

Maybe she should call for Anna.

"You ignored the brick through your window."

Was Anna upstairs or in the kitchen?

"You got me fired from my job, and you're ruining my liquor business saloon by saloon. It's only fair that you make restitution."

Would Anna be able to help, or would she end up hurt?

"I'm not making any more requests, Mrs. Ashier. I'm telling you to stop the marches. And reimburse my loses."

She was considering stopping the marches but wouldn't be pushed into it by this brute. "Get out of my house."

He slammed her against the foyer wall, knocking the breath from her lungs. "Don't push me. Your watchdog isn't here to save you this time."

Her chest cramped as she struggled to draw in air, but nothing trickled into her paralyzed lungs.

"I'll make your husband look like a saint, lady." He jerked her chin up. "I was at the bar when the sheriff told his brother about your husband drowning. Tell me, Mrs. Ashier, where were you when he was sucking river water?"

Terror knifed through her. What did he know? That she'd been there? In the water with Jack? That she'd...

"I think you could have helped him, but I'll keep my suspicions to myself for one-hundred dollars."

"What?" She glared at him. "How dare you threaten me with blackmail."

"Lady, my mother is going to lose her house tomorrow if I don't come up with the money to pay off my loan. Believe me, I'll dare anything right now."

Outrage overrode Claire's common sense and she stared at him. "Let me guess. You risked your mother's house at the gaming table on a sure bet." The surprise on his face made her laugh derisively. "You're as sick as my husband was."

"I'm not sick!" He slugged her and drove her head against the wall.

Pain exploded in her skull and she felt herself falling. Her arms flailed as she fell sideways into a nest of coats and bedding items hanging in the closet.

"Claire?" She heard Anna's voice, but it sounded far away, as if she were standing at the end of a long tunnel. Karlton jerked her upright by her coat lapels, bringing her face close to his. "You'd better make sure you get to the bank early tomorrow morning, and that every woman in this town stops marching, Mrs. Ashier, or I'll come back and finish this."

"Claire!"

Anna's voice grew louder, and the sound of shoes striking the floorboards echoed in the tunnel. Dazed, Claire stared up at the beast panting above her, and saw flashes of Jack's enraged face glaring down at her.

"If you and your friends cost me one more cent, I'll kill you." His gaze raked her breasts. "After I get my money back."

He was enjoying this. He intended to hurt her. He grabbed her throat and squeezed. "I'll meet you at the bank at ten o'clock,"

She jammed her hand in the corner of the closet, grasping for the gun, feeling her windpipe close beneath his clenching fingers. The feel of hard steel gave her hope, but she couldn't grip the gun properly with her mittens on. She scraped her hand against the shelf, trying to rake the mitten off, but it twisted around her fingers. Darkness bled in from behind her eyes. She was seconds from passing out.

She shook her hand, but the mitten stayed on.

A buzzing filled her ears. She remembered that sound. It was the noise she always heard just before she passed out.

She spread her fingers inside the wool mitten and clamped her hand over the gun. The buzz grew louder.

She swung the heavy revolver toward Karlton's head.

The impact against his skull jarred her entire forearm, He grunted and staggered back a step, his hand raised to his bleeding head. Claire sucked in a breath and gripped the doorframe to keep from falling.

"Claire!" Anna gasped, her eyes filled with horror.

Claire staggered toward the door. "Get Boyd," she croaked then lurched outside.

Anna's scream turned Claire's blood cold. She yanked off her mitten and turned back, the revolver in her shaking hand. Karlton leapt forward and hit her in the chest.

Claire stumbled backward, her arms flailing and her hands hitting the railing as she fell. The revolver went off as she plunged to the floor.

From behind Karlton, Anna raised a shovel and struck him across the shoulders. The man turned.

"Get out of here," he said, wrenching the shovel away and shoving her down the steps.

"Run, Anna!" Claire tried to push away, to warn Anna to go for help, but Karlton gripped her throat again.

"You just made a big mistake, lady."

She couldn't move, couldn't breathe. The shadows grew deeper and weakness saturated her body. She wanted to tell Karlton that she would never give in to a coward like him, but the world was turning black. His voice came from that long, dark tunnel. "I'll bet this is how your husband felt when he was drowning."

Chapter Thirty-three

B oyd clenched his hand around his carving knife, feeling an insane urge to start hacking at the statue. The block of basswood was misshapen and changed, but still a hunk of wood.

Dead.

Just like his talent.

He couldn't see the statue.

It wasn't there.

With a vicious stab, he thrust the knife into the wood, startling Sailor who'd been asleep on the floor. The dog scrambled to his feet and gave him a bewildered look.

He stood up and turned out the lantern. "Come on, Sailor." He would chop the block into kindling tomorrow and get it out of his sight. *Why torment himself? Why keep trying to revive something that was long dead?*

He slapped the wood dust off his trousers and headed downstairs with Sailor panting at his heels. He had a saloon that needed his attention.

Claire and her temperance friends had stirred up a hornets nest by shutting down three more saloons. Three!

His patronage had doubled because of the other saloon closings, but each day more men were taking the pledge and encouraging their friends to do the honorable thing and follow suit.

Boyd didn't care about the profits anymore. He just wanted some peace for one night.

The sound of a gunshot jolted him. Sailor tore across the room, barking and lunging at the front door in a frenzied attempt to get out. Boyd sprinted across the room then yanked the door open as his patrons pushed from behind.

Anna was running up his steps, yelling for help. "He's beating her," she cried, terror filling her voice, "Hurry."

Ice rushed through Boyd's veins. Sailor raced across the snow-covered street and bounded onto Claire's porch with a ferocious growl. A man's howl of pain filled the night, and Boyd saw the man kick the dog across the porch.

Karlton! The bastard was on Claire's porch.

Shouting at the man, Boyd bolted across the street.

As Claire reached out to protect Sailor, Karlton kicked her in the ribs and drove her against the railing.

Molten rage flooded through Boyd as he leapt the porch steps. He drove himself into Karlton's broad chest and slammed him against the wall. The house shuddered, the cannon-like sound echoing through the neighborhood as Boyd pummeled the man who had beaten Claire.

Karlton grunted and fought back, shoving Boyd backward as he crashed his beefy fists into Boyd's shoulders and chest.

Boyd felt nothing but rage as he tore into Karlton with deadly intent. He shot his long arms out, swinging his fists into Karlton's face. Each blow snapped Karlton's head back, driving the man back until he fell over the railing and sprawled in the snow.

But that wasn't enough punishment for what he'd done to an innocent woman. Boyd leapt the railing and landed in knee-deep snow.

Hands pulled at him, shouts filled his head, and he continued to strike. Finally, he realized he couldn't get to Karlton anymore. A group of bloody men formed a circle around him, another around Karlton, who was bleeding a river in the snow.

"Somebody get a doctor!"

Pat Lyons's voice cut through the melee, and Boyd spun toward the porch where Pat was bending over Claire. Anna knelt beside them, her face streaked with tears.

Boyd's heart clanged as he vaulted the steps and fell to his knees beside Claire. "Jesus, God in Heaven, please let her be all right," he whispered. He pushed her hair out of her face, and his stomach clenched with fear. Her left cheek was mottled, and her lip was bleeding. "Open your eyes, sweetheart."

"M-my gun." She struggled against his hands. "Where's my gun?"

"You don't need it."

She pushed his hands away, her own shaking uncontrollably as her frantic gaze swept the porch floor. "Where's my gun?"

"The boys got Karlton. They're taking him to my bar until Duke gets there. Anna has your revolver."

She struggled to sit up, but gasped in pain and sagged back to the floorboards in a near faint. Sailor whimpered and nudged Claire's shoulder with his nose. Her moan sent a river of dread through Boyd.

"The doctor's on his way," he said, barely able to speak through his fear.

"He was going to kill me," she whispered, the effort to talk almost more than she could manage.

"Karlton will never touch you again. I vow it."

Anna touched Claire's shoulder. "Be still. Please."

Boyd sat on the snow-covered porch and carefully lifted his beloved's head onto his lap. He wanted to hold her, to take her inside where it was warm, but he was afraid to move her.

"You're safe now," he said. But Karlton wasn't. Duke had better have the wretch long gone when Boyd got to his saloon, because he would honestly kill the man.

Claire gripped his hand. "He knows about J-Jack."

"Shhh..." He brushed the tears off her lashes, feeling helpless and sick to his soul. He should have recognized Karlton's anger, his veiled threats, his hatred of Claire as something that would need to be ended. He should have been paying attention instead of drowning in self-pity.

He yelled to the group of patrons who were milling around the perimeter of the porch. "Someone get some blankets out here. And go see what's taking the doctor so long."

Anna and a man from the crowd ran to do his bidding. A few seconds later Anna brought two thick quilts. She and Boyd tucked them around Claire's shaking body, and Boyd winced each time she moaned in pain.

"The doc's coming up the street now," Pat said, rubbing Sailor's head.

"Jack would have sold Grandma's house," Claire said. "It was all I had." Tears flooded her eyes and she sobbed.

Boyd stroked her hair. "It's okay. Jack's not here. You're safe now. You'll be all right," he said, but she was beyond calming.

"No, I won't. I'm not all right." She shook her head. "I'm not... I'm not."

Tears streaked her temples, but Boyd let them fall. There wasn't a single thing he could do for her. And that was the worst feeling he'd ever experienced.

She sobbed and turned her face into the crook of his arm. The doctor climbed the steps and crossed to where they sat.

"Why is this woman outside in the cold?" he demanded, scowling fiercely.

Boyd was as outraged as the doctor, but at his own lack of attention. If Claire hadn't fired her revolver, they might have been calling the coroner rather than the doctor.

"She was kicked in the ribs, Doctor. I was afraid to move her."

"Kicked?" The doctor glanced at Claire then back at Boyd. *"Kicked?"*

Boyd nodded. Acknowledging the beastly act sent rage roaring through him again. He would kill Karlton.

He and Pat lifted the quilts and helped the doctor as best they could. Gently, the doctor ran his fingers over Claire's rib cage.

She moaned and flinched away.

"You'll have a nasty bruise, Mrs. Ashier," the doctor said, "but I'm fairly certain your thick coat saved you some broken ribs."

As soon as the doctor deemed it safe to move Claire into the house, Boyd and Pat helped her to her feet, feeling it would be less painful for her to walk than be carried. Anna followed them in and put the revolver on the desk in the foyer.

Claire refused to be put in bed, so the doctor allowed her to sit on the sofa in the parlor. While he finished examining her, Boyd and Pat made sure Anna hadn't been injured when Karlton shoved her down the steps. When she assured him she was fine, Boyd knelt beside Sailor. The dog's eyes and mouth were free of blood, and his breathing chugged like a well-fed steam engine.

Boyd rubbed Sailor's ears, feeling gratitude and love for his brave dog.

A horrendous uproar from his saloon brought Boyd to his feet. He and Pat raced for the door together.

"Stay with Claire," he told Pat then bolted outside.

He saw Karlton leap down the saloon steps. Two men grabbed at him, but Karlton swung out his arm and hit one of the men in the head. He shot the second man.

Boyd stared in disbelief. A howl of outrage came from the men surging out the door of his saloon.

Karlton darted past Levi. The deputy and several other men pursued him, but Karlton was getting away. Boyd tackled him in the street, before he could take one step closer to Claire's boardinghouse.

But Karlton's desperation and bulk made pinning him impossible. The gun in his hand made him twice as dangerous. Boyd wrestled his arm around Karlton's neck, hoping to hold him long enough for Levi to cuff him.

"Look out!" someone shouted, just before Boyd felt the gun in Karlton's fist connect with his temple. Lights exploded inside his skull, and weakness stole over him. Karlton wrenched loose from Boyd's arms and ran toward Claire's porch.

"Get him," Boyd shouted, struggling to his knees. He couldn't let Karlton inside her house. If he got to Claire...

Shouts filled the street.

Boyd staggered to his feet.

Levi pointed his revolver at Karlton's back. "Stop, or I'll shoot you, Karlton!"

Karlton swung his arm and fired at Levi then leapt toward the porch steps. Boyd's heart stampeded his chest, and he lurched forward on unsteady legs.

"Stay back," Duke called out, shoving Boyd back into the street as he sprinted past.

Boyd gripped his bleeding head and ordered his legs to move. The deep snow felt like thick mud sucking at his feet, making him stumble and go down on one knee.

Pat stepped outside Claire's boardinghouse and planted himself in front of the door. Karlton raised the revolver and pointed it at his chest.

"Look out!" Boyd yelled, but his warning was lost in the noise filling the street. Karlton was going shoot him. Boyd's best friend was going to die, and he couldn't make his legs move fast enough to save him.

The deadly blast of a revolver ripped through the night.

A collective grunt came from the shocked crowd, and Boyd's gut twisted.

"Pat!"

He surged forward, and stumbled onto Claire's porch.

Chapter Thirty-four

Numb, Boyd went back across the street to close down his saloon. He felt no rush of relief, no sorrow, no satisfaction—just hollow disbelief that Karlton was dead. Duke had shot him.

He'd had to, of course. Karlton would have pulled the trigger and killed Pat—and anyone else who'd gotten in his way. He'd set his course and gone too far to turn back. For Karlton, it seemed, there had been no choice but to play out his hand and hope to use Claire as a wild card.

Boyd hadn't known that desperate, deadly side of Karlton. His throbbing temple was proof of that. His head pounded and gut felt queasy. But Claire had to feel a hundred times worse.

After the ruckus from Karlton's charge, the bar seemed strangely quiet. Boyd climbed the steps to close it down for the night.

The instant he stepped inside, he slammed to a stop. The back bar shelf his father had built lay in broken pieces across the floor. Mugs were toppled, and shards of glass littered the room. Everett and Zach, two of his regulars, stood in the middle of the mess, their faces filled with anguish.

"Karlton did this while we was waitin' for the sheriff to come get him," Everett said. "He jumped the bar and wrenched the whole thing right off the wall. Then he grabbed a gun from behind the bar and shot Peter right in the chest."

So that's where Karlton got the gun. From Boyd's own bar. Not a word, not even a breath, escaped Boyd's throat as he stared at his father's destroyed masterpiece.

The men stood in the silence, seeing only a part of the destruction one man had caused that night.

Everett gave a helpless shrug. "We told everyone to leave, and that we'd wait for you to come back. We didn't know what else to do."

Boyd felt sick to his soul. "Thanks, boys. I'll take care of the mess."

"We can help you lay this stuff out on the floor. Maybe you can salvage it."

"No, it's too—you've done enough."

The men glanced at each other and hesitated. "We'll come by in the morning and give you a hand cleaning up."

"It'll be a few days before I can get to it," he said. He appreciated their offer, but he didn't want anybody touching his father's work.

"All right then. You let us know."

Boyd nodded. After they left, he surveyed the damage. Broken glass was scattered over the stools and floor. Huge pieces of wood lay in broken sections over and around the bar. His heart cramped with pain. The back bar shelf had been his father's last project. It was his masterpiece. It was one of the treasures that marked his existence in this world—in Boyd's life.

Boyd moved forward, but the sound of his boots crunching through glass stopped him. He looked down, horrified that he was stepping on pieces of the back bar.

A two-foot section of mirror lay on the floor in front of him, broken in half. He knelt and lifted the pieces. His reflection flashed back at him, and he saw the broken man who had failed both his father and the woman who'd deserved more than any other to be cherished and protected. His hands shook as he struggled to fit the halves together. The glass edges grated and shifted and sliced his skin as he fought to make them fit. They had to fit. He had to fix this.

The glass plates wobbled, and he grew frantic in his effort. They clanked together and chipped, causing a jagged gap to open between them.

He gripped the pieces with his bloody fingers. "I can't fix it. I can't fix this."

He hurled the pieces of mirror against the wall. They shattered with a violent crash that brought him to his feet, lusting for an outlet for his frustration and heartache.

He kicked over a stool then swung his arm and slugged mugs off the bar. They flew in several directions and smashed on the floor. He overturned the billiard table then kicked over the bucket of kindling beside his stove. His fists blasted the walls with shuddering force. He busted bar stools over the bar and kicked chunks of firewood across the floor.

"I can't fix it!" he shouted, his voice circling the room and returning to torment him.

He'd failed everyone. He couldn't fix his father's masterpiece. He couldn't fix Claire's injuries or the pain he brought her, any more than he could fix his father's shredded pride.

Tears flooded his eyes and burned down his cheeks. "I can't fix any of it," he whispered, his throat so clogged with remorse he couldn't breathe. He fell against the wall, his chest gripped by a relentless claw that crushed the air from his lungs.

"I can't fix this," he sobbed, "I'm sorry." He slid down the wall and crouched beside the piano, bleeding and weeping and wishing he could take back all the mistakes he'd made in his life.

⟞⟝ ⟞⟝

The sound of a crash startled Claire. She'd been sitting on the sofa with Anna, trying to calm down after the deadly scene with Karlton. Sailor barked and raced to the foyer.

Anna followed him. The doctor was upstairs working on the two men Karlton had shot.

Claire clutched her sore ribs and stood. Her head grew light from the pain, but she hobbled to the foyer to look out the window. The saloon was dimly lit, but someone was definitely in there.

What if one of Karlton's friends was angry with Boyd for helping her? She looked at Anna. "Something bad is happening over there."

"Stay here," Anna said. "I'll get Pat." She hurried toward the kitchen where he was filling the stove.

Claire took her revolver off the desk then opened the door. The cold blast of air took her breath away, but it cleared her head and helped steady her as she stepped outside. All she could think about was someone driving their fist or foot into Boyd's body like Karlton had done to her. Boyd had no one to step in and help him.

Sailor sprinted across the street and bounded onto Boyd's porch. Gasping in pain, Claire hobbled behind him and climbed the steps.

She marshaled her strength and entered the saloon with her gun held directly in front of her. She would pull the trigger if necessary.

But as she surveyed the destruction, her breath rushed out and her arms fell to her sides. What on earth happened here? The sight sickened and terrified her. Who'd done this awful thing? And where was Boyd?

A hoarse sob from the corner of the room startled her. Sailor bolted forward with a yelp. Boyd was crouched against the wall, bleeding and sobbing.

She went to him. "Are you hurt?" she asked, lowering herself to her knees with a jerky, pain-filled movement.

He looked up, his eyes ravaged with tears and sorrow. "I can't fix this."

"Can't fix what?" she asked, her hard breathing wrenching her bruised ribs, the pain so sharp it made her nauseous.

"You. My father. My bar." Tears streamed down his face. "I'm sorry, Claire. I should have protected you. I should have hugged my father. I didn't do either."

Pat rushed into the saloon, his stance indicating he was ready to take on an army of men. But when he saw Claire kneeling beside Boyd, he stopped and stared. "What is going on?"

Boyd gawked at Claire as if just realizing she wasn't safe on her sofa where he left her, but was here kneeling in the debris on his saloon floor. He looked at Pat. "Why did you let her come here?"

"He didn't," she said in Pat's defense.

Boyd raised his bloody hand to stop her explanation. "Never mind. I'm taking you back right now." He dragged his shirtsleeve across his eyes then reached for her hand.

She drew away and spoke to Pat. "Will you please wait outside with Sailor?"

"The doctor said—"

"Please," she interrupted. "Give us a minute."

He nodded and took Sailor outside.

"Boyd, wait." She laid a hand on his arm to stop him from standing. She put the revolver on the floor and pointed it away from them. "What happened here?"

"It's not important. You need to be in bed."

"I feel better sitting on the floor. Really," she said. It wasn't an outright lie. She was in extreme discomfort, but nothing worse than she'd experienced at home on her sofa. She leaned her shoulders against the wall, fighting to disguise her pain and the raspy sound in her voice. "You can take me back as soon as you tell me what happened."

"I can pick you up and carry you home."

"Please don't. It would be painful to be manhandled again."

He sagged back against the wall and released a weary sigh. "This should have never happened. And it's my fault, Claire."

"You didn't beat me."

"I may as well have." Tears filled his eyes, but he seemed unaware of them. "I should have protected you. I'm so sorry I didn't." He slipped his blood-splattered fingers over her hand. "Karlton should never have been able to touch you."

"It isn't your job to protect me."

"The hell it isn't. It was my own bartender who was threatening you, and I didn't know until it was too late." He met her eyes. "I'm sorry I didn't get there before he attacked you."

"So am I," she said wryly.

He leaned his head against the wall, as if he were too weary to move.

"Boyd, why didn't you... hug your father?" she asked, sensing this was Boyd's cross, that this was what had taken him to his knees tonight.

"Because that would have given him permission to die." He pulled his handkerchief out of his pocket and blew his nose. "Let me take you home now."

"Please don't. I'm fine. Really." She squeezed his wrist to keep him still. "I can put the ice pack on my face when I get back. And my ribs are going to ache whether I'm sitting on my sofa or on your floor. Tell me about your father."

"Will you go home then?"

"If you want me to."

He bent his knee and draped his elbow over it. "My father had a disease that crippled him. None of the doctors he saw were familiar with the disease, but it was something that attacked his muscles."

"I've never heard of such a thing."

"None of us had." He sighed and pushed his hair off his forehead, showing a smear of blood where Karlton had struck him with the gun. "What I didn't realize," he said, "was that while Dad was growing weaker, I was growing stronger. When I was fourteen, we were horsing around and I caused him to fall. He broke his hip. When he learned he'd never walk again, he said it was time for him to leave us. He asked me to give him a hug. In other words, he wanted my blessing to die." He sighed and stuffed his handkerchief back into his pocket. "I wouldn't hug him."

"Of course not. You were a boy who needed his father."

"My brothers hugged him. They understood what it would cost him to live. I thought he'd heal, that he'd learn to walk despite the doctor's diagnosis."

"Did he?" she asked, suspecting she knew the answer.

"He tried, but the disease wrung every bit of strength from his body, and every drop of pride from his soul. He got so weak we had to help him on and off the commode."

"How sad for all of you."

"The day before he died, I went to the bathroom to check on him, and he was sitting on the commode with tears running down his face. Paper was scattered over the floor near his feet, and I knew he'd been unable to take care of himself."

Claire's heart filled with sympathy for a man she didn't know, but somehow cared very deeply about.

"He said—" Boyd's voice cracked and his lips pursed as if he were holding back a sob. He inhaled and continued, but his voice came out in a pain-filled whisper. "He said, when a man can't wipe his own ass, it's time to die."

Her eyes watered with sympathy. "That poor man."

"I couldn't help him, Claire. I walked out of the house and didn't come home until the next morning." Tears slipped down his face, but she couldn't think of a single word that would offer him comfort. In the awkward silence Boyd grew eerily calm. "He was dead when I got back."

A wave of sorrow filled her throat and choked off any words of comfort she might have offered.

"Mom said he understood why I wasn't there, but how could he? A son is supposed to be at his father's side at a time like that."

The self-condemnation in his voice broke her heart. He was falling apart, and she had no idea how to help him. She wanted to put her arms around him, to assure him he was a decent, honorable man, but that wouldn't be enough. Because nothing right now would be enough.

"Surely your father understood you were scared?"

"I was his son. I should have been there."

They sat in silence, Claire feeling a fierce need to relieve the pain in Boyd's eyes. But words were inadequate.

He reached out and picked up a piece of broken mirror. "It took me and my Dad two days to piece these sections of mirror into that shelf that used to hang behind my bar."

She saw the gaping, empty space on the wall and the twisted pieces of wood lying across the bar. "What happened here?"

He shook his head, as if he couldn't bring himself to say. "It took us half a year to build it, and one long, sweaty day to hang it." His lips tilted to one side. "He bought me my first ale that day, and we sat right over there at the end of the bar." He pointed to the place where she'd seen him sitting the night she brought Sailor back and had her first nasty confrontation with Karlton. "That afternoon, I promised myself I would someday own this place and the back bar we worked so hard on."

Now she understood Boyd's attachment to his saloon. He became a man while building the huge shelf with his father. He celebrated that passage in this bar by drinking an ale with his dad. To preserve that memory, and the masterpiece he and his father had built, Boyd had bought the saloon.

He slipped his blood-spattered fingers over hers. "I didn't realize it would cost so much, Claire. I would change it if I could, but I can't undo it. I can't go back and hug my father and let him die with his pride intact. I can't take back Karlton's beating or the pain I've caused you. I'd sacrifice anything to do so."

"We all do things we wish we could change," she said, knowing she would undo her own mistakes if it were possible. "Most times we do those things with good intentions. What boy wouldn't want his father to live?"

He tipped his head back against the wall and closed his eyes, his cheeks wet from grief.

"Boyd, sometimes it's not enough to know what you've done," she said softly, "but to know why you've done it."

"I do. Everything I've done has been for selfish reasons."

"I don't believe that." She shifted her weight to her left hip, trying to relieve the pain in her ribs.

He stretched his legs out, unmindful of the glass and debris scattered across the floor. "I'm closing the saloon," he said, pools of sadness in his eyes.

At one time his statement would have thrilled her. Now, she felt a deep sympathy for all he lost. He lost his business, his income, and his refuge, the place where his patrons—many of whom were his friends—had gathered. Worst of all, he lost the project he'd made with his father.

"Will you go to work for Addison Edwards now?" she asked, shifting her weight again but finding no relief from the throbbing ache in her side.

"I'll go back to the mill. I've missed it, and there's more than enough work waiting for me."

"What about your carving?"

He stared at his wrecked saloon. "I can't see the treasures in wood anymore."

She felt her heart sink. "Maybe you're trying too much. Maybe you should do what Michelangelo did with his block of marble, and just chip away everything that isn't David."

He brushed his thumb across her knuckles. "I wish I could. More than you know." He got to his feet and held out his hand. "Let me take you home."

Pain radiated through every bone in her body and spilled out through her pores in a cold sweat, but her heart hurt the worst. Too much had been lost this night. And she was responsible for all of it.

Chapter Thirty-five

Claire woke to bleak sunshine and a bone-deep pain she'd thought she'd never have to experience again. She picked up her house robe, but was too stiff and sore to pull it on. She hobbled to the window to see what was going on outside. The sound of several raised voices had jarred her awake, but she couldn't see through the frosted panes.

Someone tapped on her door. She turned, expecting the doctor, who'd been checking on her and his other patients throughout the night. He kept the injured men at her house, explaining that they needed a day or two of healing before he could move them. She didn't mind; but their presence, and the sight of her bruised, swollen cheek in the mirror, was a frightening reminder of last night's violence.

Anna entered the room, brow creased with worry. "How are you feeling?"

"Miserable. What's going on outside?" Claire scrubbed her fist over the window, trying to clear a section of the glass.

"Our temperance friends are down there and they're outraged. They heard about Karlton attacking you last night, and they're outraged with the saloon owners for serving men like him liquor. They're blaming Boyd because the trouble started at his saloon."

Claire frowned then winced at the soreness in her cheek. "This wasn't Boyd's fault. Karlton doesn't even drink."

"Our friends don't know that."

"Then it's up to me to set them straight. Help me get dressed."

"You're in no condition to go outside."

"Help me, Anna. I'm too sore to dress myself."

Anna got Claire's day gown, but Claire's ribs were too tender to suffer the tugging and pulling motions of getting dressed. "This isn't going to work." Anna tossed the garment onto the bed then left the bedroom. She returned a minute later with Claire's longest wool coat and her highest pair of boots. "No one will be able to tell that you're wearing your nightrail under this."

Under other circumstances, Claire would have called Anna crazy, but in her present condition, she thought her friend was brilliant. Gritting her teeth, she struggled into her boots and her coat; then, with Anna's help, she slowly made her way down the stairs. The noise outside grew louder in the foyer, nearly overwhelmed her when she opened the door.

"You saloon owners should be ashamed of yourselves!" someone in the crowd yelled at Boyd.

He was coatless, but seemed oblivious to the cold wind cutting across the porch. He acknowledged the group of women with a sweeping glance. "Karlton's attack was unforgivable. No one could regret this more than I do. That's why I'm shutting down my saloon."

The ladies cheered and chattered to each other happily.

Claire felt bereft and sad. It wasn't Boyd's negligence, or his saloon, that had gotten her hurt. It was her own meddling that had put her into a precarious position with Karlton. Boyd had saved her. He'd been with her all night, smoothing her brow when the pain would wake her, holding her hand because she needed him to.

Unwilling to let Boyd accept the blame for what happened, she stepped onto the porch. A collective gasp rippled through the crowd then it grew eerily quiet as they all stared at her. Claire cursed herself for not pulling her hood up to hide her bruised face. She didn't want to incite them further.

Desmona Edwards stood with her daughters at the bottom of the porch steps, with her hand pressed to her heart. "This is an outrage."

Elizabeth's eyes flooded with tears of compassion as she looked at Claire. A murmur of assent hummed through the mass of women crowded around the porch and in the street.

"Any man who would do that to a woman deserved to die," someone said.

Claire glanced at Boyd. His head was bruised and his knuckles were covered with red scabs. He fought to protect her last night, He punished himself because he felt he'd failed, She'd been wrong about him. She'd been wrong about saloons and the men who frequented them. She couldn't allow any more heartache or loss to happen because of her personal ideals."You shouldn't be out here," he said, scowling in displeasure.

"Neither should you," He shouldn't be held accountable for Karlton's actions, or for her own bad decisions. Of all of them, Boyd had lost the most. He'd lost something irreplaceable last night. Because of her.

Anna stepped up behind Claire, "The doctor is coming down."

Claire acknowledged Anna's warning with a slight nod. If the doctor found her outside, he'd haul her right back to bed and give her enough opiate to keep her there.

She faced the women she'd been marching with and scanned the sea of winter hats and outraged upturned faces.

"What Karlton did was wrong," she said, wincing at the pain in her ribs. The effort of raising her voice wrenched her side and made her lightheaded, but she had to end this battle here and now. "But I was wrong too. I wanted to help protect women and children from being beaten or neglected, but I've caused more harm than good. We all have."

"We've shut down the rum holes," Desmona said. "How can that be bad?"

"Those rum holes provided an income to the owners and their families. We were destroying Karlton's life, and that's why he retaliated."

An indignant murmur rolled through the crowd.

"Karlton Kane wasn't a drunkard," she said, gripping the railing to steady herself. She raised her hand to quiet the women, "He attacked me because he was angry, not because he'd been drinking. I'm not saying he was justified in hurting me. But perhaps we were wrong to march against these men."

Another burst of disagreement came from the women.

"What good have we accomplished?" Claire asked.

"We've gotten men to sign our pledge and stop drinking," one woman said.

"We've closed down four taverns," another woman added.

Claire nodded to acknowledge the truth of their comments. "But has that served the women and children we were trying to help?" No one answered.

"That's my point. We aren't accomplishing what we set out to do. I thought closing the saloons would force men to spend their time at home with their families, that it would keep some men from drinking and gambling. But I've learned that a man who drinks isn't necessarily violent or bad, and that a man who abstains from drinking can be unforgivable cruel. In other words, our battle isn't about stopping men from drinking liquor. It's about stopping the violence in our homes." She paused to catch her breath. "All we've accomplished is to shut down businesses that provided income, and a gathering place, for many decent, hardworking men in this town. Men who weren't abusing alcohol or neglecting their wives and children,"

"Are you suggesting we let these rum holes stay open?" Desmona asked. Her voice was filled with curiosity rather than antagonism.

"I'm suggesting that instead of solving a problem, we're creating one. I'm to blame for that," Claire admitted. "I'm the one who wrote to Dr. Lewis and started these temperance marches."

"That doesn't make you responsible for Karlton's actions," Boyd said, moving to stand beside her. It was as if he knew she was clinging to the railing because she was faint. "There was nothing wrong with your intentions," he said to the women gathered below them. "None of us saloon owners could fault you for wanting to assist those people who need help. Some men do need to be stopped from drinking."

"But we are at fault," Claire insisted. "Our cause is good, but our marching has split the community. We must find a way to bring our town back together. That's the best way we can help our neighbors. Antagonizing business owners isn't productive. It's destructive. One man is dead, and two others are severely injured and lying upstairs in my boardinghouse because of the mess our marches have caused. My conscience can't bear any more of this." Her body shivered and she bit down on her lip to stop a groan of pain.

Mrs. Cushing and Mrs. Barker moved to stand beside Desmona and Elizabeth. "What are you saying?" Mrs. Cushing asked.

"That our efforts are misdirected. Our mission should be to protect the home." Claire drew her elbow against her aching ribs. "Marching may be beneficial in other towns, but I think we can find more effective means to help the women and children who need us. Dr. Lewis has his heart in the right place, but I've come to realize stopping the sale of alcohol will not stop the majority of beatings and neglect. I'm sorry, but I can no longer support his methods."

Mrs. Cushing's mouth fell open. "Are you quitting?"

Claire nodded. "Too much has been lost. I can't bear being the cause of any more pain. And nothing has been gained by our marching that I can see."

Mrs. Barker scowled, but a new light seemed to fill Desmona's eyes. She nodded as if agreeing. Claire could hardly believe Desmona was the same bitter woman who had held a gun to her ribs only a week before.

"What are you proposing?" Desmona asked, stepping forward and taking charge.

"I'm suggesting that each of us consider how we might better contribute to our town, as individuals, and as a group. Consider whether or not closing the saloons is the right course. It isn't to me, and I don't think it's the answer for our town."

"Are you quitting because you were attacked?" Mrs. Barker asked, her eyes and voice sympathetic. "I can certainly understand why you might be afraid to go on."

Sadness snaked through Claire, and she shook her head. "I've suffered worse than Karlton's attack, Mrs. Barker. I was once one of those women we are trying to help."

A sympathetic and mildly horrified sigh rippled through the group, but it was the compassion in Boyd's eyes that made Claire's sinuses sting.

"I'm one of those women, too," Elizabeth said, her voice trembling as she stepped forward. The crowd of women stared, the expressions on their faces a mix of surprise, horror, and pity. "My husband isn't a drunkard. In fact," she said, averting her eyes from Desmona's shocked stare, "he never drinks liquor. Shutting down the saloons won't change him."

The crowd fell dead silent. Their frosty breaths clouded the air, but not a sound came from them.

Desmona cried out, and reached for her daughter.

Elizabeth's cheeks flamed red, but she kept her head high and let her mother hug her.

Claire met Elizabeth's eyes and gave her a nod of support. It had taken immense courage for Elizabeth to take a stand and make her confession.

"My husband was a drunkard," Claire said, purposely drawing the women's pitying attention away from Elizabeth. "He wanted to be successful, but his addiction to alcohol and gaming was too strong. My husband was a conflicted and angry man. Liquor exaggerated those traits and made him controlling and violent."

Boyd touched her arm, the tenderness in his eyes silently letting her know that she didn't need to continue, but that he was there for her if she chose to do so.

She had to continue. She had to convince the women in front of her to see the real problem and to turn their efforts toward helping women like Elizabeth and Anna.

She hugged her arms to her nauseous stomach. "My husband grew more violent each year of our marriage," she continued. "I learned to stay silent. That's what happens to women who are beaten. They grow silent. They disappear." She inhaled and winced at the pain in her side. "Living with Jack was like being caged. We lived in hovels and moved every few months. When my grandmother willed me this house, I believed Jack and I could come here and build a better life. But Jack saw Grandmother's gift as a way to make money. He wanted the deed to use at the gaming tables."

The memory broke her heart again, and she struggled for several seconds to control her rush of tears. The women waited quietly, and when Claire lifted her head, she saw their concern and sympathy.

"I refused to give the deed to Jack."

"Good for you," one woman declared, starting a ripple of murmurs through the crowd.

Their support encouraged Claire to continue. "My husband beat me for defying him," she said, struggling to keep her voice loud enough to be heard. "Grandmother's house was all I had left. It was my only hope for a decent life. So I fought back." The tears she'd been fighting welled up in her eyes. Boyd rubbed her shoulder, but she forged on. "We fell into the river and Jack tried to drown me."

A horrified gasp burst from the women, and they pushed closer to the porch. Elizabeth broke away from Desmona and climbed the steps to stand beside Claire.

Her show of support brought more tears to Claire's eyes, but she let them fall without shame. "Jack couldn't swim. The first time he pulled me underwater, I thought he was panicking. The second time I knew he was trying to drown me. My own husband was..." She bit her lip and tears streaked down her cheeks. "I swam away and left Jack in the river. God forgive me, but I don't regret it. I wanted to live!" she said fiercely. "I wanted to come to my Grandmother's house and build a new life, one where I wouldn't be beaten or caged or fear for my life each day. That's all any woman in that position wants," she said, her voice breaking on a sob.

"That's right," Elizabeth declared, her voice strong with conviction. "We just want a safe place to go." She faced the crowd, her eyes meeting Desmona's before looking at the rest of the women. "It doesn't matter if the man beating you is a drunkard or a pastor. It hurts either way. I'm supporting Claire in her decision to quit marching and find a better way to protect our homes."

"I support both of you," Anna said then patted Claire's shoulder. "The doctor is coming."

The doctor's voice cut through the sudden silence. "What in blazes are you doing outside in this wind, Mrs. Ashier?"

She ducked her head to hide her tears.

Boyd slipped his arm around her shoulders as though to protect her from the doctor. "She wanted to thank her friends for their support," he said then moved her toward her front door and spoke over his shoulder. "Mrs. Ashier needs to be in bed, ladies."

"Yes, she does," the doctor said. "You ladies get on home now. This gal needs rest."

Claire went inside, but she stopped in the foyer to let Boyd remove her coat. Anna shooed the doctor to the kitchen, promising that Boyd would get Claire back to her bedchamber.

Boyd hung up her coat, not even seeming to notice that she was in her house robe and nightrail. He stood by the closet, his eyes dark with compassion and sadness. "I finally understand," he said, his voice low and gentle. "If Jack was worse than Karlton then I can only imagine what you suffered. I understand why you won't marry again."

Instead of feeling shame or embarrassment, she felt relief. She was finally free of her secrets, and nobody had run her out of town.

Boyd brushed his knuckles across her jaw, careful not to touch the injured side of her face. "I wish I had been there, that I could have saved you from Jack and that life. I wish I could have saved you from Karlton and the pain you're suffering now."

"You did save me." She cupped his knuckles and pressed his palm against her wet cheek, awed that his hand could be so powerful and yet so gentle. "They say what doesn't kill you makes you stronger."

"You don't look very strong right now," he said, drawing his thumb across her jaw bone before lowering his hand to his side.

Her body felt like one big bruise. But she would heal, and she would be stronger for surviving. "I'll be fine," she said, wondering why the look in Boyd's eyes was so... bereaved.

"If you need anything, let me know."

"I'd love for you to stay another night or two," she said, hoping she didn't sound like she was begging, even though she was close to doing so. He was leaving her. He was going to walk out her door and never come back. She could tell.

"Now that you've quit marching, I won't have to watch over you. You won't be in danger."

She felt sick, hollow, the pain in her ribs dull compared to the pain in her heart. "I have gotten used to you watching over me," she said. "I've come to value your friendship."

"I'll want more than friendship if I stay."

"So will I," she said shamelessly. She wanted the comfort of Boyd's arms, his playful humor that had taught her how to laugh again, and his radiant light that filled her life with warmth.

"I'm too selfish, Claire. I want more than that. I want your friendship, your love, and your trust. You're not ready to give that. And I understand that you may never be ready."

Chapter Thirty-six

"Are you saving this scrap?" Kyle asked, nudging the toe of his boot against a pile of broken back bar bits lying on their father's wood shop floor. Boyd had brought the pieces, and his massive hunk of basswood here after leaving Claire's house. He had to get out of there before he started begging her to trust him, to marry him, to love him. The doctor had warned everyone not to upset Claire, that she needed to heal. Boyd needed to stay away and let her do that.

Pat had promised to stay in Boyd's rented room at the boardinghouse for a few nights, just to make certain all the danger was really past. Anna and the doctor were there as well. At Claire's request, Boyd had left Sailor to boost her spirits.

He stared down at the broken pieces of wood on the floor and saw a reflection of his life. "Maybe I should just burn it all." He turned to his brothers, who were gathered there with him.

"Don't." Duke knelt beside the pile. "Don't burn it. You might be able to use these scraps to make other things."

The back bar was ruined beyond repair, but for some reason it brought Boyd a measure of peace to know the pieces were stored safely in his father's wood shop.

He pushed the shop door closed against the cold wind, shutting out the bleak afternoon sunshine. "I'm surprised you're here, Duke."

"There's nothing for me to do in town," his brother said. "It's been quiet as a morgue all day."

Despite the nonchalant response, Boyd knew it had torn a hole in his brother to shoot a man, especially a man he knew. There had been no choice, but that didn't make it any easier to pull the trigger, or to deal with Karlton's death afterward,

"It's about time things quieted down." Boyd started a fire in the stove with some old scraps of wood then slapped his palms across his thighs to brush off the wood dust.

"Look at this," Radford said, picking up a long stick from the workbench.

Boyd's stomach clenched when he saw it. He made the one-of-a-kind walking stick out of diamond willow, and presented it to his dad for a birthday present. His dad had loved it and had made a great show of chucking his old cane into the stove. The day his father died, Boyd had hurled the cane into a field behind the house. Whoever had found the walking stick had brought it here where it would be safe.

His throat closed as he took the cane from Radford. He inspected it and found himself proud of his early work. If only he could reclaim that confidence and the plain joy of carving without worrying about the results.

Would that feeling ever come back?

"What's wrong?" Duke asked, seeing Boyd examine the walking stick.

Boyd leaned the cane against the block of basswood and faced his brothers. "I'm shutting down the saloon."

His brothers stared at him, a mixture of surprise and suspicion in their eyes.

"I figured I'd come back to the mill full time."

Kyle slapped Boyd's shoulder. "Well, my day just improved one hundred percent."

"Why are you closing?" Radford asked, his gaze shrewd and assessing.

"I'm ready to do something different."

"You've worked the mill since you were eight years old. How will that be different?"

"I meant different from saloon-keeping." Boyd realized he wasn't convincing his brothers. "You should be happy, Radford. You and Kyle won our wager. The ladies closed me down just like you said they would."

Radford crossed his arms over his chest. "What's going on?"

Boyd huffed out a breath and leaned against the workbench. "I don't know." He'd just laid the truth on the line with Claire. He could do no less with his own brothers. "How could you three have hugged Dad, knowing you were giving him permission to die?"

His siblings glanced at each other, but said nothing.

"I can understand why you did, Radford. You were older. You'd been through a war. You must have known what it would cost Dad to fight to stay alive. But how did you know, Kyle? How did you know that it was time to let him go?"

Kyle shrugged. "It seemed like it should be his decision, not mine."

"You were barely sixteen, Duke. How did you know to let him go?"

"I didn't." Duke hooked his thumbs in his coat pockets. "I hugged him because Radford and Kyle did."

"Why didn't you make me hug him?" Boyd stared at them. "You three taught me everything. Why didn't you teach me to let a man die when it's the kindest thing to do?"

"So that's what this is about." Radford sighed and braced his hand on the metal vise at the end of the workbench. "Boyd, none of us knew what to do when Dad broke his hip. I had my own battle going on in my head, but I understood what it would mean for Dad to lose his ability to walk. I didn't want him to die. None of us did. But I couldn't ask any more of him than he'd already given. I was undeserving of his pride. I was willing to let him go because that's what he wanted."

"I wish you would have explained that to me. Maybe I could have hugged him." Boyd picked up a chisel and balanced it on his palm. "I just wanted him to live. I had no idea he'd grow so weak."

"You asked him to fight for us. Where's the sin in that?" Duke asked. "Dad understood why you didn't hug him."

"The sin is that I could barely even touch him," Boyd said, his gut twisting with shame. "I said I was afraid I'd hurt him again. But truthfully, I couldn't stand to feel his bones poking through his skin and feel how that disease was sucking the life out of him."

"That was one of the reasons I couldn't stay either," Radford admitted. "I couldn't stand watching him waste away."

Boyd glanced up, expecting to see loathing or pity in his other brothers' eyes. He saw understanding and sympathy. "If I could, I'd go back and give him that hug, you know."

"I don't know why you're killing yourself over this," Radford said. "You were closer to Dad than any of us. And you know what? You brought that man more joy than the three of us could ever have hoped to do."

"No, I didn't."

"You did," Kyle said, opening the stove door. He chucked in a small chunk of firewood. "Dad was always laughing over something you said or did."

Boyd shrugged. "I don't remember a day where Dad wasn't threatening to break a board over my ass."

"I offered to beat you numerous times, but he wouldn't let me lay a hand on you." Not a touch of remorse tainted Kyle's grin. "You irritated me endlessly, Boyd, but you made Dad happy."

"You made us laugh," Radford said. "All of us. I honestly don't know how he would have borne his illness without you there to lighten his days. He understood why you didn't hug him that day. And I think he was touched to know you loved him enough to ask him to fight a little harder."

A wad of emotion clogged Boyd's throat. He stood in the little shop with his brothers, feeling intense love for them, but unable to speak a word. He owed them, and his mother, so much. They were his strength, his safe harbor when he needed one, always standing beside him, never judging him, always there no matter what.

"As far as I'm concerned," Radford said, "only God had control over whether Dad lived or died. You made the time he had bearable for him. Feeling guilty isn't serving any of us. I say it's time you honored Dad and got on with your life."

Kyle and Duke nodded in agreement.

Radford's words of wisdom rang true to Boyd. He would always regret asking so much of his father, but he had acted out of love. Now he understood the cost of his actions, but at the time, he only knew he couldn't bear to lose the man.

"Thanks," he said, forcing the word past the burrs in his throat.

"You want a ride back to town?" Radford asked.

Boyd shook his head. He needed to stay here, in his father's shop, a place he hadn't set foot in since his father died.

After his brothers left, Boyd stroked the scarred pine workbench. He'd spent countless hours standing here beside his father. He balanced his father's metal carving knives in his palm, remembering the weight and feel and angle of each. His father had taught him how to hold a chisel and grip a carving tool, how to eye a piece of wood for grain and balance. He'd also taught Boyd how to work to the level he was truly capable of.

His father's words filled his mind as Boyd stood alone in the small shop. After years of not being able to remember the sound of his father's voice, he now felt a sense of coming home.

He stepped three feet to the right, and smiled when the pine floorboards gave a hard creak.

"I guess the only thing that's changed is me, Dad," he said, smoothing his palm over the heavy iron vise mounted to the end of the workbench.

As if his father nudged his shoulder, Boyd turned to the block of basswood that had been haunting him for years. It stood in the shadows, as if leaning on the walking stick, watching. Boyd finally saw more than a block of wood. He saw his own potential.

Chapter Thirty-seven

The dust-covered windows of the wood shop looked fogged in the morning light, but Boyd kept the stove and the lanterns burning as he continued working. He was carving by feel again, sensing what to keep and what to chip away.

His father's personality quirks and nuances had streamed into his mind during the long, silent night. Boyd remembered everything, the way his father would bite his lower lip while carving intricate details in wood; the sly, just-between-us winks he would give Boyd that made him feel grown up and manly. Boyd could even remember his dad's favorite expletives. His father had become so lifelike, Boyd felt they were working side by side.

He worked his knife around the intricate peaks and valleys he'd formed in the wood then paused to brush away the tiny wood shavings. He used a curved gouge to remove a small section of wood then switched back to the carving knife to smooth out the rough edges.

As the statue slowly emerged from the block of wood, Boyd felt something new emerging inside himself. He'd spent uncountable hours in this wood shop helping his father. He'd worked the mill each day after school for his father. He'd fetched and carried for his father. He'd done everything and anything a boy could do to please his dad. Because he'd loved him.

Love. It was a word he was finally beginning to understand.

As his mother had explained, love didn't mean never asking too much, never being selfish, or never hurting another. Love meant staying during the hard times, looking for the humor in life, encouraging and supporting the other. It meant making a commitment to be there no matter what.

Boyd had been there for his dad in the only way he could as a boy of fifteen. Right, wrong, or otherwise, he'd done his best.

He wanted to be there for Claire, too. Night and day. Every day. He loved her.

But she was afraid. He understood why, but her inability to trust didn't make it easier for him to accept her rejection. He thought his blocked talent had created the emptiness in his life, but now he knew he'd been missing love.

A love Claire had but was afraid to give him.

━━◦┼◦◦┼◦━━

Claire reread the last page of her grandmother's journal then closed the leather cover. The love story wrenched her heart more severely this time.

She knew what it was like to be married to a man who cheated. Jack had slept with other women. Each night he hadn't come home, it had broken Claire's heart. But she was sure Jack hadn't loved those women. He hadn't loved anybody, including himself.

Abe had cheated with one woman and had loved her with all his heart. No wonder Desmona had been bitter.

Claire felt a deep sympathy for Desmona, but she also empathized with her grandmother and Abe, who had eventually sacrificed their love for duty.

How had her grandmother and Addison survived five decades of such wrenching torment? They must have crossed paths with each other every week. How could they not throw themselves into each others' arms at those moments?

That's how Claire felt when she'd seen Boyd climbing his porch steps late last night. He'd barely been home during the past week, and when he had, he and Sailor had stayed inside. When she saw him on his porch, she wanted to race across the street and hug him and kiss him and beg him to be her friend again.

But that would be unfair. He stood by her through everything, protected her when she needed protection, and taught her how to laugh again. She couldn't take any more without giving more in return.

And that was the crux of her problem.

Her father had called her a foolish chit for spurning Boyd's proposal. Addison's words were kinder, but he told her she was letting love pass her by, and without love, what point was there in living?

She'd wanted to argue that she had her friendship with Anna, her charity work, and her boardinghouse, but not one of those things brought her the love Addison was talking about. After reading her grandmother's journal again, Claire knew that life wasn't worth a plug nickel without love.

As she'd been learning, living scared wasn't living.

Anna entered the parlor with a cup of tea, and kept her concerned gaze on Claire as she sat on the sofa. "You look... upset. Are you all right?"

Claire shook her head, unwilling to pretend that everything was fine when her heart was crumbling. She wasn't all right. "I'll be back shortly," she told her friend then went to the foyer.

Her ribs weren't as tender anymore, but they still ached when she pulled on her coat and boots. She tucked the journal under her arm and left the house. Ten minutes later, she knocked on Addison and Desmona's door.

Addison answered her knock, and frowned when he saw her. "What are you doing out on this wretched afternoon?"

"I'd like to talk to you and your wife."

He hesitated, but Desmona's voice came from behind him. "For mercy's sake, Addison, invite her in. You're letting the heat out."

He stepped back so Claire could enter their small but surprisingly cozy home. Had Desmona decorated it to give her the comfort Addison's arms hadn't?

"Come in," Desmona said, her voice surprisingly cordial. Claire stepped into the kitchen. Desmona was sitting near the stove with an afghan draped around her shoulders. "How are you feeling?" the woman asked, her eyes roving Claire's face and body as if genuinely interested.

"Sore, but the doctor assures me I'll feel much better by next week."

Desmona nodded in approval. "I've been wanting to call on you," she said, "but I assumed you weren't up to receiving callers."

"I wasn't. Today is the first I've been outside since I was... since you ladies gathered at my house."

"That man did a terrible thing to you." Desmona's shoulders drooped and remorse deepened the grooves in her face. "I did a terrible thing too. Nothing can excuse my awful behavior, but I do apologize for pushing into your home and threatening your life." She glanced at Addison then lowered her lashes as if deeply ashamed. "I embarrassed my husband and myself, and treated you in a most dreadful and disrespectful manner." She looked up, her brown eyes filled with regret. "I'm deeply sorry."

Claire was too. She was sorry for Addison and her grandmother, who'd loved so deeply and made the ultimate sacrifice for their families. And she was sorry for Desmona who had lived an empty, loveless life. Most of all, she was sorry for herself because she'd been a coward.

She believed a solitary life was a safe life, and it had brought her more pain than Jack and Larry and Karlton combined.

She didn't have the courage to say yes to love, to trust, to believe in Boyd when he asked her to marry him. She let her fear stop her. She was no smarter than Desmona, who had allowed her painful past to ruin what could have been a decent life. Claire was doing the same thing, and if she didn't change, she would spend her life alone like Desmona had spent most of hers, a pathetic, lonely, old crone.

Claire had to change. She had to stop hiding in her cage and peeking out at world around her. She needed to step right into the middle of life and embrace it all, the risks, the excitement, the loss and sorrow, the joy and the love.

She could only do that by putting her past behind her.

She looked at Desmona, who seemed to be waiting for her forgiveness or condemnation. "I've made mistakes of my own, Mrs. Edwards. And now I realize how deeply you've suffered over my grandmother's affair with your husband."

Desmona's mouth opened at Claire's bold statement.

"I'm sorry for the worry and heartache this journal has caused you," Claire said. "I came here to put your fears to rest." She pulled the journal from her pocket and looked at Addison. "I'm going to burn my grandmother's diary."

Pain and shock flashed in his eyes. Surprise lit Desmona's.

"It's the compassionate thing to do," she went on, hoping she could forgive herself for desecrating something so beautiful.

The darkness slowly receded from Abe's eyes, and the lines in his face smoothed out. She knew that he understood. She was protecting the love he shared with her grandmother, keeping it pure and away from gossips who might call their grand passion a sin. It was also the right thing to do for Desmona, who had spent fifty years knowing her husband loved Marie Dawsen.

"I understand," Addison said, giving her a decisive nod.

Claire leaned down and opened the stove door.

"No!" Desmona's gnarled fingers clamped around Claire's wrist.

Claire was too shocked to keep the woman from slipping the diary from her hand. But when she flipped it open, Claire's heart stopped. To burn it was one thing, but Desmona had no right to read it.

Desmona tore out the first page and threw it into the fire. "Is your grandmother's name written anywhere else in this book?"

"No."

"Is my husband's name in here?"

"No."

"Then there's no need to burn it." She handed the journal back to Claire, her eyes filled with a depth of understanding and compassion Claire had never seen there. "I'm entitled to some peace of mind. You're entitled to your grandmother's life."

Desmona's selfless gesture overwhelmed Claire, and she hugged the journal to her stomach. "Thank you."

Addison sank into a chair beside Desmona, neither of them speaking, but they seemed to be a couple for the first time in Claire's memory. Desmona had softened toward Addison, and Claire suspected they would share their remaining years on friendlier terms.

———⊱ ⊰———

As she walked home, Claire thought about the two people who'd survived decades of heartache, and yet had found the courage to open their hearts again. She climbed her porch steps, realizing that she'd already opened her heart to Boyd. She'd fallen in love with him. But she hadn't let herself trust him. What had begun as a test of wills between them had deepened into a test of courage.

Sailor's happy bark and nudge against her leg lifted her heavy heart. She hadn't seen the dog in days. Snow speckled his nose, and his tongue lolled from the side of his grinning mouth. When Claire looked down into his adoring brown eyes and considered a life without him, she burst into tears.

She knelt and hugged his knobby head to her breast. "Oh, Sailor, I'm such a fool..."

Her sobs pained her ribs, but she couldn't stop crying or hugging the dog. She found passion and love with a decent, honorable man then turned him away and locked herself back in her safe little cage. Boyd had asked her to spend her life with him and his silly dog. And like a fool, she'd said no.

Chapter Thirty-eight

Boyd climbed his porch steps with bone-weary slowness but a deep sense of accomplishment. The hunk of basswood had yielded its treasure.

All the years of anguish, of false starts, of fear, had taken their toll on him, but time had honed and focused his skill. The lessons and losses had brought wisdom and a keen vision he hadn't possessed. He couldn't have carved the statue without first being reshaped himself— by life, by loss, by love. The love of an independent and beautiful woman.

He thought about Claire constantly since walking out of her house nearly two weeks ago. He wanted to see her, to make her laugh, and to make love with her, but he stayed away because he was afraid of pushing her into a commitment she would later regret. But coming home to an empty saloon and an empty life was torture.

Even Sailor preferred to stay at Claire's house.

Boyd twisted his doorknob and heard the crinkle of paper. He looked down to find a note in his hand.

Dear Mr. Grayson,

I am writing to complain about the lack of noise from your saloon. You haven't disrupted my life in almost two weeks. I let the best thing in my life slip away when I acted the coward and rejected your proposal. If you're still interested in sharing bawdy songs and leisurely body rubs, please come see me.

With love, Cold Claire

Boyd read the note twice because his tired brain refused to believe it was real. His heart demanded it was, clamoring so hard it left him short of breath.

He pushed inside and straddled a bar stool, afraid he would fall on his backside if he didn't sit down.

He read the note again. Claire had written it, and she wanted to see him. She wanted to share "bawdy songs and leisurely back rubs." But what did that mean, exactly? Was she still suggesting an affair? Or had she finally changed her mind about marrying him?

He leaned over the bar and rummaged around for a pen and paper, but Sailor's impatient scratching on the door made him give up his quest and let the dog inside.

As if Sailor knew something big was in the air, he wheezed and circled Boyd's legs.

"I know, I know, she's waiting for an answer." Boyd rubbed Sailor's head. "I'm looking for a pen."

Sailor followed him behind the bar, sniffing pails and empty liquor bottles while Boyd scrounged up a writing implement and a stained piece of paper.

Dear Claire, I have found my David, and my treasure—you.
But I'm lost without your love and your trust.
Marry me and I'll promise the fairy tale (as long as your version includes a clumsy saloon hound).
Our bruises should be gone by Friday. Will you marry me in four days? Say yes, Claire, and I'll send a telegram to your parents.
With love, Boyd

Boyd knelt and tied the note to Sailor's neck. "Let's see what Claire will say to our proposal."

The instant they stepped outside, Sailor raced across the street to Claire's porch, barking like a hound on a scent. Boyd grinned, gaining a new appreciation for the lack of subtlety in children and animals.

Claire opened her front door and gave his dog a smile that warmed Boyd clear to his soul. She looked across the street and waved.

Boyd waved back, but was too on edge to return her smile.

Sailor nudged Claire's legs and barked until she knelt beside him.

Boyd held his breath while she opened and read his note. She asked him to come see her, but that didn't mean she was ready to commit to marriage.

She stared at his note then pressed her fingers to her mouth. She stood and waved the note in the air. "Yes," she shouted then laughed and waved him over.

━◆━◆━

Claire watched Boyd—her friend, her lover, her future husband—crossing the street. She loved his long-legged, confident stride and the way his golden gaze drank her in as he climbed her steps.

He stopped in front of her, and Claire realized how much she missed him, and that he seemed taller, and more handsome, and that his hair had grown an inch past his collar.

"Is this real?" he asked, the hoarse uncertainty in his voice melting her.

For her, it was a dream come true, and she nodded. "I've got a note to prove it."

"Will you feel well enough to marry me Friday?" "

I'm healthy enough to start our honeymoon tonight," she said with a boldness that flushed her face. But she didn't care, because she ached to be held and loved by him.

"Don't tempt me," he said. Then he pulled her into his arms and kissed her.

She moved closer to his warm, hard body. He cupped her bottom and pulled her against him, fitting her to his groin, his body telling her how much he wanted her. Anyone and everyone could see them standing on her front porch, carrying on like young lovers, but Claire didn't care. Let the neighbors talk.

"You're shivering," he murmured against her temple.

"I'm nervous and excited and I... I don't want to wait one minute longer to make love with you."

He kissed her forehead, her eyebrows, the tip of her nose. "You're worth waiting for. From this moment on, the only woman I'll ever make love to is my wife."

She clutched the lapel of his coat, ashamed of her neediness but desperate for reassurance. "Please make that a promise."

"I promise," he said, brushing a kiss to her mouth. "Only you, Claire, for now and forever. And I'll make you my wife in all ways on Friday evening."

She drew back and looked at him, needing to ask the question that had been plaguing her since Boyd returned from Buffalo. "Did you see Martha when you went to Buffalo?"

"Yes, why?"

Her heart plunged. "You know why."

The hint of a smile lifted his lips. "Do you remember the night of the cantata when Martha threatened to reveal 'our little secret'?"

Claire nodded, but it hurt to remember that night and what she'd suspected happened between Boyd and Martha.

"Martha was threatening to reveal that she's my cousin."

Claire's jaw dropped. "Your... cousin?"

His smile deepened, and he nodded.

"You rat." She tried to pinch his side, but pinched his wool coat instead. He chuckled and pulled her back into his arms.

"Why did you let me think she was your companion?" she asked.

"Because I liked that jealous sparkle in your eyes."

"I was not jealous."

"You were."

She buried her face against his chest. "I was."

He chuckled and eased her away from him. "Ah, Claire, from the minute I saw you, there was no one else for me. There'll never be anyone else for me. Ever."

"I couldn't bear it if—"

He placed his finger over her mouth. "I love you. Only you. For the rest of my life."

She kissed his fingertips then raised up on her toes and kissed his warm neck, inhaling the scent of soap and bay rum cologne on his skin, and the ever-present smell of fresh cut wood that clung to his coat. "I love you." She kissed his whisker-shadowed chin. "I can't wait to be your wife," she whispered. Then she covered his firm, gorgeous lips with her mouth, overcome by her need for him, surprised that she was no longer afraid.

Once she made up her mind to say yes to Boyd, and to the myriad of experiences that would come with loving and living a full, robust life, something miraculous happened. The fear that had darkened her life and clouded her judgment dissipated, leaving behind a clear view of her future—one filled with light, laughter and love. With Boyd at her side, life couldn't be any other way.

He tightened his arms around her and deepened the kiss into a slow, seductive mingling of tongues. She moaned into his mouth and slipped her fingers up through his soft thick hair.

"Am I hurting your ribs?" he asked, his breath hot against her cheek.

"No, but you're killing me with need."

A laugh rumbled in his chest and he looked down at her, his eyes lit with humor and heat. "This is a fine time for you to fall into my arms. I spent weeks trying to seduce you, and you'd have none of it."

"I didn't want to be seduced," she said, unable to keep from spilling her heart out to him. "I wanted to be loved."

"You are." His earnest eyes never wavered from hers. "You are loved."

Her heart swelled with joy, and she felt honored and blessed to be loved by such a handsome and noble man. Their gazes locked, and she pressed her palm to her palpitating heart, knowing she would remember this moment and this intense feeling for the rest of her life.

"You're crying," Boyd said quietly, lifting his hand to wipe away the tear that had slipped from her eye.

"Because I never thought I could be this happy."

"We'll always be happy. We'll always be in love. We'll always have this," he said, dipping his head to capture her mouth in another hot, languorous kiss. It sparked a strong blaze in her already aroused body.

"I don't want to wait any more," she panted against his lips.

He opened his mouth, but before he could speak or kiss her again, the front door opened and Anna stepped out. She spotted them, her eyes rounded, and her glance instantly assessed the heated moment she'd just interrupted.

"Oh! I'm sorry. I didn't realize you were out here." With flushed cheeks and the hint of a smile on her face, she stepped back inside and closed the door.

Boyd grinned. "You almost convinced me."

Claire leaned her forehead against his chest. "Does this mean I'll have to start all over again?"

"No," he said, easing her away. "It means I'm going to leave before I act the cad and take advantage of you."

"Wait." She caught his hands but allowed him to put some distance between them. "I can't ask Anna to leave," she said, praying Boyd would understand her need to help Anna start a new life.

"I know that, Claire. She can live in my apartment. You and Anna can turn my saloon into a safe house for those women and children you want to protect."

"Oh, Boyd." She was too overcome by his generosity to adequately express herself. "You have no idea what this means to me."

"I'm afraid I do." He gathered her close and stroked her back. "I understand why you need to help women like Anna. And you'll never have to worry about me standing in your way." He gave her a gentle, rocking hug then eased back to see her face. "I admire your compassion and courage, Claire, and I'll support you in whatever you do. If you want to take in strays then I won't care if we have a house full of them. If you want to give women and children a safe place to stay then the Pemberton Inn is yours."

She was touched beyond words, in the deepest part of her soul where flowers of hope and joy were beginning to grow again. Boyd would nourish her spirit; he would be her light and her love, her slayer of dragons, her knight in shining armor, her prince, her friend, her lover, her husband—her *everything*.

Chapter Thirty-nine

———◈———

"Be careful where you grip it," Boyd warned as his brothers helped him lug the huge, cloth-wrapped statue into the office at the sawmill depot. "Set it on that pedestal."

"What is this?" Kyle asked, huffing as he stepped away from the monster they just stood upright on the four-inch oak base.

Boyd's nerves jangled with apprehension and excitement. "Something I've been working on for a long time."

Duke groaned and arched his back. "It had better be worth my strained back muscles."

Radford pulled out a pocket knife and handed it to Boyd. "Cut this behemoth loose, and let us see what we've been busting our backs over."

Boyd couldn't disguise the tremble in his hands as he cut the cords. He finished the final touches on the statue just before dawn, and had roared like a madman, screaming out all the joy and anguish he'd experienced while carving the piece. He laughed and cried and gotten down on his knees and thanked his father for the gifts he'd given his son.

But now, Boyd wondered if it was any good. Had his moment of jubilation clouded his judgment? Should he have waited? Was there more work to do?

Bat wings beat inside his chest.

Kyle smacked him on the shoulder. "Unveil the thing before it mildews."

Before he lost his nerve, Boyd yanked the canvas off and dropped it on the floor.

Radford, Kyle, and Duke stared in awe at the statue of their father leaning on the diamond willow cane Boyd had made for him, giving them a just-between-us-boys wink.

Kyle's mouth hung open, his gaze glued to the wooden replica of the man they had loved so dearly.

"If Dad could see this—" Radford compressed his lips, and clipped off his words. Moisture edged his eyes and he looked away.

Boyd's heart swelled with pride and love and a hundred emotions he couldn't name. That block of wood had been riding his shoulders for seven long years, and he was finally free.

Radford hooked his arm around Boyd's shoulders and gave him a brotherly squeeze. "Dad would love this."

It was one of the nicest things Radford had ever said to him, and it warmed Boyd clear through to be able to share this moment with his brothers.

Almost reverently, they smoothed their callused palms over the statue, as if touching it would, allow them to touch their father again.

"This is incredible." Wonder filled Kyle's eyes as he touched the statue's face—their father's face. "It's so life-like, I'm waiting for Dad to tell us to get our asses back to work."

Their laughter cut the cords of tension gripping Boyd's chest. Finally, he could breathe again. It felt good to laugh with his brothers. For so long he felt unworthy of even walking in their shadows, but today, he could stand beside them and feel proud of himself. Today he was whole again. He'd chipped and carved and smoothed and sanded his way to the heart of his "David."

His brothers clapped him on the shoulders and praised him for his masterpiece. "Dad would be honored," Radford said, leaving the office with moisture still beading his eyes.

Kyle thumped him on the shoulder. "He'd be pretty impressed. I sure am." He followed Radford outside.

Duke stayed behind, shaking his head as he eyed the statue.

"Dad wasn't a vain man," he said, "but if he were alive, he'd make sure every person in town saw this." He turned, pride in his eyes. "This is an impressive tribute to a man who loved you."

Then he stepped outside, as if he knew Boyd needed to be alone.

His brothers' words warmed Boyd, but as he stood in front of the statue, in front of the man he'd loved with all his heart, he knew the statue wasn't just about honor and pride, but about letting go. Unashamed, he embraced the statue and gave his father a hug.

Chapter Forty

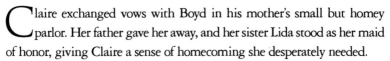

Claire exchanged vows with Boyd in his mother's small but homey parlor. Her father gave her away, and her sister Lida stood as her maid of honor, giving Claire a sense of homecoming she desperately needed.

Duke had traded his sheriff's badge for a handsome black suit and starched white shirt to stand as Boyd's best man.

Anna stood behind them in her magic dress, slowly but surely building herself a new life. With the help of Duke's lawyer friends she was trying to divorce Larry, who had been convicted of two murders and would spend his life in prison.

Claire's mother, and Lida's husband and three children, were comfortably ensconced in the warm, welcoming bosom of Boyd's family.

Claire stood beside her future husband, eyeing him with open admiration as she spoke her vows. He looked tall and proud in a full-dress black suit and a snow white shirt, his eyebrows black slashes above warm honey-brown eyes as he promised to love, honor, and cherish Claire until death parted them. When he added his promise not to be a toad, the room filled with laughter.

Claire cried. She couldn't name a time she'd been this happy.

After their vows, Boyd's brothers slapped his strong shoulders to congratulate him. And one by one, each tall, dark, handsome brother-in-law kissed Claire's cheek to welcome her to the family. Her parents hugged her and wished her well. Her sister and Anna cried. And by the time Boyd's family finished introducing themselves and congratulating her, Claire's head was spinning as if she'd had too much wine.

But she hadn't had a drop, because tonight she wanted to savor every minute of her husband's lovemaking.

They spent the evening getting to know each other's family, but exchanged private looks of longing while trying to be gracious to the people they loved. After three hours of being pulled in opposite directions, Boyd caught Claire's waist and directed her to his mother's small foyer. "That's a lovely bouquet you're carrying, Mrs. Grayson."

She glanced down at the tiny carving she'd held while speaking her vows. "You weren't supposed to notice."

"I notice everything about you." He squeezed her fingers. "I am shocked, though, that you like such naughty art."

"There's nothing naughty about this carving. It's beautiful."

A wicked grin climbed his cheek, and Claire's heart stuttered. "What's wrong with this carving?" she asked, dreading his answer.

"Turn it upside down."

She lifted her hand and turned the carving so the roses were at the heel of her palm. "It's an upside down bouquet."

"Roll it a bit to your left."

She did. And she gasped.

Turned upside down, the carving resembled the nude backside of a woman. The bouquet of roses formed her rounded bottom, the stems her narrow waist, and the trailing ribbon resembled two arms lifted and bent as if tucked behind her neck.

"I showed this to your family!" she said, mortified by the dual image she'd never noticed.

His hoot of laughter drew everyone's attention to the foyer. Her face burned, but she forced a smile. "Boyd Grayson, you are a scoundrel," she said through her false smile. "You'll pay for this."

Boyd pulled his bride into his arms for a playful kiss. "I'm looking forward to it," he said—and he really was.

Claire was his passion, his love. He would take anything she would give him. And he would give her anything she asked for.

He chafed through supper and cake, and enough well wishes to last him a lifetime, before he could finally secret his bride away to his apartment. They would spend their honeymoon night here. Anna and Claire's family were staying at Claire's house. Tomorrow her parents and sister would leave, and Anna would move into his apartment. But for tonight, his old apartment where they'd first made love was their haven.

And to honor that first night, they sat at the bar in the glow of gas lighting, drinking wine together. But when Boyd reached for his wife, she danced away from him with the wine bottle in her hand.

She set it on the billiard table. "Time to pay the piper, Mr. Grayson."

"For what?"

"For that naughty little trick you played on me with that carving."

He grinned. "I'll make it up to you by rubbing your back."

"I don't think so." She stepped away from him. "If you want a willing bride, you have to play 'Cold Claire' for me."

"You're jesting."

She lifted her chin. "You have to play it all the way through without making a mistake."

"That's a peculiar request for your wedding night, Mrs. Grayson."

"And a simple one."

"As you wish." He took a seat on the piano bench and lifted the cover. "Do I have to sing the lyrics too?"

"Of course."

Her impish smile put him on guard. "What mischief are you up to?"

"I just want to hear my favorite song." She nodded at the piano. "Start whenever you're ready."

He started. The quicker he played her song, the sooner he could make her sing:

I once had a lover with gorgeous blond hair, but the lady was so—

Claire's stocking-clad foot landed on the piano bench right beside him. Boyd banged to a stop and stared at her.

"What's the matter?" she asked, standing with her foot planted on the edge of the bench, her skirt hiked clear to her naked thigh. "I'm just going to take off my stockings."

The lacy edges of her drawers peeped out at him. "Let me give you a hand." He smoothed his palms up her shin, but she gave his knuckles a playful whack.

"Start over at the beginning."

"With your ankle?"

She smiled. "With my song."

He'd rather pull her pretty wedding dress off her gorgeous body and ravish her, but he dutifully fingered the keys. "You're a cold woman," he said, his gaze glued to her slender legs.

She smiled and slipped her delicate fingers under the white lace edge of her fancy stocking then slowly slid it down her long leg. "Start singing, Mr. Grayson."

I once had a lover with gorgeous blond—

She leaned forward and dropped her stocking in his lap, her cleavage nearly brushing his lips.

But the lady was... um, something

"Ornery," she said, near his ear. "Start over."

"You're joking."

"Not even a little." She jerked her thumb toward the keys. "Play my song through without a mistake, and we can go upstairs."

"Is this some sort of challenge?"

"You teased me earlier with that little piece of art. It's my turn to tease you with a bit of my own art. Unless you don't have the nerve to watch."

Laughter burst from him and echoed through the saloon. "By all means, darling, show me what you've got."

"Start the song."

Now that he knew her game, he was more than willing to play. He made it through the first verse without a hitch as she slipped her other stocking off. Then he started the second verse.

She taunted and teased,
while I begged and... sweet Savior!

Her skirt hit the floor.

but the lady, hum, hum...
and I don't remember a word.

She burst into laughter, her eyes sparkling with triumph. *"'The lady didn't dare, so I called her Cold Claire',"* she said, supplying his missing lyrics.

This lady did dare, and it was shattering his concentration. He closed his eyes and banged down on the keys, determined to finish the song then carry his luscious bride upstairs to bed.

He made it to the third verse when her hand stroked the inside of his thigh. He slammed his fingers down on the keys so hard, the sound vibrated the window panes.

She knelt at his side, gazing up at him with a sultry half-smile that fired his blood. Her petticoats were gone, and the only thing covering her creamy skin was her lacy drawers and corset. "Did I distract you, darling?"

Oh, he loved her sense of humor.

She stroked his thigh again. "I was just going to ask you to unlace my corset."

How far would she go if he kept making mistakes?

"I can move away if I'm bothering you."

He brushed his knuckles over the swell of her breasts. "I like you here."

"Will you unlace me before you start my song again?"

"Of course, darling. Anything for you." He freed her from the grip of her corset then willed himself to put his hands back on the keys.

"You're not singing," she whispered, nibbling his earlobe with her sweet lips.

I once had a lover,

She sat back on her heels, gripped the bottom of her chemise, and pulled it over her head.

with gorgeous—
Breasts...

She moaned and stroked her palms up over her full bare breasts. "It feels lovely to be free of that corset."

Boyd slammed the piano lid and swept her into his arms. Her laughter rang through the room as he whirled her in a circle.

He kissed her, loving her, needing her more than air.

Finally she broke away panting. "Take me to bed."

"Every night for the rest of our lives," he said, carrying her toward the stairs. She snagged the open wine bottle as they passed the billiard table and took a drink.

He grinned. "I can't offer you a castle, Claire."

"I don't need one."

"The prince may have a bad day slaying dragons on occasion."

"The princess will have her own dragons to slay," she said.

His body burned. His heart beat with happiness. He took her upstairs to their bedroom, eager to love her and give her pleasure and make her his wife.

Sailor leapt to his feet at the foot of their bed, and greeted them with a happy bark that made Claire flinch in Boyd's arms.

Then a tiny, fuzzy-headed kitten popped up off their pillow, and Claire's mouth and eyes rounded.

"Meet Sergeant," he said. "Your wedding present, and the newest member of our family."

"Oh, Boyd..."

He knew he would never forget the tender look in Claire's eyes or her beautiful face illuminated by joy.

She hugged his neck. "Sergeant is darling."

Sailor gave a petulant bark and nudged her bare side with his cold nose. Claire gasped then reached down to pet him. "No need to feel jealous. I have more than enough love for all of you." She turned her beautiful blue eyes to Boyd and pressed a tender kiss to his mouth. "Thank you. I'm overflowing with love and happiness."

So was Boyd, but he was too absorbed in watching Claire dribble burgundy wine down her ivory cleavage. It pooled in her navel in a purple pool he wanted to lick dry.

She grinned at him. "Care for a drink, Mr. Grayson?"

"Claire... He kissed her wine-flavored mouth, her full breasts then he hefted her up in his arms to kiss her navel.

She laughed and squirmed away from his tongue. "That tickles."

Boyd moved toward the bed, but Sailor wasn't about to be ignored. The mutt wheezed with such excitement, his entire rump wagged. The kitten leapt off the pillow and batted his tiny white paws at Sailor's swinging tail. Sailor nudged the kitten away with his nose, sending Sergeant tumbling across the fluffy quilt. Sergeant was tiny but determined and he came back swiping his paws at Sailor's whipcord tail.

Claire's laughter rang through the bedroom, and the empty place that had been in Boyd's chest for so long overflowed with happiness. He'd reclaimed his art. He'd found love.

He had Sailor and Sergeant—and his beautiful, loving and courageous Claire with her amazing sense of humor. They were his family, his life, his treasure.

⇥ THE END ⇤

Dear Reader,

Thank you for taking the time to read *Lips That Touch Mine*. The Grayson family has taken up permanent residence in my mind and they are all clamoring for their stories to be shared. Duke's book *Kissing in the Dark* is next in the series, and this sexy sheriff is in for the shock of his life when he marries Faith Wilkins. If you would like to spend more time with the Grayson family, receive a notice when the next book is coming out, or learn more about the books in this series, please visit www.wendylindstrom.com and sign up for New Book Alert!

I sincerely hope you enjoyed *Lips That Touch Mine* and consider it a 5-star keeper that brought you many enjoyable hours of reading. If so, and you would be willing to share your enthusiasm with other readers, I'd be very grateful. Telling your friends about my books and posting online reviews is extremely helpful and instrumental in elevating this series. It not only helps other readers find my books more easily but enables me to publish books more frequently. I have many wonderful stories to share with you, so please continue to spread the word.

Even with many layers of editing, mistakes can slip through. If you encounter typos or errors in this book, please send them to me at www.wendylindstrom.com (use contact link).

Thanks again for your enthusiastic support. I'm wishing you many blissful hours of reading.

Peace and warmest wishes,
Wendy

About the Author

Wendy Lindstrom is a RITA Award-winning author of "beautifully poignant, wonderfully emotional" historical romances. *Romantic Times* has dubbed her "one of romance's finest writers," and readers rave about her enthralling characters and the riveting emotional power of her work. For more information about Wendy Lindstrom's other books, excerpts, and sneak previews, please visit www.wendylindstrom.com.

Please remember to sign up for New Book Alert! and post your online review!

[8]